Also by Harold Robbins

Goodbye, Janette

a novel by

Harold Robbins

SIMON AND SCHUSTER
NEW YORK

Published by Simon and Schuster
A Division of Gulf & Western Corporation
Simon & Schuster Building
Rockefeller Center
1230 Avenue of the Americas
New York, New York 10020
SIMON AND SCHUSTER and colophon are trademarks of
Simon & Schuster
Designed by Irving Perkins
Manufactured in the United States of America
10 9 8 7 6 5 4 3 2 1

Library of Congress Cataloging in Publication Data

Robbins, Harold, date
   Goodbye, Janette.

   I. Title.
PS3568.0224G6   813'.54   81-4774
                                    AACR2
ISBN 0-671-22593-6

THIS NOVEL IS DEDICATED WITH LOVE TO
Zelda Gitlin ·
WITH GRATITUDE FOR THE FAITH, LOVE
AND SUPPORT SHE HAS SO FREELY GIVEN
TO ME, BOTH AS A NOVELIST AND AS A
HUMAN BEING THROUGHOUT THE YEARS

Book One

Tanya

HE WAS NERVOUS. She could see that in the way he paced around the room, occasionally going to the window and lifting the lace curtain to look out at the rain-swept Geneva street. He turned to look at her. "The Frenchman isn't here yet," he said in his harsh Bavarian German.

She did not look up from her knitting. "He will come," she answered.

He walked back to the sideboard and poured himself a schnapps, swallowing it in one gulp. "It wasn't like this in Paris. Then he would come running whenever I snapped my fingers."

"That was three years ago," she said calmly. "The Germans were winning."

"We were never winning," he said. "We only thought we were. The minute America came into it, we all knew in our hearts it was over." The faint sound of the doorbell came from downstairs. "He's here now," he said.

She rose to her feet, laying the knitting on the table next to her chair. "I'll bring him right up."

She went down the staircase to the foyer. He was already in the house, the maid taking his coat. He turned, hearing her footsteps, his small white even teeth showing in a smile when he saw her.

He advanced toward her and took her hand, raising it to his lips. She felt his thin moustache prickling the back of her fingers. "*Bon soir*, Anna," he said. "You are as beautiful as ever."

She returned his smile and answered in the same language. "And you are as gallant as ever, Maurice."

He laughed. "And the litte one?"

"Janette is five. You would not know her now, she is so big."

"And beautiful, like her mother."

"She will have a beauty all her own," Anna said.

"Good," Maurice said. "Then since I cannot have you, I will wait for her."

Anna laughed. "You might have to wait for a long time."

He looked at her strangely. "Until then I shall have to content myself with what is available."

"Wolfgang is waiting in the library," she said. "Follow me."

He waited until she had gone up a few steps before following her. And all the way to the top of the stairs he was aware of the sensuous movements of her body delineated by the clinging silk of her dress.

The two men shook hands, Wolfgang clicking his heels, with a nod of his head, Maurice, very French, with a slight bow. They spoke in English, a neutral language that each thought he spoke better than the other, since neither would give the other the advantage of speaking his own language.

"How is Paris?" Wolfgang asked.

"Very American," Maurice answered. "Chocolate bars, cigarettes, chewing gum. Not the same."

Wolfgang was silent for a moment. "At least the Russians are not there. Germany is finished."

Maurice nodded sympathetically without answering.

Anna, who had been watching, turned toward the door. "I'll get the coffee."

They waited until the door closed behind her. Wolfgang went to the sideboard. "Schnapps? Cognac?"

"Cognac."

Wolfgang poured Courvoisier into a snifter and handed it to him, then took a schnapps for himself. He gestured to a chair and they sat down opposite each other, the small coffee table between them. "You brought the papers?" he asked.

Maurice nodded and opened the small leather briefcase he carried with him. "They're all here." He placed the blue paper documents with the official *notaire*'s seal in three stacks on the coffee table. "I think you will find everything in order. All the companies have been placed in Anna's name, as you requested."

Wolfgang picked up one of the papers and looked at it. It was the usual legal gibberish which rarely made sense, whatever language it was written in.

Maurice looked at him. "Still sure you want to do it? We can burn the papers and it will be as if it was never done."

Wolfgang drew a deep breath. "I have no choice," he said. "There is no way the French will allow me to keep those companies, even though I acquired them legitimately during the occupation. The Jews will come back, screaming that I forced them to sell."

Maurice nodded in agreement. "Ungrateful bastards. It would have been better if you were not so honest. There were others who not only took the companies but sent them to the camps as well. At least you let them get away with their lives."

They were silent for a moment.

Maurice looked at him. "What are your plans now?"

"South America," Wolfgang said. "My wife and children are already there. I can't stay here much longer. It's only a matter of time before my name comes up, then they'll want me back for trial in Germany. And the Swiss will suddenly find me persona non grata."

"Does Anna already know?"

"I told her. She understands. Besides, she is grateful to me for saving her life and the life of the child. When I found her in Poland, she was already on the way to the camps, her husband, the young count, was dead on the battlefield, the rest of her family gone in the blitz."

He paused, remembering the day he first saw her, almost five years ago.

It was a small house in the fashionable residential area on the outskirts of Warsaw. Small in comparison to the houses that most of the other high-ranking German officers chose to occupy during their stay, but Wolfgang was another breed. He had no reason to display himself or assert his importance, coming as he did from an old, impeccably aristocratic industrial family. His basic concern was not military or political; it was his job to see that local industry was absorbed into the Reich war industry. The job, here in Warsaw, was mainly a cleanup operation, the preliminary studies and work already done. It would be up to him to make the final decision on the disposal and integration of the various companies and industries. He estimated that it would take him between a month and six weeks to complete his assignment, then back to Berlin to await a new assignment. Only thirty-four, he had already been given the temporary rank of Generalmajor to enable him to deal with his Wehrmacht counterparts on an equal level. His personal secretary, Johann Schwebel, was made a sergeant so that he could accompany him.

It was Schwebel who saw her first. He was standing in the doorway of the small house when the truck pulled up in front and the women began to climb down from it. He stood there, marveling at the efficiency of the S.S. It had been just yesterday that they asked procurement to locate a housekeeper for them, one who spoke German as well as Polish so that there would be no language difficulty in running the house; and now six women were getting out of the truck for him to make a choice. They stood nervously in the yard as the guard with a machine pistol on a sling over his shoulder came up to the doorway.

The guard stopped in front of Schwebel. "I've got the women here for you to make your pick," he said flatly.

"Do you have their papers?" Schwebel asked.

The guard nodded and took them from a pouch. "Here they are." He noticed Schwebel looking over his shoulder and turned.

A seventh girl was getting out of the truck. There was something different about her. Certainly it wasn't the clothing. They all wore the same drab gray prison dress. But it was something that she did with it. Maybe it was the way she carried herself. Straight and tall. With an air of indifference, of pride. Her hair, long and chestnut brown, brushed neatly, fell just below her shoulders with not a strand out of place. She glanced around coolly, then stood there next to the truck, waiting. She made no move to join the other women, who had begun to chatter nervously among themselves.

"That's the princess," the guard said.

"The princess?"

"That's the name they gave her in the camp. She came there ten days ago and I don't think she's spoken a word to any of the other girls in the whole time. She keeps to herself. And you know how Polish girls love to fuck. The minute you take it out they start coming and when you stick it to them they go crazy. This one, zero. About fifteen of us fucked her already and it was the same with every one of them. She laid there without a movement until it was over. Then it was as if nothing had happened. She would wipe her cunt without saying a word and go about her business."

"Which paper is hers?" Schwebel asked. "I'd like to see her first."

"The one with the red band on the corner and the A in a circle. She's already scheduled for Auschwitz next week. We don't need girls like her around." The guard laughed coarsely. "My advice is not to bother with her. She pisses ice water."

Schwebel sat at the small table in the foyer which served as his desk, the files in front of him. He opened the folder with the red band.

Tanya Anna Pojarska b. Kosciusko, 7 Nov. '18, Warsaw. Widow, husband ded. Count Peter Pojarska, Capt. Polish Army in Jan. 1940. One child, daughter, Janette Marie, b. Paris, France, 10 Sept. '39. Rel. Catholic. Father, Professor of Modern Languages, Univ. Warsaw, ded. All known family, ded. Educ. B.A. Univ. Warsaw, Mod. Lang, '37, M.A. Sorbonne, Paris, Mod. Lang, '39. Fluent Pol. Fre. Eng. Ger. Rus. Ita. Spa. All family assets and properties forfeited to State, 12 Oct. '39. Guilty treason, subversion. Gestapo file Warsaw–72943/029. Sentenced labor camp #12. Perm. gtd. for daughter to accompany.

Schwebel finished leafing through the other folders. He had already come to the conclusion that she was the only one qualified for the job. The others were ordinary. Despite the fact that they had some knowledge of German, they had very little in the way of educational background to offer. When he looked up, she was standing in front of his desk.

"Sit down, Frau Pojarska," he said in German.

"Dankeschön." She sat down quietly.

He continued in German. "Your duties will consist of running the house and keeping order. You will also be asked to assist in the translation and writing of certain documents. Do you think you're capable of this?"

"I think so," she nodded.

"It will be for six weeks only," he said.

"In these times," she said, "six weeks can be a lifetime." She took a deep breath. "Am I permitted to bring my daughter with me?"

He hesitated.

"She will not be any trouble," she said quickly. "She is really a very quiet baby."

"I can't make that decision," he said. "It is up to the general."

Her eyes met his across the desk. "I will not leave her there," she said quietly.

He was silent.

"There are still ways I have to show my gratitude," she said quickly.

He cleared his throat. "I will do what I can. But it will still be the general's decision." He rose to his feet. "Wait here."

She watched him go up the stairs to the general's room. A moment later he came out on the landing. "Come up here."

He opened the door for her and she entered before him. The general, who had been standing near the window, looking at her folder, turned to her. Her first thought was one of surprise. He was so young. Maybe thirty-five. Not much older than Peter.

Schwebel's voice came from behind her. "Generalmajor von Brenner, Frau Pojarska."

Wolfgang looked at her. He felt a tightness come into his gut. He could sense the woman beneath the drab prison dress. His voice was suddenly hoarse. "Schwebel thinks you can do the job, but there is a complication."

Her voice was clear. "It does not have to be one."

He continued to look at her silently.

"I promise," she said. Her voice suddenly grew strong. "I cannot leave her there to die."

He thought of his own two children, going to school in Bavaria, far from the war and untouched by it. He turned away so that she could not see the expression in his eyes. What was it that Schwebel told him she had said? Six weeks could be a lifetime. It was only six weeks. There was no reason why she could not have it. He turned back to her. "You have my permission to bring the child."

He saw the sudden mist in her eyes but her voice was controlled. *"Dankeschön, Herr General."*

"Do you have any other clothing?"

She shook her head. "They took everything away when I came to the camp."

"We'll have to get some for you," he said. "It will be up to you to receive guests and make them comfortable. We'll

15

also need two more women. A cook and a maid for cleaning and laundry. You choose them."

"*Jawohl, Herr General.*"

"I'll have Schwebel write an order approving the child and the others. Then you will go shopping with him. You will buy clothing for yourself and uniforms for the others. You will have everything in order for dinner tonight, which will be at eight o'clock. I will leave the menu up to you."

He watched the door close behind her, then went back to his desk and sat down. What was it Schwebel had told him? Fifteen men. He couldn't believe it. None of it showed on her face. No anger, resentment, subservience. It was as if nothing could touch her that she did not want to feel.

Dinner surprised him. Vichyssoise. *Gedämpftes kalbfleisch,* with a delicate horseradish dressing, boiled potatoes, fresh stringbeans. A garden salad with cheese. Finally, coffee and cognac.

At the end of the meal she came into the dining room. "Was the dinner to your satisfaction, *Herr General?*"

"Very good."

She allowed herself a reserved smile. "I am pleased. Thank you. Is there anything else I can get you?"

"That will be all, thank you. Good night."

"Good night, *Herr General.*"

It was almost midnight and he still tossed sleeplessly on his bed. Finally he got out of bed and put on his robe and went out into the hall. The light still shone from under Schwebel's door. He opened it.

Schwebel jumped to his feet from his bed, the book he was reading still in his hand. "Herr von Brenner," he stammered. "I mean, *Herr General.*"

"Her room," Wolfgang said.

"The first one at the top of the stairs on the next flight up."

He closed the door behind him and went up the next flight of stairs. No light came from under her door. He hesitated a moment, then opened it and stepped inside.

16

In the faint moonlight from the window, he saw her sit up suddenly. A moment later a small light from the bed lamp went on. Her hair was long and dark, falling well below her shoulders, her eyes wide. She did not speak.

He saw the makeshift crib next to the bed and went to it and looked down. The infant was sleeping peacefully, her thumb in her mouth. He bent over the crib and gently withdrew the thumb. "It's bad for her teeth," he said, straightening up.

She still did not speak.

"What's her name?"

"Janette."

"It's a pretty name," he said. He looked down at the child again. "She's beautiful."

"Thank you, *Herr General.*" She looked up at him. "You have children?"

"Two," he said.

"It must be difficult being away from them."

"It is."

"And your wife?"

"That, too," he said. Suddenly he felt awkward. He turned back to the door. "Well, good night."

He had been back in his bed for about ten minutes when she came into his room. He sat up. "Yes?"

"Turn on the light," she said. "I want you to see me."

He pressed the switch on the bed lamp. She was wearing a full-length white nightgown, her hair falling around it. "Look at me," she said softly, beginning to slide the gown off one shoulder.

His breath caught in his throat as one breast appeared, full and strong, the strawberrylike nipple jutting forth from the purple-red areola, then the other breast leaped free as she pushed the gown down to her waist. His eyes followed her hands as she slowly moved them down across her rib cage past her flat, softly muscled belly, pushing the gown suddenly tight across her wide hips until at last it fell to the

17

floor around her, her dark curly pubis pointing like an arrowhead down between the columns of her legs.

She came close to the bed and moved the sheet away from his legs. She pulled at the tie string of his pajamas and his phallus sprang free. She knelt beside the bed, looking into his eyes for a moment, then down at him. Gently she peeled the foreskin back from his throbbing red glans. Her tongue flicked snakelike over it.

Suddenly her hand tightened over his phallus, holding it in a viselike grip. She looked up at him. Her voice was imperious. "Don't come yet."

He couldn't speak. All he could do was nod.

Her face bent back to him. "I'll tell you when," she said as she once again took him in her mouth.

Six weeks later when he boarded the train for Paris, she and the child went with him.

Silently Wolfgang finished signing the last of the documents. He looked up at Maurice. "I think that does it," he said.

"Technically, yes," Maurice answered. "But there are other problems."

Wolfgang looked at him.

"Her French resident's permit was issued by the Pétain government. It may not be acceptable to the present regime."

"Why not? It was a permanent permit recognizing her status as a displaced person. She was even graduated from the Sorbonne before the war. Besides, her daughter was born in France before the occupation."

"There have been many cases where they have withdrawn permits because the holders were considered collaborationists. And there are many in Paris who know of her relationship with you."

Wolfgang thought for a moment. "What can we do about that?"

18

"I've given it some thought, but I've come up with no firm solution. The only thing that could work is if she held a valid French citizenship."

"Shit." Wolfgang got to his feet. "What do we do now?" He crossed to the sideboard and poured himself another schnapps.

Maurice turned and looked at Anna, who had been sitting silently while Wolfgang had been signing the papers, the coffee service on the small table in front of her. She raised her head from the needles in her hands and met his eyes. They stared at each other for a long moment, then his eyes fell away and she returned to her knitting.

Wolfgang swallowed his schnapps, refilled his glass, came back to the couch and sat down heavily. "Maybe it's not worth the effort. Maybe we should just sell the companies and get rid of them."

"You'd get nothing for them right now," Maurice said. "The French are bankrupt. Five years from now, when things are normal, they'll be worth a great deal of money."

"Five years," Wolfgang said. "Who the hell knows where we'll be in five years?"

"If we're dead it won't matter," Maurice said. "But if we're alive, it will."

"If they withdraw her permit, we lose it all anyway. They'll take the companies back."

"It's a chance we have to take," Maurice said.

Anna spoke softly without looking up from her knitting. "If I were married to a Frenchman, I would automatically have citizenship."

Wolfgang stared at her for a moment, then turned to Maurice. "Is that true?"

Maurice nodded.

"Then find someone we can trust and Anna will marry him."

Maurice gestured to the papers. "I know of none I can trust with these. Do you?"

19

Wolfgang looked down at the papers, then up at him. "You're not married."

Maurice shook his head. "It would be too dangerous. There are still many Gaullists who are suspicious of me. After all I still did not jump across the Channel until the last possible moment."

"But they bought your story. And the information you brought them as well as the explanation that you stayed undercover in order to help them."

"True. But that was while the battle was still going on. Now questions are beginning to be asked."

"I'm sure your uncle could take care of that," Wolfgang said.

"My uncle is dead. He died four months ago."

"Then who is the Marquis de la Beauville now?"

"There is none. He died without issue."

"What happens to his property?"

"It will go to the state. Unless someone comes forward to pay the inheritance taxes on it. Someone in the family, of course."

"Do you think anyone will?"

Maurice shook his head. "I'm the only one left. If my father, his brother, were alive, he would have succeeded to the title. But now it will all be gone—property, title, everything."

Wolfgang pursued it. "If you paid the tax, could you claim the title?"

Maurice thought for a moment. "If the government accepted my payment, I suppose I could."

"How much is involved?"

"A lot of money. Five million francs. Nobody really knows. The government records are hopeless."

Wolfgang got to his feet. He was excited. "Let me think for a minute."

They watched him walk back and forth across the room and finally come to a stop in front of Maurice. "If these companies were in the estate would their ownership be valid?"

"Absolutely," Maurice said. "There is no one who would dare to challenge my uncle's integrity and loyalty. After all, he was one of the few Frenchmen who dared to remain in France, still defying Pétain's authority. And even they did not dare touch him, though he remained virtually a prisoner in his country home."

Wolfgang smiled with satisfaction. "That's it then. All our problems are solved. You and Anna will be married. I will see to it that you have the money to pay the taxes and claim the title. Then the companies will be transferred into the estate and everything will be in order." He picked up his schnapps and tossed it down his throat. "I dub thee the Marquis de la Beauville," he said, tapping Maurice lightly on both shoulders.

Maurice looked past him at Anna. He thought he saw a faint smile on her lips as she continued to look down at the knitting needles flying in her hands. It was the same enigmatic smile that very first time they had met in Paris, in the autumn of 1940.

He walked up the small flight of steps from the street to the door of the small town house, sandwiched and almost lost among the large apartment buildings on the avenue d'Iéna, and pressed the doorbell.

A maid in uniform opened the door and looked out at him. "Monsieur?"

He took a card from his pocket and gave it to her. "I have an appointment with General von Brenner."

She glanced down at the card. "*Entrez*, M'sieur."

He followed her into the hallway and waited while she disappeared into another room of the house. He looked around the walls. They were bare and there were still faint discolorations where pictures had once hung. Idly he wondered what unlucky French family had been summarily evicted from their home to make way for their Prussian conquerors. And the paintings that had once adorned the walls—had the Frenchmen been able to take them or

21

were they now somewhere in the general's house in Germany?

The sound of a man's footsteps came from behind him. He turned. The soldier wearing a Wehrmacht sergeant's uniform raised his hand in a salute. "Heil Hitler."

Maurice raised his hand. "Heil Hitler."

"The general will be with you in a few minutes." Schwebel opened a door. "Would you be kind enough to wait in the drawing room?"

"Avec plaisir." Maurice went into the room and the door closed behind him. The furniture in this room seemed to be untouched, as were the paintings on the wall. A small fire burned in the fireplace.

He crossed to the fire and warmed his hands in front of it. Even now, in early fall, when Paris was normally warm, there always seemed to be a northern chill in the damp air. The French were sure that it was the Germans who caused it.

He heard the door open and turned back to it, expecting the general. Instead it was a tall young woman, her long brown hair brushed carefully back in a quiet chignon that accented her high cheekbones and large dark eyes. She was wearing a chic dark afternoon dress that accented her full figure while at the same time playing it down.

"Monsieur de la Beauville?" She spoke in accent-free Parisian.

He nodded.

She came toward him. "I am Madame Pojarska. The general asked me to make you comfortable. He may be detained longer than he thought. May I order coffee or a drink for you?"

"Coffee would be fine."

"And some pastry perhaps. Our *pâtissier* is one of the finest in Paris."

He smiled. "You have uncovered my weakness, Madame." It was true. Since the Germans had come to Paris there wasn't a decent piece of pastry to be had anywhere.

A few moments later, he was seated on the couch, a cup of fragrant real coffee in front of him, his fork crinkling through the flaky leaves of a *millefeuille*. "This is delicious," he said.

That faint smile curved the corners of her mouth. "Some things in France will never change."

He looked at her in surprise. It was not the kind of remark he had expected to hear in the home of a German general. "You lived in France before, Madame?"

"I went to school here," she answered. "The Sorbonne." She placed another *millefeuille* on his plate. "My daughter was born here. Just after the war broke out."

"Then your daughter is French," he said.

"Polish. My late husband and I are Polish."

"Under French law your child has the right to French citizenship unless her parents have notified the authorities differently."

She thought for a moment. "Then she is French, because my late husband went back to Poland the day war broke out and we never filed any papers at all."

He raised a questioning eyebrow. "Your late husband?"

She nodded. "He died defending his country."

"I'm sorry," he said.

She was thoughtful for a moment. "It was fated," she said. "I am not the only widow this war has produced, and I will not be the last. Poland was not the only country to fall before the Germans, and France will not be the last."

He was silent.

"But people survive—even if it means they have to learn to live with a new order," she continued.

He nodded. "That is true. The circles of power are far beyond us. We must learn to live with them, not them with us."

There was a knock at the door. The sergeant came into the room. "The general is free now. He asks that you bring Monsieur de la Beauville to his study."

He followed her through the bare hall to another room.

She paused, knocking on the door and then opening it without waiting for a reply.

General von Brenner was a much younger man than he had expected. At most he was no older than Maurice himself, who was thirty-seven. He did not offer the usual salute; instead he held out his hand. "Monsieur de la Beauville. I have been looking forward to meeting with you." His French was tinged with a heavy German accent.

Maurice replied with his French-tinged German, "It is my honor, General."

The two men stared at each other; then suddenly the general grinned. "My French is as bad as your German."

Maurice laughed. "Not quite."

"Do you speak English?"

"Yes."

"Then suppose we converse in that language. Then neither of us has to feel embarrassed. And if we have any problems in understanding each other, Anna, here, can help us out."

"Agreed," Maurice answered in English.

"Now to work," the general said. "The French Industrial Board has assigned you to work with me so that we may better mobilize industry into the war effort against our mutual enemy. Our first priority of course will be heavy industry that can be used to manufacture weapons and equipment."

"That, too, was my understanding, and with your permission I have already prepared a number of files which at this very moment are on their way here by special couriers. I am at your disposal to begin work with them immediately."

But in the course of the three years they were to work together during the occupation, both saw other opportunities begin to develop. Non-war-related businesses that were begging to be taken over, because under the new order there were many owners who were not acceptable. A large, well-known vineyard, a company that bottled natural mineral waters, another company in the south that manufactured bases for perfumes and cosmetics. All at bargain prices. Low cash and liberal exit visas for the former owners which enabled them to seek freedom elsewhere. Since these companies' true ownership was always hidden by the laws affecting French *sociétés anonymes* there was never an overt record of the real proprietors. Still, when decisions regarding the companies had to be made, the owner had to reveal himself, if only within his companies. To forestall any criticism, Wolfgang placed the management of record in Anna's name. All were quiet companies which did little business during the war. It was for the postwar period that Wolfgang had acquired them—for a time when the need for their products and their market would expand.

It was slightly more than two years later on a hot humid day in the summer of 1943 that Wolfgang returned from a meeting at H.Q. West. She saw that he was upset, but kept silent until he was ready to talk. That did not happen until after dinner as they sat in the study and he smoked his cigar and sipped his coffee.

"I'm called back to Berlin," he said heavily.

She looked at him. "For how long?"

"Permanently," he said. "My job here is finished. There are production problems in the Fatherland they want me to look into."

She was silent for a moment. "I'll begin packing immediately."

"No." His voice was abrupt. "You're not coming with me."

She looked at him without speaking.

"I can't bring you to Germany," he said awkwardly. "My family—"

"I understand," she said quickly. She took a deep breath, then forced a smile. "I have no complaints. At first it was only for six weeks, remember?"

"It is not over," he said. "I have plans."

"I don't want you to endanger yourself," she said.

"There will be no danger," he answered. "I have asked Maurice to join us at breakfast tomorrow and I will explain them all to you."

She was silent for a long moment. "When do you have to leave?"

"Friday."

She looked deep into his eyes. "This is Tuesday," she said, rising. "Come to bed. We have not much time left."

Wolfgang waited until the maid had cleared the breakfast dishes and left the room before he spoke. Maurice and Anna sat around the small table. "Germany has lost the war," he said flatly.

Neither of them spoke. He continued. "War is like business. When you stop going forward, you lose momentum. Then you lose control. The Führer made a critical error. Instead of pressing forward across the Channel to England, he turned toward Russia. At that point it was all over."

The others were still silent. "Now it's only a question of time and we must make plans. There will be many opportunities after the war and it will be up to us to take advantage of them." He looked at Maurice. "We will begin with you. If we want to keep the properties we have acquired here in France you will have to change sides. Cross the Channel and join the Gaullists."

"Impossible!" Maurice protested. "They will shoot me on sight."

"Not if you follow my plan. I will make available to you certain information that will be invaluable to the Allies. Information on manufacturing and production facilities that they have not as yet learned about. You will go to your uncle, the marquis, whose reputation is unassailable and explain to him that you have been secretly working with us to gain access to this information. Now that you have it, you need his help to get it across the Channel. I'm sure that he has contacts, and with my help, I can guarantee you safe passage across the Channel within a month."

Maurice hesitated. "It will be dangerous."

"It will be more dangerous to remain. When the French return you will be shot as a traitor and collaborationist."

Maurice was silent.

Wolfgang turned to Anna. "For many years my family has owned a small town house in Geneva. I have already secured a Swiss residency visa for you to work there as my housekeeper, and for Janette. You will remain here for about a month after I leave. Then you will move to Switzerland. Schwebel will remain here with you to help organize the necessary files and papers that you are to take with you, then, acting as your chauffeur, he will drive you to Geneva. The excuse will be that Janette is ill and the doctors have advised her to recuperate in the Alps. When you are safely in the house there, he will return to Germany to join me."

Anna looked at him. "And what will you be doing all that time?"

"I will be making plans to get my family out of Germany. Because of my position, we will all be targets for Allied vengeance."

"Where will they go?"

"There are several countries in South America which offer us shelter. For a fee, of course. But that is only money."

"And what will happen to you?"

"As soon as I see them safely away, I will join you in Geneva."

She was silent for a moment. "There is no other way?"

He shook his head. "No other way. The end may come in a year, two years, maybe even three. But it will come, believe me."

They were all silent for a moment, each with his own thoughts. *"Merde!"* Maurice exclaimed suddenly. He looked at Wolfgang. "I had foolish dreams of one day being a rich man."

Wolfgang smiled. "Do as I say and you still may be a rich man."

After Maurice had gone, Wolfgang got to his feet. "Come to my study with me."

She followed him up to the small room which he used as his private study. He closed the door and locked it behind him. "What I am about to show you, no one else in the world knows, neither Maurice nor Schwebel, not even my family. No one. Just me. And now, you."

She watched silently while he moved his chair from behind the desk and lifted the rug from the floor beneath it. His hand searched for a wooden slat on the floor, and finding it, pressed it. A small trapdoor, little more than a foot wide, sprang up. He reached inside and took out what looked like a tin safe-deposit box and placed it on the table. He lifted the latch, opened it and beckoned to her. "Look."

She walked to the desk and, standing beside him, looked down. The box was filled with shining gold coins. She was speechless.

His face was serious. "Gold louis. There are forty boxes like this here. One hundred thousand in all."

Her breath rushed from her. "My God! I had no idea." She looked at him. "How—?"

"No questions," he answered. "I have them. That's all that matters. And you're going to bring them to Switzerland."

"How?" she asked. "You know all the luggage is searched when we cross the border."

"I thought of that," he smiled. He gestured to her and she followed him to the window. He pointed to the Mercedes limousine standing in the courtyard. "It looks like just any other car, doesn't it?"

She nodded.

"It's not," he said. "The side panels around the doors and sides are hollow and lined with soundproofing material so that the coins will not rattle and make noise. I had it specially built."

"What if the men who built it talk?"

"They won't talk," he said. "They were Jews. And they are long since gone."

"Dead?"

He didn't answer. He went back to the desk and placed the box back in the trap, then covered it again with the rug and moved the chair back into place.

He sat down in the chair. "You will have to transfer it alone. I will show you how to gain access to the panels. But no one must see you do it. No one. Your life and your daughter's will be worth nothing if you are seen. I do not have to explain what people will do for that kind of money."

She nodded. Murder had been committed for far less.

"You will have to arrange at least one or two hours each night to be alone in the house. It does not all have to be done in one night. You have a month. When it is all in place you will be ready to leave."

"Will Schwebel be the only one going with me?"

"No. There will be another man with him. An ex-paratrooper. Tough and a trained killer. If there is any real trouble he knows how to handle it."

"And what do I do with it when I get there?"

"Rent a numbered box at one of the Swiss banks. Then remove the gold in the same way you placed it there. A little at a time. When the car is empty, Schwebel and his assistant will then drive the car to me in Germany."

She sank into a chair. "For the first time, I am frightened."

He looked at her steadily. "So am I," he said heavily. "But we have no choice. There is nothing else we can do if we want to have any life together after this is over."

Not once in all the time they had been together had he ever told her that he loved her—not even when his passion burst and flooded her with his seed did he ever do more than groan, trembling in the grip of his ecstasy until she feared that the crush of his body would thrust its way deep into her womb. And even now, as they stood in the doorway of the small French house, the gray of morning spilling through the open door, he was still erect and reserved.

Politely he leaned forward and kissed her formally on both cheeks. "Be careful," he said.

"I will." She nodded.

Then he turned to Janette, who had been standing next to her mother, her eyes wide, and picked her up in his arms. He kissed the child's forehead, then her mouth. "*Auf Wiedersehen, Liebchen,*" he said. "Be a good girl and do as your mother tells you."

The child nodded. "Yes, Papa General."

He smiled and gave her to her mother. "I will see you soon," he said, then turned and marched out the door, getting into the car that was to drive him to the train without looking back.

Anna waited until the car left the driveway before closing the door and turning back into the house. She put the child down.

"Mama?"

Anna looked down at her.

"Will Papa General come back?"

Anna was surprised. "What makes you ask that?"

"Nana says that he is going and that Monsieur Maurice is going to be the new papa."

"Nana is stupid," Anna said. "She does not know what she is saying."

"But Nana said that Papa General is going to Germany and that we can't go with him. And now, Monsieur Maurice is going to be in charge."

"Nana is wrong. When Papa General is away I am in charge. No one else. Not Monsieur Maurice, not anyone."

"Then Papa General is coming back," Janette said.

Anna hesitated a moment, then nodded. "Yes, he will come back. And you can tell stupid Nana that."

30

Two hours later when Schwebel returned from the train station, she called him upstairs into the general's study and closed the door. She sat in the chair behind the desk. "I think we may have a problem."

He was silent, waiting for her to speak further.

"The child's nurse. She talks too much. She has already told the child that the general will not return. If she talks to the child, who knows who else she might be talking with?"

Schwebel nodded.

"A word in the wrong place could endanger the general's plans," she said.

"I will take care of the matter, Countess," he said.

She looked up at him in surprise. It was the first time he had ever addressed her by title. Until now it had always been Frau Pojarska.

There was no change in the expression on his face. "Is there anything else, Countess?"

"Nothing else," she said, shaking her head. "Thank you, Johann."

He bowed politely and left the room. Two days later the nanny had her day off. She never returned to work.

Maurice's voice was guarded on the telephone. "I must see you."

It had been three weeks since Wolfgang had left Paris and this was the first time she had heard from him in all that time. "I am here," she said simply.

"You don't understand," he said. "I may be under surveillance. Now that I have made my overtures I do not dare come to your place."

"Can't we discuss it on the telephone?"

"There are certain papers I must turn over to you. Exit visas for yourself and Janette approved by the French authorities and the Germans. Other matters concerning mutual affairs."

"I'm sorry," she said. "There is no way I can come to see

31

you. Schwebel is under orders to accompany me every time I leave the house."

"*Merde!*" He fell silent.

She waited for him to speak.

"There is not much time left," he said. "The day after tomorrow I will be gone."

She still did not speak.

"After midnight tonight," he said, "be at the back door of your house. If I am not there by half past the hour do not wait for me."

At ten minutes past midnight she heard a light tapping on the service door. Quickly she got to her feet and opened it. He stepped inside and shut the door quickly.

"Is everyone asleep?" he whispered.

She nodded.

"Schwebel?"

"Since the general left, he spends the night in the small apartment over the coach house."

"I need a drink," he said abruptly.

"Come," she said. She led him through the darkened house to the small study on the second floor. She opened the cabinet and took out a bottle of cognac and a snifter. Quickly she filled it almost to the brim and handed it to him.

He drank half of it almost at one gulp and let out a deep sigh. Slowly he seemed to relax. "It's been like walking a tightrope," he said. "Questions. Always questions. Traps in every corner."

She didn't speak.

He took another sip of the cognac. "Have you heard from Wolfgang?"

"No. Should I have?"

He looked up at her. "I suppose not. Still, I thought he might have gotten word to you somehow."

She changed the subject. "You said you had some papers for me."

"Yes." He opened his jacket and took out an envelope.

"The exit visas for you and Janette all countersigned and approved by the French and Swiss authorities."

She opened the envelope and looked at the papers. They were in order. She put them down on the desk. "You said there were other matters."

"They were not things that could be committed to paper," he said.

"I don't understand."

"The gold," he said.

"Gold?" She hoped the puzzled sound in her voice was convincing. "What gold?"

"I have heard rumors at different times that Wolfgang had been buying up gold louis."

"That's the first time I heard of it," she said. "And I thought I knew everything that was going on."

"He never said anything to you?"

She shook her head.

"Strange," he said. "The information came from usually reliable sources."

"You'd better check them again," she said. She paused, then as if she had a sudden idea. "Could it be that it is another form of trap they are setting for you? To discover how close you really were to the general?"

"I never thought of that. It is possible." He looked at her with open admiration. "I am beginning now to understand why I have been attracted to you from the very beginning."

She smiled, keeping the relief from showing in her eyes. "You're being very French. And very gallant."

"Not true," he said, reaching for her hand. "I'm sure you know how I felt about you."

She allowed her hand to rest in his. She did not want to seem too abrupt. After a moment, she spoke. "It is getting late. It might be dangerous for you to remain too long."

"No," he said. A flush surged into his face. "This time may not come again. I want you to know how I feel."

"Maurice—" She tried to keep her voice light as she withdrew her hand. "We're not children. This is neither the time nor the place."

His voice was challenging. "I am not a one-meter-eighty Boche general but I have a power that none of them have, a strength that all of them envy." His hand moved quickly, unbuttoning his fly. "Look!" he commanded.

She stared down at him, unable to keep the look of surprise from her face. It was as if whatever growth had not gone into his slight frame and height had all gone into his phallus. It seemed almost as thick as his wrist and half the length of his thigh.

"Touch it!" he ordered. "You will need more than two hands to hold all of it."

"I can't," she said, shaking her head but unable to take her eyes from it.

"Why?" he demanded.

She forced her eyes up to his face. "Because I have my period. And if I touched it I am afraid I would not be able to stop."

He searched her eyes. "You're not lying to me?"

"I'm not lying." She forced a smile. "Who could lie with a monster like that threatening me?"

He took a deep breath, then turned away for a moment. When he turned back to her his clothing was rearranged. "There will come a time," he said. "You will not be able to forget this."

One week later she drove across the border into Switzerland, Schwebel and the ex-paratrooper in the front seat, she and Janette, wrapped in blankets, in the back. The border guards waved them through without even a cursory inspection of her luggage.

And now, more than a year later, as she listened to Wolfgang arrange her strange betrothal, she remembered the words Maurice had spoken that last night in Paris. It was at that moment she first realized that he had been right. She

34

had not been able to forget. As much as she tried to concentrate on the knitting needles in her hands, all she could see was that monstrous phallus, the swollen red glans glistening moistly at her.

Wolfgang snapped the valise shut and straightened up. He turned toward her. "That does it."

"Yes."

They were standing on opposite sides of the bed. "It will be a long time," he said. "Perhaps years."

"I know."

He forced a wry smile. "I won't even be here for your wedding."

She didn't speak.

He made no move to come around the bed to her. "I never told you that I love you, did I?"

She shook her head. "No, never."

"But you know that I do, don't you?"

"Yes."

"Maybe not the same way that other people love each other. But in my own fashion."

"I know," she said. "As I love you. In my own fashion."

He glanced at his watch. "I guess it's time."

She opened the door and signaled to Schwebel, who was waiting. He picked up the valise and they followed him downstairs. At the halfway landing, she placed a hand on Wolfgang's arm, stopping him. She waited until Schwebel had gone outside before she spoke. "The gold? What do you want me to do with it?"

"Leave it where it is," he said. "As soon as I get settled I will write you and let you know."

She still held on to his arm. "I wish you were going directly to South America from here, not back to Germany."

"There are still things I must do there," he said. "But do not worry, I will be safe. I will remain in the French zone, where Maurice has everything arranged for me."

"I still don't trust him," she said.

He tried to joke. "Fine way for a woman to talk about her future husband."

She didn't smile. "That makes no difference."

"He's greedy," he said. "He wants the title and the money. And he knows there's no way he can get either except through us. Nothing will happen, believe me."

She looked into his eyes. "I don't want anything to happen to you. You have been too good to me."

He cleared his throat of a sudden tightness. "You have been good to me also."

"Be careful anyway."

He thought for a moment. "You be careful too. Remember what I told you. No matter how much he insists, after you are married do not transfer the companies into his name. Just have him appointed the managing director of them. If he asks why you won't do it, tell him that I did not leave the transfer papers with you."

"I'll remember."

"That should keep him in line," he said. "He wouldn't dare try anything unless it's all in his hands."

"I understand," she said.

This time he kissed her on the mouth. There was a faint saltiness to her lips. He drew back and looked at her. "No tears."

She shook her head. "No tears."

"Strange things happen during a war," he said. "But you made some of it beautiful." He kissed her again. "That's for the little one. Tell her that I was sorry I could not wait for her to return from kindergarten."

"I'll tell her."

They went down to the front door. Once again, he kissed her. Gently this time. "*Auf Wiedersehen, mein Liebchen.*"

M AURICE'S VOICE CRACKLED with pleased excitement through the telephone lines from Paris. "The De Gaulle government accepted my proposal. You are now talking to the Marquis de la Beauville."

"M'sieur le Marquis," she said. "May I offer my congratulations?"

"Madame la Marquise," he said. "That is not all I expect you to offer."

She laughed. "That is good news."

"There is even more," he said. "I managed to have your old papers disappear from the files and have a whole new set for you."

"How did you manage that?"

"Don't ask how. It was expensive but it was worth it. Now there is no one who can point a finger at you. The new papers are in the mail to you. Now all you need are new photographs to attach to them, then go to the French Consul and sign them and it's all over."

"But there are still some people in Paris who might recognize me."

"I thought of that too. Dye your hair blond and change the style. Shoulder length with waves is the latest thing in Paris right now and it would be perfect for you. Plucked eyebrows are also in fashion, as are dark eye makeup and blush-accented high cheekbones. Do that before you have the photos taken. And one more thing. You will notice your residency permit is made out in the name of the Countess Tanya Pojarska. I've dropped the Anna for a reason. Just as Wolfgang had you drop Tanya because it was not a German name, I want you to go back to it, just in case anyone does try to put two and two together."

"I'll go to the beauty parlor first thing in the morning," she said. A thought flashed through her mind. "You seem to know a great deal about the latest fashion."

He laughed. "We own a perfume factory in Grasse, remember? It would be a simple step to jump from there into cosmetics. I've been studying the market. After all the drabness of the war years it's ready for a tremendous expansion —women are just bored with being plain."

"I think you're right," she said.

"I know I'm right," he said. "And I'm making all the contacts I can in that field."

"I hate to bring it up," she said, "but there's one thing you seem to have forgotten."

"What's that?"

"Our marriage."

There was a moment's silence. "I thought we'd be married when you came to Paris."

"No," she said. "I know the French. There will be too many papers to fill out and too many questions to answer. They will want to check everything and that will take forever. Besides, who knows what they might discover? Then all our plans will be for nothing. We'll get married up here as soon as I have the papers completed. It will be much simpler." She laughed. "Besides I like the idea of coming back to France as the wife of the Marquis de la Beauville."

She could almost see him preening over the telephone. "Of course, my dear," he said quickly. "Anything you want."

"By the way," she asked, "have you heard anything from your friends in Berlin about Wolfgang?"

"Not a word," he said.

"I'm worried about him," she said. "It's been more than two months."

"I'm sure that he's all right. If anything had gone wrong, I would have heard. By now he's probably out of the country."

"I hope so," she said.

"Call me as soon as you have the papers in order," he said.

"I will," she said, putting down the telephone.

The door opened and Janette came into the room. She was waving a paper in her hand. *"Maman!"* she exclaimed in French. "Look at this drawing of a bird that I made. The professor gave me an *A*. He said he has never seen a bird like it."

She took the paper from the child's hand. The professor was right. There never was a bird like it. Except maybe in nightmares. It was a cross between a pterodactyl, an eagle and a bat, all in bold vivid frightening colors.

"Isn't it beautiful?" Janette exclaimed.

Tanya nodded. "Very." She gave it back to the child. "You'd better put it in a safe place so that you don't lose it."

"I would like to put it in a frame and hang it on the wall over my bed."

Tanya forced a smile. "All right."

"You were speaking in French on the telephone," Janette said. "Who were you talking to?"

Tanya picked the child up. Now was as good a time as any to tell her. "Mama is getting married."

Janette's face broke into a happy smile. "Papa General is coming back?"

"No," Tanya said. "We're going back to Paris to live. I'm marrying Maurice."

A startled expression crossed Janette's face, then suddenly she began to cry. "No, *Maman*, no! I don't like him. He's a bad man."

"He's not a bad man," Tanya said patiently. "He's very nice. You'll see. He likes you very much."

"He does not!" Janette cried. "He hates me. He always pinches me when you're not looking and he hurts me."

"He doesn't mean to hurt you," Tanya explained. "It's just his way of showing that he likes you."

"No, it's not!" Janette said emphatically. "I can tell from his face that he wants to hurt me, and when I don't cry out he pinches even harder." She began to cry again. "I don't want you to marry him. I want you to marry Papa General."

"I'm sorry, Janette," Tanya said firmly, putting her down.

"There are some things you know nothing about. I am
going to marry him, and that's the last word I'll have on the
subject. Now you go up to your room and calm down."

Still sobbing, the child went to the door. At the door, she
turned back, wiping her nose and face with her forearm.
"I don't care," she said defiantly. "Even if you marry him, I
still won't like him."

They were married three weeks later, and despite the fact
that Tanya had bought Janette a new white dress for the
wedding, she refused to go to the registrar's office with
them.

She stared at herself in the mirror. She still was not used
to seeing herself with blond hair. In a strange fashion she
almost felt as if she had become someone else. Before she
had felt her sexuality as subtle and quiet. Now it was overt
and strong, almost as if it had a force of its own—a force
she could not control.

Slowly she brushed her hair, feeling the soft sensuality of
each silken strand. She paused, looking in the mirror.
Something wasn't just right. Then she knew. The white silk
gown she had chosen for her wedding night was all wrong.

She turned to the small valise she had packed to take to
the hotel. Quickly she went through it. A moment later she
had changed gowns. Now when she looked in the mirror
she understood the impulse that had made her place the
black lace gown in the valise. Now she was different. Now
she was someone else. The thought jumped through her
mind. Lilith.

Again she looked at herself. Now she was ready. Suddenly she felt her legs begin to tremble and placed both
hands on the sink to steady herself. In the mirror she saw
the nipples of her breasts jutting suddenly forward, almost
forcing their way through the filmy lace.

She shook her head violently to clear it. What was wrong
with her? It wasn't as if he was the first man for her. She

closed her eyes for a moment. The knowledge came to her. The monster phallus danced before her closed lids. The ultimate symbol of man's power. The man himself was nothing. It was Priapus with all the worship he inspired. She felt the wetness flooding into her loins.

She waited until she felt she could control the trembling of her legs, then turned off the bathroom light and opened the door to the bedroom. It took a moment for her eyes to adjust to the dim light.

He was standing, naked, next to the bed, his back toward her. Without moving from the bed, he turned slowly toward her. At first all she saw was his hard glittering eyes and the lips drawn back tightly across his small white teeth; then her eyes fell, drawn inexorably to his phallus. She felt the trembling begin again in her legs, her mouth suddenly dry with the breath catching in her throat.

Without speaking, he gestured with one hand for her to come to him, the other hand concealed behind his back.

Silently she moved toward him, feeling as if she might fall with every step she took. At last she was before him, her eyes still cast down. She felt as if she were hypnotized by his manhood.

Suddenly he moved and with one hand tore the black gown down the front of her body until it lay on the floor around her feet and she was naked in front of him. Still he didn't speak.

She felt her wetness running down the inside of her thighs. But there was no way she could move. It was as if his phallus had taken over all the strength in her body. She did not see his other hand come from behind his back. It took a moment for the shock wave of pain to travel from her body to her brain. Then the agony was so intense that a scream involuntarily tore its way from her throat.

For the first time she saw the cat-o'-nine-tails in his other hand, the small metal tips at the end of each thong gleaming in the light. She looked down at herself. The lash marks were already rising across her breasts, her belly and thighs,

41

and blood was beginning to seep through the skin where the metal had torn into her flesh.

Before she could speak, his harsh voice tore at her. "Whore of the Boche! Do you think I will be like the others? Slave to your cunt?"

She could only shake her head. There was no way she could speak. Her voice had gone with shock.

Again the lash. Again the pain. Then his hand was in her hair, cruelly forcing her to the floor before him. She tried to cover her face with her hands but he forced her head back so that she could look at him. His phallus, fully erect now, hung over her face like a giant snake.

His voice was harsh and cruel. "You are the slave and he is your master. Look at him and know that you are nothing but his whore."

She tried to turn her head away but his hand gripping her by the hair would not let her move. Then the cat fell again. This time across her back. Twice. The pain engulfed her and she screamed, her voice almost raw with hoarseness.

It was as if her scream of pain triggered him off. His phallus began to leap like an angry cobra as his semen came spurting over her. Angrily he lashed at her again and the pain and the semen seemed to be flowing all together over her body.

Then it was over and he thrust her violently to the floor. She sprawled, sobbing, at his feet, unable to move. He stood silently for a moment, breathing heavily, looking down at her. Then he prodded her with his foot until she rolled over on her back, her face staring up at him.

His voice was normal now. "Go to the bathroom, whore, and clean yourself."

She didn't move.

Again the lash. Her body jumped with the pain. "Do as I say!"

Slowly she rolled to her hands and knees and began to crawl to the bathroom door. She heard his voice from behind her. "Wait!" She stopped. She saw his feet walk around her and stop in front of her. She didn't raise her head.

"Look at me!" he commanded.

She looked up. He was holding his penis in one hand. Suddenly the urine gushed forth from him, its hot burning saltiness bringing a new dimension to the raw bleeding pain of her wounds. "No!" she screamed, trying to move away. But the lash fell again and the pain beat her to the ground, sprawling at his feet.

Then he was finished and he laughed. "Now you can go."

Somewhere inside she found the strength to look up at him. Her voice sounded like an animal's, deep and husky in her throat. "I'll kill you for this!"

He laughed again. "No, you won't," he said contemptuously. "Because if you do, both you and your child will die. You must think I am a fool. I'm not. All your records are in a safe place, and if anything should happen to me, they will be turned over to the authorities."

Slowly he went back to the bed and sat down on it. His voice was relaxed, almost gentle now. "After you clean yourself and this mess, come to bed. I'll be waiting for you." Then he stretched out and pulled the sheet over him. "You don't have to rush. I think I'll sleep for a while."

She pulled herself to her feet by the doorknob. She leaned against it for a moment, then opened the door. It was daylight before she came out and he seemed to be still asleep. She moved quietly to a closet door to get a dress.

His voice came from behind her. "Come here."

She made no move toward him.

He sat up in the bed, holding the cat in his hand. "I said, come here."

Slowly she moved toward him.

"Lie down and spread your legs."

"No." The cat tore at her. Silently she got into the bed.

He threw the sheet from him. He was already erect. He poised himself over her and tried to enter her. But she was dry and closed to him. He spit into his hand and rubbed it on himself then with one violent motion thrust himself deep inside her.

She screamed again in pain as the immenseness of him tore its way through her. He began to move and she continued screaming at the growing intenseness of his mounting passion. It was an agony she never dreamed she could ever feel. Finally he exploded inside her.

For a moment, he lay gasping on her breasts, then raising himself on his arms, looked down at her. He was smiling. "Isn't that what you really wanted? A cock like a horse's?"

She stared into his eyes with hatred. Her voice was cold. "I've seen horses' cocks bigger than yours but I've never wanted to fuck them."

His hand flashed across her face. She could feel the white finger marks begin to flush with pain. Her voice was still cold. "Are you finished?"

He nodded.

"Then get off me," she said. "I want to wash you out of me."

He watched her walk to the bathroom door. "Tanya."

She turned to look back at him.

He seemed genuinely puzzled. "I don't understand you. What is it that you want?"

She took a deep breath. "A man," she said, then closed the bathroom door behind her.

The chauffeur opened the door and Maurice got out first, turning to give her his hand to help her down. She avoided his hand, steadying herself by his wrist, and waited until Janette was beside her before she turned to look at the house. "It's a big house," she said.

"It was a steal," he said. "The owners wanted to sell quickly."

She felt Janette clutching her hand. It was a large gray stone house, more than twenty meters wide, set back behind

44

a wrought-iron fence in a tiny garden facing the street. Behind the giant center gates was a small walk, leading up to the entrance of stained-glass doors protected by a wrought-iron grille into which already had been set the Beauville coat of arms.

She followed him to the door as the chauffeur began to unload their baggage from the car. The door was opened by a butler in full livery before Maurice had a chance to ring the doorbell.

"Shall I carry the bride over the threshold?" Maurice asked sarcastically.

She didn't bother to answer and went into the house. As was the custom, the household staff was lined up in the reception hall to meet the new mistress. There were six of them, all in household uniform. Henri, the butler, his wife, Marguerite, who was the cook, and four young girls, maids who would take care of the cleaning and other services. René, the chauffeur, was still outside.

She shook hands with them one by one, acknowledging their curtsies with a slight nod of her head. "Madame la Marquise," they murmured respectfully.

Just as the introductions were completed, a young man came from one of the closed doors leading to the hall, carrying some papers in his hand. He stopped when he saw them. "Excuse me," he said in English. "I didn't realize you were already here."

Tanya didn't have to hear his accent to know that he was American, she could tell from the cut of his suit. She glanced from him to Maurice.

"My dear," Maurice said. "May I present my executive assistant and secretary, Jerry Johnson? Jerry, Madame la Marquise and her daughter, Janette."

Awkwardly, the American bowed. "It's a pleasure, Madame la Marquise."

Tanya didn't offer her hand. "Mr. Johnson."

"Would you like to see the house, my dear?" Maurice asked.

Tanya shook her head. "I'm a bit tired from the journey. I would like to rest and freshen up a bit first."

Maurice nodded. "Very well." He turned to the butler. "Will you take Madame la Marquise to our suite and see to her comfort." He turned back to Tanya. "I have some papers to go over with Jerry. I'll join you in a little while."

Tanya glanced at the young American. Suddenly many things began to come together in her head. She nodded slowly, no sign of her thoughts showing on her face, then, taking Janette by the hand, began to follow the butler up the stairs.

Slowly Tanya got out of the tub and reached for the giant terry bathrobe and wrapped herself in it. She dried herself quickly, then dropping it on the floor, stood in front of the mirror. The welts and cuts of her wedding night had gone from her body but not from her mind. She slipped into a silk robe and went into the bedroom. She pressed the button for the maid and sat down at the dressing table. There was a discreet knock at the door. *"Entrez."*

The maid came in and curtsied. "Madame."

Tanya looked at her. She was a young girl with dark curly hair and large brown eyes. "What is your name, child?"

"Louise, Madame."

"Louise, would you bring me some tea, please?"

"With pleasure, Madame." The maid curtsied again and left the room.

Tanya turned back to the mirror. Idly she touched her hair. The trouble with being a blonde was that it needed touching up every few weeks. She hated the ugly look of dark roots, though many women didn't seem to mind it. Again there was a knock at the door. Thinking it was the maid returning with the tea, she called out, *"Entrez."*

In the mirror she saw the door open. Quickly she pulled the robe closed around her breasts, as Jerry came into the room, a file of papers in his hand. She looked at him questioningly. "Yes?"

46

"The marquis would like you to sign these papers," he said.

She nodded. "Put them on the table over there and I'll get to them."

He stood there, hesitating.

"Anything wrong?" she asked.

"The marquis said it was important that you sign these right away."

She rose to her feet and faced him. "Tell the marquis that I will sign nothing until after I have read them." She held out her hand. "You can leave them with me."

Automatically he placed them in her hand and turned toward the door. Her voice stopped him.

"By the way," she asked in a casual voice, "how did you happen to meet the marquis?"

"Several years ago in England," he said. "I was attached to GHQ as a liaison officer with the Free French forces. When the war was over and I decided to remain in Europe, the marquis was kind enough to offer me this job."

"I see." She nodded thoughtfully, then smiled. "That must have been a very good thing for the both of you."

"It was," he said, feeling more at ease now and smiling. He turned once again, reaching for the doorknob.

"Jerry."

He looked back at her, his hand still on the doorknob. "Yes, ma'am?"

Her voice was artless. "How long have you and Maurice been lovers?"

She saw the flush creep up into his face and his normally blue-gray eyes grow green with hatred. Then his lips tightened against his reply and he left the room abruptly, the door almost slamming shut behind him.

She was seated at the small breakfast table near the window, sipping tea and reading the file when Maurice came into the room. She glanced up at him. "You could knock," she said casually. "It's the polite thing to do."

His face was flushed and angry. "Jerry told me that you said you wouldn't sign the papers."

"Not until after I'd read them," she said, her voice still casual. She glanced down at the file in her hand. "Now that I have, I won't sign them at all."

"Everything was supposed to be transferred into the estate after we were married," he said. "That was what Wolfgang said we were going to do."

"That's what he said," she agreed pleasantly.

"Then do it," he said.

She shook her head. "No."

"You have to," he said. "I have assumed many financial obligations based on that agreement."

"That's unfortunate," she said.

"Even this house was bought on that assumption," he said.

"I noticed that," she said. "In your own name personally, but to be paid for out of Wolfgang's companies with his moneys. I don't think his intention was to enrich you at his own expense."

"Then you intend to keep it all," he said balefully.

"Until I hear from Wolfgang to the contrary."

"What if you never hear from him?"

She shrugged her shoulders.

"Under French law you're liable for the money in any case," he said.

"I know that," she said calmly. "But tomorrow I will get in touch with the *notaire*, and when he makes the necessary changes in the papers, I will make the payment."

"And what am I supposed to do?"

"Just what we agreed on. You will be the director general of the companies. Manage them well and there's no reason why you too cannot be rich."

"You won't get away with it," he said balefully. "You can be deported."

"And where will you be if you open that can of beans?" she asked with a faint smile. "Especially when I tell them of the circumstances that led to our marriage."

He stared at her without speaking.

"You can go now," she said calmly, dismissing him. "And on your way downstairs inform the butler that I will be ready to look at the rest of the house in a few minutes."

"Is there anything else Madame la Marquise wants me to do?" he asked sarcastically.

"Yes," she said. "Tell your boy friend to get his things out of the house before dinner. You know how servants love to gossip. I don't think it would be an especially nice thing to have them spreading the word all over Paris that Monsieur le Marquis is a pederast."

She waited until the door closed behind him, then went into the bathroom and opened her cosmetic case. She lifted the top shelf out and placed it on the marble countertop next to the sink. Quickly she emptied the jars of cream and lotion from the bottom of the case until the leather case resting on the bottom was revealed. Then she took the leather case and held it in her hand.

The gold-tooled lettering shone at her. *W v B Schweringen.*

She snapped open the case. The silver-steel razors gleamed. Seven of them. One for each day of the week. Labeled in black on the ivory handles. Monday through Sunday. She had found them in the bathroom of the Geneva house and on an impulse had packed them in her case. Now she knew it wasn't an impulse at all. Suddenly the thought flashed through her mind that Wolfgang hadn't forgotten them at all. That he had deliberately left them where she could find them.

Quickly she went back into the bedroom and stood in the center of the room. A moment later she had made up her mind. One on either side of the mattress behind the two sets of pillows between the mattress and the headboard. Then one under the mattress on each side at the foot of the bed. One under the cushion of the small couch in front of the coffee table, one more under the cushion of the chaise longue and the last behind the curtain on the window near the breakfast table.

She took one last look around, then returned the leather case to the bathroom just as the butler's knock sounded on the door.

It took more than two hours for the butler to show the house, and when at last they returned to her room, she complimented him. "You have done very well, Henri. I am pleased."

He bowed. "Thank you, Madame. Is Madame ready to proceed with the unpacking of her luggage?"

"Yes, thank you."

"I will inform Louise to come and assist you. She should be finished in your daughter's room by now." He hesitated a moment. "And what time would Madame like dinner?"

"Eight o'clock."

"In the dining room?"

She looked at him questioningly. "Why do you ask?"

He was uncomfortable. "Monsieur le Marquis informed me that he would not be taking dinner at home tonight."

She was silent.

"Perhaps you and the child would be more comfortable in the breakfast room. It's very cozy in there and looks out on the garden."

She nodded. "A good idea, Henri. Thank you."

"Thank you, Madame." He bowed again and started for the door.

"Henri."

He stopped. "Yes, Madame."

"You've shown me all the rooms except my husband's. I would like to see that now."

"Excuse me, Madame," he said uncomfortably. "I thought—"

"No. I haven't seen it. I don't even know where it is."

He gestured to a narrow door on the far wall of her room. "If Madame will follow me."

She looked at the door. Narrower than normal, until now

she had thought it was a closet. The door opened into a narrow corridor, slightly less than a meter wide and a little more than a meter long, at the end of which was another narrow door.

He opened the second door and she walked into Maurice's room. She stood there for a moment. She should have known it. Maurice had taken the best room for himself. All four windows facing the front of the house overlooking the park across the street. And newly decorated in a fashion that was somehow even more feminine than her own room. She walked into the bathroom. Even that was more than twice the size of her bathroom.

She came out of the bathroom to find the butler standing in the center of the room watching her. "Very nice, Henri."

His voice was guarded. "Yes, Madame."

"I've changed my mind. You do not have to send Louise to unpack me today. Tomorrow will be soon enough."

"Yes, Madame."

"We will also be changing rooms tomorrow," she said. "I will occupy this suite, my daughter will move into mine and you will move the marquis' things into my daughter's suite."

"But, Madame—" His voice was shocked.

"Yes, Henri?" Her voice was cool.

"Monsieur le Marquis. *Le patron.*" He was stammering. "He would not like it."

She met his gaze steadily. "If I am correct, Henri, *le patron* is your employer, the person who pays your wages. *N'est-ce pas?*"

"That is correct, Madame."

"Then you have nothing to concern yourself about," she said, her voice still cool. "Since I am the person who is paying your wages, not Monsieur le Marquis, I am *la patronne.* And the only person you have to please."

His eyes fell before her gaze. He bowed. "Yes, Madame."

"One more thing, Henri," she added. "Tomorrow when you change the rooms you will also have a locksmith change the door locks."

"Yes, Madame. Will there be anything else, Madame?"
She started back through the narrow corridor. "Let me
know as soon as Mr. Johnson has removed his things."

"He has already left the house, Madame. About an hour
ago while we were upstairs on the fourth floor."

"Good," she said. She had made her point and knew that
he didn't miss it. "Thank you, Henri."

"Isn't Monsieur Maurice having dinner with us?"

Tanya looked across the small table at her daughter. "No,
darling. He went out."

Janette's voice was curious. "With that girl?"

Tanya was puzzled. "What girl?"

"You know." Janette's voice was guileless. "That one. The
one that dresses in men's clothing."

Tanya stared at her daughter. "He's not a girl. He's a
man."

"If she's a man, why did you send her out of the house?"
Janette asked pointedly.

Tanya was surprised. The child saw more than she
thought she did. "We need the room for someone else," she
explained, sensing the lameness of her words.

Janette was silent as she finished her soup. She looked up
again after Henri had removed her plate. "I still think she's
a girl."

"What makes you think that?"

"I was downstairs in the kitchen when Monsieur Maurice
came down and told her that you ordered her to leave."

"That doesn't mean he's a girl."

"Then when I was going back up the stairs, I passed her
room. She was crying and Monsieur Maurice was kissing
her and telling her that everything would be all right. He
acted just like she was a girl."

Tanya was silent. "Maybe he just felt bad," she finally
said.

Janette shook her head. "She was taking dresses out of

her closet and putting them in the valise. When they saw me standing there, Monsieur Maurice kicked the door shut with his foot. But they couldn't fool me."

"It doesn't matter anyway," Tanya said with finality. "Either way, he is gone and will not be back in the house."

They were silent until after the entree had been served. Janette cut into her meat. "This is good, isn't it? French cooking is better than Swiss."

Tanya smiled. "Yes, darling."

Janette took another mouthful of food. "I really like it." Then without changing the tone of her voice, "Does it hurt when Monsieur Maurice puts his big thing in you?"

"Janette!" Tanya was shocked. "Where did you ever learn such things?"

"In school," Janette answered casually. "All the kids talk about it. Some of them have even seen their mothers and fathers doing it. Do you think sometime you can let me watch when Monsieur Maurice does it to you?"

"No," Tanya said sharply. "And that's not a nice thing to talk about. Nice girls never talk about it."

"I came into your room one night when you and Papa General were doing it. But you didn't see me, and I went out." She took another forkful of the meat. "But Monsieur Maurice's thing is twice as big as Papa General's. That's why I thought it might hurt."

"How do you know such things?"

"Monsieur Maurice always left his bathroom door open when he took a pee. I couldn't help seeing it. He even knew that I saw him and he used to smile."

Tanya didn't know what to say. Maurice had only stayed in Geneva for a week after they were married and then had gone back to Paris to put the house in order, and until he met them at the train today she hadn't seen him. "Well, that won't happen any more," she finally said. "Tomorrow you're changing rooms to the room next to mine."

"Where will Monsieur Maurice be staying?"

"He'll be moving into your room."

"Then he won't be making a baby in you with his thing?" Janette asked.

"No," Tanya said definitely.

"Why not?"

Tanya looked at her daughter. Her voice grew gentle. "Because you're the only child I want. I don't want any other baby but you."

A smile suddenly broke over Janette's face. She left her chair and ran to her mother, throwing her arms around her. "Really?" she exclaimed.

Tanya hugged her. "Really. You're all the babies I need."

"I'm glad, *Maman*," Janette said. "I don't want you to have any other baby except me."

It was almost midnight when she turned the bed lamp off. Her eyelids felt as if they were lead-weighted. It had been a long day, starting before six o'clock in the morning in Geneva. The nine-hour train ride hadn't been that restful either with its many stops and starts. She had wanted to be awake when Maurice returned but there was no use. She had to get some sleep.

The faint sound of voices and laughter filtered through her sleep. She stirred restlessly, trying to block out the sound, but it was persistent. Finally she opened her eyes and stared at the radium numbers glowing on the alarm-clock dial. It was ten minutes to three. She rolled over on her back, listening to the noise.

It seemed to come through the narrow corridor connecting their rooms. Someone was in there with Maurice but the sound was too blurred for her to tell whether there was one person or more. She lay quietly in the dark. After a while the sounds seemed to die down and her eyes closed and she drifted off.

She didn't know how much later it was that the sharp click of the light switch and the sudden flooding of light into the room woke her up. She sat up in bed, her eyes blinking against the blinding lights. Quickly her eyes adjusted.

The connecting door was partly open and Maurice was standing behind it, looking at her.

"Get out!" she said coldly.

Instead he threw the door wide and stepped into the room. He was completely naked and the cat-o'-nine-tails trailed along the floor as it fell from his right hand. He stopped in the center of the room, staring at her, and with his left hand began to stroke his penis into an erection.

She glanced up at him, then up into his face. "It won't work this time," she said, her voice still cold. "Get out."

He laughed suddenly, then turned and called. "Come in, Jerry darling. Let me show you how to treat a German whore."

Jerry appeared in the doorway. He, too, was naked and holding a bottle of cognac. He stared at her and giggled drunkenly.

The cat snaked across the bed at her. She threw up her hands, catching most of the lashes across her arms, shielding her face. The cat snaked again, falling across her breasts, still covered by the bedsheet.

"Get out of bed, whore cunt!" Maurice snarled.

Silently she got out of the bed, her white cotton nightgown touching the floor. She stood erect, facing him.

"Jerry, tear off her gown," Maurice commanded.

Still giggling, Jerry minced toward her. "Like a drink, darling?" he asked, waving the bottle of cognac.

She stared at him without answering.

"Give her shit!" Maurice snapped. "Tear off her gown. I've got what she wants."

She said nothing as Jerry tried to rip the gown from her. But the cotton was too strong and wouldn't give. Finally he pulled it down over her shoulders and it fell to the floor. He stared at her, then reached out and touched her breasts. "She has big tits," he said almost enviously.

Angrily she slapped his hands away from her.

He giggled. "Don't worry, darling. Another year and they'll begin to fall down to your belly. Big tits always do. Then you won't be so proud of them."

The cat slashed across her. She bit her lips against the pain. "Come over here," Maurice commanded.

Silently she moved toward him, stopping directly in front of him, her eyes fixed on his face. He gripped her by the hair, forcing her to look down at him. "Look at your master, slave bitch!"

She tried to turn her head away from him but the cat slashed across her shoulders as he angrily forced her to her knees before him. He pulled her head back against her neck, forcing her mouth open. "Suck it!"

She tried to close her mouth. This time the cat fell across her back and she gasped in pain. "Now. Will you do as I tell you?"

Slowly she reached for his phallus with one hand as she inched closer to the small couch next to where he was standing. She closed one hand around it, drawing it toward her mouth, as with the other hand she searched between the cushions and found the razor.

Maurice laughed triumphantly. "I told you I knew what she wanted."

Jerry giggled. "She'll never get it in her mouth. That's the biggest cock in Paris."

Now the razor was in her hand. The silver blade flashed briefly in the light. A line of blood suddenly appeared on Maurice's body reaching from his bellybutton down into the hair over his pubis.

Maurice screamed in sudden pain. He stared down at himself. "What have you done to me, you bitch?" Then he saw the blood. "You've killed me!" he screamed and fell to the floor in a faint.

She got to her feet, staring down at him, the razor still bloody in her hand, then she turned to look at Jerry.

He was suddenly sober, his face white, as if he were going to be sick. He stared at the razor in her hand and tried to speak, but no words would come to his lips. Then his eyes fixed on hers with horror.

"I could have killed him but I didn't," she said calmly. She stepped across Maurice and started for the bathroom. At the door she turned back to Jerry. "You'd better call a doctor. He'll need some stitches or he could bleed to death."

"What are you going to do?" he asked hoarsely.

"I'm going to my daughter's room to sleep," she said. "After all, I'm not responsible for what you two do to each other when you get drunk."

It was about ten o'clock the next morning and she was seated at the breakfast table having a cup of coffee after dropping Janette off at her new school when he came into the room. She glanced up at him. "You'd better sit down," she said calmly, as if nothing had happened the night before. "You don't look too well."

He dropped into a chair. "The doctor says I might have the scar the rest of my life."

"Too bad," she said noncommittally.

He reached for the coffee and filled his cup. He took a sip and looked at her. "Now what do we do?"

She met his eyes. "We stop playing games and go to work. Isn't that the reason for this whole arrangement?"

He nodded morosely into his coffee cup.

"You're a good businessman," she said. "Wolfgang said that a long time ago. I respect that and I respect your abilities. I haven't changed in that regard."

He raised his eyes. There was a growing respect in his voice. "You're a strange woman, Tanya."

"Maybe," she said. "But there is one thing you and I have in common."

"What's that?"

"We're both survivors," she said slowly. "We've come this far together and there's no reason to let a moment's stupidity fuck us up and keep us from going a long way further."

57

He took a tentative sip of his coffee. It was already cold. He put it down. "And you're not angry over what has happened?"

"Should I be?" she asked. "As far as I'm concerned it's over. Are you angry?"

He thought for a moment. "Yes. And no. But you are right. It's over."

"We can still make it the good life, Monsieur le Marquis." She smiled. "For both of us."

He raised his head and looked at her intently. Then he nodded his head slowly. "Madame la Marquise, I'm beginning to believe you are right."

"Of course, I'm right, Maurice." She smiled. She picked up the service bell. "Now, let me call Henri and get you some hot coffee and breakfast."

THE VOICE CAME through the telephone, echoing through a corridor ten years long. "This is Johann Schwebel."

Maurice felt the knot tighten in his stomach. Even after ten years, fear gripped him. He couldn't speak.

"Remember me?" The German accent was faint. "It's been a long time."

"Yes," Maurice answered. "It's been a long time."

"I called Madame la Marquise but she was not in. They transferred me to you."

"Yes. She had a luncheon appointment."

"We should arrange a meeting," Johann said.

"Of course," Maurice answered. "Where are you?"

"I'm in Paris."

"Let me check with Tanya and I'll get back to you," Maurice said.

"No, I'll be moving around too much. Let me call you tomorrow morning about eleven o'clock."

"That will be fine," Maurice said. The telephone went dead in his hand. He stared at it for a moment, then slowly returned it to the desk. He took a cigarette and tried to light it. It wasn't easy. His hands were shaking.

The doctor was silent as he helped her remove her legs from the stirrups on the examination table. He stepped back as she swung around sitting up, her white cotton examination gown falling shapelessly around her.

"Get dressed," he said as the nurse moved to help her. "I will see you in my private office in ten minutes."

He left the room before she could ask him a question.

59

The nurse opened the small closet in which her clothing had been hung and moved around behind her to untie the strings that held the gown fastened behind her back.

She was seated in the comfortable leather chair in front of his desk as he came into the small office. Carefully he closed the door behind him and sat down behind the desk, facing her.

"You look very serious, Doctor Pierre," she said.

He nodded. "You're pregnant."

She smiled. "That's all? I was worried for a moment. We can take care of that."

He shook his head. "Not this time."

Her voice was shocked. "Why not? We've done it before."

"You've waited too long. The fetus is fully developed. It's about fifteen weeks old."

"Damn," she said.

"Why didn't you come earlier? As you did before? Four, five, six weeks, and there's no problem."

"I was busy," she said. "Besides I didn't pay any attention. I skipped several periods many times and it came around."

"You were wrong," he said.

"I've heard of abortions when the fetus was this old," she said.

"Yes. But it is very dangerous. Besides, you have several factors militating against it. One, you have had three abortions in the last seven years that I have known you and they haven't done you any good. Two, you're not a kid anymore. Thirty-eight, and physiologically speaking, your body is not that strong, neither do your womb and ovaries have the elasticity to withstand a violent shock like that. You could very well rupture and bleed to death before we could even find out what it is we have to repair."

She took a deep breath. "Could I have a cigarette?"

He pushed a pack across the desk and lit it for her. He waited a moment. "The marquis should be pleased."

She laughed shortly. "You know better than that, Doctor Pierre. The whole world knows better. They all know what he is. It will be the biggest joke in Paris."

"You don't have any choice," he said. "Unless you prefer dying."

She shook her head slowly.

"You could go away for a while," he said. "Have the child and no one would know."

"For how long would I be gone?" she asked.

He looked at her critically. "You're not showing yet. With diet you can stay small, and with the right clothes no one would know. Maybe only the last three months."

She shook her head violently. "Impossible. I have too much to do. I can't be away from the business that long. There would be too many problems."

"Then I suggest you have a talk with the marquis and see what you can work out. I'm sure that the two of you can get together on a story that would pass public muster."

She laughed. "Maybe the public. But not the world in which we live."

"Your life is more important than what people think."

She nodded. "That's the truth."

"Do you know the father?"

She looked at him. "Why do you ask?"

"It would be helpful if we could get a blood type from him. Just for the RH factor. After all it's been almost seventeen years since your daughter was born and there could have been many changes in your system."

She thought for a moment. She had been with two men that month. But logically it had to be the American. She had been with him steadily the last three weeks of the month she had missed her first period. "Yes," she answered.

"Would he give you his blood type?"

She shrugged her shoulders. "Who knows? He's back in America now with his wife and children. I couldn't write him, it might be embarrassing. I would have to call."

"It would be worth the call," Doctor Pierre said.

She nodded slowly and started to her feet. "I'll do it."

He rose from his chair. "The nurse will give you a printed diet on the way out. Follow it carefully and you will keep your weight down. You will also get a supplementary list of vitamins and minerals to take every day to maintain your strength and energy. I would like to see you again in about a month."

She looked at him. "Are you sure we can't do an abortion?"

"It can be done but I don't advise it," he said. He met her gaze. "And don't do anything foolish, because there are nine chances out of ten that you might die."

"I won't do anything foolish, Doctor Pierre," she said. "I promise."

"Good." He smiled. "And send me the blood type if you get it." He came around the desk and kissed her on the cheek. "And don't worry, Tanya. We've all been through worse things."

She nodded. During the war he had been in a concentration camp. He still bore the numbered tattoo on his arms. Only the fact that he had been a doctor saved him from the gas chambers. Impulsively she kissed his cheek. "That's true, Doctor Pierre," she said. "Thank you."

Janette folded the blouse carefully and placed it in the valise, then stepped back. That was the last of the packing. She looked around her room carefully. Satisfied that nothing had been forgotten, she closed the valise and locked it, then placed it on the floor next to the other valise. Tomorrow morning at seven thirty she would be on the train to Switzerland and school.

She walked back to her desk near the window and called her friend Marie-Thérèse. The telephone rang a few times before Marie-Thérèse picked it up. As usual, she sounded breathless. "Hello."

"I'm finished packing," Janette said.

"Oh, God," Marie-Thérèse exclaimed. "I haven't even started yet."

"Would you like me to come over and help you?" Janette asked.

"I sure would." Marie-Thérèse giggled. "But then we'd never get finished. Like last night."

Janette remembered. In the afternoon they had gone to an American movie on the Champs-Elysées. *Rebel Without a Cause*, featuring a new American star, James Dean. It was the fourth time each of them had seen the movie and it was about American kids just like them. Their parents didn't understand them either. And there was something about James Dean that reached inside them. All either of them had to do was to close her eyes and she was Natalie Wood being held roughly in James Dean's arms.

This time on the way out of the theater, Marie-Thérèse had bought a poster of James Dean. He was standing there in tight, worn jeans, skinny hips, and legs slightly bent, his face surly and angry, eyes peering defiantly out at them under a shock of brown-blond hair falling over his eyes. She wanted it for the wall over her bed in school.

When they got home, Marie-Thérèse took a valise from her closet and placed it on the bed. She opened it and placed the poster, still folded inside. "Might as well begin packing," she had said.

Janette nodded. "I've already started. One bag is finished and I just have one more to do."

Marie-Thérèse looked at her. "I wish I could be like you. You're so organized. I always wind up rushing at the last minute."

Janette laughed. "But you always manage to get it done."

Marie-Thérèse giggled. "Yes. But I don't know how." She opened a bureau drawer and took out an armful of underwear and dumped it on the bed next to the valise. She began to separate it into stacks—brassieres, panties, slips. She stared down at them with distaste. "Aren't they ugly?"

Janette shrugged her shoulders. White and beige cotton. "It's regulation," she said. "The school wants it. We don't have any choice."

"I hate them," Marie-Thérèse said. "I don't think Jimmy Dean would like these, do you?"

Janette laughed. "I don't know what he would like."

63

Marie-Thérèse giggled suddenly. "Let's show them to him and see what he thinks." She took the poster, opened it up and stuck it against the wall with two thumbtacks. He stared down at the two girls with an angry look. Marie-Thérèse picked up a brassiere and panties and held them across her over the front of her dress. "Do you like these, Jimmy?" she asked.

After a moment she turned to Janette. "See? I told you he would not like them. You take a pair, see if it's any better."

Janette picked up a set and did the same thing that Marie-Thérèse had done. Marie-Thérèse looked at her, then at the poster, and shook her head. "No better." She threw the garments back onto the bed. "Stupid school."

Janette folded her things neatly and placed them back on the stack from which they had come, then turned to take the poster down from the wall.

"No," Marie-Thérèse said quickly. "Maybe the reason he does not like it is because we have it on outside our clothes." Quickly she pulled her dress over her head and stood there in brassiere and slip; a moment later the slip joined her dress on the floor. She stood in front of the poster, her full breasts straining against the beige cotton brassiere. "Is this better, Jimmy?"

She turned to Janette. "Take off your dress."

Janette felt the warmth of her body rush into her face. "That's silly."

"No, it's not," Marie-Thérèse insisted. "How else can he make a fair judgment? Besides I haven't seen you since school closed. I want to see if you've gotten any bigger."

Janette looked at her. Marie-Thérèse had gotten bigger. Her breasts were at least a full size larger. Staring at her friend she felt the warmth inside her growing more intense. Slowly she took off her dress.

Marie-Thérèse's voice was surprised. "Silk! Black silk! You sneaky thing, you never told me! Take off your slip, I want to see your panties."

Silently Janette let the slip fall to the floor and stood there facing the poster, not looking at her friend. The warmth inside her was going into her groin and legs now.

"Black silk panties too!" Marie-Thérèse exclaimed. "Where did you ever get those things? They're so beautiful and sexy."

Janette still did not look at her. "My stepfather gave them to me. He said he hated the cotton things I wore."

"When did he ever see you?"

"In the summer it's so hot I leave my door open for some air. He saw me when he walked by. One day he came in and threw a box of lingerie down on my desk. 'From now on, you wear these when you're home. The other things are ugly.' Then he walked out."

"My God!" Marie-Thérèse breathed. "Did he ever do anything else?"

Janette was still looking up at the poster. She felt the warmth turning to wetness inside her. "After that, he would come to my room sometimes when my mother wasn't home and sit down in the chair and make me walk up and down the room in these things in front of him. Then after a while he would make me take them off and give them to him and he would make me watch him while he took his thing out and jerked off into them. When he was finished he'd give them back to me, slap me hard across the face and say, 'Slut! Wash these filthy rags!' and walk out of the room." She turned to Marie-Thérèse. Her friend's mouth was open, her eyes wide and round. One thing she couldn't tell her. The intensity of the orgasm that swept through her when Maurice slapped her face left her so weak and drained that she would sink to the floor until her legs regained the strength to carry her.

"That's all he did?" Marie-Thérèse asked. "Nothing else?"

Janette laughed. "You know better than that. He's the most famous queer in Paris."

"Still?" Marie-Thérèse wondered. Her voice was hushed. "Is it true what I heard? About the size of his thing, I mean?"

Janette nodded. "It's big all right."

"Bigger than Donald the flasher?"

Donald the flasher was an English boy at the school across the lake in Switzerland whom they met at the weekly dances. He was always getting the girls to go outside with him so that he could show it to them and tell them how big he was. Janette laughed again. "It made his look like a toy."

"My God!" Marie-Thérèse breathed. She began to rub herself. "I think I'm going to come. Let's get on the bed and do it to each other."

They moved toward the bed and began to masturbate each other to a climax. It wasn't the first time they had done it. But this time somehow it seemed even more exciting with the poster of James Dean scowling down at them from the wall.

"Finish packing then," Janette said into the telephone. "And I'll come over after dinner and we'll go to a movie."

"No chance," Marie-Thérèse said. "The night before I leave for school I always have to stay home with my parents."

"Okay, then," Janette said. "I'll meet you at the train seven thirty tomorrow morning."

She put down the telephone and turned to find Maurice standing in the open doorway to her room. She glanced at her watch. Five o'clock. He was home early. Usually he never got home before seven.

"Who were you talking to?" he asked suspiciously, coming into the room.

Her eyes fell and she looked down at the floor. "Marie-Thérèse."

"How can you find so much to talk about with such a stupid girl?" he asked.

She didn't answer, her eyes still cast downward.

"Where's your mother?" he asked.

"I don't know," she replied.

"Hasn't she come home yet?"

She shrugged her shoulders.

"Why don't you look at me?" he demanded.

66

She raised her eyes, feeling the flush creep into her face. "Has she called?"

"I haven't spoken to her."

His lips tightened in an angry narrow line. "The slut's probably fucking away the afternoon with one of her gigolo friends," he snapped. "She's never around when something important comes up."

Her eyes fell again. She didn't answer.

"If she calls and you should speak to her, tell her it's important that I see her."

She nodded.

"Important. You understand. I must speak to her."

She nodded again without looking at him.

Angrily, he slapped her across the face. "Look at me when you answer me!"

She looked at him, feeling the trembling in her legs.

He slapped her again. "It's important. Do you understand?"

"Yes," she whispered, her voice tight in her chest. "I understand."

He stared at her balefully. "Someday you'll all have to pay for what that whore has done to me." He turned and went out of the room, slamming the door angrily behind him.

She sank trembling into the chair, the beginning shudder of her orgasm sending the wetness down her shivering legs.

Jacques Charelle saw her as she came through the doors of the Relais Plaza. The room was crowded at cocktail hour, the hum of conversation filling the room as if a swarm of bees were passing. He got to his feet, gesturing.

Tanya made her way to his table, nodding to several acquaintances as she moved through the room. Jacques kissed her hand politely, held the table so that she could sit on the banquette, her back to the window, facing the room while he sat down opposite her.

"You look absolutely radiant, my dear," he said. "You grow more beautiful every day."

She smiled inwardly at that. What was it they said, women never looked more beautiful than in the early days of their pregnancy? *"Merci,* Monsieur," she said. "It does not get easier as one grows older."

He laughed. "Some women never grow old. You're one of them. And how was your day?"

She shrugged her shoulders. *"Comme ci comme ça."* She looked up at the waiter. "A martini, please." She turned back to Jacques. "And what did you find out?"

He made a subtle gesture at the table next to them. She looked and saw one of the directors of Balmain's salon seated with three other people. "Not here," he half whispered.

She nodded. She could understand his caution. Overtly Jacques was a fashion reporter for one of the news syndicates, but his real money came from his private occupation as a sort of fashion spy. Somehow he managed to know before anyone else what each designer would come up with for the next showing and who would make it that season or not. He had been on her payroll for the last three years and the information he had supplied had been invaluable. "We'll have a quiet dinner," she said.

"Tonight at my apartment," he said. "I have a beautiful *côte d'agneau* I can do for you, with *herbes de Provence* I just received this morning from my mother in the south."

She almost agreed, then remembered. Tonight was Janette's last night before leaving for school. "I can't tonight," she said. The waiter placed the martini before her. "How about tomorrow night?"

"My editor is in town tomorrow," he said apologetically.

She took a sip of the martini, then remembered the doctor's instructions. No alcohol. She put down the glass. "Damn!"

He was sympathetically silent.

"I guess it will have to be tonight then," she said. She looked at him. "But I can't stay late. My daughter's leaving for school tomorrow and I want to spend some time with her."

"You'll be home by ten o'clock," he promised.

The waiter came to the table and placed a calling card in front of her. She glanced down at the German gothic print on the card, then up at the waiter. "The gentleman who gave you this card," she asked, her heart suddenly beating rapidly. "Where is he?"

"He just left," the waiter said. "He said he did not want to disturb you."

Still holding the card in her hand, she got out of her seat and almost ran out the door. A taxi was just pulling away from the curb but she could not see who was in it and the street was almost empty. No one she knew was there. She looked down at the card again.

JOHANN SCHWEBEL
FINANZEN DIREKTOR
VON BRENNER GmbH

Montevideo	Munich
Uruguay	F.W.G.

She turned the card over. Johann's precise handwriting never changed. "I will be at this number at 0900 tomorrow. Please call me. J."

Slowly she walked back into the Relais Plaza. Jacques was standing. "Is there anything wrong?" he asked in a concerned voice.

"No," she answered, taking her seat. "Nothing's wrong. It's just someone I hadn't seen for a long time and I would have liked to see him again."

"An old lover?" Jacques smiled.

She shook her head. "Not really."

"Take my advice, my dear," he said with typical French sagacity. "Never chase an old love. They are never like what you remember when you catch them."

She looked at him. Suddenly the information she sought from him wasn't that important anymore. "Look," she said. "I've thought it over. Let's skip tonight. I think it's really more important that I spend the evening with my daughter."

It was slightly after seven o'clock when she arrived home. Henri opened the door. *"Bon soir,* Madame."

"Bon soir, Henri," she said. "Any messages?"

"No, Madame," he said. "But Monsieur le Marquis is already at home."

She nodded. "And Janette?"

"She is in her room, Madame." He paused for a moment. "What time would Madame like dinner?"

"Eight thirty," she said, starting up the staircase. She walked down the corridor and stopped in front of Janette's room. Quietly she knocked at the door.

Janette opened it. She smiled. *"Maman!"*

Tanya leaned forward and kissed her daughter, then followed her into the room. Quickly her eyes took in the closed valises standing near the door. "You're all packed?"

"Ready to go," Janette said. "Seven o'clock in the morning."

Tanya smiled. "Anxious to get back to school?"

"In a way," Janette answered. "Truth is, I'm getting tired of vacation. There's nothing really much to do around Paris in the summer. Most of the girls were away."

"Maybe next summer I won't be so tied up. Then we can go away too."

"Maybe," Janette said. "By the way, I forgot to tell you. Maurice came home early. He was looking for you. He told me to tell you it was very important that you speak to him right away."

"Okay," Tanya said. "I told Henri to have dinner ready at eight thirty. Is that all right?"

"It is with me," Janette said. She looked at her mother. "Just the two of us? Or is Maurice eatimg with us too?"

"Just the two of us if that's what you want," Tanya said.

"I'd like that."

"Just the two of us then," Tanya said. She started from the room. "I'll call you when it's time."

She walked down to the other side of the hallway and stopped in front of Maurice's door. She knocked, and at the muffled sound of his voice coming through the closed door, went into the room.

Maurice was sitting in a lounge chair, a half-empty cognac snifter in his hand. He stared up at her balefully without getting up. "Where the hell have you been all afternoon?"

She ignored his question. "You wanted to see me?"

"Whose prick were you sucking this afternoon?" His words were slurred.

"If I were," she answered, "it wouldn't matter to you anyway. It would be someone who definitely wasn't your type. Now, you either have something important to tell me or you haven't. If not, let me go and take my bath."

His voice was angry. "You'll never guess who called today."

Suddenly she knew. Even without his telling. She was silent.

"Johann Schwebel," he snapped. He studied her face. It was expressionless. "Aren't you surprised?"

"Should I be?" she asked ingenuously.

"Maybe that's the wrong word," he said. "Concerned should be more like it."

"I see no reason for that either," she said. "We've kept the books honestly. Wolfgang's share is intact."

"You're stupid," he snarled. "What if they want to take over? Take everything back? Then where will we be?"

"Did he say that?" she asked.

"No. He merely wanted to arrange an appointment with the two of us. I told him to call back tomorrow at eleven o'clock."

She looked at him. His face was flushed with liquor and she knew that he never drank that much in the daytime unless he was upset. "You could have called him back and made an appointment."

"He said he would be moving around too much and would call us."

She nodded. "That's possible. After all, we don't know

71

what other business he has in Paris." Johann had to have a reason for what he did. He knew about the call at eleven, yet he had asked her to call him at nine. She started from the room. "At any rate we'll know more tomorrow."

He rose to his feet. "I was only waiting to give you the news. I'm going out to dinner. Will you be using the car?"

"No. Take it," she said. "I'm having dinner in tonight with Janette."

Johann came out of the Georges Cinq and waited for a taxi. Paris. It never changed. Not even in all the years since the war. Like the French themselves. Selfish, expedient, demanding, egotistical. Standing there saying, Look at me. Am I not beautiful? The most beautiful in the world? And the trouble was that it was the truth. The truth, if you had the price to pay for it.

The doorman opened the door of the taxi, managing to pocket the five-franc coin and tip his hat all at the same time. Johann gave the driver the address, then settled back into the seat and took a folder out of his briefcase and opened it.

Inside were credit reports gathered for him by his bank on the French companies. He glanced down at the top sheet.

Eau de la Vie Minérale S.A. Mng. Dir. Marquis de la Beauville. Product, bottled mineral water sold in 1 liter bottles, principally to small hotels and restaurants, very few retail outlets. Mgnt. pursues noncompetitive policy, no advt., depending on price (30% to 40% less than Evian, Vittel, etc.) for sales. Est. avg. gross 3 yrs, F. 10M; net, F. 1,5M. Est. value, property and plants, equipment and inventory, F. 45M. No record or est. available on acct's rec. or debt. Est. C.O.H. on deposit F. 40M. All bills pd. pmpty, 10 to 30 days. Credit rating, AAAA to F. 25M.

He slipped the top sheet under the others and began to read the second report.

Domaine Marquis de la Beauville S.A. Mng. Dir. Marquis de la Beauville. Product, mid-range quality wines, champagne, cognac sold in quantity (bbls) to other vineyards and bottlers. No retail sales or labels established. Est. avg. gross 3 yrs, F. 125M; net, F. 25M. Est. value, property and plants, equipment and inventory, F. 400M. No record or est. available on acct's rec. or debt. Est. C.O.H. on deposit F. 250M to F. 325M. All bills pd. pmpty, 10 to 30 days. Credit rating, AAAA to F. 200M.

He reached for a cigarette, lit it and turned to the last report.

Parfum Tanya S.A. Mng. Dir. Marquis de la Beauville. Product, perfumes, colognes, perfume bases, scents, sold in bulk to various companies for bottling and incorporation into cosmetics under their own label. No retail sales or labels established. Est. value, property and plants, equipment and inventory, F. 110M. Est. avg. gross sales, F. 100M, net, F. 45M. No record or est. available on acct's rec. or debt. Est. C.O.H. on deposit F. 350M to F. 400M. All bills pd. pmpty, 10 to 30 days. Credit rating, AAAA to F. 100M.

He closed the folder and stared thoughtfully out the window at the passing traffic. In many ways none of the companies were operated in the typically French manner. For one thing, no French company, large or small, ever paid its bills on time. And no French company ever maintained a cash balance so far in excess of its annual needs. It had to be Tanya. Maurice would never do it. He did some rapid mental calculation. Of course, it was Tanya. The money was there because she was holding it for von Brenner. In that balance was his 50 percent share of the profits.

The taxi pulled to the curb and he got out. He looked at his watch. Five minutes to nine. He paid the driver and hurried upstairs to the lawyer's office. His hunch had been right. He was glad that he had asked her to call him there. He had a feeling he should see her before he met with Maurice.

He opened the door in answer to the soft knock, then stepped aside to let her walk into the living room of the hotel suite. Slowly he closed the door behind him and turned to look at her. For a long moment they looked silently at each other; then he cleared his throat. "Old friends should not meet each other in restaurants or in attorneys' offices."

She nodded without speaking. He could see the tears welling into her eyes and felt a choking in his own throat. He held out his hand. She ignored it. Her voice was husky. "Old friends do not merely shake hands."

He threw open his arms and she came into them. He kissed her cheek, tasting the salt of her tears. She rested her head against his chest. "Dear Johann," she murmured. "Dear kind good friend."

He raised her chin to look into her eyes. "Anna—" He hesitated. "Tanya."

"Tanya." She smiled.

"I am glad to see you," he said, nodding his head.

"It's been too long," she said. "Ten years and no word. I thought we'd be in touch long before this."

He looked at her, strangely puzzled. He really didn't understand why she had thought that. "Come," he said. "Let me get you something to drink."

She followed him to the couch and sat down. "I really don't want anything, thank you."

"I'll order some coffee," he said, pressing the signal for the room-service waiter. A few minutes later, a cup of coffee in his hand, he nodded, pleased. "Now, tell me about Janette. She must be a big girl now."

Tanya smiled. "Sixteen. And she just left for school in Switzerland this morning."

"I'm sorry I missed her," he said. "I would have liked to

see her. If she takes after her mother, she has to be beautiful."

"She is," Tanya said. "But in her own fashion, not in
mine."

"I suppose you're wondering why I'm here?" Johann
asked.

"Only why it took you so long," she said. "You'll find the
books in order. And the money in a separate account."

"What for? There's no money owed to the von Brenner
Gesellschaft." Then it all came together in his head. He
stared at her with suddenly dawning comprehension.
"Wolfgang—" he began, but his voice failed him.

"That's it," she smiled. "I put half the profits in a special
account for Wolfgang just as I promised him."

His voice was strained and strangely tortured. "You
didn't know?"

"Know what?" Something in the expression in his eyes
reached into her heart with a cold chill. Then she knew.
Her clenched fist went to her mouth so that she wouldn't
cry. "Wolfgang is dead. When?"

He put down the coffee cup with shaking hands. "Ten
years. I thought you knew."

"I didn't know." Her voice reached for control. "How did
it happen?"

"He was killed by the Russians when they came to arrest
him. He always said that he would not allow himself to be
taken alive and tried as a war criminal. He was never a
member of the Nazi party."

"He was supposed to be safe in the French sector. How
did the Russians get him?"

"Nobody really knows," he said. "Apparently he went to
a meeting in the Soviet zone."

She was silent for a moment. "Maurice knew," she said.
"He knew it all along."

"I don't know," he said.

She met his eyes. "I do. He knew that if I learned Wolfgang was dead I wouldn't stay married to him."

"And now?"

"It's over. I'll divorce him."

"But the companies? Aren't they in the Beauville estate?"

She shook her head. "No. I kept them in my name. I had the feeling that if I ever did transfer them, Wolfgang would be the first to be cheated."

"That was lucky," he said. He smiled suddenly. "You're a rich woman now. Everything. It all belongs to you. You don't owe anything to anybody. And I think that was what Wolfgang really wanted."

"Yes." She remembered the gold louis in the vault in Switzerland. Even after they had lived there together, he had never asked her to give them to him. Or even place his name on the vault card. He had meant for her to have it all along. She felt the moisture in her eyes. Poor Wolfgang.

"Are you all right?" Johann asked anxiously.

She held up her head. "I'm fine now." No wonder Maurice was upset at Johann's call. It was as if the day of reckoning had come. "You started to tell me why you wanted to see me."

He nodded. "I know of a company that is interested in buying the wine company for a lot of money. They want to take the company into retail sales."

"Should I sell it to them?" she asked.

"Of course, it's up to you. But I wouldn't."

"What would you do then?"

"What they plan to do. And make ten times as much money as the company is making now."

"But we deliberately stayed out of the public eye. We thought that the less attention we called to ourselves the better."

"That was ten years ago. But now nobody gives a damn."

She met his eyes. "I'm pregnant. In March, I'm going to have a baby."

Surprise echoed in his voice. "Then you can't divorce until afterwards."

Her voice was strong. "I'm divorcing now. I won't let a child of mine bear his name. After the divorce I'm going to America to have the baby. The father is American."

"Will you marry him?"

"It doesn't matter," she said. "But I won't be able to run the businesses myself. I still need a man in there."

He was silent.

"What about you, Johann?" she asked. "That's what you did for Wolfgang. And it would not be just a job, you would be a partner."

"I don't know," he said doubtfully. "I might not be the right man for you. Basically I'm an accountant. You need someone more than that."

"We can hire anyone else we might need," she said. "But you can't buy trust. That only comes with time."

"No!" Maurice's voice was shrill. He was near hysteria. "I won't give you a divorce! I worked just as hard to make those companies as you did. You're not just going to pay me off and throw me out! Just because you know you can keep it all for yourself."

"You make me sick," she said, her voice cold with contempt. She rose from her chair. "Divorce or not, you're out of the companies."

He stared up at her from behind his desk. His voice was quieter now. "It won't be that easy for you. Under French law a wife's property automatically comes under her husband's control. I'll hang you in court for twenty years. By that time the companies will be worth nothing."

"The hell with them! I don't need them."

"You have a lifestyle you've become used to," he said shrewdly. "You won't be able to afford it any more. And you're not as young as you used to be. There are younger, fresher girls around. You'll still be able to find a man to fuck with you, but you won't find a man to keep you. When it comes to that, Tanya, you're over the hill."

She looked down at him. "What are you trying to say?"

"I'm saying we can approach this reasonably, calmly. Like two sensible adults, without flying off the handle and destroying ourselves in the process."

"And what's your idea of working this out reasonably?"

He took a deep breath. "First, no divorce. We stay married. There's nothing wrong in that. It works for both of us. Money alone won't keep you in the world in which you live if you relinquish the title. Tanya, Marquise de la Beauville goes a lot further than Tanya Pojarska, even if you should decide to use your former husband's title, which at the moment is being used by at least three other people. Polish titles aren't worth a sou for a dozen in Paris. Do you think that school in Switzerland would have even accepted Janette if it weren't for the Beauville name?"

She was silent. He pressed on. "You were prepared to give me twenty-five percent of the total net worth of all the companies in cash. That has to be somewhere between one hundred and one hundred twenty-five million francs. Instead of cash, you quit-claim one company to me; in exchange I will quit-claim the other two to you. That way our property rights will be clear and incontestable. And to show you that I am not greedy, I'll accept the smallest company of them all. The mineral-water company. Its net worth is far less than the amount you would give me in cash."

She stared at him. "What makes you so generous?" she asked skeptically.

"I'm not generous. Just practical. I need something to work at and something to save face. And I can live comfortably on that company's earnings. Once that is done, we separate. I go my way, you go yours. And it becomes what it always has been. A marriage of convenience."

"Let me think about it," she said.

"What is there to think about?" He was more confident now. "At this moment, you're angry. About many things. Wolfgang. Allowing yourself to become stupidly pregnant."

Surprise was in her voice. "How do you know about that?"

"There are no secrets older than twenty-four hours in Paris," he said. "So you're angry and lashing out at the only one available to you. Me. What you don't see is that in the process you are also hurting your own children. Janette and the unborn baby."

Again she was silent. He got to his feet. "Tanya," he said quietly, "wouldn't it make more sense for your child to be born de la Beauville than a fatherless bastard?"

She was still silent. He managed a faint smile and a Gallic shrug of his shoulders. "Who knows? If you have a son, he automatically becomes the next Marquis de la Beauville."

For the first time since Janette had begun going away to school, her mother was not at the train station to greet her when she returned to Paris. René, the chauffeur, was waiting for her on the platform, his coat collar turned up against the Christmas-holiday cold.

"Where's Mother?" she asked as she came down the steps from the train.

He reached for her valise. "She's not feeling well, Mademoiselle Janette," he said. "She is waiting for you at home."

"What's the matter with her?" she asked, falling into step with him.

He shot her a curious glance. "It's nothing serious," he said evasively. She followed him through the station outside to where the black Rolls-Royce limousine was parked in a No Parking zone confident that no mere mortal gendarme would dare disgrace it with a contravention. He opened the door for her. She got into the car and he placed the valise in the front seat beside him and pulled the car away from the curb.

It was rush hour and the streets were busy with people going home from work, and as usual traffic was backed up at every corner. He glanced into the rearview mirror and saw her sitting forward in her seat, looking at the shop windows as they moved past. "The Christmas shopping rush is on," he said.

"Yes," she answered.

79

"The *météo* says we might have snow."

"It's been snowing in Switzerland since the last week in October."

"Have you been skiing?" he asked.

"Of course," she said. "There's not much else to do."

Then he ran out of conversation and they were silent until he stopped the car in front of the house. Before he had a chance to open the door for her she was out of the car and up the steps, pressing the doorbell. Henri opened the door and she ran past him with a quick *"Bon jour,"* up the steps to her mother's room. Outside the closed door, she stopped and knocked.

Her mother's voice answered. *"Entrez."*

She opened the door and ran into the room. *"Maman!"* she exclaimed. Then stopped suddenly, her mouth partly open in amazement.

Tanya saw the expression on her face. She tried to treat it lightly. "I'm really not that big yet. Only six months."

There was a shocked note in Janette's voice. "But you never said anything to me."

"What was there to say?" Tanya asked. "These things do happen."

Janette's voice was suddenly angry. "I'm not a child. You could have told me."

Tanya was silent, surprised at Janette's anger.

Janette searched her mother's eyes. "He raped you. That's why you didn't tell me. You were ashamed."

"No, Janette," Tanya said. "It wasn't like that at all."

A note of repulsion came into Janette's voice. "You mean you let him do that to you?"

Tanya was silent. For the first time she really didn't know what to say to her daughter. She found her voice. "Maybe you'd better go to your room and have a quiet relaxing bath. We'll talk afterwards."

Janette's lips tightened. "Once you told me you didn't want any other children."

Tanya's voice grew firm. "Do as I say, Janette. Go to your room. We'll talk later when you've calmed down."

80

Janette turned and started for the corridor connecting their two rooms.

Tanya stopped her. "Not there. Maurice's suite has been redecorated for you."

"And who's in my room?" Janette asked angrily. "Maurice?"

"No," Tanya said. "He doesn't live with us anymore. The room is being fixed up as a nursery for the baby."

Janette stared at her, tears beginning to well into her eyes. "Merry Christmas, Mother!" she cried bitterly, turned and ran sobbing from the room.

Tanya stared at the closed door. She heard Janette's footsteps running down the hall. For a moment she thought of following her but then sank wearily into a chair. Janette would get over it. Later when she had calmed down they would talk, and Tanya would explain to her what had happened.

But Tanya was wrong. Janette wasn't waiting for an explanation. Instead of going to her room, she ran out of the house, took a taxi to the train station and made the night train back to her school in Lugano.

"It will take two years," Johann said. "Next year is impossible. Our entire production is already committed to our regular customers."

She glanced at the report in front of her and nodded. "Maybe it's just as well. It will give us more time to develop the label and publicize it."

"I have several interesting possibilities," he said. "There are two bottling plants on the market right now. I think we can get them for a price."

"Get into it," she said. "And let me know."

"Another thing," he added. "I think we should forget about the domestic market. We'd have to fight our way through the established wineries, and you know the French. Snobbery and tradition, they don't like to change. My feeling is that we should aim at America. The wine market there is just beginning to open up and we can compete pricewise in their medium range. A French label there is instant status."

"That makes sense."

"There are several large American distributors already interested. Schieffelin, Bronfman, even Twenty-One Brands. They're talking big money and big promotion. I feel we can even get a large enough advance from them to finance the acquisition of the bottling plant."

"We don't need their money," she said.

"True," he agreed. "But it always is better to work with someone else's capital than your own. Besides that would free more of our own money to acquire a *maison de couture* and also to operate it. I don't know of one that makes money, they're constant losers. Even Chanel."

"But she makes it all back on the perfume. Plus. We know that. After all, we can't even supply her with all the essences she needs for the base. Sooner or later all the couturiers will be into it. I want to be there first."

"I'm worried about that," he said. "Operating losses on one of those houses could be a disastrous drain. And everyone I spoke to wants an arm and a leg for nothing, just their name."

"I have one company in mind that I think we can get at the right figure," she said. "Shiki."

His eyes opened wide. "The Japanese? His shows were the biggest hit of the last season. *Vogue* and *L'Officiel* are filled with nothing but him. Even the papers say that he is the rage."

She laughed. "That's the press. His things are outrageous and they love it. But there's no way anyone can wear his clothes. They're just not practical and not really selling. Jacques Charelle says his ass is out and he's in debt up to his ears."

"If that's the case, why do you want him?"

She smiled. "The name. If he gets the space, we can find a way to make him work. Tone him down just a little. And, don't forget where the money is. Coco Chanel doesn't. The perfume. If we do twenty-five percent of Chanel Number Five we make nothing but money. And after that, who knows? Maybe an entire line of cosmetics." She took a deep breath and looked at him. "What a stupid thing it is to be a woman. There is so much to do, and here I am, pregnant."

He nodded sympathetically. "Only two more months."

"Seems like eternity."

"It will pass quickly enough," he said.

She fell silent, thinking. Finally she took a deep breath. "I'm worried."

"There's nothing to worry about," he said quickly. "You're just fine."

"One never knows," she said. "I'm not as young as I was when Janette was born. There could be problems."

He was silent.

"I've never made a will," she said. "If anything should go wrong, what happens to Janette? Or the new baby? I'm still married to Maurice. He might get everything."

"Under French law," Johann said, "the children have specific inheritance rights."

"They would still need a guardian or trustee until they are of age," she said. "And Maurice adopted Janette and will be legally the father of the other. Automatically it would make sense that he would control not only his share but their share too. I don't want that."

He was silent.

"You're the only one I can trust to protect the children," she said. "Would you be willing to be my executor if I should die?"

"Of course," he said. "But we both know nothing will happen to you."

"There's too much at stake," she said. "I don't want to take any chances. Arrange for the lawyer to come here in the morning. I want my house to be in order."

"I'll take care of it," he said. He looked at her. "Just one thing puzzles me. What happened to your idea about taking that young man at Christian Dior's and starting a new house with him?"

"You mean Yves St. Laurent?"

"That's the one."

"I gave that up for two reasons. First, Dior and Boussac won't let him go. Second, he hasn't established his own name yet and it could take a fortune to get him known as widely as we need him to be. I spoke to Jacques about it. Despite the boy's talent, nothing will happen until Dior lets him come out from under his shadow. Good or bad, at least Shiki's name is on everybody's lips."

"Okay," he said doubtfully. "I hope you know what you're doing."

She smiled at him. "I do too. I've spent years cultivating Charelle and learning from him. He may be greedy, but season after season, he's picked the winners."

"What's he going to get out of this?"

"Director of Public Relations. At five times the money he makes and can steal from the crummy news syndicate he works for."

Johann laughed. "You've thought it all out."

"That was easy," she said. A troubled look came to her face. "I wish it were as easy to understand Janette."

"You haven't spoken to her yet?"

She shook her head. "She won't even answer my telephone calls."

"She'll get over it when the baby comes. You'll see."

"I don't know," she said thoughtfully. "Janette's a strange child. There's something about the way she keeps to herself. I have the feeling I don't know her at all."

The little Japanese was both stoned and drunk at the same time. He held a glass of wine in one hand and a hashish cigarette in the other. "Schiaparelli, Balmain, Maggy Rouff, they've all had it. They're still designing ball gowns for yesterday's dowagers, who are growing too old to even wear shrouds. Even Dior knows when he's had it, he admits that Yves did more than half of his last collection. Today's women want more excitement in their clothes. There's a whole new world coming and they want to be there first."

The host, Juan Delgado, was in full drag. His long Schiaparelli gown trailed the floor behind him. "And I suppose you're going to be the one who leads them there?" he asked sarcastically.

"Damn right I am," Shiki retorted.

"Horseshit!" Juan snapped. "You haven't even got enough money to pay your fare on the Métro."

"That's how much you know," Shiki retorted with a superior air. "Just this morning I signed the papers which will make me independent for life."

"Now, I'll tell one," Juan said.

"I'll prove it," Shiki said, looking around the room. He saw Maurice and Jerry Johnson standing near the bar. "Come with me."

Juan followed him across the room. Shiki stopped in front of Maurice. "Juanita doesn't believe that we made a deal. Tell him."

Maurice was puzzled. "What deal?"

Delgado chortled. "I told you you were full of shit. He doesn't even know what you're talking about. You have to be stoned out of your head."

"I'm never that stoned," Shiki said, standing on his dignity as much as his four feet nine inches would allow. He turned back to Maurice. "I signed the papers this morning with your man, Schwebel. It's with one of your companies. Tanya Parfums or something like that."

"That's one of my wife's companies," Maurice said. "I have nothing to do with that. It's all her affair." He looked at Shiki curiously. "You say Schwebel signed the papers? Where was Tanya?"

Shiki was surprised. "I thought you knew. She went to the clinic last night to have your baby."

"Last night?" Maurice was incredulous. "She wasn't expecting for another two weeks yet."

Delgado broke up. He turned to the room, announcing in a loud voice, "Our good friend, the marquis, is about to have a baby and his wife hasn't even bothered to inform him." He paused for a moment. "But, then, why should she? She never even bothered telling him that she was making a baby when she was off fucking that American."

"You son of a bitch!" Maurice said angrily. "Why don't you just suck my cock?"

Juan fell to his knees on the floor before him. He held up his hand in mock prayer. "Thank you, God," he said, rolling his eyes heavenward. "You've just made my dreams come true."

Maurice shoved him and he rolled backward on the floor, laughing, while Maurice, followed by Jerry, stalked angrily from the party.

It was two o'clock in the morning when they got out of the car in front of the small private clinic. They crossed the deserted sidewalk and pressed the night bell. Maurice tried the door impatiently. It was locked. He put his finger on the bell and kept it there.

A few moments later a sleepy concierge opened the door. "Monsieur, Monsieur," he protested. "Patience. There are sick people in here." He looked around behind them. "Where is she?"

"She?" Maurice asked. "Who?"

"The patient," the concierge answered. "This is a maternity clinic. Only expectant fathers ring the bell like that at night."

"My wife is already here," Maurice snapped. "I want to see her."

The concierge began to close the door. "Impossible, Monsieur. Visiting hours are finished at ten o'clock. Come back in the morning."

Maurice put his foot in the door, blocking it. "I want to see her now. I insist. I am the Marquis de la Beauville."

"I don't care if you're Charles De Gaulle," the concierge said. "You come back in the morning."

A banknote appeared in Maurice's hand. "If you would be kind enough to speak to the head nurse," he said in a more reasonable voice, "I would appreciate it."

86

The banknote disappeared in the concierge's pocket as quickly as it had appeared. "If Monsieur would be kind enough to wait. I will return in a moment."

The door closed, and Maurice and Jerry stood there. "Maybe we should come back in the morning," Jerry said.

"No. We'll see her tonight." Maurice's voice was tight.

The door opened again. This time a gray-haired nurse in a heavily starched uniform stood next to the concierge. "I am sorry, Monsieur," she began to explain. "But the rules—"

Maurice interrupted her. "I know the rules, Sister. But please take mercy on a poor man who just at this moment arrived back in Paris and longs only for a moment's glimpse of his wife and child."

The second banknote in Maurice's hand disappeared into the pocket of the starched uniform. "Very well, Monsieur," she said, admitting them into the hallway. "But we must be very quiet."

They followed her down the long hospital-smelling corridor and stopped outside a room. She turned to look at them. "Madame la Marquise had a very difficult labor. We have given her very heavy sedation and she is sleeping. You can look in from the doorway but please do not enter."

Maurice nodded. The nurse opened the door. There was a very dim light in the room. He peered past her. Tanya was lying in the bed, her eyes closed. Even in the small light, Maurice could see her face was pale and drawn. He stepped back and turned to the nurse. "And the baby?" he whispered.

The nurse closed the door softly. "Follow me, Monsieur."

They walked down to the end of the corridor and turned right. They stopped in front of a large double-paned window. Looking through the window they could see about seven or eight tiny cribs on small wheels, a baby in each.

Maurice looked at the nurse. "Which one is mine?"

"Just a moment, Monsieur," the nurse said. "I will go into the room and hold her up so that you can see her."

"Her?" Maurice's voice was incredulous. "You mean it's a girl?"

The nurse smiled. "Yes, Monsieur, the most beautiful girl you ever saw. Golden ringlets of hair the color of the sun, the bluest eyes that sparkle like aquamarines and will be blue all through her life. Wait just a moment, you will see for yourself."

She left them to enter the nursery. But when she came to the window with the child in her arms, they were already gone.

Maurice drove wildly through the deserted streets. "The bitch!" he swore angrily. "The bitch! She couldn't even do that right!"

"Take it easy," Jerry said. "Or you'll get us both killed."

"The least she could have done was have a son." Maurice was still angry. "Someone to carry on the name. But no, another fucking cunt! Blond and blue-eyed on top of it all. Paris will break up with laughter. There has never been a blue-eyed blonde in the seven-hundred-year history of my family."

"What difference does it make?" Jerry asked. "Everyone knows it's not your child anyway."

"That makes it even worse," Maurice said. "They all know the only reason I stayed with her was to get a son."

He raced across the small bridge over the Seine to the Ile Saint-Louis and down the narrow streets to a stop in front of their apartment. He got out of the car and slammed the door angrily. "The bitch!" he swore again. "I'll make her pay for this. You'll see."

Dr. Pierre came into the room. He stopped at the side of the bed and looked down at her. "How are you feeling?" He smiled.

"Tired," she said.

He shrugged. "That's normal." Quickly he checked her heart, pulse and blood pressure. "You're okay."

"And the baby?" she asked.

"Perfect," he answered. "One couldn't ask for any more. You fed her this morning?"

"Yes."

"Good. We'll put her on a formula for lunch. She'll have that every other feeding time for a few days, then when she's adjusted to it, we'll take her off the breast completely."

"How long will that take?" she asked.

"Three, four days."

"I don't want my breasts to get too large," she said.

"Don't worry about it," he smiled. "I'll give you a series of shots that will stop the lactation and bring your breasts back to normal in no time."

"How long do I have to stay in here?"

"About a week. Then you'll be able to go home."

"I have a lot to do," she said.

"It will wait. Your health is more important. But you can begin walking around a little this afternoon. Just don't overtire yourself." He snapped his small medical bag closed. "I'll be back this evening before you go to sleep."

"Thanks, Doctor Pierre."

The chief night nurse came into the room just as he left. *"Bon jour,* Madame la Marquise." She smiled.

"Bon jour, Soeur."

"I just came by to see how you were."

"I'm fine, thank you."

"By the way," the nurse said, "did anyone tell you that your husband was here?"

Tanya was surprised. "No. No one mentioned it. When?"

"Two nights ago," she said. "It was about two in the morning. The reason I didn't say anything was because yesterday was my day off."

"Did he see the baby?"

"No. Funny, because when I went to show her to him, he had already gone."

Tanya was silent.

"Don't worry about it," the nurse said in what she thought was a comforting manner. "I've seen that happen many times with husbands. Frenchmen are always upset when they get a daughter instead of a son. But he'll come around, you'll see."

Tanya forced a smile and nodded.

The nurse looked at her watch. "I've got to go now and get some sleep. I'll see you tonight."

"Thank you, *Soeur*."

The door closed again. Tanya looked across the room. The flowers on the dresser were from Johann. Another vase filled with roses had come from Jacques. So Maurice had been here. Strange that there had been no word from him. Not that she expected him to send flowers. There was another knock at the door. *"Entrez."*

Johann came into the room followed by Jacques. Both were carrying more flowers. They smiled as they approached the bed. "You look marvelous," Jacques said.

"Don't tell me," she said. "I look awful and I know it."

"No, really," Johann said. "You look wonderful."

"You're both prejudiced." She laughed. She looked up at them. "What brings you both here this early in the morning?"

"We have two problems," Johann said. "We need your decision before we can do anything."

"Bien," she said. "What's the first?"

Jacques spoke. "We have to make a public announcement about our deal with Shiki. He wants to do it immediately. I want to wait at least a month for several reasons. One, because you'll be in shape to appear with him at the press conference. I think it's very important that we establish immediately your presence in the concern. Two, because it will bring us that much closer to the showings for the fall season and will spark a great deal of interest and publicity to see exactly what we come up with."

Tanya's voice was definite. "I'll go with your plan. Tell Shiki we'll make the announcement later. Now, what's the second problem?"

They glanced at each other a moment, then Johann spoke. "It's Maurice again. Jacques tells me that he's going all over Paris saying that he's filing for divorce on the grounds of adultery."

She looked at Jacques.

He nodded. "That's what I've heard. Not just once, but many times."

She thought for a moment. "I don't see where it matters," she said. "Originally I wanted a divorce anyway. If he files, let him have it."

"It could get complicated," Johann said. "He's also claiming that you fraudulently misstated the assets of the companies in making him accept the mineral-water corporation."

"Did you talk to the lawyers?" she asked.

Johann nodded. "He can't make it stick but it can create problems. Just from a public-relations point of view."

She turned to Jacques. "Do you think you can contain it?"

"I won't be able to keep it out of the papers," Jacques said. "But I think I can get you a fair amount of space to counter his stories. After all, he's not exactly a closet queen. If we let him know that we plan to open the door wide, maybe he'll have second thoughts."

She nodded. "Okay. Make sure that he hears we're going to do that. Meanwhile ask my lawyers to file a countersuit for divorce, charging him with pederasty, and have it ready to serve the moment he files against me."

Johann looked at her. "You don't need this. You have enough to do."

"There's nothing we can do about it," she said. "It's one of the facts of life."

"I suppose so," he answered. "Have you spoken to Janette yet?"

She shook her head. "She still won't take my calls. I told her friend Marie-Thérèse to tell her that she has a sister."

"Have you decided on a name for the baby yet?"

"Yes," she nodded. "I'm going to call her—Lauren."

"Lauren? That's a strange name."

"It's after my grandmother. My father's mother. She was

91

American and I always loved her name. When I was little I used to pretend that it was mine."

Marie-Thérèse came into their room "The headmistress wants to see you."

Janette looked up from her book. "What for?"

"She didn't say. Just come down right away."

Janette closed the book and put it down. "I'll see what the old biddy wants and be right back."

Janette knocked at the office door and then went in. The headmistress was seated behind her desk. A man, his back toward the door, was seated opposite her. As the door opened, he rose to his feet, turning to face Janette.

"*Bon jour,* Janette," Maurice said.

Janette stared at him for a moment, then she curtsied as school protocol demanded. "*Bon jour,* Papa."

The headmistress smiled. She was fluttery as usual when parents were around. "Your father has come to take you down to Paris to see your mother and your new baby sister. Isn't that nice?"

Janette looked from one to the other. "I won't go. I have too much studying to do."

"But your mother wants to see you," Maurice said. "She's still in the clinic."

"I don't want to see her," Janette said defiantly.

"That's no way to talk to your father," the headmistress said sharply.

"I won't go," Janette repeated stubbornly.

Maurice's hand moved quickly, the slap stinging her cheek sharply. She met his eyes for a moment, then her gaze fell to the floor. She felt the flush creeping into her cheek, its warmth radiating through her. She stood there absolutely motionless.

"Now go upstairs and pack a few things and be down here in ten minutes," Maurice said with authority.

She did not raise her head, her eyes still cast downward. "Yes," she murmured, then turned and left the room.

Maurice turned back to the headmistress. He smiled apologetically. "I regret the display, Madame, but children today need a firm hand. They're not like we were when we were young."

"I understand, Monsieur le Marquis," the headmistress gushed. "You wouldn't believe some of the things we have to go through with them."

The conductor examined their tickets, then handed them back to Maurice. "Everything is in order, Monsieur le Marquis," he said. "The dining car will be open for dinner at six o'clock. If there is anything I can do to make your journey more comfortable, please call on me."

"*Merci,* Monsieur," Maurice said, giving him a banknote.

Deftly the conductor palmed it and left the private compartment, closing the door carefully behind him. They sat on opposite banquettes next to the window. Maurice picked up a newspaper and looked over at her. "Might as well make yourself comfortable," he said. "We're not due to arrive in Paris until midnight."

Janette looked out the window. The train was beginning to wend its way through the mountains. Though it was three o'clock in the afternoon, there wasn't much light. The day had been overcast with clouds and occasional showers. She reached for a book, opened it and began to read. But her eyes skimmed the pages and the words did not make much sense. After a while she just gave up and pretended to be reading.

They had been traveling almost an hour in silence. Finally Maurice put down his paper and stood up. He went to the small toilet compartment and opened the door. He didn't bother closing it as he lifted the toilet seat and stood there relieving himself.

Janette looked up from her book. The inside of the toilet door was a full-length mirror and the angle of the door was such that she could see the water gushing from him as if from a giant garden hose. At the same moment, he turned his head and caught her eyes in the mirror. She dropped her gaze immediately, feeling the flush creeping up into her cheeks. She kept her eyes steadfastly on the pages of the book as he came back and sat down opposite her.

Silently he took a cigarette from his gold case, lit it and sat there studying her. She was still wearing the school uniform—white middy blouse and blue skirt. Knee-length white socks and black shoes completed the picture. But here in the dim light of the compartment it seemed incongruous. Already she had the full figure of a woman, and it seemed as if she were trying to hide the fact in child's clothing.

"Janette." His voice was sharp. "Are you wearing the underwear I gave you?"

She didn't look at him. "No."

"Why not?" he asked. "Didn't I tell you to always wear it when I'm around?"

"It's against school regulations."

"You're not in school now," he said. "You should have put them on."

She looked at him. "You didn't give me time. I had to be ready in ten minutes."

"Do you have them with you?"

She nodded. "Yes. In the valise."

"Put them on."

"Now?" she asked.

"Now," he said.

She stood up and took the valise down from the overhead rack and opened it. Quickly she took out the black lingerie and started for the toilet compartment.

He stopped her. "No. I want you to put it on here in front of me."

She glanced at him silently, then at the open windows of the compartment.

He read her glance. "You can pull down the shades. And lock the door."

She didn't move.

He raised a threatening hand. Quickly she pulled down

the shades and locked the door. She turned back to him. "Now," he said.

Slowly she undid the buttons of her middy blouse and shrugged it from her shoulders, then the side buttons of her skirt, and let it fall to the floor. She stepped over it. She picked her clothes from the floor and folded them neatly, placing them in the open valise. With her back to him, she began to undo the brassiere.

"Turn around and look at me!" he snapped.

She met his gaze for a moment, then her eyes fell, and still looking down, she undid her brassiere and stepped out of the panties. Silently she put on the black lace brassiere and sheer silk panties. She turned to pick up the middy blouse.

"You're not finished yet," he said. "Where are the garter belt and silk stockings?"

Without answering, she took them from the valise. She snapped the belt closed around her hips, then sat down to put on the stockings. A moment later she stood up again to fasten the clips to the stocking tops. Again she reached for the middy blouse.

"No," he said. "Go back to your seat."

"Like this?" she asked.

"Like that," he said shortly. "I'll tell you when to get dressed."

"But it's cold," she said.

"You'll get used to it," he said.

Silently she sank back on the banquette opposite him. He sucked on the cigarette, letting the smoke drift idly from his nose as he looked at her. "Your tits have grown too big for your brassiere already," he said almost conversationally. "You've got a whore's body, just like your mother."

She didn't answer.

"Spread your legs!" he snapped.

Automatically she opened her knees. She felt the pull of the thin silk moving to one side and put a hand down to cover herself.

He slapped her hand away. "I didn't tell you you could

do that." He laughed suddenly. "You've got a big bushy whore's cunt too. Just like your mother."

She felt the tears coming to her eyes. She kept her mouth tightly shut as they began to roll down her cheeks.

"Tears?" he asked sarcastically.

She didn't answer.

He leaned forward and unexpectedly thrust his hand between her legs. Startled, she almost jumped, then the hot wave of an instant orgasm left her weak and trembling while the wetness of her flooded down on his probing fingers.

He leaned back on his banquette, laughing. "You are like your mother, Janette. Wet eyes and wet cunt."

The sound of the first call for dinner came from the corridor outside. He got to his feet and went into the tiny toilet where he began to wash his hands meticulously.

He looked over his shoulder at her reflected in the mirror. "You can get dressed now, Janette," he said casually. "I'm hungry and I find it's always best to eat early on these damn trains. If you wait too long, you'll find the best dishes are always gone."

The train arrived in Paris an hour and a half late due to the pouring rain. Jerry was on the platform waiting for them and it was two o'clock in the morning when he stopped the small car in front of the apartment on the Ile Saint-Louis.

"I have some cold cuts if you're hungry," he said in the small elevator as they made their way up to the fifth floor.

"I'm not hungry," Janette said. She looked at Maurice. "Why didn't you take me home?"

Maurice's hand flashed across her face. "Nobody spoke to you," he said. "You speak when I tell you to."

She stared at him silently as the elevator stopped, then followed them out onto the landing. Jerry fumbled with his keys and opened the door. She was surprised at the lavishness of the apartment. From the outside of the building it seemed like nothing, but inside there was everything. The finest of furnishings, carpets, even new American heating-air-conditioning units in the walls.

Maurice led the way through the living room and the dining room, then through his bedroom to a small room located in a corridor between his room and Jerry's. There was no door on the room and the only furniture was a small bed, a chair and a washstand in the corner of the room. It was obviously a servant's room. "Put your things in here," Maurice said.

"When am I going to see my mother?" she asked.

He looked at her. "I'll let you know when." He turned to Jerry. "I'm hungry."

"I'll get the food out of the refrigerator," Jerry said.

"No," Maurice said. "You show her where it is. She'll do it."

"I'm tired," Janette said. "I want to sleep."

Maurice slapped her. She half fell across the bed. "That will wake you up," he said. "Now, get out of that stupid school outfit and come and set the table."

"But I didn't bring anything else to wear," she cried.

"You'll wear what you wore on the train," he said. "You won't need anything else." He turned to Jerry. "Wait here for her. Then show her what to do. I'm going to have a shower and get out of these clothes. They stink from the train."

After Maurice left the room, she got up from the bed. Jerry stood there, watching her. "Turn around," she said.

"What for?" Jerry grinned. "I'm going to see you anyway."

She stood there without moving.

"Maurice wouldn't like it if I have to call him back," he said.

Quickly she undressed, her back toward him. When she finally turned around, he let out a low whistle. "Maurice was right. You are built like your mother."

She stared at him. "You saw my mother too?"

"Yes," he said. He was silent for a moment, then turned. "Come."

She followed him into the kitchen. They had just finished setting the table when Maurice came into the dining room, wearing a black silk robe and velvet slippers.

He looked down at the table. "Where are the candles?"

"I forgot them," Jerry said quickly. "I'll get them." He went to the sideboard. A moment later the candles were glowing on the table. He turned off the electric lights.

Maurice reached for the bottle of wine. "We'll have a glass of wine while you change," he said to Jerry. He filled two glasses and held one toward her as Jerry left the room. "Here."

She shook her head. "I don't want any wine."

"I didn't ask you," Maurice said. "Drink it."

She took the glass and held it to her lips and sipped slowly, then began to put it down.

"All of it," Maurice snapped.

She picked up the glass again and drained it, feeling the warmth of the dark red wine seeping into her. She put the glass down.

Maurice refilled it. "That's better," he said. "Just do as I tell you and we won't have any problems." He began to fill his plate with cold ham, tongue, pâté and cheese. Breaking off a piece of bread, he began to eat hungrily. "This is good," he said. "Why don't you have some?"

"I'm not hungry," she said. "Just tired."

"Food will make you feel better," he said as Jerry returned.

Janette stared at him. Jerry was in drag, wearing a sheer paneled chiffon dress with nothing underneath that exposed his privates with every motion. He had made up his face—lipstick, mascaraed lashes, shadowed eyes, rouged cheeks.

Maurice saw the expression on her face and laughed. "What's the matter? Don't you think he makes a pretty girl?"

She didn't answer. Jerry laughed, a thin falsetto laugh, and sank into a chair, his legs akimbo. The panels of the

98

dress fell open away from his hips, revealing the pale length of his penis.

Maurice smiled, still eating. "Don't you think he has a pretty prick?" he asked. "Not as large as mine, of course, but quite graceful."

She took a deep breath. "Maurice," she said.

He shook a gently chiding finger. "Papa."

She met his eyes. "Papa."

"That's better, Janette. Now, what is it you want to say?"

"Why?" she asked. "I don't understand. Why?"

"There's nothing to understand, Janette," he said. "Your mother is a whore. And when you leave here, you'll be even a bigger whore than she is."

"You can't keep me here!" she cried, starting to run from the room.

With one leap, he caught her arm before she reached the door. He dragged her back into the room. "It seems to me, Janette, that you're acting like a baby. And you know what they do to babies when they don't behave? They get spanked!"

He sat down on a chair and pulled her across his lap face down. His hand rose and fell with an even rhythm. At first there was pain, then she felt a warmth spreading through her buttocks into her loins. Her cries began to turn to a soft moan.

Maurice laughed. "Do you want to be spanked?"

She shook her head violently.

He laughed again and suddenly thrust his hand between her legs underneath her and began to massage her vulva at the same time continuing the rhythmic slapping on her buttocks. She began to gasp for breath, unable to control her spastic reactions.

"Look what you've done, you naughty girl," Maurice said. "You've gotten Jerry all excited and jealous. He's got a big hard on."

Suddenly she was aware that Jerry was standing in front of her, masturbating his penis violently. She shook her head to turn away from him.

"Stick it in her mouth, Jerry!" Maurice almost shouted. "Choke her with it!"

Jerry grabbed her by the hair, pulling her head back, forcing her to open her mouth. He pushed his penis into her mouth just as he began to come.

She began to choke and gasp trying to cry out when suddenly she felt herself in the grip of an orgasm so violent, so strong, that she had never imagined anything could have ever created such spasms of agony, pleasure and pain.

Suddenly, Maurice stood up, spilling her from his lap to the floor. She lay there, gasping and crying, unable to move. He smiled down at her. "That's lesson number one, dear child," he said. "There will be many more. And you will learn to love all of them in time. You'll see."

He turned to Jerry. "Get her into her bed."

Jerry picked her up and carried her into the bedroom and threw her down. Maurice came from behind him and picked up her arm. She heard a click. Then stared at her arm. A handcuff fastened her to the brass bedpost. She turned to look up at Maurice.

"That's just so that you don't get any funny ideas in the night," he said. "Like trying to run away."

Then he turned and left the room, followed by Jerry. The light suddenly went out, leaving her sobbing alone in the night.

She never knew whether it was day or night. When they came to take her from the bed, the drapes were always closed; even the bathroom windows were covered. The meals seemed to be always the same. Never a breakfast, lunch or dinner. A variety of cold cuts on the table. Bread. Wine. Strange things were happening in her head. Now the only thing she resented was lying alone, handcuffed to the bed in the dark. She began to await the times they would come for her. Even to look forward to the pain, because always with it came the exquisite agony of release.

100

Maurice's words kept turning over and over in her mind. "Remember, Janette, without pain there is no pleasure. The two go together, heighten each other, each contributing to the ultimate bliss."

It always began with a spanking. Once she had heard Jerry ask, "Why don't you use the cat?"

"There must be no marks," Maurice had answered.

That had been the first time they had taken her to Maurice's bed, her hands tied with long silken ropes to the wooden bedposts. "You take her first," Maurice said. "Get her ready for me."

He held her legs apart while Jerry knelt on his knees before her. Quickly he masturbated, trying to make himself erect, then suddenly pushed himself into her. She cried out with the sharp quick pain but then Jerry went suddenly limp and fell out of her. He turned to Maurice. "I told you I can't make it with a woman!"

With an angry gesture, Maurice pushed him away. He dropped his robe and got on the bed, positioning himself between her legs. He was already erect.

Janette stared up at him, unable to take her eyes from his phallus. "I'm afraid," she cried.

Maurice put his hand down between her legs, then brought it up and looked at it. His fingers glistened with moisture and a faint tinge of pale blood. "Your big wet whore's cunt belies your words," he said.

"You'll hurt me!"

He smiled. "Remember, Janette, without pain there is no pleasure." He put his hands under her buttocks and raised her toward him.

She stared down with wide eyes as he slowly moved himself into her. She could not believe that she could open wide enough to receive him. He seemed to pause for a moment as he came to an obstruction. He looked into her eyes, then, without warning, gave a violent shove.

The pain tore through her and she screamed. He put a hand over her mouth, holding her motionless against him with the other hand. After a moment, she opened her eyes, staring up into his face, then slowly lowered her gaze. He felt her lungs fill with air as she came to the realization that he was completely buried inside her. Her eyes slowly moved back up to him, beginning to fill with a strange kind of wonder. He stared at her for a moment, then took his hand away from her mouth and pulled the cords that bound her to the bedposts, freeing her hand.

She stared at him for a moment more, then, suddenly, threw her arms around him clinging to him tightly. She began slow tentative movements, then as she grew more frenetic, she squeezed her eyes tightly shut so that the tears forced their way through her closed lids. Her voice was a whisper turning to a screaming shout in his ears. "Papa! Papa! Papa!"

Her eyes opened staring up at him. "Slap my face!"

His open hand cracked across her cheek.

"Again!"

This time there were white handprints on her cheek. She smiled up at him. "You do love me, don't you, Papa?" she asked.

He laughed aloud. "You're Papa's little whore!" he said.

"Yes," she whispered. "Yes. You knew it all the time. That's what I always wanted to be."

After that she never went back to the bed in the small room. She slept in Maurice's big bed with the two of them. One morning she woke up and there was daylight flooding into the room. She blinked her eyes.

Maurice was standing next to the bed, already dressed. "Your mother came home from the clinic last night," he said. "I'll have Jerry drop you off at the house."

"I don't want to see her," she said.

"Then you'll have to go back to school," he said.

"Can't I stay here?" she asked.

He shook his head. "No. If you don't go back to school there will be too many questions."

"But I want to stay with you," she said.

"You can't," he said. He put his hands in his pocket and came out with a key ring. "But I had a set of keys made for

102

you. Next month when you have the Easter holidays you can come down here, and if we're not home you can let yourself in."

That afternoon she boarded the train back to school.

The late April sunshine was fading from the windows when Jacques sank exhausted into a chair in the large flower-filled living room. He looked up at Tanya and Johann. "I'm dead. I'm glad it's over."

Johann nodded. "I thought the press conference went very well."

"The best idea I had was holding it here in your house," Jacques said to Tanya. "I think everyone appreciated the personal touch. They're so bored with salons and hotel conference rooms."

"Do you think they liked the advance preview of some of Shiki's designs?" Tanya asked.

"From what I heard," Jacques answered, "they all loved them. Now they'll all turn out for the showing at collection time. They know you're serious."

"Did Shiki leave already?" she asked.

"Yes," Jacques answered. "He was gone as soon as the last reporter disappeared." He got to his feet. "And that's what I'd better be doing. Let you get some rest. It will be a hectic day at the office tomorrow."

"I'll be leaving too," Johann said. "Congratulations."

Tanya smiled. "It's too soon for that. We'd better wait until after the showings."

"I'm not worried any more," Johann said. "It will be all right."

She saw them to the door, they kissed her cheek goodbye, then she turned and started for the staircase. Henri came toward her. "Madame," he said hesitantly.

"Yes?"

"Mademoiselle Janette is in her room," he said.

"Janette! Here?" The surprise echoed in her voice. "Why didn't you tell me before?"

"She arrived in the midst of the conference, Madame, and asked me not to disturb you."

Without another word she ran up the stairs. The door to Janette's room was closed. She knocked politely, then entered. Janette was standing at the window, looking out. "Janette!" Tanya exclaimed.

Janette turned toward her mother. Her eyes were expressionless. "Hello, Mother," she said in a dull voice.

Tanya stared at her. The girl's face was thin and drawn and there were deep blue circles under her eyes. "Janette," she cried. "What's the matter with you?"

Janette made no move to come toward her. She met her mother's eyes defiantly. "I'm pregnant," she said.

"No," Tanya said. "No."

"Yes, Mother," Janette said.

Tanya moved toward her. "My poor baby."

Janette avoided her arms. "I'm not your poor baby, Mother. Not any more."

"Why didn't you call me? At least answer my calls?" Tanya asked.

"What difference would it have made?" Janette shurgged. "You would have had the baby anyway."

"You have a sister, Janette."

"And my sister will have a sister," Janette said.

Tanya stared into her daughter's eyes. "I don't understand."

"Don't be stupid, Mother," Janette said. "The same man that made you pregnant made me pregnant."

"That's impossible!" Tanya said.

"Is it, Mother? That week you were in the clinic, Maurice came up to the school and brought me to Paris to see you. But he never took me to the clinic. Instead I spent the week in his apartment and on the day you came home, I went back to school."

"Maurice?" There was a note of incredulity in Tanya's voice. "I can't believe even he would do that."

"No, Mother?" Janette opened her small purse and took out a set of keys. She threw them down on the table next to her. "He even gave me a set of keys to the apartment so that I could come back there at Easter."

Tanya stared down at the keys, then up at her daughter. The tears began to flood into her eyes. "Why didn't you let me talk to you? Why? I was going to tell you. Maurice is not Lauren's father. I've never let him come near me since the day we were married."

"You're lying, Mother," Janette said.

"I'm not lying," Tanya said. "One look at your sister and you would know that. Blond and blue-eyed. Why do you think Maurice is suing me for divorce charging adultery? There's never been a blond blue-eyed child in his family for generations."

Janette stared at her. "I didn't know that, Mother. No one ever told me."

Tanya took a deep breath. She felt as if her insides had turned to stone. "It doesn't matter now," she said. "It's done and can't be undone. We must make plans for tomorrow. The first thing to do is to see Doctor Pierre."

Suddenly the tears sprang into Janette's eyes. "Oh, Mother," she cried. "I'm sorry."

Then they were in each other's arms, their tears running down each other's cheeks. For a long while they stood there, clinging together without words until the daylight had faded from the windows.

Two days later, Tanya waited in the small office of Dr. Pierre until he came from the operating room of his clinic. She rose to her feet as he entered. "How is she, Doctor Pierre?"

"She'll be all right," he said. "It's all taken care of. She's resting now."

"Thank God," she said.

"Yes, thank God," he said solemnly. "If she had had the baby she would have died."

Tanya stared at him.

Dr. Pierre shook his head. "I don't know what kind of an

animal she was with but she was all torn apart inside. He must have used a battering ram on her. Not only were the vagina and tubes torn apart but her anus and part of her bowel were ripped. I couldn't believe it." He looked into Tanya's eyes. "I repaired her as best I could. At least she won't have any problems from it." He paused, letting out a deep breath.

"There's something else you're not telling me," she said in a tense voice.

He hesitated a moment. "Janette will never be able to have a child," he said. "I had to remove all but a part of one ovary."

It was two o'clock in the morning, exactly ten days later, the day after Janette had returned to school, that Tanya parked the small car in the street in front of the apartment building on the Ile Saint-Louis. The street was deserted as she got out of the car. Automatically she locked it, putting the car keys in her purse, at the same time taking out the keys to the apartment. She looked up at the building. All the windows were dark. Slowly she made her way to the outside door.

It was the big key, always the big key for the street door. It turned easily, sliding back the bolt, and she stepped into the dark hallway. She had to stop herself from reaching for the hallway lights automatically. One thing she didn't want was to call attention to herself. She waited a moment until her eyes became used to the darkness, then moved toward the elevator.

The noise the old creaking elevator made as it ascended seemed loud enough in her ears to wake up all Paris. She held her breath until finally it came to a stop. Then, with a feeling of relief, she stepped out. There were two apartments to a floor. She hesitated a moment, then struck a match. There it was. A small brass plate over the doorbell. Le Marquis de la Beauville.

She closed her eyes for a moment and thought. Was there

anything she had forgotten? Her will had been properly signed and executed. The instructions to the Swiss bank regarding the vault in which the gold was kept had been received and acknowledged. If something should happen to her, Johann would take care of everything. The children would be protected.

The first key made no sound as she turned it slowly. She heard the faint click of the bolt. Good. Now for the second key. It squeaked faintly. She stopped. There was no other sound. She turned the key the rest of the way slowly. It clicked and the door swung open slowly.

She took a tentative step into the apartment, then stopped, listening. There was no sound. Quietly she shut the door behind her. Now she waited while she got her bearings.

She tried to remember what Janette had told her about the apartment. Straight ahead through the big archway would be the living room. To the right, a small door led to the service entrance and the kitchen. Beyond the living room through another smaller arch would be the dining room. Maurice's bedroom was through a door on the far end of the dining room.

Carefully she moved through the rooms, moving slowly so that she would not stumble against an unseen piece of furniture. Now she was in front of the door to the bedroom. She opened her purse again and took out the razor. It was only right that it should be Wolfgang's razor. There was no doubt in her mind now that it had been Maurice who betrayed him to the Russians.

She opened the razor so that the cutting edge faced outward away from her hand and turned the doorknob softly. The door swung open and she stepped into the room, moving softly on the carpeted floor. She didn't bother to close the door behind her.

She could see the bed in the faint luminescence that filtered through the draperies from the street lights outside. She walked toward the bed. She sensed, rather than saw, the huddled mass beneath the blanket. She paused over him, looking down, trying to see him. The heavy sound of breathing came to her ears but she did not know whether it was his or her own. "Maurice!" she said softly.

He turned, starting to sit up. Then she struck. With all her strength she ripped the razor down his body. A strangled scream rose in his throat and he rolled frantically away from her, his hand pulling something from the table at the other side of the bed. Angrily she kept on slashing as he tried to turn. She saw the glint of something hard and metallic in his hand but kept on slashing and striking.

A roar exploded in her ears and blue fire seared her eyes at the same time that a sledgehammer blow seemed to strike her in the chest, almost throwing her backward, but still she pressed on, the razor rising and falling. At last he collapsed inertly on the sheets.

She stood there breathing heavily, then put her hand down to touch him. Her fingers seemed to sink into a morass of blood-sodden sheets. She pulled her hand back quickly, the razor falling from her fingers. The pain in her chest was growing more intense now. She pressed her hand against her breast and felt the warm blood seeping through her dress onto her fingers. For the first time, she realized she had been shot.

Slowly she turned and made her way back through the apartment, the pain growing more agonizing with every step. It seemed to take forever for her to reach the apartment door. Now the pain was rolling in waves through her body and she felt dizzy and wavering, as if consciousness were draining from her through the blood running down her fingers.

She reached for the door. Suddenly the light in the hallway outside flooded on and the door sprang open in her hands. He stood there in open-mouthed shock, the light spilling from behind him across her face.

She stared at him in wide-eyed horror. "Oh, no, Maurice!" she screamed. "You're dead! I just killed you!" Then she began falling as consciousness left her, never to return.

Book Two

Janette

SHIKI STOOD IN front of the easel studying the design critically. He heard the door close behind him and the girl's footsteps approaching. "Take off all your clothes," he said without turning around. "Let me know when you're naked."

A moment later he heard the low voice. "I'm naked."

He penciled in a small adjustment to the drawing and turned around. "*Merde*," he said, his jaw dropping.

Janette laughed at his consternation.

"Why didn't you tell me who you were?" he asked.

"I thought if you were switching," she smiled, "I would like to be the first."

He reached for a robe on the chair next to him. "Put this on," he said uncomfortably.

She didn't take it. "Come on, Shiki. Wouldn't you like to eat my pussy? You might even like it."

"Cut it out," he said, annoyed. "I'm working."

"I won't tell anyone," she replied.

"I thought you were the model I sent for to try on a new design," he said.

"You can try it on me."

He shook his head. "It won't work."

"Why not?"

He looked at her critically. "You're too much of a woman. Your tits are too big, your ass is too big and your *mons veneris* sticks out further than most men's cock and balls. You're just not the model type, that's all."

"What type am I?" she asked.

"You're like your mother," he said. "Big and strong. An earth type. Pure animal sex. You walk out on a runway and automatically every other woman in the place would hate you, which means no matter what you wore they wouldn't buy it. You're too much of what each of them would like to be."

"That's a backhanded compliment if ever I heard one," she said, reaching for her jeans, which she had thrown over a chair, and getting into them. She slipped into a large man-tailored shirt and tied it around her waist.

"What are you doing down here?" he asked.

"I had an appointment with Johann," she said. "But he was in a meeting so I thought I would drop in on you."

"It's always good to see you," he said.

She smiled. "Even if I'm not the model type?"

He laughed. "Even so."

"Maybe you ought to change your models," she said. "There are more girls like me than there are like them."

"Most girls like you can't afford the kind of clothes we make," he said.

"That could be what's wrong with our business," she said. "Too many *haute couture* designers fighting for too small a market."

"We're doing all right," he said half defensively.

"I'm sure we are," she said quickly. "I was just thinking out loud."

The telephone on his desk rang. He picked it up, then looked at her. "Johann's meeting is over. You can see him now."

"Thank you." She blew him a kiss and left the room.

He stared at the closed door for a moment, then locked it and went back to his desk. He sat down behind it, took a joint from the neat cigarette case and lit it. He leaned back in his chair and let the smoke drift thoughtfully from his nose.

Like mother, like daughter. Like mother, like mother, like mother. But even more, like daughter.

"Two years at the *Université* is enough," she said. "I'm not going back."

Johann's face was expressionless. He looked at her across his desk. In a way he wasn't surprised. She was nineteen now and there was very little of the child left in her. More and more each day, she reminded him of her mother. Tanya had been about the same age when they first met, the same reddish-brown hair, long and falling down her face, partly concealing her high cheekbones and dark eyes in the fashion of the day. "What would you prefer doing?" he asked carefully.

"I think it's time I became involved in the business," she said. "After all, in two more years I will be responsible for the whole thing. I think it's about time I learned something about it, don't you?"

She was like her mother. Johann nodded. "I agree with you. Now the question is, where would you like to begin?"

"Maurice says that more than sixty-five percent of our gross income comes from the United States," she said. "Yet I've never been there."

"That's true," he said.

"He's planning to go there next month and has offered to take me with him and show me around."

Johann didn't let his surprise show in his face. It was the first time he had learned that she had even been talking to Maurice. "That's kind of him," he said cautiously. "How do you expect that to help you? After all, he's not involved in any of our companies. His own is quite separate."

"That's true," she said. "But he does know everybody."

He was silent for a moment. "I don't object to it," he said. "And you certainly don't need my permission to go on a trip. But don't you think it might be a better idea to come into the office for a few months first and get some grounding? Then when you go you'll be better equipped to relate."

"I'd like to go," she said. "I think I would go out of my mind sitting in the office. It reminds me too much of being in a classroom back at the *Université*."

113

"Sooner or later, you're going to have to do your home-work," he said. "Running a business isn't all fun and games."

"I know that," she said. "But isn't that what you do? I would like to become more involved with the creative and marketing side of it. Here in France we still do things in the same old-fashioned way. America is way ahead of us in many ways. I have a feeling we can learn many things from them."

"I would still like it if you could spend some time in the office before you go," he said.

"Maurice isn't planning to leave before the end of next month," she said. "That gives me six weeks. Is that enough for you?"

"It's better than nothing," he said. "I just hope it's enough for you."

"I'm a quick study. I'll make it enough," she said seri-ously. She got to her feet. "What time would you like me to come in tomorrow?"

"Nine o'clock," he said. "I think the best place for you to start is with the controller."

"I'll be here." She smiled. "Thank you, Johann."

He came out from behind the desk. In a curious sort of way he felt good about her wanting to come into the com-pany. Something had been missing ever since Tanya's death. Now, perhaps, it would be whole again. "How is your sister?" he asked.

She looked at him. "Fine. Growing. I haven't seen much of her since I came down from school. Her nanny hovers over her like a blanket."

"It might be a good idea if you could spend some time with her," he suggested. "So that at least she feels she has a family."

"I'm afraid I haven't much of a mother instinct," she said. "To me, she seems like every other child."

"Too bad," he said.

"Yes," she said. "The poor can offer their children for

114

adoption when they're not equipped to bring them up, no matter what the reason may be. But what do the rich do?"

He was silent for a moment. "What we're doing, I suppose. Hire nannies and hope they provide a love substitute."

"Maurice said something about maybe we could work out an agreement and he would move back into the house. That would provide a more normal family life for her. After all, legally he *is* still her father."

"And yours too," he said.

"That's right," she said. "But in two more years, I'll be legally of age, and free of him. Lauren still has a long way to go."

He was silent.

"If something should happen to us—you and me—who would get her?" she asked.

"Maurice, I imagine," he said. "There's no one else."

"*Merde,*" she said. She thought for a moment. "I wonder what he has on his mind. Why do you think he's being so nice to us all of a sudden?"

"I'm sure I don't know," he answered.

"I don't trust him," she said. "But then I never did."

"In time we'll find out," he said. "Until then, be careful. Just don't sign any papers, that's all."

She laughed. "Don't worry. I know that much." She started toward the door, then stopped and turned back to him. "Johann, you're a nice man, why is it you never married?"

He looked at her without answering.

Suddenly she understood. "Mother. You were in love with her, weren't you?"

He still didn't answer.

"She's dead now," she said. "That's over. Find yourself a good woman and marry her. Then you could give Lauren the kind of home she needs."

He smiled suddenly. "I might surprise you."

Impulsively she went to him and kissed his cheek. "It

would be a lovely surprise," she said, then went out the door with a wave of her hand. "Tomorrow morning. Nine o'clock sharp."

He went back to his desk and sat down heavily. After a moment he reached for the telephone and dialed a number. A woman's voice answered. He spoke in German. "Heidi? Eight o'clock all right for dinner? I'll pick you up."

"He's too conservative," Jacques said, placing the chilled glass of kir on the cocktail table in front of her. He sat down beside her, taking a small vial from his pocket. She sipped her drink, watching him as he skillfully spilled some of the white powder from the vial on the glass tabletop, then separated it carefully into four thin lines. Expertly he rolled a hundred-franc note into a straw, then sniffed one line of cocaine into each nostril. He held the bill toward her. "It's good coke," he said. "A friend of mine just brought it in from the States."

Quickly she did the two lines and handed the bill back to him. She felt her pulse quicken as the coke exploded in her head. "It is good."

"It's not the crap they sell here in Paris," he said, picking up his drink. "Cheers."

"Cheers." They sipped at their drink.

"When your mother was there it was different," he said. "She had ideas, there was a feeling of excitement. We were doing things. Now all that is gone. All Johann wants to do is keep steady, just hold on to what we have. Expansion costs money and he won't take any chances."

"But we've been making money, haven't we?" she asked.

"Of course," he said. "But we should be making a lot more. Compared to some of the other companies we've been standing still." He looked at her. "Are you really serious about coming to work here?"

She nodded.

He smiled. "Then maybe there's a chance for us yet. With you around Johann might be more venturesome."

116

She looked at him. "I didn't come up here to talk business."

He pulled at the knot that tied her shirt closed. It fell open revealing the nipples already distended with excitement. "Jesus!" he said, leaning forward to take one in his mouth.

She turned his face up to her. "Shiki said my breasts were too big."

"What the hell does he know?" he asked, burying his face between them, pressing them against his cheek with either hand. "They're beautiful."

"I asked him to eat my pussy," she said. "But he wouldn't."

"You don't have to ask me. Just get out of those damn jeans."

She rose to her feet in front of him. She pulled the snap and then the zipper and pushed the jeans down over her hips. "He said my ass was too big too," she said, turning away from him and bending slightly forward so that her buttocks were practically thrust into his face.

He was silent.

"Slap my ass," she said.

He hit her playfully.

"Harder," she said. "Like you mean it."

"I don't want to hurt you," he said.

"You won't hurt me," she said. "Do what I tell you. Hit me hard."

His open hand cracked across her buttock. He could see the white handprint on it. He hesitated.

"More," she said fiercely. "Don't stop."

His hand began to rise and fall rapidly. He could see the white handprints turning red on her buttocks and suddenly he realized that she was grinding her hips and moaning, masturbating herself at the same time. Excitement began to rise in him and suddenly he was angry. The bitch was just using him to get off. Now he really began to hit her.

"I'm coming," she cried. "I can't stop coming!"

Angrily he spun her around to face him. There was a

strange inner look on her face. She didn't even seem to see him. Without thinking, he slapped her face. "What about me, you bitch?"

She stared at him, suddenly silent, then her eyes fell before his gaze. She sank to her knees before him, her fingers quickly opening his trousers. She thrust her hand into his trousers, freeing him, and then further underneath him until a finger found his anus. "I want you to come in my mouth," she said, covering him with her lips.

A moment later he felt his testes explode and the semen bursting forth. The orgasm wracked his body and began to subside, but still she didn't stop. With one hand she held him still rigid and kept drawing on his glans until he could no longer bear the agony, his penis feeling like nothing but raw nerve ends. He sank his hand in her hair and pulled her away from him.

Her cheeks and chin were covered with semen that had escaped her mouth. For a long moment he stared at her until he caught his breath. "You're crazy," he said.

Her eyes suddenly turned cold. "I'm not like my mother," she said angrily. "Don't every say that to me again."

She started to get to her feet. His hands on her shoulders kept her down. "I didn't mean that kind of crazy," he said quickly. "I meant crazy great."

He felt the tension leave her. "You fucked with my mother, didn't you?"

He nodded.

"Was she good?"

He looked at her. "Yes. But not like you. You're fantastic."

"She wasn't really crazy," she said. "She had a nervous breakdown. She was working too hard and there were too many things on her mind."

"I know that," he said.

She rose to her feet. "Christ, I'm soaking wet. I must have come a thousand times." She wiped herself with her fingers then raised them to her mouth and sucked them. Again she

118

pressed her fingers into herself. This time she held them out to him. "Taste me."

Slowly he licked her fingers.

"Good?" she asked.

"Like honey."

"As good as my mother?"

"Better," he said.

She laughed aloud and pulled his face toward her. "Then eat me," she said.

Johann parked the car in front of her apartment house. He sat there a moment with the motor running, then reached across to open the door for her.

"It's early yet. Why don't you come in for a nightcap?" she asked.

He smiled to himself as he always did when she spoke German. The faint American accent gave the language a strange musical sound, a softness it did not ordinarily have. He answered in English, "Thank you," as he switched off the motor.

The light scent of her perfume and the warmth of her body seemed to permeate him as they stood in the tiny elevator barely large enough for the two of them as it took them up to her apartment on the third floor. He felt a slight sense of relief when it finally stopped and he could hold the door to let her out. He followed her to her apartment and waited while she opened the door with her key, then followed her inside.

It was a small apartment, what the French called a "studio," which consisted of a fair-sized room with a bed that doubled as a couch during the day, a kitchen in a double-doored closet, and a separate bathroom. A lamp was glowing in the far corner of the room, and that, more than anything else, showed that she was basically American. No Frenchman or other European would leave a light on while he was not at home.

119

She gestured toward an armchair. "I have whiskey, gin, vodka and cognac."

"Cognac, please." He watched while she opened the small kitchen doors and took down the bottle and two glasses from the closet over the sink. She poured the golden liquor into the glasses, then came back to him. He took one from her hand. "Thank you," he said.

She smiled. "Are you always so formal when you come to a lady's apartment?" she asked, speaking in English now.

"Habit," he answered. He held up his glass. "*Santé.*"

They clinked glasses and sipped. "You can sit down now," she said, crossing to the couch and sitting opposite him.

He sat down carefully as the chair was fragile and might break under him. It was deceptively comfortable and he sank into it. He swirled the cognac in his glass and sipped at it again.

"Dinner was lovely," she said. "I really enjoyed it."

"You didn't eat much."

She laughed. "I have to watch my diet."

"Why? You look perfect to me."

She laughed again. "That's why I have to watch it. Every ounce I swallow turns into a pound on me."

He was silent for a moment. "Anyway, I'm glad you enjoyed it."

"I did, really." Then she too was silent.

He sipped at his cognac again. "I suppose I'd better finish my drink and go," he said. "I have to be at work early tomorrow."

"Johann," she said. "I'll be going back to the States next week."

He nodded slowly. "I thought you might be. When do you plan your next trip back here?"

She met his eyes. "I don't think I'll be coming back. At least not for a long time."

He felt a sinking feeling in his chest. "I'm sorry, Heidi. I've come to look forward to your visits."

"I am too," she said. "But only because I'll miss you."

He was silent again, swirling the amber liquid in his glass. "I've been coming to Paris every third month for two years now, Johann," she said. "And each time we see each other. Lunch, dinners. I can't count how many times. I know how you feel about me, yet you never say anything. Never. Why, Johann? I don't understand, why?"

He took a deep breath, meeting the hurt look in her blue eyes. "I'm forty-six years old, Heidi. Seventeen years older than you."

"Sixteen," she said quickly. "I'll be thirty next month."

He didn't smile. "I'm a serious man, a respectful man. I'm not a playboy who would have a casual affair with you. I like you too much."

"I'm not a child, Johann. I'm a woman. And a divorced woman at that. Don't you think that I have feelings too? And desires?" She shook her head. "But you never said anything. And you still haven't told me why."

"I have responsibilities, heavy responsibilities," he said.

"I know about that," she said. "Janette and Lauren. I haven't been deaf and you've certainly talked enough about it. But does that mean that you cannot have a life of your own? Or a family of your own if you should want it?"

"They have no one but me to protect them. I made a promise. First to von Brenner. Then to Tanya. I can't go back on my word."

"I'm not saying you should go back on your word," she said. "I'm only saying that you're entitled to have a life of your own, that's all."

"Heidi," he said.

She heard the pain in his voice and rose from the couch. She sank to her knees in front of him and looked up into his face. "I love you, Johann. Do you love me?"

"Yes." The words tumbled from his lips. "Yes, I love you."

"Then, for God's sake, kiss me," she cried. "You know in all the two years, you never even once kissed me."

He leaned down toward her as her arms went up around his neck, his mouth searching her soft lips and tasting the salt of her tears.

She found a place to park, jumped her car onto the sidewalk and got out and locked it. She smiled, pleased with herself. That was one of the advantages of a mini—it could be parked anywhere.

It was a little after eleven o'clock at night but in La Coupole it was high noon. The theaters were just beginning to empty and already the brasserie was jammed with people. She pushed her way through the crowds waiting for a table and went to the back of the restaurant. There was a table in the far corner that had everything but their names on it. From seven in the evening on, one or the other of their crowd was always sitting there. They had an unspoken rule that until two o'clock in the morning whoever was at the table could not leave until someone came in to take it over. If it was empty for even one minute, it would be gone, and then they would have to stand in line like the rest of the crowd.

Marie-Thérèse and Françoise were sitting at the table, Coca-Colas in front of them, staring at Jean, whose head was resting on his folded arms on the table, his untouched pastis next to his elbow. She bent over and kissed both girls on the cheek, then straightened up. "What's the matter with him?" she asked.

"He's out of it," Françoise said in a disgusted voice. Jean was her boy friend. "Some Moroccan laid a cube of black hash on him. I took two hits and was high as a kite but he wouldn't quit until it was almost all gone. I don't know how he even made it to the table."

"Asshole," she said, sitting down next to him.

The waiter appeared as if by magic. "*Bon soir,* Janette," he smiled. "What'll it be tonight?"

"*Bon soir,* Sami," she smiled back up at him. "I'm hungry tonight. I'll have a hamburger *au cheval, frites* and a beer."

"Right away," Sami said, disappearing as magically as he had come.

She looked around the restaurant. "Anybody around?"

"Nobody." Marie-Thérèse shrugged her shoulders. She looked across the table at Janette. "Where have you been? Your eyes look funny."

Janette laughed. "It's just the light in here. It always takes me a few minutes to get used to it."

"Don't give me that shit," Marie-Thérèse said. "I know you. You're on something."

Janette felt good, strong and full of energy. She laughed again, patting the shirt pocket over her breast. "Coke," she said, lowering her voice to a whisper. "And I've got enough here for all of us."

Sami came back to the table and put her hamburger and beer down in front of her. She began to eat voraciously. "I'm starved," she said between mouthfuls.

"I don't get it," Françoise said. "I heard coke was supposed to kill your appetite."

"Nobody told me," Janette said, picking up some of the *frites* with her fingers and dipping them into the mustard before placing them in her mouth. "As soon as I finish we'll get out of here and go over to my place."

"What about Jean?" Françoise asked.

"The hell with him," she answered. "Let him sleep. They'll throw him out in the morning."

"I couldn't do that," Françoise said hesitantly. "He'd never talk to me again."

"You wouldn't be missing anything," Janette said. "I've never heard him say anything that made sense."

Françoise was beginning to get angry. "You don't like him because he won't jump when you snap your fingers."

Janette stared at her. "I don't like him because he's stupid," she said flatly. "And I have no patience with stupid people." She wiped the last of the egg yolk from her plate with two *frites* and pushed the empty plate away from her. She held up her hand for the waiter. "I'm getting a coffee and then I'm going. Either of you like anything?"

"No, thanks," Françoise answered. She glanced at Jean. "I'm getting worried. I can't sit here all night with him."

Sami did his magic act. Janette wiped her fingers with her napkin and handed it to him. "Two double espressos and another napkin, please."

"Right away," he said, clearing the plates away from in front of her. He was back in a moment with the coffee. He put one down in front of her and looked around the table questioningly.

"It's for him." Janette gestured at Jean.

Sami looked, then shrugged his shoulders and put the coffee down. He began to turn away but Janette stopped him.

"Check, please."

Sami flipped open his little order pad, made a note with his pencil, then tore out the sheet and gave it to her. "Thirty-eight francs," he said.

She gave him a fifty-franc note. "Keep the change."

Sami smiled. "*Merci,* Janette." Then he was gone.

Janette gulped her coffee and put the empty cup down.

"How are you going to get him to drink the coffee?" Françoise asked.

"Easy," Janette answered. Casually she picked up the pitcher of water from the center of the table and poured it over Jean's head.

He came up sputtering, knocking his books from the table. He shook his head groggily. *"Merde,"* he muttered.

Janette gave him the napkin and pushed the coffee toward him. "Dry yourself and drink your coffee, sleeping beauty."

He rubbed at his face with the napkin. "What did you do that for?"

Janette laughed. "Your girl friend was worried that you might sleep here all night." She got to her feet. Marie-Thérèse got out of her chair. Janette looked down at Françoise. "He's awake now. You can come if you like."

Françoise looked at Jean, then up at her. "I think I'd better stay."

"Suit yourself." She turned away. "Let's go, Marie-Thérèse."

They left so quickly that they pushed right past a young man who was coming toward the table. He stopped at the table, looked after them, then sank into a chair. "What's with Janette?" he asked. "She almost knocks me down and then doesn't even say hello."

"I think the dike bitch is in heat," Françoise said snidely. "She couldn't get Marie-Thérèse away from the table fast enough."

"Just my luck," the young man said. "Do you think if I went after them, they'd let me watch? I'd love to see them get it on."

"Me, too, Michel," Jean said, suddenly awake. "Let's all go after them."

"You sit there and drink your coffee," Françoise said angrily.

"Where have you been all night?" Marie-Thérèse complained as Janette backed the car onto the road. "You told me you would be there at nine o'clock."

Janette flashed the headlights, then cut out into traffic, ignoring the squeal of brakes and the blaring horns behind her. She gunned the car into the center lane, then turned left at the corner past the restaurant without signaling in order to beat the traffic light, which was just beginning to change. She double-shifted into third and settled into the wide boulevard at a steady sixty kilometers.

"You are high," Marie-Thérèse said. "You're driving like an Italian."

Janette didn't answer. She switched on the radio and the music of Europe 1 flooded into the small car.

"You know how Sami hustles," Marie-Thérèse said. "I drank so many Cokes I'll be pissing mud for a week." She took out a package of cigarettes and lit two, passing one over to Janette. "You still didn't tell me where you were."

"I told you I was going up to the office to see Johann," Janette said.

"The office closes at six o'clock. You didn't get to the restaurant until after eleven."

"You're worse than a cop," Janette said. She stopped for a traffic light and looked across at her friend. There was a hurt look on Marie-Thérèse's face. She dragged on the cigarette and put the car into gear as the light turned green. "If you must know the truth, I ran into Jacques Charelle on the elevator leaving the office and we wound up at his place."

Marie-Thérèse's voice was shocked. "How could you, Janette? Wasn't he your mother's—?" She didn't finish the sentence.

"Lover?" Janette laughed. "Of course he was. But he wasn't the only one. She had others. So what difference does it make?"

"You're too much," Marie-Thérèse said. "He gave you the coke?"

"That's right."

"How is it?" Marie-Thérèse asked. "I never had any coke."

"Neither did I until tonight," Janette said. "But it's great. It really gets you up there."

"Did he know that you never had any?"

"Of course not. And I wasn't about to tell him either. I just acted as if I had it all the time. I watched how he did it and then copied him. As a matter of fact, I think that the only reason he gave me some coke to take with me was to get rid of me. Otherwise he was afraid I'd be there all night." She glanced over at Marie-Thérèse. The tears were rolling down her friend's cheeks. "Now, what the hell is the matter?"

"I don't understand you, Janette," Marie-Thérèse sniffed. "I love you and I can't make love with anyone but

126

you. You say you love me but you can make love with any-body."

"How many times do I have to tell you it's not the same thing?" Janette said in an annoyed voice. "Making love and fucking are two separate things."

"Not for me," Marie-Thérèse said.

"I don't get it," Janette said. "We've made love with others many times together."

"That's just it," Marie-Thérèse said. "We were together. Sharing each other's pleasures. But the idea of you coming to me second just to finish off the night because you didn't get enough and you're still horny doesn't appeal to me."

Janette was angry. "If that's the case, why don't I just drop you off at your place?"

"I think maybe that's the best thing to do," Marie-Thérèse said tightly.

They didn't exchange another word until Janette pulled the car to a stop in front of Marie-Thérèse's house. Marie-Thérèse sat for a moment, then turned to Janette. "I love you," she said. "But you always find new ways to hurt me."

Janette didn't look at her, just kept staring through the windshield. "I have nothing to do with it," she answered. "You invent ways to hurt yourself. Next time, if you don't want to hear the truth, don't ask questions."

Marie-Thérèse got out of the car. She looked in at Janette. "I'll feel better tomorrow by the time I see you at the *Université*."

"You won't see me there tomorrow," Janette said shortly.

"Why not?"

"Because I've quit the damn place. I'm going to work in the office tomorrow morning."

"Oh, no, Janette." Marie-Thérèse's voice was almost a wail. "What will I do if I can't see you every day?"

"Get used to it. We all have to grow up sometime," she said flatly. She reached across the seat and pulled the door shut, then pulled the car away from the curb leaving Marie-Thérèse still standing there.

127

"Stupid cunt," she muttered angrily. For a moment she thought of going back to La Coupole. She could always find someone there. But then she changed her mind. She had had enough of a man's hardness for one night. What she wanted was the softness and sensitivity of a woman. Abruptly she slammed on the brake, then threw the car in reverse and shot back to where Marie-Thérèse was still standing in the street, crying.

She stopped the car and pushed open the door. "I'm sorry," she said. "Get in."

"A hundred million francs a year," Maurice said. "That's what's in it for us if we get that fucking Nazi out of there."

Jacques stared up at him. His head was still fuzzy with sleep. It was after two o'clock in the morning when Maurice woke him up with a telephone call. And he had been too punchy to tell him he would see him in the morning. Besides, it probably wouldn't have done any good because Maurice was calling from the lobby downstairs. "Excuse me a minute," he said, getting up from the couch. "I'm going to splash some cold water on my face. For a hundred million francs a year I want to be awake."

He padded in his bare feet into the bathroom, turned on the light and closed the door. He put his hands on the sink and leaned on it, staring at himself in the mirror. He looked awful. Like death warmed over. That bitch never wanted to stop. He couldn't remember when the last time it was that he had four climaxes in almost as many hours. And for the fifth time, he was happy that he could just manage to achieve an erection. By then it didn't seem to matter to her whether he had an orgasm or not. He doubted that she even knew the difference, she was so into her own.

He turned on the cold water and splashed his face and neck. It helped a little but not that much. Slowly he dried his face. The demanding bitch. She wasn't at all what he

128

had expected when he saw her in the elevator at the office. He had grown used to mature women, to more considerate and gentler affairs.

Still, there was that scent of sexuality about her that reminded him strongly of her mother, and that was what had led him to ask her home for a drink. It would be amusing, he had thought, having made love to the mother, now to make love with the daughter. It wasn't until later that he realized she had had the same thought.

She had her car outside and she drove them to his apartment. It was when he asked her what she had been doing at the office that she had told him she was going to work there beginning tomorrow morning. And all the while, as they talked about what she planned to do in the office, when she shifted gears her hand managed to brush lightly along the side of his leg. He shifted uncomfortably as his erection began to press against his trousers.

She noticed it and laughed. "If you take it out," she said, "I'll shift both gears at the same time."

He smiled. "You won't have to, we're there already."

On the way up in the elevator, she looked at him. "My mother liked you. I heard her speak of you often."

"I liked her too," he said.

She nodded as the elevator doors opened and silently followed him to his door.

He stared into the mirror. He still felt awful. Thank God for the cocaine. At first he had hesitated about using it. The French were about twenty years behind the times. When it came to *la drogue* they were horrified, no matter what other excesses they were into. But apparently she had done it before. Quite a bit from the way she had him putting down lines for her.

A little now wouldn't hurt, might bring him up so that at least he would know what the hell Maurice was talking about. Fortunately he always kept a spare vial in the medicine cabinet. There was no way he would put down a line in front of Maurice. He was too French.

He took the vial and tapped two good snorts onto the back of his hand then quickly did one in each nostril. He felt it go right up to his head. He looked in the mirror as he returned the vial to the cabinet. He looked better already. His eyes were brighter.

He walked back into the living room. Maurice was standing at the window, looking out. He turned as he heard Jacques enter.

"At least I'm awake now," Jacques smiled. "Forgive me, I didn't ask if you would like a drink?"

"If you have a whiskey?"

"Of course," Jacques said. "With ice?"

"No, thank you. I developed a taste for it in England during the war. They drink it neat."

"Of course," Jacques said, despite the fact that he preferred it with ice, American fashion. "It's the only civilized way."

He poured a whiskey for Maurice and a cognac for himself. They sat down. *"Santé."* They both sipped, and he waited for Maurice to lower his glass. "Now what was it you were saying about a hundred million francs a year?"

Maurice smiled to himself. What was the saying the Canadians had? The Mounties always get their man. Money did it faster. "Janette was here from six ten this evening until eleven oh five. I assume that you didn't spend all that time in conversation."

Jacques stared at him. "How do you know that?"

"Since I'm the one who has been urging her to leave school and go to work in the company, I make it my business to know exactly what she's doing. All the time."

"You're having her followed?"

Maurice nodded.

"I don't quite see what that has to do with all that money," Jacques said.

"You will when I explain it to you," Maurice said. "She

needs education, to be made aware of the potential of the business that is not being taken advantage of. In my own way, I have begun. You can add a lot more to that because you know more than I do about many aspects. Maybe when she learns enough she will take some action against the Boche."

"Even if she did, it might not work," Jacques said. "She doesn't reach her majority until she is twenty-one, and then Johann has all the years after that until Lauren reaches her majority. So that's at least two more years until Janette can even question his decisions."

"It doesn't have to be two more years," Maurice said, looking at him. "Under French law, control of her estate automatically goes to her husband the moment she marries."

There was a knock at the door. Johann looked up from his desk. "Come in."

She came into his office, the tweed skirt falling straight across her hips, the man-tailored silk shirt and tweed jacket fighting a losing battle to restrain her full breasts. She came to a stop in front of his desk and looked down at him, smiling. "The six weeks are up."

"Yes," he nodded.

"Things are not as simple as I thought they would be."

He smiled. "They seldom are." He picked up a pencil from his desk. "But you've done well. I've had nothing but good reports on your work. You've managed to ask all the right questions."

"I still have a great deal to learn," she said.

He looked up at her for a long moment. "Then you've also come up with the right answer." He put the pencil back on the desk. "But don't feel too disappointed. All of us have a great deal to learn."

"I've changed my mind. I'm not going to America with Maurice next week."

For the first time surprise came into his voice. "What caused that?"

"I've learned enough to know that I'm not ready for that yet. When I do go I want to be able to project the kind of image the Americans expect from someone in our business."

"I'm afraid I don't understand," he confessed.

It was her turn to smile. "May I sit down?"

"Of course," he said, suddenly flustered. "I'm sorry. I just didn't think." He watched her sink into the chair opposite him.

It was almost as if she were picking up his thoughts. "Do I remind you of my mother?"

"Yes," he said. "Very much. Especially seeing you sit there."

She smiled. "I thought so. Many people have said that. I know they meant that as a compliment, but that's one of the reasons I'm not going to the States just now. My mother never had to look French for what she did, but if I go to the States, I'd better look the way Americans expect a Frenchwoman to look or I'll never be able to convince them that I represent the fashionable things of French life. Beautiful clothing, high fashion and good wines. I'm just not the type physically."

"What makes you think that?" he asked.

"I've been going to the fashion shows with Jacques," she said. "And I've seen what the American buyers look for and expect. And I'm not the type. I'm just too big. In every way. Shiki was right."

"There's not much you can do about that," he said.

"To start with I can lose some weight," she said. "Sixty-six kilos is too much, fifty-five is maximum for my height if I want to look right."

"You can also wind up very sick," he said.

"I don't think so," she said. "There's a clinic in Switzerland not far from where I went to school. They do some wonderful things and it's all under medical supervision.

Ten kilos less, and I can wear anything Shiki can throw on me."

"It's not that important," he said.

"I think it is," she said seriously. "If I'm going to be in this business, the main thing I have to do is look like I belong in it."

He was silent for a moment. "Have you told Maurice yet?"

She shook her head. "I've told no one. Not even Jacques. You're the first one to know."

"Jacques will be more disappointed than anyone," he said. "He was planning to meet you in New York about a month after you got there."

"I know," she said, smiling suddenly. She rose to her feet, the smile disappearing as suddenly as it had come. Her voice turned almost cold. "He had some stupid idea about taking me to Las Vegas and getting married. He said I wouldn't need anyone's consent there, being over eighteen."

He looked up at her silently.

"He's a fool, a fortune hunter," she said.

Johann still did not speak.

"I'll be gone for two months," she said. "That's how long the doctors at the clinic say it will take to get me in shape without damage to my health. No one will know where I am except you. I want you to get rid of him while I'm away."

"But I thought you—" He tried to keep the surprise from his voice. There were no secrets. By now the whole office knew about the affair she had been having with Jacques.

Her voice was almost clinical. "He was using me just as he used my mother. I'm sure that she tolerated him for good reason. And so did I. But I have no further use for him. I have learned all he has to teach me."

"But he does an important job," Johann said. "He will not be easy to replace."

"It will be very easy," she said confidently.

"I'm not that sure," he said hesitantly. "Do you have someone in mind?"

"Of course I do. Do you think I would ask you to do something like that if I didn't?"

"Who?" he asked.

She looked down at him and for the first time he saw the impenetrable hardness in the coal black of her eyes. There was a complete lack of expression in her voice. "Me."

He went deep inside himself for the strength he knew he would have to have. "I'll take your suggestion under advisement," he said. "I'm not convinced yet that you can handle the job."

For the first time there was surprise in her voice. "How can you put up with him? Do you know what he calls you behind your back? A Nazi, a Hun, a Boche?"

He smiled slowly. "That's not a valid reason. If it were, there wouldn't be a single person in the office left to work for us. I'm German. I don't expect them to love me—just to do their jobs."

She thought for a moment. "What would it take to convince you that I can do the job?"

"When you come back, you can go to work as his assistant. If after six months I am satisfied, we'll do as you suggested."

She took a deep breath. "He'll expect me to go on fucking with him."

"That's your problem, not mine," he said.

She was angry suddenly. "I could say the hell with it and marry him!"

Surprisingly, he laughed. "I can't stop you," he said. "But then you'd never get rid of him."

She was silent for a moment, then she too laughed. "Now I know why Mother chose you as she did," she said. "We'll do it your way, Johann."

"There's no other way," he said.

"I still don't want anyone to know where I am," she said.

"No one will know," he said.

He watched the door close behind her and sat there a

long moment, then reached for the telephone and placed a long-distance call to the United States. While he was waiting for the call to go through he kept remembering the coal-black wall in her eyes. Someday it would be his turn. He knew that now. In a way, he had always known it.

But there was no way he could turn away from it. Even when Janette reached her majority, there would still be Lauren to protect. If there were only a way to take Lauren out of it without sacrificing the child's equity, he would feel free. It seemed, somehow, that all his life he had been paying debts to the dead. Maybe, now, it was time that he made an investment in his own life.

She came out of the shower and wrapped the oversized bath sheet around her, then turned toward the mirror as she shook her hair free of the shower cap. It fell damply to her shoulders and she reached for another towel to rub it dry. In the mirror she saw the bathroom door behind her open. She turned around.

Lauren was standing there looking up at her. The child's blue eyes were dark and somber in her face framed by the golden ringlets of hair. She was silent, just staring up at Janette.

Rubbing her hair with the towel, she asked, "What is it, *chérie?*"

"Monsieur le Marquis is in the library. He would like to see you."

"Okay. I'll be down in a minute," she said, turning back to the mirror. In the mirror she could see that Lauren still waited there. Then tears welled up into the child's eyes. Janette turned quickly and knelt beside the child. "What's wrong, *chérie?*"

"What is a half a sister?" Lauren asked, holding back a sob.

"Half a sister?" Janette echoed. "I don't know what that means."

"That's what Monsieur le Marquis said you were. He said, Go tell your half sister that I'm waiting for her. He also said it was not polite to call him Monsieur le Marquis, I should call him Papa. I said that you don't call him Papa and he said that was because he was not your father as he is mine, and that's why you're my half sister." Lauren was really crying now.

"Merde," Janette said, taking the child and hugging her close. "Don't you pay any attention to him, darling. I'm your big sister and that's all there is to it. And you don't have to call him Papa, because he's not your father any more than he is mine."

"Then why does he say he is?" Lauren asked with a child's directness.

"Because that is what he would like to be. But he isn't."

"Then who is my Papa?" Lauren asked.

"Your Papa went away, just as my Papa did."

"Did you know my Papa?" Lauren asked.

"No," Janette replied. "But then I didn't know my Papa either."

"Then why are we sisters? How do we know that?"

"Because we have the same mother," Janette said.

"Did you know her?"

"Yes, darling," Janette said.

"Why didn't I know her?" Lauren asked.

"She had an accident when you were still a baby," Janette answered.

"She's dead, isn't she?" the child asked. "Like our Papas?"

"Yes," Janette said gently. She kissed Lauren's cheek. "But that's nothing to worry about. We have each other."

Lauren pulled back and rubbed her nose with the back of her hand. "Was our mother a nice lady?"

"Very nice."

"Was she beautiful?"

"She was one of the most beautiful ladies in Paris," Janette said. "She loved you very much."

"Did she love you too?"

Janette nodded slowly. "Yes."

Lauren thought for a moment. "I'm sorry I didn't know her. Someday I would like to have a Mama."

Janette was silent.

The child looked up into Janette's eyes. "Do you think you could be my Mama?"

"How could I be? I can't be your sister and your mother all at the same time."

"I don't mean for real, Janette," the child said quickly. "I mean play mother. Just sometimes when the two of us are alone. We won't tell anybody. Even if it's just pretend it would be nice to have a Mama."

Janette thought for a moment, then nodded. "Okay. But it's just pretend, remember?"

A radiant smile broke across Lauren's face and she threw her arms around Janette, kissing her cheek. "Thank you," she said.

Janette hugged her tightly for a moment, then let her go. "Okay, baby," she said. "Now off to bed with you."

Lauren kissed her again. "Good night, Mama," she said and ran from the room.

She turned back to the mirror and finished drying her hair, then brushed it and dressed slowly. It wasn't until she was on the staircase that she suddenly realized that she had automatically put on the black brassiere and panties that Maurice always wanted her to wear.

He was standing behind the library door when she opened it and did not see him until she closed the door. Before she had a chance to speak, he slapped her viciously on the cheek, knocking her backward to the floor, her skirt flying up over her hips.

He stood over her for a moment, staring down at her, then abruptly thrust his hand between her legs. The black panties were soaked with moisture. He squeezed her pubis in a viselike grip, watching the pain contort her face as more moisture flooded into his hand. "Whore!" he said, a note of satisfaction in his voice. He straightened up and prodded her with the tip of his pointed shoe. "Whore!"

She stared up at him silently as he walked away and sat down on a couch facing her. She took a deep breath and got to her feet. She could feel her legs still trembling.

"Bitch!" he said in a normal tone of voice. "What kind of games are you playing with me?"

Her voice was almost dull. "I'm not playing any games."

"I've made all the arrangements for America," he said. "And now I hear you're not going."

"I've changed my mind," she said.

"You've changed your mind?" he echoed mockingly. "I thought you wanted to learn something more about your business."

"I'm bored with it," she said. "Why should I work? It does all right. I have enough money."

"And you're willing to let that Nazi continue to bleed you?"

She didn't answer. Instead she turned and walked to the sideboard near the fireplace. She poured some pastis into a glass and added the water, shaking it gently until a milky-white cloud filled the glass. She sipped it slowly, turning back to him, feeling her strength return. "I'm just not interested, that's all," she said.

He moved quickly, the glass went flying from her hand almost before she realized he was upon her. She turned her face, trying to avoid being hit again, but not quickly enough. She crashed to the floor in front of the fireplace. Through pain-filled eyes she saw him approaching.

She rolled over and grabbed a small iron poker from the stand. Gripping it with both hands, she rolled away from him to her feet. Wildly, she swung at him.

He sprang out of the way just in time and the poker flailed through the empty air. He stared at her, almost in shock at the raw nature of her violence.

She spat the words at him. "You touch me again and I'll finish what my mother started!"

"You're crazy!" he said. "Just like she was!"

"Get out!" she screamed, moving toward him. "Get out!"

He fled toward the door and turned, looking back at her, his hand on the doorknob. "Listen to me," he said. "I was only trying to keep you from losing everything."

"I'll take care of myself," she said. "Just keep away from me, this house, and my sister or I'll kill you! Now, get out!"

"Someday you'll be on your knees begging for my help," he said, slamming the door behind him.

She stared at the closed door for a moment, then her legs gave way and she slumped onto the couch, the poker falling to the floor from her hand. She closed her eyes, giving in to the pulsing waves of heat surging from her loins. Almost automatically she slipped her hand inside her panties. An orgasm swept through her almost as soon as her fingers touched her moist, swollen clitoris. "Oh, God!" she exclaimed, then turning face down on the couch and burying her head in her arms, began to cry.

Heidi saw him standing just beyond the railing as she approached the police at immigration. She waved to him as she pushed her passport through the narrow window. He smiled and waved back. It wasn't until then that she noticed the small bouquet of flowers he held in his other hand. The policeman pounded her passport with his stamp and pushed it back to her. She took it and almost ran as she came through the railing.

For a moment they paused awkwardly, looking at each other, then he proffered the bouquet almost shyly. She took it, then looked up into his face and went into his arms.

His voice was husky as he whispered into her ear. "Until this moment I was afraid you would not come."

Her voice trembled between laughter and tears. "Until you called, I was afraid you'd never ask me."

They drew apart. She looked down at the bouquet. "The flowers are beautiful. You didn't have to."

He laughed as he reached for the small valise she was carrying. "Come, let's get the rest of your baggage."

Traffic moved slowly on the *autoroute* leading from Orly into Paris. "It's still the morning rush hour," he explained.

"I don't mind," she said.

"Did you sleep on the plane?"

"A little," she said.

"You'll have a bath once we get home. Then a little rest and you'll feel better."

"I feel fine," she said quickly. "Just excited."

He laughed. "I hope you weren't too excited to bring all your papers."

"I brought them all," she said.

"Good," he answered. "I have a friend in the *mairie*. He said he would rush everything through for us. It shouldn't take more than ten days."

"That long?" Her voice echoed her dismay. "In the States it would only take overnight."

He laughed again. "This is France. Remember?"

She nodded and reached for his arm. "I don't care. Even if it takes forever. As long as I can be with you."

"You'll be with me," he said. He glanced at her again. "I had the apartment cleaned and painted, but if it's not right, you can change anything you want."

"I'm sure it will be okay," she said. "After all, it will only be for two years."

He was silent.

"You meant what you said?" she asked quickly.

He nodded. "I meant it. I think by the time Janette is twenty-one she'll be only too glad to have me step out."

She studied his face as he drove. "You're not upset over it, are you?"

"Not really," he said. "The only thing that disturbs me is the little one. Lauren. I will have to find a way to see that she is protected."

"You have two years to work that out," she said. "And I'm sure you will." She paused for a moment. "I'm looking forward to meeting Janette."

140

He laughed. "You'll have to wait another month. Right now she's in Switzerland at a clinic."

"Is there anything the matter with her?"

"Nothing," he said. "She thinks it's time she looked more like a fashion model."

"Is she heavy?"

"Not at all," he said. "But she's like her mother. She's a big girl."

"Children get all sorts of strange ideas," she said.

He glanced at her. His voice was thoughtful. "Janette is not a child. I don't think she ever was."

"Johann is getting married this week," Jacques said.

"I don't believe it," Maurice said, signaling the waiter for another drink. "Anyone I know?"

Jacques shook his head. "None of us know her. She's American. Her father is supposed to be very rich."

"Is she young?"

"About thirty, I think. She was in the office the other day. Very attractive. I think her parents are German."

"What kind of business are they in?" Maurice asked.

Jacques shrugged his shoulders. "I don't know."

"It might be a good idea to find out," Maurice said. "Johann is not stupid. There might be some connection to his future plans with the companies."

"I'll see what I can learn," Jacques said. "Have you had any luck discovering where Janette is?"

"Zero," Maurice said. "She just seems to have dropped out of sight. I wonder if anyone knows."

"Johann knows," Jacques said confidently. "He's the only one who isn't curious. But he's not saying anything."

"It may all tie together," Maurice said. "We'd better keep our eyes open or we may discover the whole thing has gotten away from us."

"Do you really think we still have a chance?" Jacques asked.

"Maybe more now than before, with Johann getting married. Janette might not like the idea that he has other interests than her own. If she gets the feeling that his concerns lie elsewhere she might turn our way."

Janette stepped down from the scale and turned to the doctor. "Only four kilos," she said. "That's not much."

Dr. Schindler smiled. "I'm satisfied. That's a little more than one kilo per week. If we try to do more, we can lose skin tone too rapidly and everything begins to sag."

"My breasts are sagging already," she said.

"Are you doing the exercises I gave you?" He clasped his hands in front of his chest and tightened the muscles across his chest so that she could see them moving under his shirt.

"I walk around all day doing them like an idiot," she said. "I don't think it's working."

"Everything takes time." He smiled. "We must have patience." He made some notes on a card. "We have to be very careful so that we don't build up muscle that would become impossible to take away."

"*Merde.*" She fell into the chair opposite his desk. "Another thing. I'm nervous all the time. Edgy."

He made another note on his card. "I'll cut down on the injections. From now on only twice a week instead of every other day. You're not feeling hungry any more, are you?"

She shook her head. "Not at all."

"That's good," he nodded. "I'll book you for two massages a day, and you increase your swimming from a half hour each session to one hour."

"It's all getting very boring," she said.

He smiled. "We never claimed to be an amusement park, Janette. This is a serious business. You come to us for help with a problem and we're working to solve it as best as we can."

"It wouldn't hurt if you provided some amusements in the evening so that people could relax a little."

"Like what?"

142

"Films. Music. Something. I don't know what. Just to take our minds off the dullness of the routine."

He nodded. "That's a good thought. We'll look into it."

"Patients wouldn't feel as if they're in a kind of prison then. After all, how many diet-and-exercise fitness lectures can anyone listen to?"

He laughed. "You're right. I just never thought of it that way."

"You would do more business too," she said. "Especially if you made it seem like fun."

He nodded and made some more notes on his card. "How do you sleep?"

"Not too well," she said. "As I told you, I'm edgy."

"I can give you a pill," he said. "But one of the possible side effects is that you might retain water, and that would be self-defeating."

"I'll manage," she said, smiling. "Masturbation is the best natural tranquilizer."

He laughed. "It's great to be young." He got to his feet. "You're doing all right. Just stick with it. It's only five more weeks." He walked to his office door with her. "I guarantee that you'll be pleased."

"I'll be happy if my breasts don't wind up falling down to my belly," she said.

"Don't worry about it," he said. "It won't happen. But even if it should, we have a cure for that too."

"It's a matter of routine, Herr Schwebel," the banker said to Johann, his voice crackling slightly over the long-distance lines from Switzerland. "Madame la Marquise left instructions with us that if we did not hear from her for three years in sequence, we were to contact you for instructions in regard to the property she has placed in our safekeeping."

Johann was silent for a moment. Not once in all the years had Tanya ever mentioned that she had property or any-

143

thing at all in a Swiss bank. "Do you have any idea of the nature of the property?" he asked, circumspect with his use of language over the telephone, even though they were speaking in German, because one could never be sure who was listening in to the line.

"Not of the contents," the banker replied. "As far as we are concerned it consists solely of six large safe-deposit boxes leased by the marquise in 1944 for a period of twenty years. The rental fees were paid in advance."

"I see," Johann said thoughtfully. 1944. That was the year they moved to Switzerland. "So there is no urgent problem at the moment?"

"None," the banker said. "As I said, this is purely routine. We are only following instructions."

"Do you have a duplicate key?" Johann asked.

"No," the banker answered. "Madame had the only key."

"You know, of course, that Madame is dead?"

"Yes," the banker said. "But again, following orders, we did not contact you until the time requested."

"Of course," Johann said. Bankers were all alike. The routine was more important than the fact. "Let me go through Madame's papers again and see if she left any specific instructions regarding this matter and I will get back to you."

"Thank you, Herr von Schwebel," the banker said.

Johann smiled to himself. Now that the banker was sure that he was in charge, he had been elevated from plain Herr Schwebel to Herr von Schwebel. Money and authority were an irrefutable combination. "I plan to be in Switzerland in a few weeks," he said. "Perhaps we could meet then to further discuss the matter."

"I am at your disposal, Herr von Schwebel," the banker said. "Meanwhile if I could impose on you to write us a letter acknowledging that we have contacted you in accordance with our instructions it would keep our records in order."

"I will dispatch the letter immediately," Johann said.

144

They exchanged polite goodbyes and Johann returned the telephone to its cradle. He stared down at the notes he had made on his scratch pad. All the information was there. The bank, the banker's name. Everything. Abruptly he tore the page from his pad and tucked it carefully into his wallet. Then he tore the five pages of the scratch pad beneath the one he had written on and crumpled them into the wastebasket. He started to call for his secretary to dictate the letter to the banker, then changed his mind. He would write the letter himself and mail it from home. He would also request that the banker contact him at home after this. There was no point in leaving any hints about this anywhere near the office.

He glanced at his watch. Heidi should have returned to the apartment by now. Like any prospective bride, she had been out shopping for her wedding dress. A dress, she had emphasized carefully, not a gown. She answered the telephone.

"Did you find anything?" he asked.

Her voice was excited. "Yes. It's beautiful."

"Where?"

"Maggy Rouff," she said. "And I got a twenty percent discount for the trade, because I mentioned your name."

He laughed. "Marvelous. When can I see it?"

"Not before the wedding," she said. "It's bad luck for a groom to see the bride in her wedding dress before that."

"Okay. I'll wait then," he said. "Have you heard from your father?"

"Just a few minutes ago," she said. "He'll be here for the wedding."

"Good. I'm looking forward to meeting him."

"And he is also," she said.

"Have you ever been to Switzerland?" he asked.

"No," she said.

"I know of a lovely small hotel in the mountains not far from Geneva," he said. "Would you like to go there for our honeymoon? It's very small and very quiet. And chances are we'll be the only ones there."

"I can't wait," she said.

"I'll make the reservations then," he said. "Where would you like to go for dinner?"

"I thought it would be nice if we ate in tonight," she said. "After all, you don't even know if I can cook."

"True," he said. "But then, that never even entered my mind. I was more interested in other things."

She laughed. "Well, I can cook too. You'll see."

He put down the telephone. Six large safe-deposit boxes. Since 1944. He closed his eyes trying to remember everything that happened that year but there was nothing he could think of that could lead to their contents. But still, there they were.

And they had to be valuable enough, and important enough, for Tanya to provide for their safekeeping for twenty years. And perhaps the only thing she had never spoken to anyone about, not even to him.

He took a deep breath. Tomorrow he would go to his bank and take out all her papers again and go through them. Somewhere in them there had to be a clue to what it was all about. And, somewhere, also, there had to be a safe-deposit key.

"He owns a brewery," Jacques said.

"Who?" Maurice was puzzled.

"Johann's bride's father," Jacques said. "He's very rich. Mayer's Breweries in Minneapolis."

Maurice was impressed. "Johann did all right by himself. I know of the beer. Twin Cities Beer, it's called. One of the most popular in the States. I wonder how he came to meet her."

"She was married before and divorced. Then she worked for several years as a fashion buyer for one of the Midwest department stores and came here four times a year. His

146

secretary told my secretary that they met at one of Shiki's fashion shows."

"Did he ever do any business with her?"

Jacques shook his head. "Not that I know of. Shiki does not do well in mid-America."

"Well," Maurice said, "wonders will never cease. Stodgy, dull, boring Johann comes up with an heiress worth more than twenty million dollars."

"You're joking!" Jacques' voice was incredulous.

"No, I'm not," Maurice said.

"I wonder if Johann knew that when he met her," Jacques said.

Maurice laughed. "It doesn't matter now." He took a sip of his drink. "Johann," he said, shaking his head in wonder.

"I also heard her father is coming over for the wedding next week," Jacques said. "Apparently she is his only child, and this will be his first trip to Europe in more than thirty years. Johann reserved a large suite for him at the Georges Cinq."

"It's getting better and better," Maurice said.

"I don't understand," Jacques said.

Maurice looked at him. "Johann may be making his own plans. Two more years and Janette is of age. She comes into the business as an owner while he is still only a part trustee and employee. He's going to do something. I feel it in my bones." He took another sip of his drink. "I wonder if Janette knows about it."

"I don't know," Jacques said. "Nobody still knows where she is. I even went over to La Coupole the other night, where her friends hang out. Even Marie-Thérèse doesn't know. And they've been inseparable since they were kids at school."

"I know about Marie-Thérèse," Maurice said. "And if she doesn't know, no one does. Still, I would like to know how Janette feels about it."

"We'll just have to wait until she returns," Jacques said.

"I suppose so," Maurice said thoughtfully. "I'm leaving

for New York at the end of the week. I'll be at the Pierre. Keep me informed as to what is happening."

Jacques smiled. "Of course. If it's anything interesting, you'll be the first to know."

The doctor peered over her shoulder at the scale. "Seven kilos," he said, satisfaction in his voice. "We're getting there." He went back to his desk and sat on the edge of it, facing her. "How do you feel?"

"I don't like the way I look," she said.

"What's wrong?" he asked.

"Even with all the exercise my breasts are sagging even more, and now my buttocks are beginning to droop. And with my face thinner my nose seems to be longer."

"It's only five weeks," he said. "Your body is still adjusting. Once we get down to the desired weight, we'll begin working on the other things."

"How long will that take?" she asked.

He picked up his chart and studied it for a moment, then picked up a tape measure. "Take off your bathing suit."

She pushed the tight-fitting one-piece suit down over her legs and stepped out of it. He indicated a small platform in the corner of the room and she stepped up on it. Quickly, impersonally, he began to take her measurements, beginning with her neck. Her upper chest under her arms, her breasts at her nipples, each upper arm, her waist, the hip at the top of the pelvic bone, then around the center of her buttocks, her upper and lower thighs, finally her calves and ankles. After each measurement he made a note on his chart. Finally he put the tape and the chart on his desk. Standing directly in front of her, he eyed her critically. "Stretch your arms over your head as far as you can reach, placing your palms together and standing on your toes."

Silently she did as he asked. Slowly he walked around her and stopped once again in front of her. She detected noth-

148

ing in his face except professional judgment. "Now put your arms at your side and stand normally," he said.

Again he walked slowly around her. "With your permission I would like to check for muscle tone."

She nodded silently.

His face still impassive, he placed a hand under each armpit, his thumb reaching around to the top of her chest over each breast. Slowly he moved his thumb, raising and lowering her breasts.

She felt her nipples begin to harden and swell and she laughed nervously.

"Don't be embarrassed," he said quickly. "It's quite normal."

She laughed. "I don't mind. It's the most fun I've had since I've come here."

He laughed too, placing an open palm against her stomach. "Try to tighten your muscle as much as you can and press against my hand." After a moment, he spoke again. "That's fine. Now do the same thing with each buttock as I place my hand on it."

He walked behind her and she felt the palm of his hand against her and tightened the muscle. Then she felt his finger under her buttock against her thigh; slowly he raised the buttock upward. After a moment he repeated the process with the other buttock. Then he was finished and went back behind his desk and sat down. "You can put on your bathing suit again."

She slipped into her suit and approached the desk. "What do you think, Doctor?"

He finished making some notes on the chart and looked up at her. "Sit down," he said.

"Anything wrong?" she asked quickly as she sat down.

"Nothing's wrong," he said reassuringly. "We're accomplishing everything that we started to do. It's just that at this stage of the game we have to explore some options that are open to us."

"I don't understand," she said.

149

He leaned back in his chair, his voice almost professorial. "What we are attempting here is almost a complete restructuring of your body. By nature you are one way and we are changing that into a more satisfactory mode. Much of the success we can achieve depends on the ability of your body to adjust to the new demands we make upon it. We train certain muscles to do more and compensate for others. Sometimes this does not happen as quickly as we would like, sometimes it does not happen at all, the muscles themselves are not capable of the demands we make on them. We are now at a point where we have to decide how far we want to go."

"Are you telling me that I can't compensate for the loss of weight?" she asked.

"I'm not saying that," he said. "I'm sure that your muscles can. But it will take time. The muscles will have to be developed over a period of several years before we can achieve the optimum results you desire." He glanced down at his chart. "At this point in time you have achieved seventy percent of the weight loss targeted and your measurements vary from eight to fourteen percent less on various portions of your anatomy than when you came in here. All of this is most satisfactory and I feel at this time that we should not try to go further in either weight loss or size reduction. I am, however, concerned about compensating appearance factors. Despite the exercises and treatments, the muscles are not responding as rapidly as we would like to the demands made. So I think we should consider other options available to us."

"What options?" she asked.

"Minor corrective surgery," he said. "It would save years of work on your part and would accomplish what you desire immediately."

"But there would be scars," she said quickly.

"Tiny ones," he said. "And they would be invisible unless someone searched for them. We do the work in natural folds and creases of the body so that they are completely concealed."

"Are there any side effects or chances that it would not work?"

"We have techniques developed during the war. So far, in more than a thousand patients we have treated, there have been no problems."

"How much time does the whole thing take?" she asked.

"The surgery itself is minimal. The recovery time is two weeks before you can resume normal activities. The scars themselves will become normal, that is, blended into your skin, in approximately three months. But since all of them are generally covered by clothing, that's no real problem."

"And if I decide to have my nose done?"

"At the most two weeks, and all the swelling and other signs will be gone, leaving no evidence at all."

She sat there quietly for a moment.

"Why don't you think about it?" he suggested. "There's no rush to make a decision."

She looked at him. "Yes there is," she said in a firm voice. "I've already made up my mind. We'll do the surgery."

He stared at her. "You're sure?"

She nodded. "When can it be done?"

"I'll get in touch with the surgeon," he said. "He'll have to examine you himself first. After that, we'll try to schedule you as soon as possible."

He stared at the door after she left his office and then reached for the telephone to call the surgeon. While he waited for him to come to the telephone he found himself thinking about her. There was a drive and sense of power in the girl. She was only nineteen and he felt it was not vanity that had pushed her into this procedure as it was with his other patients. They were generally older and wanted to be younger. Her motivation went deeper than just that. She was creating a new image with a purpose in mind. What the purpose was he did not know. But whatever it was, it was strong enough to make her want to change her whole life.

Henri opened the door. "Monsieur Schwebel," he bowed. "Please come in."

Johann let Heidi precede him, then followed her through the door. "My dear, this is Henri," he said, introducing them. "Henri, my fiancée, Mademoiselle Mayer."

Henri bowed. "*Enchanté*, Mademoiselle. *Félicitations.*"

"Thank you, Henri," Heidi said.

The butler turned to Johann. "I have all the boxes in the library. We brought them up from the basement. I also had the desk cleared for you."

"Thank you," Johann said. Perhaps what he sought would be here. There was nothing in the company records that had been kept in the bank vaults.

They had begun to follow Henri to the library when the small voice came from the staircase. "Uncle Johann!"

"*Mein Schatzi!*" There was genuine pleasure in Johann's voice as he turned and the child flew across the room, leaping into his arms. "I thought you would be in bed already," he said, kissing her cheeks.

"Nanny told me you were coming, so I waited up," Lauren said. She turned to look at Heidi. "Is she going to be my new aunt?"

Johann laughed. "Yes."

"She's very pretty," Lauren said seriously. "What's her name?"

"Heidi."

The child looked at her. "May I call you Aunt Heidi?"

Heidi smiled, holding out her arms for the child. "Of course, darling." She took the child from Johann and held her tightly. "You're very pretty too, Lauren."

"You smell nice," Lauren said. "Will you come to visit me?"

"If you like," Heidi answered.

"When?"

Heidi laughed. "Whenever you want."

"That's good," the child said. "It's very lonely here now that Janette has gone away to school again." She turned in

Heidi's arms, looking at Johann. "When is Janette coming back?"

"In a few weeks."

"How long is that? More than two days?"

"More than two days, darling," Johann said.

"Oh." The disappointment was evident. She turned back to Heidi. "Janette is my big sister. Sometimes we play that she's my mother. Just pretend. We have no mother."

Heidi was silent. She had all she could do to keep tears from welling into her eyes. She hugged the child closer while looking at Johann. "Perhaps I can come and play with you until your sister returns."

"That would be nice," the child said. She looked at Johann. "Would it be all right if I showed Aunt Heidi my room and my toys?"

"I'm sure it would," Johann said.

Lauren slipped out of Heidi's arms and, taking her by the hand, led her to the stairway. Johann stood there watching them go up the steps, then turned and went into the library.

It was over an hour later that Johann rose wearily from the floor where he had been kneeling as he meticulously went through each of the packing cases spread before him. Nothing. They were all personal articles. Mostly clothing. Several sets of toilet articles, brushes, combs, some valueless costume jewelry. Shoes. No papers, no notebooks, no diaries. Nothing to indicate that Tanya had kept any records other than those that he had already obtained from the company's bank vaults. He pressed the call button for the servant.

Henri came through the door. "*Oui*, Monsieur?"

"I'm finished with them." Johann indicated the boxes. "You can send them back downstairs."

Henri nodded. "Would Monsieur care for a drink?"

"A good idea," Johann said. "Cognac, please. Is my fiancée still with the child?"

Henri smiled. "Yes, sir. I went by her room a moment ago. Lauren has all her toys all over the floor and they are

153

sitting together looking at each one of them." He went to the sideboard and returned with a cognac. "*C'est triste*, Monsieur," he said. "The child needs someone. And she has no one."

Johann sipped at the cognac. "What about Janette?"

Henri shook his head. "It's not the same thing. A mother is a mother. That's what the child needs. That's what she really wants."

Johann nodded heavily. "I suppose so."

"Perhaps when the little one is old enough to go away to school, it will be better for her," the butler said.

"Perhaps." The servant left the room and Johann sank into a chair thoughtfully. He sipped the cognac. Suddenly a picture leaped before his eyes. The two of them standing there. Lauren in Heidi's arms. How much alike they looked. Both blond, both fair, both blue-eyed. They could almost be mother and daughter. He shook his head. It really wasn't fair. Life never organized itself in a reasonable fashion. Everything was always fucked up.

He finished his drink and went up the stairs to the child's room. The two of them were still sitting on the floor surrounded by the toys and stuffed animals. "What's happening?" he smiled.

Heidi looked up at him. "Lauren has been introducing me to her menagerie. The lions are her favorites."

"Why is that?" he asked the child.

"Because it was my mommy's favorite too," Lauren answered, holding up a small scruffy lion obviously many years old. "This was my mommy's. Janette told me that she gave it to me."

"Really?"

"Yes," the child said, holding it out to him. "Touch it. It's very soft."

He took it politely and stroked it. "It is very soft."

"I told Lauren that we would take her to lunch on Sunday and then spend the afternoon at the zoo and she could see real lions," Heidi said.

154

"That would be wonderful," the child said happily.

"Yes," Johann said, still stroking the stuffed animal. Suddenly he stopped and looked down at it. He thought he had felt something inside. He squeezed it. There *was* something inside. Slowly he turned the toy over in his hands. Underneath the soft matted hair covering its belly there was a series of cross-stitches where it had been opened and then resewed.

"Would you excuse me a minute?" He went into the bathroom, closing the door behind him. Quickly he took out his pocketknife and cut a few stitches loose, then probed inside with his fingers. A moment later he held it in his hand. A small safe-deposit key, wrapped in a piece of parchment paper. There were several numbers in tiny letters written on the paper on one side. On the other just four words. Swiss Credit Bank, Geneva.

He let out his breath. Tanya. In her own way she was still here. Slowly he put the key in his pocket and went back into the bedroom. He put the little stuffed lion on the bed. "I think it's time you went to sleep," he said.

Lauren got to her feet and came toward him. "You won't forget about Sunday like Aunt Heidi promised?"

"No, darling," he said, bending to kiss her. "We won't forget."

She turned back to Heidi. "Would you tuck me in, Aunt Heidi? Like my Mama would if she were here."

Heidi looked at Johann. He nodded imperceptibly. "Of course, darling," she said.

Johann bent to kiss Lauren's cheek. He straightened up. "I'll wait downstairs." He turned and looked back before he closed the door behind him.

Lauren was already in bed, the covers pulled over her chest. She raised her arms toward Heidi. "Would you tell me a story, Aunt Heidi?"

He closed the door gently and went down the staircase. In the library he poured himself another cognac and sipped it slowly. For the first time in days he thought about Janette.

He hadn't heard a word from her since she had gone to the clinic. Suddenly he realized that she knew nothing about his coming marriage. He took a deep breath. Tomorrow he would call her.

The surgeon came into her room and looked down at her. "How do you feel?" he asked.

She looked up at him. "Lousy."

He smiled. "I would be worried if you felt any different. After all, it's only three days. Come, get out of bed. I want to have a look at you."

He held out his hand as she sat up and stepped out of bed. He led her across the room to a full-length mirror. "I'm going to remove the bandages from your bust and hips. I don't want you to get upset when you see the stitches and the bruises. They're completely normal and will disappear a few days after the stitches are removed."

"My eyes are still black and blue and my nose is still swollen," she said.

"That's normal too," he said. "Just keep on with the ice packs every two hours. They'll be gone in two or three more days. The swelling should go down in another week.

"Take off your gown," he said, at the same time signaling to the nurse. The nurse came forward holding a tray of instruments. He took a small scissors from the tray as her gown dropped to the floor. "Don't be afraid," he said. "I won't hurt you."

"I'm not afraid," she said, looking at herself in the mirror. "I'm just curious to see what I look like."

"I don't know how much you'll be able to tell," he said. "It's still very soon. All I want to do is check the stitches and see that everything is all right." He snipped the bandage just under her left arm and then slowly, gently, began to unwind it.

She watched the mirror as her breasts appeared. He took the last of the bandages off. Her breath caught in her throat. Her breasts looked ugly, covered with black-and-blue marks and dried blood. "Don't be upset," he said quickly. "They'll look better as soon as I clean them up."

He worked rapidly with cotton and alcohol. In a few seconds the dried blood and scabs were gone and all that remained were the tiny cross-marks of the stitches. He stepped backed and looked at her. "Beautiful," he said. "You're healing better than I had hoped for."

"Beautiful?" Her voice was angry. "You didn't tell me there would be stitches around my nipples."

"Areolae," he said. "When your breasts were reduced in size we saw that your nipples were too much toward the sides of your breasts. It wouldn't have looked natural so we just lifted them and moved them to their proper location. But there won't be any scars, they will become lost in the natural folds of the areolae."

She was silent, studying her breasts. "Can I touch my breasts?"

"Yes," he said. "But gently."

Lightly she cupped them in her hands. They felt smaller, lighter. "What size am I?"

"Thirty-four B," he said. "You were thirty-eight C."

"And the scars beneath them and under my armpits?"

"They'll heal and disappear too in the natural folds of your body."

"How long will that take?"

"Several months," he said. "But after a few weeks you will hardly see them, and if you don't like the way they look until then, you can always cover them with a little makeup."

She let her hands fall to her sides and turned so that she could look at herself sideways in the mirror. She nodded slowly. The look was right. She looked slimmer, more graceful.

"Okay?" he asked.

"Okay," she answered.

Taking the scissors again, he snipped at the bandages around her upper thighs and buttocks. This time she was

157

prepared for the bruises and dried blood and said nothing until he had finished cleaning her skin. She turned and looked over her shoulder in the mirror. She ignored the thin line of stitches that ran in the fold of her flesh between each buttock and thigh. Again she nodded. Her buttocks looked smaller and also higher and firmer.

"What size?" she asked.

"Thirty-five," he said. "And you're still swollen. You may go down to thirty-four. You were almost thirty-nine."

She turned to him. "It's like a miracle."

He smiled. "It's not a miracle. It's modern surgery. But we did have one advantage."

"What's that?" she asked.

"You're young," he said. "Generally when we do these things, our patients are much older and their bodies don't have the resiliency to heal and mend the way you do."

She looked at herself in the mirror. "And the scars will all disappear?"

"They won't disappear," he said. "But they will conceal themselves and in a few months, you'll need a magnifying glass to find them."

"I'm glad I did it," she said.

"I'm happy that you're pleased," he said. "I'm going to replace the bandages once again just to make sure that you don't do any damage to yourself while you're asleep. I think in another three or four days we'll be able to remove the stitches. And you don't have to remain in bed, you can move around as you like. Just remember not to bend, stretch, or lift anything heavy." He gestured to the nurse, who came forward with another hospital gown. He helped her into it, then walked back to the bed with her. "I'll see you at the end of the week."

The telephone began to ring as he walked to the door. She picked it up. "Hello."

"Janette?" She recognized Johann's voice.

"Johann!" she exclaimed. It was the first call she had received since she had been at the clinic. "Where are you calling from?"

"Geneva," he said.

"What are you doing there?"

He laughed. "I'm on my honeymoon."

"I don't believe it," she said.

"It's true," he said. "Remember what you told me in the office? I decided to take your advice."

"How wonderful," she said. "Do I know the bride?"

"No," he said. "But I'm anxious for you to meet her. I thought we might take a drive out to see you."

"Oh, no," she said quickly. "I'm not going to have anyone meet me for the first time out here. I'm right in the middle of my treatments."

"Are you all right?" he asked. "Your voice sounds strange."

"My nose is stuffed," she said. "But I'm fine, really I am. Tell me about your wife."

"She's American. She's beautiful. I know you'll like each other. What more can I tell you?"

"Have you known her a long time?"

"Three years," he said.

"Johann, I'm very happy for you," she said. "Congratulations, and I can't wait to meet her. I really mean it and I will as soon as I come home."

"When will that be?" he asked.

"I'll be here a little longer than I thought," she said. "About another month."

He was silent for a moment. "Too bad. Lauren misses you. She's very lonely in that big house."

"It can't be helped," she said. "But even when I'm home we don't see that much of each other. She's usually in bed by the time I get in."

"Heidi and I took her out to the zoo last Sunday," he said. "Heidi adores her. Maybe we'll try to keep her a little company until you get back."

"That will be lovely," she said. "Please thank your wife for me."

"It's nothing," he said. "I'm anxious to see you, to see what you look like."

She laughed. "I think you're going to be surprised. But it all can wait. After all, you're on your honeymoon."

He laughed. "That's right."

"A big kiss to you and your wife," she said. "And I look forward to seeing you both in Paris."

Slowly she put down the telephone. Johann married. Strangely, she found it hard to believe.

J ACQUES WAS at his usual table in a corner against the wall at the front of the Relais Plaza at lunchtime. Usually he sat there sipping his white wine, casually watching everyone as they entered or left the restaurant, but today he had the *International Herald Tribune* and *Vogue* open on the table before him and was studying them carefully. The showings were over and the verdict was in. Yves St. Laurent. As far as the press was concerned there was no one else. Even the photographs of the young American Presidential candidate and his wife standing in front of the Elysée did not attract as much attention.

It had been just a little more than four years ago that Michel de Brunhof, the editor of French *Vogue*, had spoken to him about finding a place with Shiki for the young boy who was living with him and attending the Académie de Couture. But even after seeing the boy's drawings and sketches, Shiki wouldn't have him. He had no time to waste on amateurs and dreamers and it would take too long to teach him the practical side of the business.

Even after that, he had taken the designs to Johann and urged him to overrule Shiki or, if not to overrule him, start another small salon to reflect a newer, younger approach to couture. Johann studied them but shook his head. They were losing enough money in the couture division without beginning another operation that would increase their losses. Reluctantly he had taken the drawings back to de Brunhof. A month later the young man was at Dior. Almost immediately the boy's name began to appear in numerous stories and articles in *Vogue,* and the rest was history. Dior had his heart attack and Marcel Boussac

161

appointed the young man as designer for the House of Dior.

Jacques stared down at the magazine. If only de Brunhof had come to him one year earlier when Tanya was still alive. She would have snapped him up. Even gotten rid of Shiki if that was the only way. Always the big *if*. But she was gone, and Johann's approach to the business was oriented to the balance sheet rather than the concept.

But perhaps it wasn't too late. This was St. Laurent's last showing before he began his compulsory military service in the French Army. Two years. Boussac was not going to mark time with the House of Dior just because of that. He couldn't afford to lose the momentum that had been created. There were a number of names that were being bruited about as St. Laurent's possible successor but he already knew who it would be. The designer who ran their house in London—Marc Bohan. He wasn't St. Laurent, but as talented and individual in his own way, and very strong. By the time St. Laurent came out of the army, Bohan would be so entrenched at Dior that it would take a nuclear bomb to get him out of there. Then St. Laurent would be forced to look for a new home. This time, Jacques was not about to let him get away. Not even if it meant that he had to go out himself and find the money to found a new house of couture.

He sipped at his kir slowly and idly kept turning the pages of the magazine. His, as usual, was an advance copy; it would not be on the newsstands for sale to the general public until next week. He always made it a point to go through the magazine thoroughly, reading the advertisements as well as the articles. In a way, the ads were even more important because they offered clues as to the directions that the various houses were taking. Almost halfway through the magazine he came to a sudden halt. He stared down at it in a sort of shock, his brain refusing to believe his eyes.

Spread across the two pages was a color photograph of a

beautiful nude girl lying on her side, facing the camera, looking down at her hand, on the engagement finger of which was a large heart-shaped diamond ring. In bold type across the two pages were the words, "A simple diamond is all any beautiful woman needs to wear." Then, in small letters, in the corner of the second page beneath the photograph: "janette marie de la Beauville for harry winston."

"*Merde!*" His lips moved silently. He was angry. More with himself than with the photograph. With all his contacts, he should have known about it before it even happened. But somehow she had managed to see that it was kept from him. Then the humor of it got to him and he began to smile. He studied the photograph. She had never looked more beautiful. He signaled the waiter.

"Another kir, Monsieur?"

"No," he said. "I'll have a whiskey. With lots of ice." He closed the magazine. To hell with Yves St. Laurent for the moment. This photograph was going to be the talk of Paris for the coming season. The waiter put the whiskey in front of him and he took a deep drink. Already his mind was working on how to capitalize on it.

Johann looked down at the magazine, then leaned back in his chair. "Quite startling," he said. "Why do you think she did it?"

Jacques laughed. "Because she's smarter than both of us. That's why. There's more of her mother in her than either of us realized."

"I still don't understand," Johann said.

"Image," Jacques said. "With one photograph she created an image. Something Shiki has not been able to do for us in five years. The day after this magazine is on the street she will be the new queen of the young Parisian *haut monde*. They'll fall all over themselves trying to be like her. Anything she does, anything she wears, anything she says will be law."

"How is that going to help us?" Johann asked.

"It's a whole new market. And we'll be there first," Jacques answered. "We won't be struggling, as we have with Shiki, trying to penetrate a market in which all we wind up with are the crumbs that fall from the tables of the other designers. We'll have to begin a brand-new line with a brand-new concept."

"And what about our investment in Shiki?"

"Finished," Jacques said. "Over. We never made any money with it so why continue flogging a dead horse?"

"But Tanya thought—"

Jacques interrupted him. "Tanya is dead. Janette is now. If Tanya were alive, she would be the first one to agree with me."

Johann was silent for a moment. "Have you spoken to Janette?"

"Not yet. I wanted to speak to you first."

"It means writing off fifty million francs," Johann said. "That's half her money now, which means the decision should be half hers. I am only responsible for Lauren's share, and as trustee I can't bring myself to accept such a loss for my ward."

"Eventually it will all be lost. Shiki will never make it. We've given him every chance he could ask for."

"I don't know," Johann said. "I don't feel comfortable in this part of the business. I never quite understood it. Nothing makes sense. Nobody seems to know what will sell and what will not. The wine business is something else. You produce so much, you sell so much, you always know what is going to happen. Even the fragrance company has a steady market. Not very big, but you can also figure on what will happen. *Couture, zero.* You spend a fortune designing a line, showing it, advertising it. Two days later it's all down the sewer and you can't even give the samples away. I'm sorry we ever went into it, but Tanya wouldn't listen to me. She had her own ideas."

"Why don't you talk to Janette?" Jacques said. "Maybe she has some ideas too."

164

Johann looked at him. "Do you really think so?"

Jacques nodded. "I'm beginning to know that lady. She never does anything without a purpose."

Johann stared down at the magazine on his desk after Jacques had left the office. The Janette looking seductively up at him from the photograph was a very different girl from the one who had told him three years before that she was going to change the way she looked. But it was more than her appearance that was changed. Something else had happened.

There had still been something of the child about the other Janette, a sophisticated naiveté. The naiveté was gone. This was a woman, aware of herself, of her body, her needs, her drives, her ambitions. But the calculation was hidden in her total look. What had emerged was the totality of her femaleness; yet, from the cut of her dark-auburn highlighted hair to the almost metallic rose-colored toenails, she was the epitome of the fashionably accepted figure, the individual flaws lost in that total look.

She had been away almost five months before she returned to the office. And then no one had recognized her; even Johann's secretary, who had known her for many years, had asked her name before she marched into his office, the shock evident in the secretary's voice over the telephone when she announced her.

He remembered looking up from his desk and just staring. She stood very still for a moment, then turned around slowly in full circle, then looked down at him with a smile. "Well, Johann, what do you think?"

He was silent, then rose from his desk and kissed her on both cheeks. "You're absolutely beautiful," he said sincerely. "But do I know you?"

"I don't know," she said with a half smile. "But then, I don't know if I know myself. I'm going to have to find out."

He went back behind his desk and sat down. "When are you planning to come back to work?"

"I'm not," she said. "I still have much to discover. About myself. And about our business. And I think I will learn more working somewhere else for a while."

He thought about the hundred thousand gold louis in the bank in Switzerland and the note of caution that Tanya had left in one of the safe-deposit boxes.

DEAR JOHANN,

One third is yours because you loved Wolfgang as I did. The remainder I place in your trust for Janette and Lauren, to be used only in case of need. I love you and trust you and apologize for placing this additional burden on your shoulders. Be good to them, my friend, because in the end, my children, like myself, have no one else.

TANYA

He looked up at Janette still standing in front of his desk. His first impulse had been to tell her, and he had telephoned her from the bank vault in Switzerland. But she had not been ready for him to come to the clinic. Only now, he understood why. What she had done was much more than just diet. But perhaps it was all for the best. There had been no need such as Tanya had mentioned. And Janette had her own idea of the direction she wanted to take.

"What are you going to do then?" he asked.

"I've already done it," she said. "I have a job as mannequin for Yves St. Laurent."

The name was vaguely familiar but he couldn't place it. "Who is he?"

"The new designer at Dior. He took over when Dior died and he's already at work on his first collection. He thinks I'm just the type he needs."

"Good," he said. Then he smiled suddenly. "It's just as well then that I did not let Jacques go."

"You were right," she said. "I know now I could never do his job as well as he does. Besides, I want something else."

"What's that?" he asked.

166

"What my mother wanted. My own fashion house. But it will take some time. I'm not ready for it yet." She stepped toward his desk and picked up the picture in a standing frame, its back to her. She turned the photograph toward her. "Your wife?"

"Yes. Heidi."

"She's lovely," she said, still holding the photograph. "When do I get to meet her?"

"Tonight at dinner, if you like."

She nodded, returning the picture to the desk. "At home, at eight o'clock. I'll have Henri do something special."

"We'll be there."

"I'll have Lauren wait up for you. She adores your wife. She speaks of no one but her."

Johann smiled. "Heidi loves her."

Janette smiled in return. "You are a lucky man. She must be a wonderful woman. Children have the greatest instincts. They're like animals. They smell out the good and the bad. And if Lauren loves her, there has to be nothing but good."

That was more than two years ago. There had been other changes since then. Six months after Janette had returned from Switzerland, Heidi had approached him with the idea of having Lauren come to live with them.

"I don't know," he had said thoughtfully.

"Why not?" Heidi asked. "She lives in that big house practically alone. She rarely sees her sister, only the servants. She needs more than that. She's entitled to more than that. She's a beautiful, warm, loving child with no one to love."

"And you don't think Janette is enough for her?"

"You're not stupid, Johann," Heidi said with a tinge of exasperation. "You know better than that. Janette is too busy with her own life. She hasn't time to give anything to the child, even if she wanted to."

He looked at Heidi. "You don't like Janette, do you?"

Heidi didn't answer for a moment. "That has nothing to do with my suggestion. It doesn't matter whether I like her or not. I'm concerned with Lauren."

"What if we have a child of our own?" Johann asked.

"It wouldn't make any difference. I would still want to give Lauren a home. I love her and she loves me."

He was silent for a moment. "If she does come to live with us, it may mean we could not move to America as soon as we had planned."

"I know now, whether she comes to live with us or not, we have to remain here. This is where your work is, this is where your responsibility lies. So that wouldn't make any difference."

He nodded. "All right. I'll talk to Janette tomorrow."

In a way he thought he detected a sense of relief in Janette when he spoke to her. Heidi found a larger apartment in the Bois de Boulogne and two months later Lauren came to live with them. The first thing Heidi did was to discharge the nanny and take over the care of the child herself. And Heidi had been right. Lauren bloomed, the dark shadows disappeared from her eyes, and now she was always happy and laughing.

He took the magazine home with him that night and after dinner he showed the advertisement to Heidi. She looked at it for a moment, then up at him. "She is beautiful."

"Jacques said the time has come to start a whole couture around her," he said.

"What does she say?" Heidi asked.

"I haven't spoken to her yet."

"What do you think?"

"It's risky," he answered. "We're not making any money with Shiki. But on the other hand we're not losing. Jacques feels that Shiki has had all the chances and is sure that he'll never make it. But I don't know. It's a hundred-million-franc gamble and if it loses, I've severely hurt the little one's inheritance."

"What about Janette?"

"In fact, I'm not responsible for her share any more. She's of age and can make her own decisions if she wants."

"But she's left that all to you still, hasn't she?"

168

He nodded.

"I wonder why?" she asked.

"I don't know," he answered. "She knows of her rights."

"If she took charge of her own affairs, could we then go to the States as we had planned?"

"Perhaps," he said, "if I could work out proper safeguards for Lauren so that she would be protected no matter what happens."

"My father said he was beginning to think of retirement. He would like you to come over and look into his business. He feels you would do well there."

"He's prejudiced," Johann said. "Besides he wants his daughter home."

"Perhaps," she said. "But I happen to think my father is right. You would do well in America." She paused for a moment. "Do you think if we did go, Lauren could come with us?"

"It's possible. I am her legal guardian still, and if there are no objections raised, there shouldn't be any problems."

"Janette is the only one who could possibly raise objections," Heidi said.

"It's just possible that Maurice might be able to do something. I don't know. But on the record he is her father. Whether he really is or isn't might not be pertinent."

"Maurice doesn't give a damn," she said.

"If he thought there was money in it, he might." He looked at her. "But we're way ahead of ourselves, aren't we? Nothing has happened yet."

She looked down at the photograph. "It may not be that far away," she said thoughtfully. "Janette would not do something like this if she did not have a larger purpose in mind."

He smiled. "Jacques feels exactly the same way."

"Jacques is right," she said. She looked down at the photograph again. "How big do you think that diamond on her finger is?"

"I haven't the faintest idea," he said.

"It has to be at least thirty carats." She looked up at him. "Any girl that would pose nude with a thirty-carat diamond has to have big ideas."

Louise came down to the mannequins' dressing room just behind the atelier, flushed with excitement. She went directly to where Janette was sitting in front of her dressing table making up her eyes for the evening. "The old man is in a rage," she said. "He just saw your photograph."

Janette looked up at her in the mirror. The blond girl was almost breathless. "It probably turned him on," she said.

"I was in Yves' office," Louise said. "And he came in screaming. He walked up and down in front of Yves' desk yelling that it was all his fault, how could he allow you to do it? The whole thing was a put-down of the House of Dior, of the whole art of couture, the entire industry."

"What did Yves say?"

"Nothing," Louise said. "He just looked down at the photograph and smiled."

Janette laughed. "I don't think he really gives a damn. He knows he's going into the army and he knows that Boussac is going to fuck him one way or the other."

"But what are you going to do?" Louise asked. "Yves goes next week, the old man's going to fire you."

"No, he's not," Janette said. "I've already handed in my notice. This is my last week here. Friday, after Yves' farewell party, I leave and never come back."

Louise's mouth dropped open in surprise. "No?"

"Yes."

The blond girl looked at her. "Do you think Yves knows that already?"

"If he doesn't, he should," Janette replied. "I gave my letter to personnel on Monday. That was two days ago."

"You have another job?"

Janette shook her head. "No."

170

"What are you going to do then?"

"First, I'm going to eat one good meal without worrying about my weight. I took a good look at that picture, and my hips are too bony. Another kilo won't hurt. Then I'm going to take a vacation. Maybe I'll go to the States for a few weeks. I've never been there." She finished her makeup and got to her feet. "I've got to run, I've got a cocktail date."

Louise looked up at her enviously. "You're lucky, Janette."

"What makes you say that?" Janette said.

"You can do anything you like," Louise said. "But I have to stay and take all this shit. They already made a date for me on Friday with that buyer from the Texas store. He'll probably paw me all evening and by the time I get back to his hotel, he'll be too drunk to even fuck, so I'll have to go down on him to keep him happy."

Janette laughed. "So what? Would you rather fuck him?"

"It might be nice for a change," Louise said. "But all any of them seem to want is to get sucked."

"*C'est la vie,*" Janette said.

"You can afford to say that," Louise said. "You're rich."

Janette stopped and looked down at her thoughtfully for a moment. "That's right. I'm rich." Then she bent down and kissed her friend on the mouth. "And so are you, Louise. In your own way."

Silently, Louise watched Janette go to the door. "*Bon soir,* Janette."

Janette smiled at her from the doorway. "*Ciao,* baby." For some strange reason there were tears running down Louise's cheeks. Slowly she began to remove her makeup.

She parked the mini in front of the gray apartment building on the Ile Saint-Louis, facing the Seine. She pressed the buzzer on the door.

An old concierge shuffled to the door and opened it, peering out at her. "Madame?"

171

"Monsieur Fayard."

He sniffed disapprovingly as he opened the door still farther. *"Le penthouse,"* he said, gesturing toward the staircase.

"What's the matter with the elevator?" she asked.

He shrugged his shoulders. *"C'est mort."*

"Merde," she said and began climbing the six flights of stairs. There was just one door on the top landing. She pressed the doorbell. She could hear a chime echoing inside the apartment door.

The door opened and a young man stood there, his fair hair tousled, a T-shirt and blue jeans seemingly glued to his body. His eyes looked at her without expression. "Hello, Janette," he said in English.

"Marlon," she said, her eyes falling for a moment to the large bulge in his jeans.

He stepped back, letting her go into the apartment, then closing the door behind him. "Shopping?" he grinned.

"No," she said. "Just curious. Is it all you in there or six handkerchiefs?"

He laughed. "It's all me. Want to touch it to prove it?"

"No, thanks," she said, returning his laugh. "I believe you." She looked into the apartment. The living room was empty. "Philippe home yet?"

"He's been home since lunchtime," Marlon said. "He didn't eat. Just went into his room and hasn't come out since." A note of concern came into his voice. "Is there anything wrong? He hasn't lost his job, has he?"

"What makes you think that?"

"I asked him about buying an air conditioner for the bedroom. The sun makes the roof unbearable. He got angry and said we can't afford it, there would be no more money for anything, we'd be lucky to have money to eat."

She looked at him. "And if that were true, what would you do?"

"Start packing," he said in a flat voice. "I didn't come all

172

the way to Paris to wind up on the same street corner I left in Los Angeles."

She smiled gently, shaking her head. "You really are a whore, aren't you?"

"I never pretended to be anything else," he said, meeting her gaze. "I also fuck pretty good."

She laughed. "I don't doubt that. But things aren't radical enough for you to consider that yet. Now, tell me, which way to the bedroom?"

He gestured to a door at the far end of the living room and followed her as she walked toward it. She turned to look at him as she raised her hand to knock at the door.

"Tell me," she asked. "Is your name really Marlon?"

He laughed. "No. I took it from the movie actor. All the guys like it better than Sam."

She laughed and knocked at the door softly.

A muffled voice came from inside the room. "Who is it?"

"Janette," she said. "We had a date for a drink, remember?"

"Go away," Philippe said through the doorway. "I don't feel well."

She glanced at Marlon, shrugged, then opened the door and went into the bedroom. She stood there for a moment. Philippe was stretched out on the bed, still in his clothes. She closed the door and walked toward him.

"I told you to go away," he mumbled, without looking up at her.

She stood next to the bed, looking down at him. "What the hell is the matter with you?"

"He doesn't love me. Nobody loves me." Philippe still didn't raise his head from the pillow.

"Don't be silly," she said. "You know that Marlon loves you."

He sat up suddenly; the tears had streaked the mascara from his lashes down his cheeks. "I know that Marlon loves me," he said vehemently. "I'm not talking about him. I mean Yves. I tried to talk to him about what I would do there while he was in the army and he wouldn't even answer me. He had enough of his own problems to worry about. And Boussac hates me, he'll never give me a chance at Yves' job. He's going to bring Marc back from London. I know it, I just know it. And then I'm finished."

"Why?" she asked. "Marc seems like a reasonable man."

"Remember the fight I had with him last year when I went over there to help him with the London collection? He said I would never understand the modifications that would have to be made for the British taste and figure. He hates me. I'm finished."

She was silent for a moment. "That's right," she said, turning and walking back to the door. "That's why I wanted to meet you for a drink. I don't hate you. I love you. I think you're a genius. An even greater genius than any of them —Yves or Marc. And I have faith in you." Abruptly she walked out of the room, closing the door behind her.

Marlon was standing there. "How is he?"

"He's all right," she said, opening her purse and taking out two five-hundred-franc notes. She put them in his hand. "You're working for me now. Whatever I tell him is the greatest idea you ever heard."

The money disappeared under his belt. "Gotcha."

She nodded. "Good. You'll get your air conditioner after all. Maybe we'll throw in a car for good measure."

He smiled. "I'm a reasonable man."

The door behind her opened. Philippe was standing there. He had washed his face, the traces of mascara were gone, and his hair was combed. "You really meant what you said?" He couldn't keep his satisfaction out of his voice.

She met his eyes steadily. "I wouldn't say it if I didn't mean it."

He nodded. "You had something in mind?"

"Yes. Would you like to talk about it?"

"I'm always ready to listen," he said. He looked at Marlon. "I'm hungry. Do you think you can fix me something to eat?"

"Ham-and-cheese sandwich? Ham and eggs?" Marlon asked.

"The sandwich. And a bottle of beer." He looked at Janette. "Would you like something?"

"I'll have a beer," she said.

"Coming right up," Marlon said, disappearing toward the kitchen.

Philippe led her to a small table near the window. They sat down and she looked out at a *bateau mouche* moving up the Seine. "You have one of the most beautiful views in Paris," she said.

"Isn't it?" he said enthusiastically. "I just love it. Too bad it isn't warm enough to sit outside on the terrace. It's really great then."

She smiled. "It's worth walking up the six flights."

"I'm sorry," he said. "The elevator was supposed to be fixed last week."

"It happens," she said. She looked across the table at him. "I'm leaving Dior this Friday."

"But you're Yves' favorite mannequin," Philippe exclaimed.

"He won't be there any more, will he?" She didn't wait for him to answer. "Besides I'm bored with it. I want to do something else. Being a mannequin does not appeal to me."

Marlon came back, placed the sandwich in front of Philippe, put three glasses of beer on the table, then pulled up a chair and sat down with them.

Philippe took a bite of his sandwich. "This is just beautiful, darling," he said to Marlon. "Just the right amount of mustard." He turned back to Janette. "What do you want to do?" he asked between mouthfuls.

"I want my own fashion house," she said.

He looked at her. "But you already have one with Shiki," he said.

"That's not mine," she said. "It was started before I had anything to do with it. And it's yesterday. I want something for today."

"Then what will happen to Shiki?"

"He goes," she said flatly. "The house stays and I change the name to mine. Not that there is anything wrong with my mother's name, Tanya, but it is already identified too strongly with the passé. I'm not interested in yesterday fashions, only tomorrow."

He took another bite of his sandwich. "Where do I fit in to all of this?"

"You're my St. Laurent, I'm your Boussac."

He was silent for a moment. "Why don't you do your own designs? I've seen some of your sketches at the couture school. They were very good."

She drank some of her beer. "They were good. But they weren't great. What I need is a touch of genius. That's you."

She glanced at Marlon and he came right in on cue. "I never heard such a brilliant idea!" His acting would have done credit to his namesake. "Do you realize what this means, Philippe? You'll have your own name, your own identity. You won't have to suck second cock for anybody."

"Do you really think so?" Philippe asked.

"You know I do," Marlon said emphatically. "Haven't I always told you that you have more talent in your pinky finger than all those guys have up their assholes."

Philippe chewed the rest of his sandwich thoughtfully. He looked at Janette. "What if you can't get rid of Shiki?"

"I'll get rid of him. Don't worry about that," she said. "What I need to know is whether you are interested or not."

Philippe thought again. "It would depend on many things. Money, position, freedom to create my own ideas."

"All of that can be worked out," she said.

"Sounds fantastic to me," Marlon said.

Philippe looked at him, then back to Janette. "I'm interested," he said, then added quickly, "but, of course, we'll have to talk some more to make sure everything is properly worked out."

"Of course," she said. "But everything will be worked out —to your satisfaction, I'm sure."

"That's great!" Marlon said enthusiastically. He raised his beer glass. "A toast! To Philippe Fayard, for Janette Marie de la Beauville!"

"In beer?" Philippe's voice was shocked. "Bring out that bottle of Cristale we have in the refrigerator."

She pulled the mini onto the sidewalk in front of her house, locked it and ran up the steps to the front door. As usual, the door was opened almost before she reached it.

"*Bon soir*, Henri," she said as she went in.

"*Bon soir*, Madame," he said politely.

She went toward the staircase. She felt tired and strangely drained. A hot tub would go far to erase her tensions. It was very important that Philippe be willing to go with her. He was the cornerstone of her plan—without him she would have to go it alone and the chances of failure were too great. And someone else always had to be there to take the blame so that her own reputation would be unassailable. Once she was established, she could always find another designer if Philippe did not work out.

"There have been many telephone calls, Madame," Henri said.

She paused at the foot of the staircase. "Bring them to my room," she said. "I'll get to them after I have a bath."

"Will Madame be having dinner in tonight?" he asked politely.

She thought for a moment, then nodded. "Yes, the usual. But I'll have only one lamb chop and a small baked potato tonight. I've already had beer and champagne and that's enough. In about an hour in my room. I'm too tired to come down."

"Yes, Madame," he said. "Would you like me to keep the telephone messages until then?"

"Please, thank you," she said and went up the staircase to her room. She began undressing the moment she went through the doorway. Her clothes felt warm and sticky even

177

though the day had been cool. By the time she reached the bathroom and turned on the water in the tub, she was naked. Quickly she creamed her face and removed the makeup, then threw herself down on the bed while the big tub filled slowly.

She felt the tautness and the tensions in her body and idly she began to stroke herself. It was at times like this she missed Marie-Thérèse the most. But the stupid girl had gone and gotten pregnant by some idiot college boy in her final year at the Sorbonne and her family married her off to him and she was now living in Lyon with a one-year-old baby and her husband like every other *bourgeoise française*.

A vision of Marlon's bulging jeans flashed before her. She could see the line of his prick running down toward one side and she knew that he wore nothing under the jeans. She wondered if his prick was as big as Maurice's. It had to be impossible. There couldn't be two like that in the world. She felt the warmth spreading through her.

Suddenly Marlon was gone and the soft sweet look of Louise's face as she kissed her jumped before her eyes. She could taste the honeyed sweetness of her lips even now, cool yet somehow warm and vulnerable. She rolled over suddenly, reaching for the telephone. She had been a fool. She had been so busy with her own thoughts that she didn't even recognize an invitation when she saw one. Quickly she dialed Louise at her home.

"Have you had dinner yet?" she asked.

"I was not eating tonight," Louise said. "I'm at my weight limit now."

"That's foolish," Janette said. "You have to eat something. But you must be sensible about it. Look, I'm having dinner in tonight. Why don't you come and join me? I guarantee you nothing fattening."

Louise laughed. "I'll have to get dressed again."

"Don't bother," Janette said. "Just jump into a pair of slacks and a taxi. We'll have dinner alone in my room and listen to the hi-fi."

She pressed down the button disconnecting the call, then pressed down another button to connect her with the kitchen. Henri answered the phone. "I'm having a girl friend over for dinner," she said. "Just put on some more chops and one more baked potato. We'll still have dinner in my room."

"*Oui,* Madame," he said.

"And, Henri," she added quickly, "please bring up the telephone messages now." She was out of the bed and into the tub before he came up to the room.

She didn't stay long in the tub, less than ten minutes, and when she came out the telephone was ringing. She picked it up, noticing the messages lying on a silver salver beside it. "Hello."

"Congratulations." It was Jacques. "I saw the Winston ad. I think we can do something to promote on it. We ought to have a talk."

"I want to talk to you too," she said.

"Why don't you come over for dinner? I'll fix something easy and we have all night to talk."

"Not tonight, Jacques," she said. "I'm just too tired. We were busy as hell at the salon today."

"I called before," he said. "Did you get my message?"

"Just now."

"Is there one from Johann?"

She flipped through the messages. "Yes."

"He wants to talk to you too," he said. "But I think it's important for us to talk before you see him."

"Okay," she said, deliberately noncommittal. But he would be an important ally. Johann valued his opinion and with his conservative approach could prove difficult. "We could have lunch tomorrow."

"Fine," he said. "My table at the Relais. Twelve fifteen."

"Right," she said.

"Come naked," he said, laughing. "You looked wonderful!"

She heard the doorbell ring faintly downstairs as she put

179

down the telephone. Quickly she glanced through the messages. The telephone buzzed.

"Mademoiselle Louise is here."

"Show her upstairs." She put down the telephone and went back into the bathroom to brush her hair. There was nothing important in the telephone messages. Time enough to answer them tomorrow. Suddenly she wasn't tired any more. She felt good. Everything was working out just the way she planned it.

By the time she appeared at the Relais everyone there had seen the advance copy of *Vogue*. A sudden hush fell over the restaurant as she stood in the doorway for a moment before turning to Jacques' table. She was wearing a loose-fitting man's shirt tied at the waist over a baggy pair of jeans that revealed absolutely nothing of her figure except what was sensed beneath the clothing as she moved through the room, her hair falling to her shoulders framing her high cheekbones and her face completely devoid of makeup.

Jacques rose and kissed her cheeks. The hum of conversation began in the restaurant again as they sat down.

"I'm sorry I'm late," she apologized. "But Boussac had me in his office. He was ranting and raving." She paused and laughed. "He fired me."

"He's an idiot," Jacques said. "But why are you laughing?"

"He didn't know it but I had already sent in my letter of resignation last Monday and no one had bothered to tell him." Louise appeared in the restaurant entrance. Janette turned to him. "I brought a girl friend along. Is it okay?"

"Of course," he nodded, rising again as Louise made her way to their table. Janette introduced them and he kissed Louise's hand as the waiter hurried up to place a chair for her. "What would you like to drink?"

"I'll have a bottle of Evian," Louise said.

"Since I don't have to go back to work," Janette said, "to hell with it all. I'll have a kir royale."

"Make mine kir royale too," Jacques said. Cassis and champagne was not a bad idea. He turned back to Janette. "What are you planning to do now?"

"I thought maybe Louise and I would take a trip to the States. Neither of us have ever been."

The waiter put down the drinks. "Cheers," Jacques said. He sipped at his drink. "I think you're making a big mistake if you go now."

Janette's voice was politely curious. "Why?"

"Now is the time to strike. While the iron is hot," he said. "Look around this room. Everybody is staring at you and talking about you. You've made yourself an instant celebrity. You can have anything and everything you want."

Janette laughed. "I don't want anything. Especially another mannequin's job."

"There are other things you can do," Jacques said. "You can come back into the business as you planned several years ago."

"And do what?" Janette was pushing. She wanted him to make the point for her. It was important that he feel it was partly his own idea.

"Move right into fashion," he said. "You could be the focal point about which everything would revolve. Something we never had since your mother died. Something Shiki never could give us."

"Shiki could never give anything to me either," she said.

The waiter came for their order. Janette and Louise ordered steak tartare, and Jacques *entrecôte au bleu* with *frites*. When the waiter had gone, Janette turned back to Jacques. "Last night you said that Johann wanted to talk to me."

"Yes," he said. "He was surprised on seeing the photo and curious as to your reason for doing it."

"I thought it would be fun," she said quickly. "Besides, I always wanted to know what it would feel like to wear a million-dollar diamond."

181

"Really?" His voice was skeptical.

She ignored this. "You had something in mind when you asked me to talk to you before I talked to Johann."

"Yes," he said. "I told Johann yesterday that we could promote a whole house based on you. A new image. But we'd have to get rid of Shiki. I agree with you when you say he's a drag."

"What did Johann say?"

"You know Johann. The first thing he thought of was that we would have to write off fifty million francs if we let Shiki go; then it would take another fifty million to get the new line started. And if it doesn't work, everything is lost."

She nodded seriously. "That's Johann all right. Always counting the numbers."

"Still, he didn't say he wasn't interested," Jacques said. "I told him to talk to you before he closed his mind to the idea."

"I don't think anyone will be able to convince him," she said. "The idea could be fun as far as I'm concerned but he's too set in his ways."

"Maybe if he thought someone else wanted to do it with you, he might be convinced."

"But there isn't anyone."

"I could arrange something," Jacques said.

She was curious. "You have someone in mind?"

He nodded.

She looked at him without speaking.

"Your stepfather for one," he said. "I spoke to him yesterday. He's very interested."

"I'm not speaking to him," she said coldly.

"I know," he said. "But that's personal. Business is something else."

"There's no way he can come up with fifty million francs," she said.

"Maybe not all of it. But I have others who would come in. An American, Charlie Carolo. He owns one of the biggest women's wear chain stores in America. He's looking to

182

upgrade his image. And there are others, but I haven't spoken to them yet. Only Maurice and Charlie."

She sat there thinking for a minute, then shook her head. "No. If I want to do it, I would only consider it with my own company. I don't want any partners."

"Then we're back to Johann," he said.

"That's right."

The waiter came with the food. They ate almost silently, each busy with private thoughts. When Louise had finished, she glanced at her watch. "My God!" she exclaimed. "I'm going to be late getting back to work."

"Take my car," Janette said. "I'll come and pick it up later."

She thanked Jacques for the lunch and hurriedly left the table. Jacques looked after her. "Pretty girl, your friend."

"Yes."

"Been friends for long?"

"We've worked together ever since I joined Dior but we didn't become friends until this week."

Jacques nodded sagely. "That happens very often. You see someone all the time but you never realize how important they are to you until the time comes to leave."

She nodded. "I never really thought about it but that's true."

He was silent while the waiter took the dishes and he ordered coffee. Then he turned to her. "Now, let's cut all the crap. Do you want the house of Tanya or don't you?"

"What makes you think I want it?" She was defensive.

"You spoke to Philippe Fayard yesterday," he said.

"How do you know that?"

"There are no secrets in the homosexual world," he said. "Your stepfather heard about it and called me."

"*Merde!*" she said. "That means Shiki already knows about it."

"That's right," Jacques agreed. "And I'll bet that right now he's in Johann's office shrieking his head off."

Janette was silent.

"Whether you like it or not," he said, "you're already committed. So now, it's up to you which way you want to go."

She looked at him. "Which way do you want to go, Jacques?"

"With you," he said. "Maybe that way the dream I shared with your mother will finally come true."

The waiter put the coffee down and she picked up her cup and looked into it. The demitasse was thick and black. Before she lifted it to her lips, she raised her eyes to him, nodding her head slowly. "Then let's go and talk to Johann right away."

Much to her surprise, Johann was calm and reasonable. He thought her ideas and plans were excellent and had a good chance for success. Only on one point was he adamant. "I have already discussed this matter with my attorney this morning," he said. "And, as trustee for your sister's share of the estate, I would be completely liable under French laws if anything should go wrong."

"What could go wrong?" she asked. "You even said you thought it was a good idea."

"We could still lose all the money," he said. "And I have no right to take that chance on Lauren's behalf."

"But what if we made a fortune?"

"That would be good. But there are no guarantees that we will." He looked across his desk at her. "I'm sorry, Janette. If it could be done with an investment of a million or so francs, that would be well within my normal jurisdiction. But this could turn out to be fifty or a hundred million. A loss like that could bankrupt the whole company and we would lose it all, not only the couture house, but the perfume company and the vineyards. You see, they're all part of one overall package and each one is pledged to secure the other."

184

She was silent, thinking. After a moment she spoke. "Is there a way I can buy Lauren's share for myself?"

"I suppose there is," he said. "But it would take a lot of money and I would still have to go before the French court for approval in order to establish that Lauren's share was properly evaluated and that she received her fair financial remuneration." He took a deep breath. "But why would you want to do a thing like that? The wine company alone guarantees you a good income for life?"

"I'm not interested in the wine company," she said. "Only the fashion house. Wines bore me. They're bourgeois."

"Even so, we would still have to follow the same procedure."

"What if I relinquished my share in the wine company to her in exchange?"

"In that case, you'd only be screwing yourself," he said. "The vineyards throw off twice the income of the fashion house, including the *parfumerie*."

"Could I sell my share of the vineyards and use the money to buy the couture?"

"I suppose you could. I know of nothing in the bylaws of the company to keep you from doing that. But I still think it would be stupid."

"Stupid or not," she said, "I would like to do it."

"Who you sell it to is also important," he said. "I have the right to reject any partner of whom I do not approve on your sister's behalf."

Her voice grew cold. "In other words, you're not going to let me do it."

"I didn't say that," he said quickly. "I'm only making you aware of my responsibilities. The same that I exercised on your behalf to protect your share. And neither you nor your sister has been hurt by it. As a matter of fact, both of you are twice as well off now as when I took charge."

"But the couture house is losing money, and for good business reasons we should sell it."

"Agreed."

"And we could sell it to a stranger?"

"Yes."

"But not to me."

"If we went through the whole process that I outlined it could be sold to you. But as your friend and former trustee, I must caution you as to the risks you would assume."

"In spite of that, supposing I say to you as a fifty percent owner of the business that I want to own the couture house alone and I'm willing to sell my share of the vineyards if necessary—what would you do?"

"I would have no choice but to hire experts to evaluate the business and try to find an equitable way of accomplishing it. After that is decided I would then have to get the approval of the courts to make the transaction."

"How long would it take?"

"I don't know," he said. "Sometimes these things take years."

"Then the only way open to me is to have a buyer for my share of the vineyards of whom you approve?"

"Perhaps," he said.

"Then that's what I'll have to do," she said.

He looked at her. "Janette, what's the rush? Why don't you take some time and think on it? If you still feel the same way, say, a month from now, come back and I'll try to help you."

"Losing a month now means losing a season. If I begin now I can make next year's spring collections."

"The fall collections are more important," he said.

"Not for me," she answered. "I'm going for another market, and if I want to reach them I have to get them in the spring in order to set them up for the fall."

"I know what she wants to do," Jacques said, finally breaking his silence. "She's got a very good chance of accomplishing it. You could wind up making millions."

"Or losing millions," Johann said. He looked at her. "I understand how you feel but I just can't do what you ask as easily as we both would like to."

186

She rose to her feet. "We're getting nowhere."

"I'm sorry," he said.

She looked down at him. Her voice was hard and determined. "I'm going to get what I want. No matter what it takes. You know that." She left the office, slamming the door behind her.

Johann looked across the desk at Jacques. "See if you can make her listen to reason."

Jacques shrugged. "Were you ever able to make Tanya listen?"

"No."

"What makes you think she's any different from her mother?" Jacques asked.

Johann arrived home at about seven thirty in the evening. Heidi met him at the door and kissed his cheek. He looked over her shoulder. Usually Lauren was right behind her at the door. "Where's Lauren?"

"She should be home any minute," Heidi said. "Janette came by and took her out for the afternoon."

"What time was that?" he asked.

"About four o'clock." She looked up into his face. "Is there anything wrong?"

He took a deep breath. "I don't know," he answered heavily. He walked into the living room with Heidi following him. "Did she say anything to you?"

"No," Heidi answered. "Just that she hadn't seen her sister for a long while and thought she should spend some time with her."

Johann rubbed his cheek reflectively. "I don't like it," he said. Quickly he told her of their meeting earlier in the day. "She said she would get what she wants, no matter what it takes," he said, finishing.

Tears came into Heidi's eyes. "She couldn't be cruel enough to destroy her sister's happiness?"

"You forget, in many ways she's not more than a child

herself. A spoiled child who's always had everything her own way. Suddenly there's something she cannot have."

"Do you think she's not going to let Lauren come back to us?"

"I don't know what to think," he said. "There's only one way to find out." He went to the telephone and dialed Janette's number. A voice answered. "Henri, is Mademoiselle Janette at home?"

"*Oui. Je vous passe,* Monsieur."

The telephone clicked and Janette came on. "Yes?"

He tried to keep his voice casual. "We were waiting for Lauren for dinner."

Janette's voice was cold. "She's not coming for dinner. She's not going back at all. She's going to remain home where she belongs. Please send her things over as soon as possible."

The telephone went dead in his hand before he could even reply. He returned it slowly to the table. "She's keeping Lauren," he said heavily.

For the first time he saw Heidi angry. "The bitch!" she swore. "The cruel bitch! Are you going to let her get away with it? After all, you're Lauren's legal guardian."

"It means bringing it all into the open. The newspapers will have a field day. They'll go back to Tanya and everything that ever happened. By the time it's finished, we'll all be covered with shit, including Lauren."

"Then why don't you just give her what she wants? Then we can take Lauren back to America with us and let Janette go to hell in her own merry way. What do you care what happens to her?"

"I don't," he said. "But it's not as simple as that. Any disposition of the assets that I make, no matter how fair and equitable it would be at the time, could be subject to misinterpretation later. If couture makes a lot of money, I've screwed Lauren out of potential benefits, if it loses and we're in it, I've permitted Lauren to be exposed·to tremendous losses. No matter which way I go, I'm damned if I do, damned if I don't."

Heidi looked him directly in the eyes. "Then if you're doomed to damnation, at least go there protecting the child who needs it most. And what she needs more than money is love and care, both of which we can give her."

He was silent.

"Why don't you buy Janette's share of the vineyards?" she asked. "My father will advance you the money. He's interested in the wine business. More than five years ago he bought a thousand-acre vineyard in California."

He looked at her, the germ of an idea taking shape in his brain. "I couldn't buy it. I would be leaving myself wide open. If that weren't the case I would have done it on my own. I have enough money. But if your father bought it, that would be a different matter. It would be a hands-off transaction that the courts and I could safely approve. Do you think he would be interested?"

"I think he would," Heidi said. "We'll call him after dinner and find out."

"He's not going to give up that easily," Maurice had said. "Not after all these years where he's had complete control. Nobody will ever know how much he made out of it for himself."

Janette looked at him. "I won't believe that Johann was ever a crook."

"I'm not saying he is," Maurice said quickly. "But he did run your business and he shared in the benefits. Who can say that he did not benefit a little more than was proper?"

She was silent.

"If you mean what you say," Maurice said, "then you'll have to go all the way. Force him out."

"How am I going to do that?" she asked.

"Make it so uncomfortable for him that he'll be glad to go. Take him into court charging him with mismanagement of your and your sister's assets, damaging your equities. You can even claim that he exerted undue influence on your mother, who was not mentally sound, to gain control of the estate. There are many things you can do."

"But how do I prove them?"

"You don't have to. That's the good thing about it." He smiled. "He has to disprove it."

She shook her head. "I don't know whether I could do that."

"Then give it all up. But it will be years before you have another opportunity like this. Did Jacques tell you that not only am I willing to back you but he has an important American also willing to invest?"

"Yes," she answered.

"Then what are you waiting for?" he asked. "Unless you really don't believe you can make a go of it."

"It doesn't make sense," she said. "I do all those things—meanwhile Lauren is living with them."

"Then take her back," he said.

"Could I do something like that?" she asked. "After all he is her legal guardian."

"But you're her sister. You can always say that you're taking her back because you're afraid that he might harm her."

Janette was silent again.

"Don't be a fool, Janette," he said. "He was a German soldier. A Boche. Nothing's changed. Only now he's occupying your business, not France."

She was silent again.

"Janette Marie de la Beauville," he said softly. "It's a good name. Did you see it on the ad? It sounds much more important than Harry Winston."

She looked at him. "How do I get Lauren back?"

"Simple," he said. "Just go to their apartment with an excuse to take her out. And then don't return her."

That was exactly what she did that afternoon. Meanwhile an appointment had been made with Maurice's attorney for

190

the following morning to begin the proceedings. By the time Johann had called it was eight o'clock and Lauren had already gone to bed.

The servants had made a great fuss over her at dinner and she loved the attention. When the suggestion was made that she go to bed she had gone happily enough. A few minutes after Johann's call, Lauren came into Janette's room.

"Aunt Heidi always tells me a bedtime story before I go to sleep," she said.

"All right," Janette replied. "Let's go back to your room and I'll tell you a bedtime story."

The child climbed into bed and looked up at her. "Tell me a story about a princess."

"What princess?"

"You know. The one who couldn't sleep because there was a pea in her bed."

Janette thought for a moment. "I don't know that one."

"Then what story do you know?"

Janette tried to remember a story from her childhood. "Once upon a time, there was an old woman who lived in a shoe—"

"I know that one," Lauren interrupted. "And that's not a story, it's a nursery rhyme."

"Oh," Janette said.

"I want you to tell me a real story," the child said.

"I'll have to think of one," Janette said. "Tell you what. Give me until tomorrow and I'll get a book with all the stories in it and tell them to you tomorrow night."

Lauren looked at her. "Are you sure you don't know any stories?"

"I'm sure."

"Not even a teeny one?"

Janette laughed. "Tomorrow night I'll tell you a dozen."

The child thought for a moment. "All right." She held out her arms. "Kiss me good night."

Janette kissed her. "Good night."

Lauren hugged her. "Good night, Aunt Hei— Janette." She put her head on the pillow and closed her eyes, then opened them immediately. "I forgot to say my prayers," she said, jumping out of bed.

She knelt at the side of the bed, clasped her hands and bowed her head. "Now I lay me down to sleep. I pray the Lord my soul to keep. God bless Uncle Johann, God bless Aunt Heidi and God bless my sister Janette." She looked up at Janette. "Amen."

Janette was silent.

"Say Amen," Lauren said.

"Amen," Janette said.

The child climbed back into the bed, lay back and closed her eyes. "Good night, Janette."

Janette walked to the door. "Good night, little sister." She turned out the light and closed the door behind her, then went down the stairs to the library. The telephone began to ring.

It was Jacques. "I just called Johann and he told me what you did. They're very upset."

"Too bad," she said. "You called him?"

"Yes."

"Why?"

"I had an idea. Perhaps a practical approach to the problem would be for Tanya Couture to enter into an agreement with Carolo for the additional financing. That would minimize the exposure."

"What did he say?"

"I never got a chance to talk about it. He told me what happened and wanted to know if I knew anything about it. I said I didn't but I don't know if he believed me."

"It doesn't make any difference," she said.

"It does to me," he said. "I've never lied to him. I wouldn't like him to think I would lie to him over this. Why on earth did you ever do it?"

"Don't be stupid," she said. "You saw the way he was at the meeting. He had already made up his mind and with his Teutonic stubbornness would never change it."

"But your sister was happy with them. There was no reason to drag her into it."

"She'll be happy here. And she was already in it. Half of the whole thing is hers."

"We would have found another way," he said.

"There is no other way," she said. "Maurice convinced me of that. I should have listened to him a long time ago but I didn't."

"Maurice's only concern is himself. He smells a chance to get back into the business. That's why he's pushing you."

"You don't approve?" Her voice grew cool.

"You didn't have to do it that way," he said.

She got angry. "Who the hell are you to sit in judgment? You've pimped and fucked for everything all your life. For your jobs, for stories, for publicity. Now you're afraid you've blown your job with Johann because you crawled too far out on the limb with me, so you're trying to crawl back into his good graces."

"That's not true!" he said vehemently. "You don't know Maurice like I do. He's trying to use you like he tried to use your mother."

"And you don't? You fucked with my mother and used her. You fucked with me and used me. How many others have you fucked and used? I don't need your fucking approval! As far as I'm concerned you can go and crawl as far back up that Nazi's ass as you want to!" She slammed the receiver back on the telephone and sat there feeling the trembling inside her.

The door opened. She looked across the room. Lauren was standing there, the tears running down her cheeks.

"What do you want?" Janette snapped.

The child stood there. "I want to go home," she cried.

"You are home!" Janette said sharply. "Now go back up to your room and go to bed."

"I'm not home. And it's not my room," Lauren said, sniffling stubbornly. "And I can't sleep. There are ghosts there."

"There are no ghosts," Janette said.

"Yes, there are," the child insisted.

"What ghosts?"

"The marquis is standing at the foot of my bed and laughing. And when I open my eyes he runs away."

Janette stared at her silently.

"Are you my sister?" Lauren asked. "He keeps saying that you're not my sister."

Janette crossed the room and knelt beside her. "Of course I'm your sister."

The child looked up into her face. "Do you love me?"

"You know I love you, *chérie*," Janette said softly.

"As much as Mommy loved you? As much as Mommy loved me?"

Janette was silent for a moment, then she felt the tears springing to her eyes. "Yes, my darling."

Twenty minutes later they were standing at the door of Johann's apartment as he opened it. He looked at them silently.

Janette's voice was strained. "I've brought her home."

There was a movement behind him. "Aunt Heidi!" Lauren cried and ran through the door into Heidi's arms.

Janette began to turn away. Johann's voice stopped her. She turned back, her eyes blurred with tears. "Yes?"

Johann blinked his eyes. "Why don't you come in?" he asked gently. "There is much we have to talk about."

Book Three

Lauren

THE CHIEF STEWARD came out of the flight deck and walked through the darkened first-class cabin to the galley that separated it from the economy class. He looked approvingly at the breakfast trays all set up and ready for serving. "We'll be in fifteen minutes early," he said.

The dark-haired stewardess filling the glasses with orange juice and tomato juice smiled. "Good. I can't wait to get home and take a bath." She turned on the heating button of the ovens. She glanced at her watch. "The eggs will be ready in twenty minutes."

"Time enough," the steward said, reaching for the telephone intercom and turning on the cabin lights at the same time. He spoke directly into the telephone, first in French, then in English. "Good morning, ladies and gentlemen. It is six thirty A.M., French time. I have the pleasure to inform you that we will reach Paris fifteen minutes ahead of schedule, eight forty-five A.M. French time. We will now begin the serving of the breakfast."

As usual, the insomniacs were the first to raise their window blinds, and the sun low over the horizon streaked into the cabin waking those who were still clinging to sleep. The rest of the passengers began to stir.

Lauren looked out the window. There was nothing to see, everything hidden by cloud cover. She turned as the stewardess gently touched her shoulder.

"Good morning, miss," the stewardess said in English. "Did you have a good rest?"

Lauren pushed her long blond hair back from her face, answering in French. "Not bad. I've been too excited. It's the first time I've returned to France in almost ten years."

The stewardess was surprised at the girl's French. It was pure, without any trace of an American accent despite her appearance, which was typically California American. Suntanned, blond hair even more whitened by the sun, large, clear blue eyes. *"Jus d'orange ou tomate?"* she asked.

"Jus d'orange," Lauren answered.

The stewardess lowered the serving tray in front of Lauren and placed the orange juice on it. "Would you like some coffee now?"

Lauren nodded. "Please." She picked up her bag and opened it. Inside was a small bottle filled with pills. She opened the bottle and shook a few into her hand, then picked up the juice.

The stewardess smiled. "Vitamins? All Americans must take their vitamins with breakfast."

Lauren smiled. "Of course." She wondered what the stewardess would think if she told her that not all the pills she took were vitamins. The red was an upper. She swallowed the pills with the juice as the girl placed the coffee in front of her. She lit a cigarette and turned to the window again, looking out. Ten years. It had been a long time. More than half her life.

Suddenly she felt a nervous tightening in her stomach. Janette would be at the airport. She wondered if Janette would recognize her. But it didn't matter. She would recognize Janette. She saw her picture a thousand times a year, in papers, magazines, even on television commercials. What was it one of the news commentators had said? One of the ten most beautiful women in the world.

She remembered one time she had been with Harvey on the beach at Paradise Cove, lying on a blanket to keep the hot sand from burning them alive. But the sun was good, sending its warmth into her body while the breeze kept her skin cool. She rolled over on her stomach and opened the magazine. Almost the first thing she saw was a color photograph of Janette. It was an advertisement for a bikini. The copy was simple. "The Briefest Bikini, by Philippe Fayard

198

for Janette." Then in smaller letters under the photograph: "At better stores everywhere from $90."

A shadow fell over the magazine. "Wow!" Harvey said. "That's a dynamite chick."

For a moment she felt a twinge of surprise. Or maybe jealousy. In some ways Harvey was an asshole. He never saw anything. He lived in a world that existed only between his surfboard and his dope collection. He never went anywhere without his surfboard—even at night there it was, tied to the roof rack of his VW. And in a cleverly concealed compartment in the door of the car were always at least twenty little plastic baggies of different kinds of grass. His mood collection, as he called it. A grass for every purpose from giggling to dreaming to fucking. Right now his primary interest was working with a friend of his up in Humboldt County to develop a grass that had no seeds, thereby eliminating the need to clean it, and of course with higher THC content than any other. It was a good thing his father never asked him what he did with his allowance, because he had already invested more than a thousand dollars in the project, which also included more than two hundred dollars which she had given him.

She looked up at him, squinting her eyes against the sun. "What did you say?"

"Dynamite chick," he said, still staring at the photo.

She glanced around the beach. It was filled with girls, alive and real, with even briefer bikinis than in the photograph, yet here he was, impervious to them and staring at the magazine. "It's my sister," she said, handing the magazine up to him.

He took it, still looking at the photograph. "Yeah," he said and then the gist of her words registered in his brain. "Did you say your sister?"

"Yes."

"You never told me you had a sister." There was a note of skepticism in his voice.

"It never came up before," she said.

"I never saw her," he said.

"How could you?" she asked. "She lives in Paris."

"France?"

"That's where Paris is," she said shortly. She was getting annoyed. There was no reason for him to make all this fuss about it. She sat up. "I could use a toke," she said.

He fished in his little paper bag and came up with a joint. He lit it and passed it to her. She took a couple of quick hits. As usual, it was the best. A Harvey special. She felt better, the annoyance leaving her.

He fell to the blanket beside her. "When did you see her last?"

"Almost ten years ago," she answered. "When I first came here."

"Did she look like that then?"

She thought for a moment, then nodded her head. "I suppose so. But I was a little girl and she was my beautiful big sister."

"When are you going to see her next?" he asked.

It was at that moment that she made up her mind. "This summer, right after graduation," she said. Ten years was a long enough time.

Long enough, she thought, looking out the window as the ground at Orly rushed up to meet the airplane. Long enough.

The immigration officer looked up at her in surprise as she passed her passport to him. "You're French?" he asked.

She smiled. "Yes." The passport she had given him was French, even though it had been issued at the Consulate in Los Angeles.

"I thought you were American," he said.

"I live there," she said. "This is my first visit here in ten years. I was only seven when I left."

He smiled and stamped the passport, pushing it back to her. "Welcome home," he said.

200

"Thank you." She picked up her passport and went to collect her luggage. In the baggage area she saw a man standing, holding a small cardboard sign in his hand: "Mlle. Lauren." She went up to him. "I'm Lauren," she said.

He bowed. "Jean Bergère, *service d'accueil*, Air France. Your sister asked me to help you with your baggage. If I may have your baggage checks, please."

"I only have one bag," she said, giving him the baggage check.

"That will be simple," he said. "Come, I will pass you through customs and then come back for your bag. Your sister is waiting outside."

She saw Janette as she cleared the customs barrier. She stopped for a moment, looking at her. There was no mistaking her. She had a presence, a quality that radiated and made her stand out from the crowd. She stared toward her almost at the same moment that Janette saw her.

She hesitated a moment, then broke into a run, coming to a halt in front of her. They stood there just staring at each other, then suddenly she smiled. "Are you really my sister?" she asked in French.

Janette answered in English, her voice trembling between laughter and tears. "You better believe it." Then she pulled Lauren close to her and hugged her tightly. "It is I who do not believe it. You're so big and so beautiful. What happened to the little girl I saw last?"

Lauren's own eyes were damp. "She grew up."

"You're taller than I am," Janette said.

"American vitamins." Lauren laughed. "But you're even more beautiful than I remembered and much more than any of the photographs that I've seen."

"*C'est pas vrai,*" Janette said. She turned and gestured. A young man dressed in a severe business suit and tie came toward them. "My secretary, Robert Bleu," Janette said.

The young man extended a delicate hand. "Pleased to meet you, Miss Lauren," he said in stiffly accented English.

"Pleased to meet you," Lauren said.

"Robert will collect your luggage and bring it to the house. This way you can ride with me to the office and then the chauffeur will take you home."

Lauren felt a slight disappointment. "Do you have to go to work today?"

"The collections are almost upon us," Janette said, taking her arm and leading her toward the exit. "We have only three weeks left to the end of July and a thousand things to get ready. We have our showing right after Dior."

Lauren found herself walking rapidly to keep up with Janette even though Janette didn't seem to be moving hurriedly. "Is July usually a busy time for you?"

Janette laughed. "The busiest time of the year."

"I'm sorry," Lauren said. "You should have told me. I could have come another time."

They went outside and a big Rolls came to the curb in front of them. The chauffeur got out of the car and opened the door. *"Bon jour,* Miss Lauren," he said. "Welcome home."

Lauren looked at him. A flash of memory echoed surprise. "René?"

"Moi-même, Mademoiselle Lauren."

Impulsively she leaned forward and kissed his cheek. "I'm happy to see you," she said.

"Thank you," he said.

She got into the car, followed by Janette. She felt an excitement she had not expected. She looked at Janette. "Are Henri and—?"

Janette's voice was hoarse. "No. They left a long time ago. René is the only one of the old ones still working for me."

"Too bad," Lauren said. "I would have liked to have seen them."

The car pulled away from the curb. Janette opened the small cupboard in the center of the passenger compartment and took a cigarette from a box there. She pressed the lighter, then held it to her cigarette.

Lauren noticed a slight trembling of her hands. "Are you okay?" she asked.

Janette glanced at her. "Of course I'm okay."

"You seem nervous."

"I'm just tired," Janette answered. "I worked until three this morning." She pointed at an attaché case on the floor in front of her. "See that? It's filled with things I have to do today."

Lauren looked down at the black crocodile case, then back up at her. "You really push yourself, don't you?"

"If you want to be a success in this business there's no other way," Janette said, dragging on her cigarette. "Someone is always out there waiting for you to fuck up. Then they can jump on you and tear you apart like wolves fighting over a carcass."

"Do you really believe that?" Lauren asked.

Janette looked at her for a long moment, then nodded. "Yes. And you will see that I'm right. You're young yet. But —in time."

Janette lit another cigarette from the end of the one she had been smoking. Lauren watched her hands still trembling. A thought flashed across her mind. "Are you wired?" she asked.

Janette was puzzled. "Wired? What's that?"

"American slang," Lauren answered. "You seem uptight. Are you on uppers, you know, reds? Black beauties?"

"I don't know what you're talking about."

"Amphetamines, speed. Mood elevators. Coke. Things like that."

"Do I look like it?" Janette asked.

"Could be," Lauren said.

"You Americans are way ahead of us in those things," Janette said. "I do some cocaine. Not much. But the French would never know it."

"You did some this morning?"

Janette nodded. "I told you I was very tired. I needed something to get me started."

Lauren nodded. "I took a red on the plane so I wouldn't fall on my face walking through customs." She searched through her tote bag and took out a small tin box. She opened the box and took from it a small, thin, tightly rolled joint. "Two tokes of this and you'll feel fine. You'll stay up there but you'll be relaxed."

"How do you know that?" Janette asked.

"I have a boy friend who's the greatest expert in the world on different kinds of grass. This is a Harvey number ten." She struck a match and lit the joint. She took two quick tokes then passed it to Janette. "Just two deep tokes. No more."

Janette held it delicately in her fingers. Slowly she drew on the joint. The odor was delicate, like none of the grass or hash she had ever smoked before. Slowly she took her second toke, then handed it back to Lauren.

Lauren moistened her fingertips and pinched out the glowing tip, then carefully replaced it in the tin box. The tin box went back into the tote bag.

"I don't feel anything," Janette said.

Lauren smiled. "You're not supposed to. But in two minutes you won't be nervous anymore."

They were silent as the big car rolled along the *autoroute* into Paris. Suddenly Janette turned toward her. "You know," she said smiling, "you were absolutely right. Everything seems better now. I shouldn't have let myself get so, how did you say it, uptight?"

Lauren laughed. "Just listen to little sister."

"I should have asked before," Janette said. "But tell me, how are Johann and Heidi?"

"They're fine," Lauren answered. "They send you their love."

"I read somewhere that Johann has become an American citizen," Janette said.

"Last year," Lauren said.

"And you? Would you like to become an American too?"

"I never thought about it." Lauren looked at her with clear blue eyes. "I feel American. But I guess I can wait until I am twenty-one to make up my mind."

"Johann has been very successful?"

Lauren didn't know whether it was a question or a statement. "I guess so," she said. "I never paid much attention to those things."

"According to the financial papers, he has one of the most rapidly growing conglomerates in America."

"I don't even know what a conglomerate is." Lauren laughed. "All I know is that he goes to work early and comes home late."

Janette was silent for a moment. "You should pay some attention to it. After all, you are a twenty-five-percent owner of the de la Beauville wine company, which is the foundation of the whole conglomerate."

"I know," Lauren said casually. "He's mentioned it several times but I really couldn't get interested. Money isn't that important to me."

"What is important then?" Janette asked.

Lauren looked at her once again with those clear blue eyes. "Discovering myself. Learning what I'm all about. Then I'll have time for other things."

"But aren't you worried that something might happen to your money?"

"What could happen to it?"

Janette didn't answer.

"Even if it were all gone, it wouldn't matter," Lauren continued. "I could still manage. I don't need very much." She caught a glimpse of the Eiffel Tower as they turned off the Boulevard Périphérique and she broke into a smile. "There it is!" she said like an excited child. "Now I really believe I'm in Paris!"

The Rolls pulled to the curb in front of the salon on avenue Montaigne. The doorman in his formal uniform opened the door. "*Bon jour*, Madame."

"*Bon jour*, Louis," Janette answered as he reached in and took her attaché case from the car. She turned to Lauren. "Try to get some rest this afternoon. I'm having a small dinner party at home this evening. There are so many people who want to see you."

Lauren looked at her. "You really don't have to do anything. I'm happy just to be here."

"Don't be silly," Janette said with a smile. "It will be fun to see their faces when they meet you. They all still think of you as a child."

She crossed the sidewalk and went up the few steps to the private entrance next to the salon. As usual, she stopped at the top of the steps and looked up and down the street.

It was early July and the street lay smoldering in the heat and the humidity left by the early-morning showers. A quick check. Christian Dior was on the corner, Nina Ricci across the street. Farther up the block was the Plaza Athénée. The street was empty; only a few early-morning tourists were coming out of the hotel to begin their pilgrimage. But there was no one in front of the salons, quiet and somnolent in the summer heat.

But she knew better. That was just the facade. Inside of each salon the pressure was building. Collections. Now, less than three weeks away. They all had to be going crazy. The scramble was on, the rumors were flying, and each house was working day and night to counter what they thought the others were doing. All were intent on grabbing the limelight, attracting the most attention from the newspapers and the publicity that resulted from the excitement. Hems up, hems down, shoulders broad, shoulders narrow, hips flat, hips round, colors bright, colors somber, silks, satins, wool, acrylics. Nobody really knew what would work, so all were going crazy.

Louis opened the door for her and she went inside. He opened the tiny elevator door, gave her the attaché case, pressed the button for the third floor where her office was and touched his cap in a salute as the door closed in front of him. Her office was at the end of the corridor. It used to be Johann's. But she had had it done over when she moved in.

The frenzy was in the air as she moved through the large general office in which the desks of the bookkeepers and secretaries and clerks ringed the walls and the doors to the private offices. A quiet murmur of *"Bon jour,* Madame" trailed her way to her own office, which was on the farthest end.

There were only three offices which had private rooms for their secretaries. Her own, Jacques' and Philippe's. She opened the door to her secretary's office and for a moment felt a twinge of annoyance at seeing a girl sitting at Robert's desk. Then she remembered that Robert was bringing Lauren's luggage home.

The girl got to her feet. *"Bon jour,* Madame."

"Bon jour, Sylvie," Janette answered, moving to her own door as Sylvie opened it for her. "Any urgent messages?"

"Monsieur Jacques wanted to see you as soon as you came in," the girl answered, following Janette into the office and placing the mail and other telephone messages on the desk.

Janette placed her attaché case on the desk and walked behind it. "Tell Monsieur Jacques that he can come right in."

The girl nodded and left the room. Janette sat down and began to leaf through the messages. Nothing that could not hold. She looked up as Jacques came into the room.

They wasted no time on greetings. "You met Lauren?" he asked.

"Yes," she said.

"What is she like?"

Janette smiled. "Beautiful. What did you expect? American vitamins never miss." She changed the subject. "Is that what is so important?"

Jacques dropped into the chair opposite her. "Philippe's hysterical again. He's screaming there's no way he can make this collection with the budget we've given him. He says that Dior, St. Laurent, Givenchy have three times as much to spend as he does."

"That's right," Janette said.

"He wants to see you right away."

"I'll see him," she said calmly. "In my own time. Right

now, he'll have to wait. We have other things to do." She opened the attaché case and took out some papers. "I want you to go over these and tell me what you think."

He glanced down at them, then back at her. "Designs? Who did them?"

"It doesn't matter for the moment," she said. "I just would like your opinion."

"I'll study them," he said. "Meanwhile what about Philippe?"

She rose to her feet. "Let's go. We might as well get it over with."

They could hear Philippe's voice as soon as they entered his secretary's office. Even through the closed door it had a shrill hysterical ring. Jacques glanced knowingly at her as he opened the door.

A mannequin was standing on the small pedestal in the middle of the room, a bored distant look on her face that only a mannequin could have while a tempest raged around her. She was draped in pieces of cloth that would later become a dress but right now were only swatches held together with pins. Two *midinettes,* their frightened faces and shaking hands reflecting their nervousness, and Mme. St. Cloud, the chief seamstress, were standing around the mannequin while Philippe was pacing back and forth in front of the girl, ranting and raving. The only person in the room who seemed unaffected by anything was Marlon, who was seated on a couch against the far wall. He was out of it.

Philippe turned toward them, throwing up his hands in a gesture of despair. "Everything's wrong," he screamed. "The material's not what I ordered, the factory said that's the best they could do with the money we're paying them, the colors are all wrong, and when the dress is cut nothing falls in the place I designed for it. Mme. St. Cloud said that she needs more money for seamstresses, what do I expect when we have only three seniors and all apprentices? I'm going mad, I tell you, stark raving mad. I can't take it anymore. I am going to kill myself. That's what I'll do. Kill myself!"

Janette looked at him for a moment, then gestured to Mme. St. Cloud. A moment later, the mannequin and the others had gone. She waited until the door closed behind them before she spoke. "What you need is to calm yourself."

"What I need is more money to be able to realize my designs," Philippe retorted angrily.

Janette stared at him. Her voice was cold. "What you need isn't more money, what you need is more creativity. Money doesn't make designs. Your problem is that you're in a rut and you're using money as an excuse."

"You saw the designs," Philippe snapped. "You thought they were great."

"They were," she said, "until you started fooling with them, reaching for materials that weren't practical—and you know it."

"What do you expect me to do?" Philippe shouted. "Have all the others making a horse's ass out of me? You know the materials that St. Laurent is using, that Bohan and Givenchy are coming out with. We'll look cheap by comparison."

"They're nothing but flash," Janette said evenly. "We can only look good by comparison."

"Dull!" Philippe snapped. He went to his desk and pulled out some folders and threw them across the desk at her. "Look at those," he said. "I paid five thousand francs to get them. Samples of materials that they're using. Every one of them cost more than twice what we're paying."

Janette picked up the folders and glanced through them silently, then passed them to Jacques. She felt a tightening in her stomach. He was right. The materials made theirs look cheap. But nothing of the way she felt showed on her face. "When did you get these?" she asked. "Why didn't you show them to me before?"

"I just got them last night," Philippe said. "I came in here at five this morning trying to work something out." He slumped into his chair. "But there's nothing we can do. We're fucked. It's too late to change now."

Jacques placed the folders back on the desk without comment. The expression on his face did nothing to encourage any of them.

Her voice was controlled. "I want to think about this." She walked toward the door, Jacques following. "We'll meet again in my office in one hour."

The house was as Lauren had remembered it. Everything was the same until she got to her room. The child's room was gone. In its place was a beautiful boudoir that seemed furnished for a princess. For a moment she stood in the doorway looking in, a twinge of regret for a memory long gone. Then she went into the room and walked directly to the window. At least the view had not changed. She still looked out at the park in which she used to play as a child.

A knock at the door turned her from the window. The door opened and Janette's secretary came in carrying her bag. Behind him were the butler and a maid, both carrying large vases of flowers. Robert put the valise down as the flowers were placed, one vase on the small coffee table next to the chaise longue, the other on the side of the dresser so that it did not block the mirror in the center.

"Claudine will help you unpack," Robert said.

"I can manage myself," Lauren answered.

"She will be hurt if you don't let her help you," Robert said in English.

"Okay, then," Lauren answered. "But I'm afraid that she'll be disappointed. There's nothing much in there."

"Madame asked me to help you if there's anything you need," Robert continued.

"That's very kind, but I can't think of anything." She had a thought. "Janette mentioned some kind of dinner party tonight. How do I dress?"

"A simple cocktail dress would be all right."

Lauren laughed. "I don't have one. Nothing but jeans and slacks."

"No problem," Robert answered. "Madame has a large

wardrobe. I'm sure we can find something in there that will be satisfactory."

The butler came toward her with two cards that had come with the flowers as the maid opened her valise. Lauren took the cards and glanced at them.

One was the card of the Marquis de la Beauville. The writing was in English. "Welcome. I look forward to seeing you this evening." The other was from Jacques, also in English. "Happy you are here. With affection."

She gave the cards to Robert. He looked at them without speaking "Are there many people coming tonight?"

"About twenty."

"Am I supposed to know them?"

"I don't know," he answered. "They are mostly friends and associates of Madame."

"Why do you call her Madame?"

"It is customary," he answered. "After all, she is the *chef.*"

"I didn't know that she was friendly with the marquis."

Robert looked uncomfortable. "She is on speaking terms with your father."

Lauren looked at him. There was no point in asking any further questions. It was obvious that he had no answers for her. She glanced past them to where the maid was taking out a man's dop kit from her bag. "Put that on the bureau," she said in French. "I'll take care of it." The kit was filled with vials containing a careful selection of Harvey's grass, cocaine and assorted other pills.

"*Oui,* Mademoiselle." The maid placed the dop kit on the dresser and continued to hang Lauren's clothing in the closet.

"I know you must be tired," Robert said. "So if you would like to rest now, I can come back later to help you select something to wear this evening."

"We can do it now while she's still unpacking."

"Very well," he said. "Come with me."

She followed him out into the corridor and into Janette's room. It was the room that had been her mother's but that, too, was now changed. Everything was now modern. White, black, bright red and polished stainless steel. It was a sybaritic room, feminine, to be sure, but with occasional hints of subdued masculinity. He led her through the room into a large walk-in wardrobe. There had to be at least two hundred dresses and outfits hanging in there. She looked at Robert in bewilderment. "I wouldn't know where to start."

He smiled. "I'll help you. The cocktail dresses are over here."

She watched while he flipped through the rack. He looked questioningly at her. She shook her head. "Not my thing. I wouldn't feel comfortable in any of them."

"They're very smart," he said.

She smiled. "Maybe that's why. I never dress like that."

"Perhaps an afternoon frock," he said, turning to another rack and starting to move the dresses apart so that she could see them.

But still she shook her head. "I'm afraid I'm not of much help, am I?" she asked. "The only dress I had on in the last three years was my white graduation dress. And you don't know what we went through until I found one that I would wear."

"Did you bring it with you?" he asked.

"What for?" she replied. "I didn't think I would need it."

"We have some white summer dresses," he said. "But they're long." He crossed to the other side of the closet where the gowns were hanging. Quickly he flipped through them until he came to the one he remembered and took it from the rack. He held it toward her. It was white eyelet cotton with white cap-shoulder sleeves, square-cut décolletage low in front, even lower in back. "This would look good on you."

"I don't know," she said skeptically. "I don't wear a bra, my breasts would fall out."

"Why don't you try it on and see?"

She took the dress from him but stood there still looking

at the racks. One section was all suits. A group, all in shiny black, caught her eye. "What are those?"

"Smokings," he answered.

"Smokings?" Her voice was puzzled.

"Tuxedos, you Americans call them. They're man-tailored especially for Madame. She wears them often. Even St. Laurent admits he got the idea from seeing her wearing one."

She moved them slowly along the rack so that she could look at each one. "It's a hell of an idea," she said. "But don't you think it's a little dikey?"

He laughed. "It depends on who wears it. They don't look dikey on Madame. As a matter of fact, in a strange way they accentuate her femininity."

"Can I try one of them on?" she asked.

"I don't see why not," he replied. "But you might have trouble with their fit. They're all cut exactly to her measure."

"We're in trouble," Janette said, sinking into the chair behind her desk. "Big trouble."

Jacques stood in front of her silently. There was nothing he could add to it.

"What happened?" she asked. "We should have known what they were doing long before this."

Jacques shrugged. "I kept after Philippe to let me get the information but he insisted that he didn't want to know what they were doing. He didn't want to be influenced."

"Since when have you taken to listening to him?" Her voice was angry. "We should have had it for ourselves."

He was silent. He couldn't tell her that he had the information over a month ago but had withheld it deliberately. He thought of Carroll sitting in his suite across the street in the Plaza Athénée waiting for a call from him. The American wanted in, but for three years Janette had consistently refused the association. Especially after Carroll had sold his companies to Twin Cities and was now a part of the conglomerate that Johann was building in the States. Carroll was no fool. Years ago, even before he had changed his name from Carolo and hit the big time—and respectability—he had recognized Janette's talent and wanted in. Now, he had real muscle behind him.

"We're going to have to take a whole new approach," she said.

"It will take a lot of money," Jacques said. "And we haven't got it. We've spent our limit on this collection."

"We'll have to find the money somehow," she said. "What's our balance in the fragrance company?"

"Negligible," he said. "We've drained it for this collection. Take any more from it and we'll bankrupt it and won't be able to deliver on our contracts."

She shook her head. If it weren't for that company, they would have been out of it a long time ago. It was the only consistent money maker she had. Just as Johann had told her it would be. "Now what do we do?" she asked.

He was silent for a moment, then took out his small vial of cocaine and the gold spoon with his initials on the stem. Quickly he did a snort in each nostril then handed it to her. "Maybe it will clear our heads."

She did the same. She felt her head lighten. "It helps," she said, giving it back to him. "You know, Lauren wasn't in the car two minutes before she asked me if I had done some coke."

He laughed. "That's America for you. They're way ahead of us."

"But she's only seventeen."

He laughed again. "You're being very French. Do you remember what you were into when you were seventeen?"

"It wasn't dope," she said. She lit a cigarette. "But that isn't solving our problem."

He tried to gauge her mood. "There's always Carroll," he said cautiously. "He's got the hots for you. He'll come up with whatever money you want."

214

"There will be too many strings attached to it," she said. "I like my independence."

"So you give him a fuck," he said casually. "Is it that important?"

"That's the easy part," she said. "What I don't want is to be back in Johann's hands. After all, he owns that company now. And I'll be right back where I started."

Jacques was silent for a moment. "Maybe it's not so bad, being bought out. Conglomerates are in these days. Maurice is making more money than ever now that he's made the arrangement with Johann to distribute the water in the States."

She was silent.

"And Cardin's making a lot of money with Bidermann. I had some talks with Bidermann but he's not interested in us, he's after St. Laurent or Dior."

"Cardin won't like that," she said.

"Cardin does not give a damn. He's well established in the States now. I hear when his contract with Bidermann is up he's going to go it on his own."

"We still haven't solved our problem," she said. She opened the folders in front of her and studied the sketches and the swatches. "Shit."

He lit a cigarette, watching her.

After a moment, she looked up at him. "I'll talk to Carroll. Invite him to the dinner tonight. But don't give him any idea of what we're thinking."

"Okay," he nodded. He kept the feeling of triumph inside him from showing on his face.

She glanced down at the folder again. "I have another idea. Call Philippe in."

He rose to his feet.

"Just a minute," she said quickly. "I want another hit before you bring him in. I want to be really up for what I have to do."

215

"Red is a whore's color!" Philippe screamed. "I won't do it!"

"Like it or not, you're going to do it," Janette said calmly.

"No, no!" Philippe shouted. "I'll quit first."

"That's your privilege," Janette said coldly. "We'll do it anyway." She turned to Jacques. "Give him that design folder I gave you."

Jacques placed the folder on the desk. Janette let it lie there closed. "There's a whole collection in that folder that I'm ready to do if you leave."

Suddenly Philippe was silent. He stared down at the folder without touching it. Then he looked at her. "Who did it?" he asked.

"What does it matter?" she replied. "But if you must know, it's mostly my designs for the *prêt à porter* line you never wanted to do because it was beneath you."

"You can't do *prêt à porter* in the *haute couture* collection," Philippe said.

"Who will know the difference?" Janette said. "Two weeks after the collections, Seventh Avenue knocks off the best things in every line. This way we're ahead, we'll be knocking off our own and marketing them directly."

Philippe shook his head. "Even if I were to agree to do it, we wouldn't have the time. We have to find the materials and the colors have to be approved as well as the designs. We're scheduled to show in three weeks."

"We'll change our date from the beginning of the showings to the end. That will give us some extra time."

"It will still be very tight," Philippe said. "And by that time all the important buyers will be gone and most of the journalists."

"I'll keep them here," Janette said confidently. "Ricci gives them a cocktail for the *ouverture,* I will give a *bal de clôture.* It's never been done before and they'll all stay just to see what's happening."

"Red! It's crazy," Philippe said. But his voice was calmer now.

"Not that crazy," Janette said. "Think about it. They all

made their statements with shapes, A-lines, trapeze lines, straight lines, hemlines up, hemlines down, shoulders broad, padded, narrow. They went so many different ways, and all we've been trying to do is catch up to them. They've been making us play their game and putting us away each time. This time, I say, we fuck them. We'll make our own statement. With a color."

Philippe was silent.

"All the shades of red, wicked and erotic, sheers and chiffons, see-throughs to layered opaques. Black underwear, bras, bikinis, chemises and camisoles, all touched with a splash of red ribbon like blood. Women will go crazy over it because it's something all of them secretly want to wear but have been afraid to. We'll make it sexually legitimate. And the men will be driven up the wall."

"You really think they'll buy it?" Philippe asked.

"They'll buy it," she said confidently. "It will be the most exciting idea in this year's collections. They'll never stop talking about it. Your name is going to be all over the papers and magazines. And I'll do something I swore I'd never do after I left Dior. I'll get back on the runway to wear the bridal gown to close the showing."

"The bridal gown in red too?" Philippe asked.

"We go all the way." Janette laughed. "Pure symbolism. Blood pouring from a broken maidenhead."

He was silent. "It will be a lot of work," he finally said.

"We'll put on as many people as you need to get it done," she said. She walked around her desk and kissed his cheek. "You can do it, Philippe. I know you can. And this time you'll really show all of them."

He looked at her. "Okay. I'll try."

"Good."

"Now I better get back to my office. I've got to begin calling the fabric houses all over the world. We'll have to get them to air express everything they have."

"Do it," she said. "If you need any help with them, call me."

She watched him leave the office, then turned to Jacques. "What do you think?"

"He's going to try." Jacques lit a cigarette. "You're a bitch, you know that. You frightened the shit out of him when you said he could leave."

"I had no choice," she said, returning to her desk. "Did you call Carroll?"

"He'll be there tonight," Jacques said. "I hope you know what you're doing. We're going to need a lot of money."

"I'm not as much worried about him as I am about Johann," she said. "He'll probably have to go to Johann for approval, and you know how Johann feels about couture."

"It has to be with Johann's approval that he's been after you," Jacques said.

"Maybe," she said. "But he still might be looking after Lauren's equity. After all she still owns twenty-five percent of this company."

"Then he's sure to go along," Jacques said. "If he wasn't interested, he might never have allowed her to come and visit."

Janette laughed suddenly. "I can always hold her for ransom."

Jacques' voice was shocked. "Not again. You tried that once."

Janette laughed again. "You're more French than I am. You have absolutely no sense of humor."

Carroll opened the door to let Jacques into the hotel suite. "I've been waiting for you," he said.

"I got over here as quickly as I could," Jacques explained. "The shit really hit the fan. It's been touch and go for the last four hours." He walked toward the bar and poured himself a whiskey on the rocks. "I need a drink."

Carroll watched him as he swallowed a big gulp. "What's been decided?"

"She junked Philippe's whole collection and they're starting over again," Jacques answered, still holding his glass.

"She'll never make it in time for the showings," Carroll said.

"You don't know her," Jacques said. "She'll make it."

Carroll looked at him for a moment. "It will take money. Where's she going to get it?"

Jacques met his gaze. "From you."

Carroll's voice was even. "And if I don't give it to her?"

"Bidermann's been knocking at her door," Jacques lied. "He'd fall on his face if she just smiled at him."

Carroll was silent. He went back to the couch and sat down thoughtfully. "*Haute couture* means nothing to me," he said.

"She knows that," Jacques said. "She's been working on a *prêt à porter* collection of her own."

Carroll was interested. "Did you see it?"

Jacques nodded. "She gave me the designs. And they're good. Very good. As a matter of fact, I think she's going to push Philippe in that direction because, she said, why wait for Seventh Avenue to knock them off when she can do it herself, quicker and better?"

"Do you think she'll want to talk about it tonight?" Carroll asked.

"I have a feeling that's why she asked you to dinner," Jacques said. "The big problem you have is Johann. She's leery about getting involved with him again. She's afraid he'll try to take over."

"Johann lets me run my own shop," Carroll said testily. "All he's interested in is the bottom line."

"That sounds like him," Jacques said. "He was always like that."

"I'll have no problem with him," Carroll said. "He knows I've been after her for a long time."

Jacques refilled his glass. He didn't speak.

Carroll looked up at him. "What's the reason for the dinner tonight?"

Jacques sipped his drink. "It's a welcome home party for her sister."

"You mean Lauren?" A note of astonishment came into Carroll's voice.

Jacques nodded. "It's been ten years since—"

"I know her," Carroll said. "I've seen her several times when I went over to Johann's house. I always had the feeling that Johann wanted to keep them apart. She's nothing like Janette."

"What is she like?" Jacques was curious.

"Very American, very California. Blond, suntanned, you know, jeans, grass, wine, very laid back like all the kids today. They think they're the first generation ever to discover youth."

Jacques laughed.

"Why are you laughing?" Carroll asked.

"Now I'm anxious to see her," Jacques answered. "Last time I saw her she was just a seven-year-old."

"You're in for a surprise," Carroll said.

"I don't like that boy Harvey," Heidi said as Johann sat down at the breakfast table.

He looked at her in surprise as he raised his coffee cup. "What brought that on all of a sudden?"

"She hadn't been gone twenty-four hours when he called and wanted her telephone number in Paris."

Johann smiled. He reached for the toast and began to butter it. "I don't see anything wrong in that."

Her voice was reproachful. "Johann, you know he's into drugs."

"So? That doesn't mean anything. From what I hear everybody's children are into drugs."

"I found drugs in Lauren's room when we went in to clean it after she had gone," Heidi said.

"What drugs?" Johann asked.

"Marijuana. Pills. I don't know what they are. I think she gets them from Harvey."

"Does your daughter look like a drug addict to you, Mama?" he asked teasingly.

220

"No, but—"

"Then stop worrying. Lauren's a bright girl. She knows how to take care of herself."

"I guess she does," she said. "I also found these." She held up a small box.

"What are those?" he asked.

"Birth control pills," she answered.

He laughed. "Then I was right. She does know how to take care of herself."

"She's only seventeen."

Johann put down his coffee. "Now stop worrying. She's all right."

"I don't like the idea of her being with Janette," she said.

"You just don't like the idea of her going off on her own. The little bird is showing signs of leaving the nest. It's normal at her age. Didn't you tell me that you did the same thing?"

"It wasn't exactly the same thing. I went away to college."

"Heidi," Johann said gently, "just relax. She'll be fine."

"She said she would call when she got there," Heidi said.

"There's nine hours' time difference between Paris and California." He glanced at his watch. "It's eight in the morning here, that makes it five in the afternoon over there. I'll bet she's sleeping off her jet lag and she'll call you when she wakes up."

"If she doesn't call me by ten o'clock, I'm going to call her," Heidi said.

"No, you won't," Johann said firmly. "She's a young lady now. Don't make her feel like a child."

The telephone on his side of the table began to ring and he picked it up. "Yes?" he said into it. "Okay, put him through." He covered the speaker with his hand. "It's Carroll calling from Paris." He took his hand from the mouthpiece. "Hello, Charles. No, it's okay. I'm just having breakfast. Sure, you can talk."

Heidi watched him while he was listening to the voice on the telephone. The maid came in and placed the ham and eggs on the table in front of him. Heidi took a cover and placed it over the plate so that it would keep warm until he had finished talking.

Finally he put down the telephone and, looking across the table, smiled at her. "There's nothing to worry about," he said, lifting the cover from his plate. "She arrived there safe and sound and Janette is having a small dinner party in her honor tonight."

"Oh, my God!" Heidi exclaimed. "She hasn't even got a dress to wear. I told her to take one with her but she said she wouldn't need it."

Johann laughed. "I wouldn't worry about that either. I'm sure that Janette would not let her come down to dinner naked."

Lauren opened her eyes. The room was dark and strange and it took a moment for her to realize she was not in her room at home. She rolled over on the bed and saw Janette sitting in an armchair, watching her. She sat up on the bed, stretching, making no attempt to cover her nakedness. "I fell asleep," she said half apologetically.

Janette smiled. "That's normal. It's jet lag. You looked so peaceful there I was wondering whether to wake you up."

"Is it late?"

"No. We have plenty of time. It will be another two hours before any of our guests arrive."

Lauren got out of bed and started for the bathroom. "I'll be back in a minute." When she returned she was wearing a Porthault bathrobe she had found in the bathroom. She sat down on the edge of the bed facing Janette and lit a cigarette. "Did you have a good day?" she asked.

Janette shrugged. "*Comme ci comme ça*. There are always problems."

Lauren giggled. "That's what Daddy—Johann—always says."

"He works very hard?" It was a question, the way Janette said it.

"All the time," Lauren said. "Even on weekends and eve-

222

nings, he always has a briefcase filled with papers that he has to go over. Sometimes I think he even takes them to bed with him."

"And Heidi? What does she do?"

"She has things to keep her busy. You know, social and charitable things, plus the houses. And she travels a lot with Johann on his business trips."

"I wonder why they never had any children of their own," Janette said.

"She had two miscarriages," Lauren said. "I don't know too much about it. It happened when I was still a kid."

"Too bad," Janette said thoughtfully. "I always thought Johann would make a great father."

"He has," Lauren said. "To me."

"I noticed that you called him Daddy. Do you call Heidi Mother?"

"Yes."

Janette nodded. "Good."

"That's the way I think of them," Lauren said.

"I don't think there's anything wrong in it," Janette said quickly. "They deserve it. They love you very much."

"I love them," Lauren said. Then she giggled. "Even if they are a little old-fashioned."

"I don't understand," Janette said.

"They still act as if I were a child," Lauren said. "They worry too much."

"Do they have anything to worry about?"

"I don't think so," Lauren answered. "I cope." She yawned again and stretched. "I can't seem to wake up."

"A hot-and-cold shower will revive you," Janette said.

"I think a toot will do it quicker," Lauren said.

"A toot?"

"A snort, coke, you know. Two toots and a red and you can take on the whole world." She got out of bed and crossed to the dresser. She opened a drawer and took out a small cosmetic bag. She turned back to Janette as she unzipped it, the bathrobe loose and open. "Want a lift?"

"I can use something," Janette said.

She took a small vial from the bag and knelt before Janette's chair. She put a small plastic straw in the bottle, took it out and held it to Janette's nostril. "Snort."

Janette felt the coke shoot back into her head.

"Now the other nostril," Lauren said, before Janette could speak.

Again Janette sniffed at the straw. This time she felt it go right up into her brain. "My God!" she exclaimed. "What the hell is in that?"

Lauren laughed. "The real thing. Pharmaceutical coke. Not the cut street stuff."

Janette watched her do two quick snorts. She could feel the sudden awakening creeping through her body. The strains of the day seemed to disappear.

Lauren's eyes brightened. She got to her feet and threw her robe on the floor. She held out her arms and suddenly danced around the room. "I can't believe it! I can't believe it!"

"What?" Janette asked.

"I'm in Paris. I'm really in Paris!" Lauren laughed. "And I'm with you. You don't know how many times I've dreamed of being here with you."

Janette laughed. "You're beautiful," she said. "I only hope that neither Paris nor I disappoint you."

The telephone next to the bed rang. Janette got out of her chair and picked it up. She listened for a moment, then held the receiver toward Lauren. "It's someone named Harvey calling you from California."

Lauren took the telephone. "Harvey, how'd you get my number?"

Harvey's voice echoed in the line. "From your mother. She sounded p.o.'d. Like she didn't want to give it to me. She also bitched because you hadn't called her yet."

"I forgot and fell asleep," Lauren said. "Why'd you call?"

"My father said if I could get the money together I could go over to Europe in August. He'll give me half if I get the other half. Will you still be in Paris?"

"I don't know," Lauren said. She looked at Janette. "Harvey wants to come over. Will we still be in Paris in August?"

"I have a villa in Saint-Tropez," she answered. "We should be able to go down there by the tenth, after the collections."

"Janette says we're going to be in Saint-Tropez," Lauren said into the telephone.

"Jesus!" Harvey said. "That's where everybody is topless and Brigitte Bardot lives."

"I guess so," Lauren said.

"Would your sister mind if I showed up?" He paused a moment. "Wait a minute. Don't ask her just yet. Let me see if I can get the money together."

"Okay."

"Is she as great-looking as she was in that picture I saw?"

Lauren laughed. "Better-looking."

"Wow," Harvey said. "Is she into anything?"

"She's hip."

"Great," Harvey said. "Tell her if I come I'll come supplied."

"When will you know?" she asked.

"I'll call you again in a couple of weeks," Harvey said. "Was the stuff I gave you all right?"

"Super."

"I've got a couple of new kinds I want you to try."

"Okay. How does the project look?"

"We're getting there. We'll be rich yet."

Lauren laughed. "Great. Just don't get yourself busted."

"I won't," he answered. "Keep cool."

"You, too. 'Bye." She put down the telephone, smiling. She turned to Janette. "He's crazy."

"Your boy friend?" Janette asked.

"Sort of," she answered. "He's a real head. But nice, if you know what I mean. He's a vegetarian. He eats nothing but raw vegetables, wheat germ, vitamins and dope. He says he's going to be a millionaire before he's twenty-one."

"How old is he now?" Janette asked.

"Almost nineteen."

"He's not allowing himself much time."

Lauren smiled. "He just might do it. He says four more crops and he'll have the right strains."

Janette was puzzled. "Strains of what?"

"Grass," Lauren answered. "He and a couple of guys are working up in Humboldt County on a strain that will have nothing but buds, no seeds at all. If they pull it off, they'll have nothing but money."

"Isn't that illegal?" Janette asked in a puzzled voice.

Lauren shrugged. "Sure. But nobody seems to pay much attention to it." She picked the bathrobe from the floor and put it around her. "Bobby gave me a few things from your closet. What do you think I ought to wear tonight?"

"Let me see what you have," Janette said.

Lauren opened the closet door. The two dresses and the tuxedo hung there. She turned back to Janette.

"What would you like to wear?" Janette asked, looking at them.

Lauren smiled. "I'd like to wear the tuxedo, if you think that's all right. I never wore anything like it before."

Janette was silent for a moment. It wasn't exactly the sort of evening for it. But if she wanted to wear it— "Okay," she said. "Let's both wear smokings."

"Fabulous!" Lauren said. "We'll do a real sister act. I'll shower and get ready. Will I have time for a joint before we go downstairs?"

"What for?" Janette asked. "Won't that bring you down?"

"Not a Harvey number five," Lauren said. "It's really mellow. Puts you in a good mood so that at least you can listen to all the bullshit that people keep laying on you without getting bored out of your head."

Janette laughed. "If it really works, I can use some of it."

"Great," Lauren said. "You come back and do it with me. It will be great going to the party stoned together." She hesitated a moment. "Is it all right if I give Mother a call? I promised I would call her when I got settled."

"Of course," Janette said. She started for the door. "Give them both my most affectionate regards."

"She's going to fuck me, I can feel it," Philippe said, putting down the telephone and staring morosely across his desk at Marlon.

Marlon's voice held no expression. "What makes you think that?"

"All the signs point that way," Philippe said. "One, she practically threw a design collection at me, daring me to look at it. I didn't, of course. But someone had to do those sketches. She *said* they were hers."

"Maybe she did do them herself," Marlon offered. "It wouldn't be the first time she showed you some of her ideas."

"Then the material manufacturers. It was as if they were all expecting my call. She had been in touch with many of them more than a month ago. They already had all the different swatches in red, which they will ship to me within a day or two."

"I wouldn't pay too much attention to it," Marlon said. "She did ask you to do the collection. No one else."

"Another thing," Philippe said. "They told me that all the materials could be available in large quantities," Philippe said. "We're *haute couture,* not *prêt à porter.*"

Marlon was silent for a moment. "Maybe there is something to the talk we've been hearing about her and Bidermann."

"Not Bidermann," Philippe said quickly. "It's the American, Carroll. You know Schwebel owns that company and he has an interest in this one. It would only be natural for him to want to put the two of them together."

"I still don't see anything to worry about," Marlon said.

"I'm not Karl Lagerfeld," Philippe said. "I'm not interested in being another Chloé or Céline."

"Janette's a long way from being there," Marlon said.

227

"Why don't you just take it easy and do your thing? Just design the things so that they won't be easy to reproduce on a mass basis, so that they will be too expensive to manufacture."

"Easy for you to say," Philippe said darkly. "You don't know how good those people are at knocking things off. And for a price."

"If you're fucked, you're fucked," Marlon said philosophically. "You have only two choices. You either do the collection or you quit."

"I can't quit now," Philippe said. "If I do, I'm finished in the business."

"Then you have no choice," Marlon said.

Philippe glowered. "That's right."

Marlon lit a cigarette and puffed on it silently.

Philippe got out of his chair. "I have a half a mind to call up and tell her I'm too busy to go to her stupid dinner party tonight."

Marlon shook his head. "That would be the wrong thing to do. You have to go along letting her think that you're cooperating. If she gets the feeling that you're sloughing off, she'll really lay it on you."

"The bitch!" Philippe swore. "The conniving lesbian bitch!"

The telephone rang just as Janette entered her room. She picked it up. A familiar British voice echoed in her ear. "What are you doing for dinner tonight?"

"Patrick!" she exclaimed. "I thought you were on safari in Africa. When did you get back?"

"Yesterday," Lord Patrick Reardon said in his rolling voice. "I thought we'd have dinner and I would show you my prize trophy."

"You got your lion?"

"Hell, no," he laughed. "My new houseboy. A black African whose cock hangs ten inches below his breechcloth. The minute I saw him I knew I had to get him for you."

228

"You're crazy," she said.

"Am I?" he asked, chuckling. "You can't say I don't know what turns you on, love. The only way a man can compete with you girls is if he has a king-size banger. And you'll never find one to beat this boy. It takes him four orgasms just to get soft again."

"Patrick, Patrick," she said. "What am I going to do with you? You're so sick."

"Aren't we all, love? Come to dinner then. Just let me watch."

"Can't do it," she said. "I'm giving a dinner party tonight." She had an idea. "Why don't you join us? If you like I can send the car to pick you up."

"I'm in London," he said.

"Then how did you expect me to come for dinner?"

"I was going to send my plane to pick you up," he answered.

"Then you can come here the same way," she said. "I'll have René at Le Bourget waiting for you."

"What time is this dinner of yours?"

"We're having cocktails at eight thirty. We won't be sitting down to dinner until nine thirty, ten o'clock. It's just going on seven now. You can make it."

"I don't know," he said hesitantly. "I know your town dinners. Usually very dull."

"This one might be a little better," she said. "My younger sister just got here from California. We haven't seen each other for ten years. Sort of a reunion."

"Is she anything like you?" he asked.

"Nothing at all. She's your type. Tanned, blond and beautiful, just like all those Scandinavian girls you're always running around with. And she's only seventeen."

"Now you've made me curious," he said. "Since you won't marry me, maybe *she* will."

"Then you'll come?"

"Have René at the airport at nine o'clock," he said.

Lord Patrick Reardon, heir to the title and to one of the richest fortunes in Great Britain, had absolutely no interest in anything except the pursuit of his almost religious form of hedonism. She had often heard him say that he had no motivation for working and adding to the fortune that had been left him when he could not possibly live long enough to spend all that had already been accumulated, no matter how many ways he could find to disburse his wealth. And he had no opposition from the executors of the estate when he had gone into the first board of directors meeting after his father's death and told them so. They couldn't ask for anything more than to be left in charge, and they happily made all the financial arrangements that were needed to keep him happy and them in control of the business.

Still, if she married him, and he allowed her to remain in her business, she would not have to make deals such as the one she was being thrust into with Carroll. Patrick could carry her business for a year with a check that amounted to a little more than one week's income to him. But that was not what he wanted. He wanted her available 100 percent of her time, without any distraction, so that they could devote themselves to nothing but what he called their whims, fancies and fantasies.

She turned on the water in her tub and added the scented musk oil especially made for her at the *parfumerie* in Grasse. Quickly she got into the tub and leaned back, letting the water flow over her body. She loved the scent and the feel of the way the tiny bit of oil clung to her skin, making it soft and smooth, like silk. *Soie*. The thought came through her mind. Someday she had to put it on the market. All the couturiers had gone into their own perfumes. Dior, St. Laurent, Givenchy and on down the list. It was a tremendous market. But she would have to do it soon—if she waited too long it might be too late. *Soie*. Silk. There was no other material, either manmade or natural, that had the same sensuous feel against the body. *Soie*. Someday soon she would do it. Maybe once this collection was over she would have time to devote herself to it.

The telephone rang again just as she came out of the bath. This time it was Stéphane. "I wanted to know what you were wearing tonight," her girl friend asked.

"I'm wearing my smoking," Janette replied.

"Good. Then I'll wear mine."

"No," Janette said quickly. "It would be too much. My sister also wants to wear a smoking. You wear that beautiful yellow gown I gave you last week."

Stéphane was silent for a moment. "Okay," she said finally.

Janette detected the hesitation. "What's wrong?"

"I'm jealous," Stéphane confessed. "Before it was always you and I who wore the smokings."

Janette laughed. "Don't be silly. There's nothing to be jealous about. After all, she's my sister."

"That has nothing to do with it," Stéphane said. "My first affair was with my older sister. We were in love for years."

"Now you're being stupid," Janette said.

"Can I stay the night?" Stéphane asked. "I want to make love to you."

Janette began to get angry. "No," she said shortly. "I told you that before she came. While she is here we play it straight."

"But she's going to be here all summer," Stéphane said. "What are we going to do?"

"We'll work something out," Janette said. "She hasn't even spent one night here."

"Is she beautiful?" Stéphane asked.

"Yes," Janette said. "But she's still just a kid."

"So was I when I began with my sister."

"If you're going to continue acting like an idiot," Janette snapped, "you don't have to come to dinner."

"I love you," Stéphane said. "There's nothing wrong with wanting to be with you."

"Then relax. Everything will work out," Janette said. She had a thought. "I'm going to seat you next to Charles Carroll. Be extra nice to him. I'm trying to work something important out with him."

"Do you want me to fuck with him?" Stéphane asked.

"If he wants to. Yes."

"I'll do it. But only for you," Stéphane said. "Just to prove how much I love you."

"That's better," Janette said. "You're still my girl."

"I'll always be your girl," Stéphane said.

Lauren was standing in front of the mirror trying to smooth the shirt front down over her breasts so that it did not keep rising out of the trousers, when Janette came into the room, still in her robe. "I thought I'd see if you needed any help."

Lauren looked at her, smiling ruefully. "I don't think it will work. My breasts are too big."

"What you need is a brassiere to hold you in," Janette said.

"I don't have any," Lauren answered. "I never wore one."

"Maybe one of mine will help," Janette said. "Come."

Lauren followed her back to her room. Janette went into the closet and opened one of the drawers. Quickly she rummaged through several brassieres, finally coming up with the one she sought. She turned to her sister. "Take off your shirt and try this."

Quickly Lauren slipped off the shirt. Janette held the brassiere cups against Lauren's breasts. "It might work. Put it on."

Lauren put her arms through the straps and fastened the brassiere. She looked in the mirror. "I can hardly breathe."

"It really looks sensational on you," Janette said.

"Really think so?" Lauren asked doubtfully.

Janette laughed. "Wear it. We'll make a hell of a team."

Lauren looked at herself again for a moment and then smiled. "Okay, but do we still have enough time for a smoke?"

"It will be a half hour before anyone gets here," Janette answered.

"Let's go then," Lauren said, starting back to her room.

"Why don't you bring the joint back in here," Janette said. "That way, we can enjoy it while I'm making up."

By the time Lauren rolled the joint and came back to the room, Janette was seated before the makeup table, her robe falling on the chair around her, carefully applying mascara to her lashes. Lauren took a small chair and sat near her and lit the joint. She puffed at it gently, then passed it to Janette. "Take tiny puffs. This is not the kind of dope you do big tokes with."

Janette did as she was instructed. After a few puffs she handed it back to Lauren. "I don't feel anything yet."

"Give it time." Lauren smiled, smoking again. "It takes a few minutes for it to work."

"How do you know it's working?" Janette asked.

Lauren giggled. "I can always tell by my nipples. They pop out and get hard like if someone is touching them, or you step into an ice-cold shower." She laughed again, looking at Janette. "It's beginning to work on you. I can see it already."

Janette glanced down at herself, then at Lauren. "But I still don't feel anything. Is it working on you?"

Lauren nodded, opening her robe. "See for yourself." The nipples of her breasts were already rising from the pale-pink areolae around them. She passed the cigarette back to Janette. "Soon you'll get a buzz on that you can feel in your head. Then that will go away and you'll just feel good. Real good."

Janette puffed slowly on the cigarette. She glanced down at herself. Her dark nipples were already jutting from her breasts. She looked at Lauren and laughed. "I guess it is working."

Lauren looked at her. "It sure is," she said. "God, you got great nipples. Mine are like nothing compared to them."

"Yours are pretty," Janette said. She laughed, beginning to feel the buzz in her head. "I prefer your kind to mine. They're more esthetic."

"But yours are sexier," Lauren said, taking the joint back

from Janette. "Harvey thinks you have one of the great bodies of all time."

"Your boy friend?" Janette laughed. "How would he know?"

"He's seen pictures of you," Lauren said. "I think that's why he wants to come over."

"He'll be disappointed if he does come," Janette said. "The photographs make me look better than I really do."

"I don't think so," Lauren said. "I don't think they do you justice." She passed the joint back to Janette and got to her feet. "I feel good."

Janette puffed on the joint. "I do too. It's very nice."

Lauren laughed. "Nice? It's great. I'm all set now. I can just fly over everything."

Janette laughed. "Just don't fly over the table at dinner. I'd have a hard job explaining to everybody what you're doing up there."

"I'll go back to my room and dress," Lauren said. "Call me when you're ready and we'll have a quick toot before we go downstairs."

Maurice was early. He made it a point to explain as he entered the library where they were waiting. "I thought it only proper that I have a moment with *mes enfants,* before the others got here."

Janette smiled. "Of course. And what do you think of the little girl now?"

Maurice turned to Lauren, a careful, observant look on his face. "She's not such a little girl now, is she? She's quite grown up. And beautiful."

Lauren laughed. *"Merci,* Monsieur le Marquis."

"Really," Maurice said. "I'm quite pleased to see you. And if there is anything I can do for you, I want you to call me."

"If there is anything, I will," Lauren said.

Maurice shook his head. "I still think of you as a little girl. But you have changed."

Lauren laughed again. "You haven't changed. You look exactly as I remembered. Not one day older."

"That's good, isn't it?" Maurice asked.

She nodded. "Fantastic. Everyone got older except you."

"I grew older too," he said. "But at my age the changes are neither as drastic or visible. And your foster parents? They are well?"

"Very well, thank you," Lauren said.

Maurice turned to Janette. "I have heard that you're going to do your whole collection over, that you've changed the date until later."

Janette nodded. "You must have spies in the woodwork. We just decided this afternoon. We have a fantastic idea and thought this would be the right time for it rather than wait until next year."

"It will be expensive," he said. "I have some extra money lying about if you should need it."

"I think we'll manage," Janette said. "But I'll bear it in mind just in case. Thank you."

Maurice smiled. "Don't thank me. After all it's family. And that's what families are for."

The faint sound of the doorbell came into the library. The other guests began to arrive, and by the time Patrick Reardon came from the airport, they were ready for dinner.

The dinner was perfect for a hot July night. The cold vichyssoise with a hint of cucumber, the delicate roast veal with the light-brown sauce tasting of Provence herbs and finely cut *haricots verts* with tiny roast potatoes, followed by a chilled lettuce salad and a perfectly ripened Brie. Still, Janette rose with a feeling of relief that it was over and led everyone back into the library for coffee and liqueurs. The table had been charged with too many tensions and nuances as all the guests seemed intent on playing games of their own. Everyone except Lauren. She had been bright and smiling, and none of the things that Janette had felt seemed to touch her.

235

Stéphane dropped behind to catch Janette in a moment alone. "Your sister is very beautiful. Everyone is very taken with her."

"I'm glad," Janette answered.

"I think you are too," Stéphane said.

Janette looked at her. "You are an idiot."

Stéphane touched her arm. "Can't we go upstairs for a moment? No one will miss us."

Janette looked at her without answering, then abruptly walked away to join Maurice and Jacques, who were talking with Jacques' date, Martine, a pretty mannequin who worked at Givenchy.

Stéphane joined Carroll, who was listening along with Philippe and Marlon to Patrick telling of his adventures on his latest African safari. She glanced around the room thinking that Lauren would be with Janette but Lauren was nowhere to be seen.

The butler served the coffee and the liqueurs, and still Lauren had not reappeared. It was not until more than ten minutes later that she came into the room, and by that time Patrick had captured everyone's attention with the story of his lion hunt.

"There I was out in the bush sitting in the Land Rover when I felt this tap on my shoulder and the white hunter sticks the big elephant rifle in my hands and points.

" 'Line the beast up in your sights and squeeze the trigger,' he says.

"The lion and I stared at each other for what seemed like ages.

" 'Shoot the fucking beast!' the white hunter shouts. 'Before the fucker comes after us!'

"I try to squeeze the trigger. But my finger can't move. It's paralyzed, and then my arm begins to shake and I can't even keep the bugger in the sights. It was right at that moment the bloody animal decided to make a run for us."

Patrick paused and held out his glass to be refilled with champagne. "Then what did you do?" Lauren asked in a breathless voice.

Patrick fixed her with a haughty glare. "What any sensible Englishman would do in a moment of danger. I ducked down between the seat and the dash and hollered to the nigger to get the fucking car out of there. Just as he started the car, the beast leaped at us. At that moment my finger caught in the trigger and the gun went off. I heard a terrible roar and stuck my head up. There was the lion rolling around on the ground, then he got up and ran off into the bush, blood dripping from the tail between his legs." He paused for a moment and sipped from his champagne. " 'You shot his bloody balls off,' the white hunter said. Right now, somewhere in Africa, there's a bloody lion, wondering what the hell happened to his sex life and wandering around the jungle trying to figure out why he would rather lie sleeping in the sun than be out hunting or fucking."

Everyone began to laugh except Lauren. Her eyes were shining moistly. "I think that's so sad."

Patrick looked at her for a moment. "Let me get you a glass of champagne."

The others broke into small conversational clusters. "No, thank you. I don't drink, I just dope," Lauren said.

"You're stoned, young lady," Patrick said with mock sternness.

"Yes," she answered.

"I'm drunk," he said.

"That's nice," she said, smiling.

"Come out onto the balcony over the garden," he said. "Maybe a bit of air will do us both good."

"Okay." She followed him through the open doors and leaned her arms on the railing. She took a deep breath. "It smells good out here. Sweet and clean."

He took a sip of the champagne he still held in his hand. "First time in Paris?"

"I was born here," she answered. "But I haven't been back for ten years. I live in California."

"I love California," he said. "Everything is so easy there."

"It's very laid back," she said.

"What do you think about us here?"

She shrugged. "It's different. Everything and everybody is very involved, very into themselves if you know what I mean."

"I'm not sure that I do," he said.

"I'm not sure that I do either."

"Do you have panties on?" he asked.

"No," she answered, looking at him. "Why do you ask?"

"I wondered if Janette talked you into wearing a smoking?"

"No. Why?"

"It doesn't help. I can still smell your quim," he said. "Makes me want to put my face in it."

She laughed. "You're putting me on."

"No. I'm not," he said quickly. "You have to realize that I have a trained nose for that sort of thing. Are you into big pricks?"

"Now where did that come from?"

"I was curious," he said. "I think if I had a big prick Janette would have married me."

"Do you *want* to marry her?"

"Yes," he said. "But she keeps turning me down."

"It has to be something else then," she said thoughtfully. "I don't think the size of your prick is the reason."

"Your sister is the most beautiful and exciting woman in the world," he said.

She turned and looked back into the room at Janette, who was talking earnestly with Jacques and Charles Carroll. Janette's face was alive and expressive as she seemed to be making a point. Lauren turned back and looked up into Patrick's face. "You're the second man I know who has said that," she said. "I think you both may be right."

Marlon joined them on the balcony, followed by Philippe and Stéphane. "Philippe wanted me to ask you if you'd consider becoming a mannequin," Marlon said.

"Why didn't he ask me himself?" Lauren asked.

"He's a little embarrassed because his English is not good enough."

238

She smiled, turning to Philippe, speaking in French. "I'm sorry. I didn't mean to be rude. I never thought that everyone was speaking English just for my benefit."

A sudden smile crossed Philippe's face. "I wanted to speak with you all evening but I was afraid that you would not understand me. I wanted to tell you how beautiful I think you are and how perfect you would be in some of my creations. You have the kind of look I have been searching for for a very long time. New, fresh, with a sophisticated innocence. I would love for you to model with some of my creations at the collection."

"I don't know anything about modeling," she answered. "But I am very flattered that you should think so."

"There is not much to learn," Philippe said. "In one week you would know everything."

"But am I not too large?" she asked.

"It's no problem," he said. "You would only have to lose two, maybe three kilos."

"Between four and six pounds," Marlon said.

"I don't know," she said. "I just never thought about it."

"Do you think your sister would object?" Philippe asked.

Lauren laughed. "I can't see any reason why."

"May I ask her?"

"If you like," she answered. "But I don't know if it's something I would want to do."

"What is it you would like to do?" Stéphane asked.

Lauren turned to her. "I haven't really given it much thought. I've been waiting to grow up first."

"It will be a full year before we're even ready to get into the market. I want ten owned and operated boutiques in the principal money areas of the States and five in the major department stores of the country. Saks Fifth Avenue, New York, Neiman-Marcus, Texas, Marshall Field, Chicago, I. Magnin, Los Angeles, Geary's, San Francisco. By that time I'm in for two million dollars. You're setting me up for a hell of a risk."

Janette looked at him. "If you press, I'm sure the department stores would go along with you this season."

"They'd take our ass," Carroll said. "They'd want everything on consignment, load all the advertising and promotion costs on us and demand the maximum discount on the clothing." He took a pull at his scotch. "We'd never make a penny."

"But we'd have a springboard to get into the market and find out exactly where we stand," Janette said.

"And what would we call our own boutiques when we do open them?" he asked. "Your name is not well enough known yet."

"I have a name for the boutiques," Janette said. "Like St. Laurent's Rive Gauche. Janette's Centre Ville, or if you think more American is better, Janette's Uptown. But that is secondary. Once we commit, I am ready to tour the country, do all the publicity, newspapers, radio, television, and by the time the stores are open there will be more Americans that know my name than there are French."

"It will all cost money," Carroll said.

"That's right," Janette answered. "That's exactly why I'm talking with you. If I had the money I would do it myself."

Carroll looked at her shrewdly. "How much would it cost to get this collection ready?"

"Maybe two hundred thousand dollars. More or less."

"Supposing I advance you that money and we see what happens. Then we can make up our minds."

Janette laughed. "I can do this collection myself in that case. It is not *that* money I'm concerned about. It's the plan beyond that interests me. If I do it myself and it's a grand success, I don't need you. Bidermann as well as others would be glad to jump into bed with me."

He took a deep breath and looked at Jacques. "That's a very tough lady you work for."

Jacques was silent.

"And if I don't agree?" he asked, turning back to Janette.

She smiled. "We are still friends."

He glanced out at the balcony to where Lauren and the others were standing. "Your sister looks very different here than she does in California. I don't think I ever saw her in anything but jeans before."

Janette laughed. "She's in Paris now." She followed his gaze. "You know, I would like to do well, not only for my own sake, but also for hers. She still owns twenty-five percent of this company and Johann is still the administrator of her interest. I have to account to him every year."

The implication wasn't lost on him. He smiled. "I don't have to be hit on the head. Why don't we meet tomorrow and discuss this further?"

"Of course," she said. "You arrange a suitable time for all of us with Jacques. But make it late in the day. I'll be busy with arrangements for the collection most of the time."

"Then you're going ahead with it?" he asked.

"*Certainement,*" she said, a faint, cool disdain in her voice. "Do you think I would depend on anyone other than myself for something as important as this?"

Maurice caught Jacques in a moment when they were apart from the others. "Did it go well?"

Jacques nodded. "I think so. The more I see Janette operate, the more I realize what a fantastic woman she really is. She has the balls of a Pampas bull."

Maurice laughed. "But what if Carroll doesn't come through?"

"Janette will find a way. I'm sure of that now. She has her mind set on it."

"I have a million francs that I'd bet on her," Maurice said. "Just bear it in mind and remind her of it, should the opportunity arise."

Jacques looked at him. "Does she know it?"

"I hinted at it," Maurice said. "But she wasn't interested —at that time. However, circumstances can change."

Jacques smiled. "I'll remember that."

Martine came toward them. "It's after eleven," she said to Jacques. "And I have to be at work early tomorrow. We're having the first fittings."

"I'll take you home," Jacques said.

"You don't have to leave on my account. I can get a taxi."

"Don't be silly." Jacques smiled. "I have to be at work early too."

The party began to break up. Jacques, Maurice and Martine were the first to leave, followed soon after by Philippe and Marlon.

"It was a lovely dinner," Philippe said. "And your sister is truly beautiful. I would like to do something with her. Maybe we can talk tomorrow."

"Of course," Janette answered. "I'll be in the office early."

Then only Carroll, Stéphane and Patrick were left. Carroll had an idea. "Why don't we all go over to Régine's for a nightcap? It should be fun there."

Janette shook her head. "Not for me tonight. I have too much to do tomorrow."

He turned to Lauren. "Perhaps you and Patrick could join us?"

Lauren smiled. "I don't think so, Mr. Carroll. I'm beginning to feel tired. The jet lag. It's been a long day."

"I'm flying back to London tonight," Patrick said. "I promised my dear old mum that I would have breakfast with her tomorrow. Some other time."

Carroll turned to Stéphane. "It looks like you and I are the only live ones in this crowd."

Stéphane glanced at Janette and smiled at him without speaking.

"Good," Carroll said, rising. "Let's go then." He turned to Lauren. "I'll be talking to your father tomorrow. Is there any message you want me to give him?"

"No," Lauren answered. "Just give him my love and tell him I'm having a wonderful time."

"Will René be able to give me a lift to the airport?" Patrick asked.

"He's waiting in the car for you," Janette answered.

They walked to the door. "Your sister is quite a girl," Patrick said to her. "I hope we'll see more of each other."

"I'm sure you will," Janette answered. "She'll be here all summer."

The sisters went up the stairs after everyone had gone. Lauren stopped in front of her door. "It was lovely," she said. "Thank you. You made me feel like someone very special."

"You are someone very special," Janette said. "You're my sister."

Lauren leaned forward quickly and kissed Janette's cheek, then went into her room, closing the door behind her. Janette, thoughtful, stood there for a moment, then slowly walked down the hall to her own room.

Jacques stood at the rear of the Lido arcade watching the crowds of people in evening dress surging toward the theater entrance, their gold-engraved invitations clutched in their hands. Beyond them he could see the Cadillacs and Rolls-Royces still lined up, discharging their passengers. It was over an hour ago that a call had gone out for extra police to control the traffic which had backed up on the Champs-Elysées. He glanced at his wristwatch. It was nearly ten o'clock and they were already running late. An hour late. Dinner was supposed to be served at ten o'clock, the collection was supposed to begin promptly at midnight.

Janette had been right. She had said that everyone would stay. And they did. Already he had seen John Fairchild of *Women's Wear* sweep into the theater with his entourage. Eugenia Sheppard, the fashion dowager of the American press, was also there. This was more than a collection—it was also a social event. Mme. Pompidou, the wife of the president, had turned up and was immediately escorted with her party to the *table d'honneur*. Mme. Schlumberger, le Comte de Paris, the Rothschilds, Dassaults and other bastions of French society swept into the theater. It was probably the first time any of them had ever come to the Lido.

There were enough film stars sprinkled through the audience to bless the premiere of any important motion picture. Brigitte Bardot, Alain Delon, Jean-Paul Belmondo, Sophia Loren, Faye Dunaway, the Gregory Pecks, the David Nivens and others—more than even he could recall. And the French press was there in force. Robert Caille of *Vogue*, almost all the editorial staff of *L'Officiel*, as well as reporters and photographers from every important paper and news service in Paris.

But the real triumph for Jacques had come the day after the invitations had gone out, when he began receiving calls from the other couturiers asking for an invitation. And when he saw Marc Bohan, Givenchy, St. Laurent, Pierre Cardin, Courrèges walking through the arcade, he knew they had it made.

He checked his watch again and started inside, when he was stopped by a maitre d'. "La Princesse Grace is here with a party of four but we have no table for her."

"Give her my table," he said quickly. "Next to Madame Pompidou."

The man nodded and hurried away. Jacques continued into the theater and keeping toward the rear behind the tables, each festooned with red balloons bearing the name Janette de la Beauville, skirted the room toward the entrance to backstage.

Snatches of conversation came to his ear. "She has to be completely crazy. This cost a fortune." "She found a money man with a bankbook bigger than his prick." "It's Lord Patrick Reardon. He wants to marry her." "Either that or Madame Poniard." And he heard the laughter as the name of the fantastically rich lesbian was mentioned.

He was stopped by Bernadine Morris of *The New York Times*. "I have to file early," she said. "Is there any way I could get an advance idea of what is coming, just in case I have to dash?"

"I'm sorry, Bernadine." He smiled. "It's impossible. Even I have not seen the collection as yet."

He continued on his way and paused at the door to look

back into the theater. He nodded with satisfaction. It was a brilliant idea of Janette's to take over the Lido for an evening. At first he had been appalled at the cost but now he was pleased that she did. The personnel of the Lido was professional. They were used to dealing with big crowds, serving dinner and getting it out of the way so that the show could go on. Dinner was under way, the dance floor was crowded, and the orchestra on the stage was playing comfortable middle-of-the-road music, no rock and roll or disco frenzy for this crowd.

"I want it to be right," Janette had said. "I want it to be elegant and Hollywood all at the same time." And that's exactly what it was. There had never been a collection with as elegant an audience and there had never been a collection with a setting as pure Hollywood as this.

He was about to open the door when he saw John Fairchild gesturing toward him. He hesitated a moment, then went to their table. The publisher gestured to an empty chair. He shook his head. "I'm working," he said.

"This party must have cost a bundle," Fairchild said. "At least fifty thousand dollars."

"Something like that," Jacques said.

"Isn't it a little heavy for Janette?" Fairchild asked. "She doesn't do that kind of business."

Jacques shrugged without answering.

"I got a cable from New York," the publisher said. "There's a rumor on Seventh Avenue that she's selling out to Carroll."

"That's not true," Jacques said firmly. "There's no way Janette would sell her house."

"Could be she's planning to go *prêt à porter* with him," Fairchild guessed shrewdly. "Carroll is sitting at a pretty important table with her father."

"Carroll belongs to Twin Cities," Jacques said. "And you know that Johann Schwebel, president of that company, has many personal and business ties with the Beauville family. And for a long time he was P.D.G. of Janette's company —from the time her mother died until she was of age."

"That's not answering my question," Fairchild said. "If she's not going *prêt à porter*, why is Carroll at so important a table?"

Jacques gestured toward another table nearby. "Bidermann is over there at an even more important table. Why don't you ask if she's not going with him?"

"Bidermann already has Cardin," Fairchild said. "And I heard he was interested in St. Laurent."

"I'm afraid you'll have to ask the lady herself what her intentions are. I have not been made privy to them yet."

"Where did she get the money for this party? I heard she was pretty strapped when she junked the whole line to begin a new collection."

Jacques held out his hands in a typically Gallic gesture. "She has other assets. Perhaps from her friendly banker. I see the Rothschilds are here in force."

Fairchild glanced around the room. "And so is half the *haute monde* of the world. Christ, I don't know if I'm seeing a collection or a Hollywood premiere."

Jacques laughed. "Janette will be pleased to hear that. It is exactly the ambiance she wanted to create. But make no mistake about it. You're at a collection. A collection like no other you have ever seen or will ever see. In this world—or the next."

Fairchild laughed. "Good luck."

"Thank you," Jacques said. Quickly he left the table and went backstage before any other members of the press could stop him. He stepped carefully over the cables lying on the floor just inside the door and made his way to the rear of the giant stage, which had been set up as a temporary dressing room for the models. It had been decided not to use any of the regular dressing rooms because they were located on various floors above the stage and too far away to allow the models time enough to make all the dress changes. In addition, Janette didn't want to take any chances that a model might fall or even catch her heel in her dress and tear it as she ran down the narrow staircase.

A black curtain had been hung completely around the

dressing area. Jacques pulled the curtain and looked in. For the moment it was calm enough. The girls sat in front of their makeup tables, the lights on around the mirror, casually applying their makeup, still in their loose, casual kimono-like wraps. Tacked to a small cork board in an upper corner of each mirror were small notes of paper, each with swatches of material stapled to it, each note containing all the information necessary to complete each model's costume down even to the color of her panty hose and jeweled accessories. Next to each girl was a rolling clothes rack on which the costumes were hanging in the order they were to be worn. The hairdresser and two makeup artists who would do the final touchup on the models for each change of costume were sitting at the end of the dressing room, looking somewhat bored and vaguely out of it, while Mme. St. Cloud and her assistants anxiously checked every costume on every rack to make sure that they were all in order. Later, just before the show would begin, Philippe would come and make a personal check of each girl and each costume, and once again, after the show had started, each girl would have to pass Mme. St. Cloud and him before she went out on the stage. But at the moment, neither he nor Janette was there.

Jacques let the curtain drop and continued on behind the stage, the faint sounds of the orchestra drifting back to the stage manager's office that Janette had taken over for the night. He opened the door and went in without knocking.

Philippe was seated on the couch, nervously smoking a cigarette, Marlon, as usual, deadpan and unconcerned. Janette was seated behind the desk, staring down at the typewritten list of the costume presentation order. She glanced up. Her voice was calm. "How is it out there?"

"It's everything you want," Jacques said. "You couldn't ask for more."

"Good." She glanced down at the list again, then turned to Philippe. "I think it might be a good idea if we show Twenty-five before Seventeen. It's a mid-length gown and would be better before we go into the full-length gowns.

Right now it's in the middle of all of them and would stick out like a sore thumb."

Philippe rose from the couch and stood behind her. He opened his folder and flipped through the sheets of designs. "You have an idea," he said. "I'll tell St. Cloud to change the order. Time I went in there to check anyway."

He left the room, Marlon following him. Jacques slipped into the chair in front of her. "I think we can use some help," he said, reaching into his pocket.

"You have to be a mind reader," she said.

"Don't worry about it," he said, passing the vial and gold spoon to her. "It's going to be all right."

"I'm not worried about it," she said with a half smile as she carefully spooned two snorts. "I'm just trying to figure a way to stay alive through the night. I'm beat."

"Do it again," he urged. "Then you'll have enough energy to live forever."

She took his advice, then handed the vial back to him and took a deep breath. He could see the color coming back into her cheeks and the brightness into her eyes. "That was good," she said. "You know, you may be right."

He just had time enough to do two snorts and put the vial away before Philippe came back into the room.

"Have either of you seen Lauren?" Philippe asked.

"No," Janette said. "Isn't she out there?"

"Madame St. Cloud hasn't seen her. She's getting worried."

"She must be somewhere around," Janette said. "She came here with me."

Jacques rose from the chair. "I'll check with the concierge at the stage door. No one can make a move in this place without him seeing it."

Philippe sank back on the couch as Jacques left. "All I need is for your stupid sister to fuck up on me," he grumbled.

"You wanted her," Janette said flatly. She lit a cigarette and they sat there in silence until there was a knock at the door and Jacques returned with Lauren behind him.

"Where were you?" Philippe asked, leaping to his feet. "I almost had a heart attack."

"I was getting nervous," Lauren said. "So I went out in the alley behind the theater and had myself a few tokes."

"Jesus! Next time at least let us know where you are," Philippe said. "Come, it's time we got you ready."

Lauren smiled. She looked at Janette. "You weren't worried, were you?"

Janette shook her head.

Lauren laughed. "I feel good now." She turned and followed Philippe through the door.

Janette looked up at Jacques, who was still standing there. "Oh, shit," she said.

Jacques smiled. "*Merde* to you too."

Despite the late start, dinner was finished at ten to midnight and the tables were cleared. The orchestra began to mute and the dancers returned to their tables as the theater gradually darkened. There was a rustle of chairs as the audience made themselves comfortable, and an air of hushed expectancy began to be felt as the theater went to black.

Softly from somewhere behind the stage the overture to *Faust* was heard. It was an almost eerie sound in the blackness. Then, suddenly, there was an explosion, almost like a thunderclap, an invisible spotlight picked up a plume of smoke in center stage before the closed scrim, and out of the puff of smoke came the devil.

He leaped high into the air, his red metallic Lurex body tights like a second skin reflecting tiny sparkling lights around him. Holding his jewel-tipped trident in one hand, he danced toward the center stage as the runway moved out into the audience on giant silent rollers, then he was out on the runway in leaps and bounds, fixing the audience with a baleful gaze and thrusting, threatening gestures of the trident. When he reached the end of the runway, he turned suddenly, knelt and aimed his trident at the curtain of the stage behind him.

A thunderous roll of drums shattered the air, then all was silent as from the projection booth high at the back of the theater came the image reflected on the translucent scrim.

Janette de la Beauville
présente
La Collection de l'Enfer

When the lights came up again the devil was gone and the curtain was rolling back to reveal a giant diorama the whole length of the stage on which had been painted in red and black an impressionistic view of Inferno as Dante might have seen it. A moving backlight gave it a strange feeling of life and reality and in the center of the diorama was an archway over two giant doors. As the doors began to open, the music softened, and the number 1 began to glow as if on fire on top of the arch.

The mannequin stood motionless for a moment, revealed by the opening doors, then stepped slowly forward, down stage toward the runway, as a voice echoed in the sound system around the theater: *"Costume en laine, rouge de sang."*

A polite wave of applause went through the auditorium as the model walked down the runway, paused, took off her jacket to show the blouse, turned in model's stylized fashion and began making her way back up the runway as the glowing number over the arch changed to 2.

Jacques, standing at the back of the theater, nodded to himself. He was pleased. The claque he had hired was also professional. He had told them to begin softly and not to really turn loose except for certain numbers and the finale.

He glanced down at the stage. The second mannequin was already on the runway and the first girl was making her exit. He looked around the audience. They watched attentively. But then, they too were professional. A great deal more would have to be seen before they would pass judgment.

He lit a cigarette. So far, so good. All had been done that could be done. The rest was in the hands of the gods. Then he looked at the stage and smiled to himself. Or the devil.

By the time they were two thirds through the collection a strange, controlled pandemonium had taken over the dressing rooms. Discarded costumes were being picked up from the floor where the models in their frantic need to change threw them and the dressers and makeup girls were frantically trying to maintain the image the mannequins had at the beginning of the show.

Philippe was white, nervous and perspiring as he checked a mannequin and sent her out on stage to wait her turn. "I'm going to be sick," he said dramatically. "I'm going to faint."

"You're okay," Janette said. "Everything's going well."

"You should never have permitted them to come," he said. "They all want to destroy me."

"Don't be silly," Janette said. "It's really a tribute. You don't see them turning out for each other."

"They're going to walk out on me," he said. "I feel it. That way they will show everyone how little they care about me."

"They're all still there," Janette said. "St. Laurent and Berge have not budged since the show began. The same with Bohan and Boussac. Givenchy, Cardin, they're all still there."

"They're planning something," Philippe said. "I feel it." He threw his hand to his forehead. "I feel faint."

Janette glanced at Marlon, then back at Philippe. "Come into my office for a moment."

"I don't dare leave," Philippe said. "Something will go wrong. I know it."

"Nothing will go wrong," she said soothingly. "We're five numbers ready. You can take a few-minute break."

"Okay," he said. "But I want them to start Lauren's body makeup first. It will take a good fifteen minutes."

Janette watched him as he went to Lauren, who was seated at her dressing table, calmly smoking a cigarette, seemingly unaware of the panic and tension around her. He whispered something in her ear and Lauren nodded casually and, rising to her feet, dropped her dressing gown around her and stood nude in the center of the floor. The makeup girl came up quickly and began to spray a base body makeup on her. Philippe said something to the girl, who nodded and continued walking around Lauren with the spray can in her hand.

Philippe came back to Janette. "Okay. I can take five minutes. But I must be back when she applies the gold flecks. I don't want too much, just enough to hint at the life beneath the sheer dress."

They went down to the room that Janette used as an office and Philippe threw himself on the couch. "Never again," he swore. "Never again."

Janette gestured to Marlon to close the door. She opened the desk drawer and came out with a small vial of cocaine. Quickly she spilled some on the glass desk top, then separated it into lines. She picked up the straw and turned to them. *"Allons, mes enfants,"* she said. "We all need the strength."

Philippe was the first at the desk. Expertly he went through four lines before she could stop him. "Leave some for the rest of us."

She did two lines, then Marlon did the rest as Philippe went back to the couch. This time Philippe did not sprawl out. The color came back into his face. He stared at her for a moment, then smiled suddenly. "Mother," he said.

Janette laughed. "My baby."

He came from the couch and kissed her cheek. "I should have known not to worry. I feel better now." He looked at Marlon. "They can go fuck themselves. All of them. Who cares what they think?"

"Right on," Marlon said.

Philippe turned back to Janette. "Another hit for the show."

"You got it," Janette said, emptying the rest of the vial on the glass-topped desk.

Jacques checked his watch. Five minutes to one. It was almost over. He took a deep breath of relief. It had worked. No one had left. They all stayed through to the end. Press and trade alike, all fascinated by something they had never seen before. Slowly he made his way down from the back of the theater to the table near the head of the runway at which Carroll, Maurice, Patrick, Stéphane and Martine were seated. He slipped into the empty chair.

Carroll leaned toward him. "What do you think?" he whispered.

"We made it," he answered. "Eugenia Sheppard and Fairchild both told their papers to hold for the story. Even Bernadine Morris sent a cable that she would file late. And none of the couturiers walked. They're all still here."

"I wonder what they'll say," Carroll said.

"It doesn't matter," Jacques answered. "This will be the most talked-about collection of the season."

"This could be twenty million dollars in the next three years," Carroll said. "It does matter."

Jacques held up a hand. "Watch. We'll talk later."

The mannequin above them was leaving the runway and the glowing number over the archway began to fade. The number was gone by the time she left the stage and over the archway this time appeared the letters glowing as if in fire. *Robe de Mariage.*

There was a momentary rustle of papers, then silence as the doors under the arch slowly opened. A single baby spot hit the bride standing there, tall, regal, hidden completely by a veil falling from a crown on her head, spilling down to the tips of her slim red shoes as she moved forward and trailing the ground behind her in a train that almost seemed to go on forever. Slowly, to the sound of Mendelssohn, she moved to the center of the runway and stopped.

For a moment she was completely still, then with her free

hand, the other still holding the tiny spray of blood-red baccarat roses, she began to raise her veil. It seemed to take almost forever until finally, quickly, she tossed the veil back over her head and it fell to the floor, revealing the translucent rose-colored gown through which shimmered her pale white body sparkling with flecks of gold. She moved her head and her long blond hair fell to her shoulders beneath the rubied tiara as she began once again to move down the runway. Now the light hit her from the stage as well as from the theater. She was naked but not nude, a bride in a gown, moving toward the altar.

"It's Lauren!" Carroll whispered. "I thought Janette was—"

"Janette thought Lauren would be better," Jacques replied.

Now Lauren was turning slowly in the model's turn at the end of the runway. Slowly the applause began to come. Jacques looked around. It wasn't the claque. They were still waiting for his signal. This was the audience.

Lauren turned and started back up the runway, again the model's turn, showing the gown, her body gleaming like ivory under the silk. She started toward the archway and stopped as if in fear, as suddenly the devil came through it.

He stood there, then gestured to her with the trident. As if hypnotized, she moved toward him. Now, they were together and he placed his arms on her shoulders and began to slip the gown down from her body. She stood as if frozen, then as her gold-flecked breasts sprang free of the gown, she flung herself into his arms. With a smile of diabolical triumph, he began to lead her back into the archway. Then, a sudden explosion, a thunderclap, a puff of smoke, and the stage went to black. They were gone.

And the audience went wild.

The houselights came up as the mannequins, each in the last costume she had worn, began coming through the archway on to the stage and down the runway. Lauren was the last to come through, once again in the bridal gown, on the arm of the devil now sporting a rakish top hat in fireman's red.

The applause kept on and photographers were now climbing on the runway, flashbulbs popping as they sought to get their pictures. Suddenly Lauren turned, ran back through the archway, then came out again, this time holding on to a seemingly reluctant Philippe, who was pale and nervous but smiling and pleased all at the same time. The applause grew louder.

Jacques caught the eye of the claque leader, who had been waiting for his signal, and nodded imperceptibly. Almost immediately, the chant began.

"Janette . . . Janette . . . Janette . . ."

Cries of bravo began to rend the air and the clapping settled into a steady rhythm. "Janette . . . Janette . . . Janette . . ."

This time it was Philippe who turned to the archway. He held out his hand and Janette came through to the stage. The glowing light over the archway began to flash her name. She stood there for a moment, smiling as a battery of flashbulbs went off in her eyes. Slim, tall and beautiful, she had dressed in anti-fashion. Red denim jeans and work shirt, calf-length red cowboy boots and a red denim locomotive engineer's work cap. Then she embraced Philippe and together they went down the runway.

More and more photographers and reporters climbed beside them. Soon they were engulfed in a press of people and they began their retreat backstage.

Jacques rose and began to make his way to the theater exit. He wanted to gauge the audience reaction if he could. Once again he stood in the arcade, this time watching them leave the theater, hearing the excited hum of voices.

But it was Fairchild who made the night for him. He took Jacques by the arm and pulled him to one side. "I don't know who's going to buy or even wear the clothes, but this is the most exciting collection in years. She'll have the front page in my paper tomorrow and I would like to talk to her for just ten minutes if you can arrange it."

"When?" Jacques asked.

"Right now," Fairchild said. "I want the first interview with her, exclusive, for the States."

"Let's go," Jacques said, beginning to push his way into the crowd. "Just hang on to my arm."

It was nearly three o'clock, and just a few people remained of the many that had crowded into the small office backstage after the presentation. Philippe was seated on the couch engaged in rapid conversation with two reporters, Marlon hovering protectively over the back of the chair.

Empty champagne bottles and glasses littered the desk behind which Janette, Jacques and Carroll were engaged in deep discussion. "I think we made it," Jacques said. "Both Goodman and Neiman-Marcus want to come in tomorrow to review the line. Saks, Marshall Field and I. Magnin's have expressed interest."

"Looking doesn't cost anything," Carroll said. "Buying is something else."

"They'll buy," Jacques said confidently. "We smell like a winner."

Their conversation came to a halt as several reporters and photographers, having completed all the photos of mannequins and costumes, came into the office wanting the last few words with Philippe and Janette.

Jacques rose to his feet. "Where's Lauren? Charles wants me to talk to her about scheduling a few photo sessions. Every photographer in town wants to do her."

"She was here a moment ago," Janette answered. "I think she went outside with Patrick." He started out but she halted him. "You might as well stay here until the interviews are over. We'll pick them up on our way out."

In the alleyway just outside the stage door, Lauren leaned against the building, drawing deep tokes from the thin joint she held in her fingers. "That helps," she said, passing it to Patrick.

256

He took a toke, then looked at her. "Very good," he said. "You didn't get that here?"

She shook her head. "It's American. Harvey number six."

He drew on the joint again and passed it back to her. "You looked bored in there. That's why I asked you to come out."

"Yeah," she said. "It's really a crock."

"Crock?" he questioned.

"You know. Phony, bullshit, cheek kissing, wonderfuls and darlings. Why do they do it? Nobody really means it. I bet if they said what they really thought, nobody would talk to anybody else."

Patrick laughed. "You don't go much for that kind of life."

"It's not my scene," she said. "I get enough of that at home. My parents are really into these business things too." A thought came to her. "You know, I never really thought that Janette was like that. Somehow I thought she would be different. The pictures I saw and the stories I read about her. She seemed to be having a good time like she never cared about anything else."

"I wish that were true," Patrick said ruefully. "But she really loves her work."

"I don't know what she has to prove," Lauren said. "She doesn't need the money."

"That's what I told her," Patrick said. "But she says that I don't understand."

"Well, I guess I don't understand either," Lauren said, passing the joint back to him. "But maybe it'll get better. She said we'd be going down to her villa in Saint-Tropez after the collections."

"Great," Patrick said. "I can fly you down. My yacht is in port there now. We'll have some fun." He took another toke. "Ouch!" he said, dropping the tiny joint. He looked down at the ground. "Burned my bloody finger. Sorry."

"That's all right," she said. "What do you say we go back into the zoo and see how the inmates are doing?"

The press had all gone by the time they got back to Janette's room backstage. Janette was behind the desk, Carroll and Jacques on chairs in front of her, while Philippe and Marlon were on the couch.

Carroll got to his feet and kissed Lauren on the cheek. "You were beautiful, sweetie," he said enthusiastically. "We've got big things planned for you."

Lauren was puzzled. "I don't understand."

He laughed. "You're a star, baby. The hit of the show. Every photographer in town wants to shoot you. I told Jacques that we do nothing but the best of them."

Lauren turned and looked down at Janette behind the desk. "You never said anything about that to me."

"I didn't know anything about it before the show," Janette answered.

"That's right," Carroll said. "Nobody could have figured it. But there you are. Like it or not, you were the hit of the showing."

"I thought we were going to Saint-Tropez after the collection," Lauren said, looking at Janette. "I told Harvey to meet us there on the weekend."

Before Janette could answer, Carroll spoke. "You can always go to Saint-Tro. The important thing to do now is to strike while the iron is hot."

Lauren was silent for a moment. "I only did the collection for kicks. If I had known there was anything more, I wouldn't have done it."

"But you did do it," Carroll said. "Now you have to stick with it."

Lauren turned back to Janette. "Do I have to? Patrick said he would take us down there on his plane tomorrow. His yacht is already in port."

Janette looked up at her. "You don't have to do anything you don't want to, *chérie*."

Carroll's voice rose angrily. "What the hell do you mean?" he shouted at Janette. "She has to do it. My PR people are

258

already planning to make her the thrust of our promotion plans in the States. I've already called and told them to go to work on it."

Janette met his angry look. "Then tell them to find another angle. Lauren didn't come here to work. She came here to visit me."

"I don't give a damn why she came here!" Carroll yelled. "I'm not blowing two million dollars on this deal to let a stupid kid decide what she should do or shouldn't. You make her do it!"

Janette's voice was deceptively soft. "And if I don't?"

"Then the deal's off!" Carroll snapped. "You might as well learn right now that you don't make decisions alone anymore and that I'm the man in charge."

Janette stared up at him for a moment, then turned to Lauren. "You make plans to go down to Saint-Tropez with Patrick tomorrow."

Carroll stared down at her balefully. "You better think that over. You're into me for one hundred and seventy thousand dollars right now and before you make any decisions you'd better have the money to come up with."

Lauren looked at her sister. "If it's that important, Janette—" she began hesitantly.

Janette stopped her gently. She spoke in French. "Don't worry about it, *chérie*. Sooner or later this pig will have to learn that there are some things his money won't buy." She turned to Carroll and continued in English, "I suggest you think about it. My decision is already made."

"Johann won't like it," Carroll threatened.

"Johann won't like the idea of your using his ward to promote yourself either," Janette said.

"We have a deal," Carroll snapped.

"The deal was with me, not my sister," Janette replied. "And besides, nothing has been signed as yet. So there is no deal really."

"You still have one hundred and seventy thousand dollars of mine," he said.

"Come to the office tomorrow and you'll have it back," Janette said.

"You haven't got the money," Carroll said sarcastically. "I ran a check on your company balances."

"That's none of your business," Janette said. "You come to the office tomorrow and you'll have your money."

He stared down at her. "You can't make a deal with Bidermann or anyone else until I get my money back."

"I know that," she said calmly.

"I'll be at your office nine o'clock tomorrow morning for your check," Carroll said.

"It will be ready," Janette said. "You can pick it up at the treasurer's office."

"It better be a good one," he said nastily, "because I'm taking it right to the bank."

Silently Janette got to her feet and walked around the desk. She stopped in front of Carroll, staring into his eyes. "You pig!" she said in a contempt-filled voice, her open palm moving almost too fast to follow, the sting of her hand echoing in the room as she slapped his cheek. He drew back, the white imprint of her five fingers showing clearly on his ruddy face. "You'd better get out of here before I have you thrown out!"

She was back behind the desk before he had a chance to reply. His hand touched his own cheek. He stared at her. "You're crazy!"

"Get out!" she screamed suddenly. "Or I'll kill you!"

Abruptly he turned and went to the door, then looked back. "Philippe, Marlon," he said. "Let's go!"

Awkwardly the designer and his friend got to their feet. Silently they moved toward the door, neither of them meeting Janette's eyes.

Carroll smiled back at her. "You've really blown it. Philippe has already signed a contract with me starting next year. I thought you might try to screw me so I took no chances."

Without a word, Janette watched the door close behind them, then looked up at Lauren. "Do you mind if Patrick

takes you home?" she asked in a calm voice. "Jacques and I
have some business to finish off tonight."

"I can wait," Lauren said.

"No," Janette answered. "It would be better if you left.
We might be the rest of the night. And you can use some
sleep before Patrick takes you down to Saint-Tropez."

Lauren came around the desk and bent to kiss Janette's
cheek. "I'm sorry. I didn't mean to cause any trouble."

"There's nothing to be sorry about, *chérie*. None of it is
your fault."

"If it will help, I can talk to Daddy," Lauren said.

Janette managed a smile. "Thanks, *chérie*, but that won't
be necessary. I can take care of that worm on my own. Now,
you go and get some rest." She looked up at Patrick. "You
see that she goes right home to bed."

Patrick smiled. "Yes, Mother."

Janette laughed. "That's a good boy. That's the right way
to talk." She turned and kissed Lauren again. "Good night,
chérie. I'll see you in the morning."

Another quick kiss on the cheek and they were gone.
Janette turned to look at Jacques. "Well, here we are again.
Nothing's changed. Just the two of us."

Jacques hit the open palm of his left hand with his right
fist. "The slimy little bastards! They never said a word to us.
I'll ruin the little creep. Wait until I get the word out that
the collection was your idea, not his. They'll all jump on it.
They already know that you rejected his original presentation."

"Philippe is the least of my concerns," Janette said. "We
can always take care of him. Right now I have to get the
money for Carroll."

"Maybe he'll change his mind," Jacques said hopefully.

"Even if he does, I don't want him. If nothing else, this
collection proves that we can make it. Once I pay him off,
I'm sure there's a better deal somewhere."

"It's three o'clock in the morning," Jacques said. "Where
are you going to find a million francs in six hours?"

"A million francs," Janette said thoughtfully. She looked

at him. "Isn't that the figure Maurice mentioned that he had to invest?"

Jacques nodded.

Janette got to her feet. "Then what are we waiting for? Let's go to the Ile Saint-Louis, wake him up and see if he meant what he said."

"You know Maurice," Jacques said. "He's not an easy man to deal with. You'll have to pay for that money. One way or the other."

"Do you have any other ideas?"

"What about your friend Patrick? His family company just bought Kensington Mills in the States. I've heard rumors that they may go into retail. They'll know a good deal when they see it."

"Patrick has nothing to do with the family business. He goes his own way and they go theirs. Neither of them wants to have anything to do with the other. Patrick is out. It has to be Maurice."

She started for the door, then suddenly stopped and looked at him. "Where did we go wrong, Jacques?"

"What's that?" he asked.

"I can't figure it out. Did we win—or did we lose?"

It was only a ten-minute drive from the Lido on the Champs-Elysées to the house and it wasn't until they were almost there that Patrick spoke. "Do you have to go to bed?" he asked. "I'm wired. I can't sleep."

"I'm beat," Lauren said. "Besides, you heard my sister."

"Yes." There was an admiring sound in Patrick's voice. "Did you ever see anything like that? The way she slapped Carroll's face? I thought she would knock his head off."

Lauren laughed. "I wish she had. My sister's got a lot of guts."

Patrick nodded. "She's a very tough lady. I wouldn't like to get on her wrong side. She could really kill a man."

Lauren laughed as the car pulled to the curb in front of the house. "I don't think she would go that far."

The chauffeur jumped out of the car and opened the door of Patrick's big silver Rolls. Lauren leaned over and kissed Patrick's cheek. "See you tomorrow."

Patrick looked at her. "How about letting me touch your quim for just a second? Then I can lick my fingers all the way home and I'll be happy."

Lauren giggled. "Don't be silly," she said, getting out of the car.

Patrick followed her up to the door and waited as she rang the bell. "I wonder what Jacques and Janette are doing right now?"

"She said they still had work to do," Lauren replied.

"I wonder if he has a big prick," Patrick said.

"I don't know. And I don't really care," Lauren said. The door swung open. Quickly she kissed his cheek again. "Good night. See you tomorrow."

"Wait a minute," Patrick said as she started through the door. "What time?"

She turned and looked back at him. "Noon, okay?"

"Noon will be fine," he said. "I'll have the car here to pick you up."

She closed the door behind her and started up the staircase. She turned as the butler called after her.

"Did everything go all right, Mademoiselle Lauren?"

"Beautiful," Lauren answered. "It was the most beautiful evening ever."

H ARVEY ROLLED FROM his mattress out of the blazing
August sun into the shade of the umbrella. "Son of
a bitch!" he said.

Lauren turned her head toward him. "Now, what?"

"Thirty francs for a mattress and an umbrella," he said.
"That's robbery."

Lauren laughed. "That's French."

"What if you just wanted to lay on the sand? Without
anything?"

"Where?" she asked, gesturing to the crowded beach
completely covered by people on mattresses.

"I saw a beach further down. People brought their own
mats and umbrellas."

"You can do that if you want to. That's the public beach,"
she said.

"Why don't we do it?" he asked. "At least, we won't feel
we're being clipped."

"We can try it tomorrow," she said.

"It's the same sun, the same sand, the same water."

"Okay," she said. "Tomorrow."

He looked at her. "Your tits are getting fried."

She sat up, reaching for a sun lotion in her beach bag.
"I'll put some more gook on."

He stared at her. "I guess I'm still not used to it. I never
saw so many tits in my life. Jesus, I wonder what they do
with all the bathing-suit tops they never use."

"I don't know," she said.

"Maybe someone ought to go around buying them up."
He grinned suddenly. "Think of it. I can get a corner on
the bikini-top market."

She laughed. "What would you do with them?"

"I don't know," he said. "I have to think of something."

264

He looked at the can of sun spray she took out. "Wait a minute. I have something better you can use." He fished in his carry bag and came out with a clay jar. He took the cork top from it and held it toward her. "Here, try some of this. But put some water on yourself first."

"What is it?" she asked, looking in the jar.

"Humboldt clay, mixed with some jojoba oil. The Indians use it to heal their skins. It also makes you tan quicker and you won't burn."

She sniffed at the open jar. "Smells funny."

"It's natural," he said. "All that crap you buy has perfume in it."

"Where'd you get it?" she asked.

"It's all over the place up at the farm. Johnny's mother mixes it up herself. They use it for everything. Cuts, insect bites, you name it."

"Does it really work?" she asked skeptically.

"I use it," he said. "And I've only been here two days and I'm darker than you are."

"Okay," she said, getting to her feet. "I'll jump into the water for a minute, then I'll be back and put it on."

He leaned on one elbow and watched her walk down to the water. She seemed different here somehow. It was strange hearing her rattle away in French. In California, the fact that she was French had never even entered his mind. She was just like all the other girls there. But so many things about her had changed in just the month she had been gone.

She even walked differently. Sort of straighter, more of a swing to her hips. Before she would stride, now she walked as if her hips were attached to her legs instead of her waist.

And she was thinner, her rib cage more clearly defined, her pelvic bones thrust forward so that the curve under her belly seemed to flow between her legs in a mound that seemed to rise from her thighs. Suddenly it dawned on him. He knew what it was. She was sexier. In California she had been a girl. Here she was a girl-woman.

Automatically he began fishing in his carry bag for a joint. Then he remembered. This was France. You couldn't smoke joints on the beach. Not only was the law rough but the people were too uptight. Nobody said a word if you drank yourself insensible or fucked your head off, and neither did they care. Neither did they give a damn whether you were gay or not. But if you were going to dope, you stayed in the closet to do it.

She came out of the water and dropped to the mattress beside him. "What do I do?" she asked. "Sprinkle it on me?"

He shook his head. "Put a little on your hands, rub them together until it's a fine paste, then apply it. Spread it very thin. A little goes a long way."

"Okay," she said.

He watched her for a moment. "I'll do your tits if you like."

She laughed. "I can do those myself. But you can do my back if you want."

"Some people are always taking the joy out of life," he grumbled. "Jesus, I'm hungry. When are we going to eat?"

"Patrick should be here any minute," she answered. "He said he would join us for lunch."

"He'll never make it," Harvey said, "the way he was when we left him last night. He was so far out of it that he'll be lucky if he wakes up by the weekend."

"He'll make it," she laughed. "But I still think you shouldn't have laid some of that number eight on him."

"He was asking for it," Harvey said. "He kept saying that none of our shit held a candle to that Moroccan hash he had." He laughed. "Did you see his face after he had just two tokes? He was out to lunch."

She laughed with him. "He sure was. I never saw him like that. But he'll get up and do a few lines. He'll be here all right." She turned away from him. "Now do my back."

Patrick struggled up from sleep. He opened his eyes slowly to the dark of the master cabin. Not a sliver of light slipped through the double curtains hiding the portholes. He reached behind him, pressing a button on the wall behind the giant circular headboard of his bed. Slowly the light began to seep in as the curtains drew back on their electric tracks.

He pushed himself into a sitting position and turned his head, staring at the bare bottom which was all that was revealed by the blankets covering the girl sleeping next to him. He slapped it gently. "Wake up, Anne."

The bottom wiggled at him and the voice came from under the blanket. "It's not Anne, it's Meg."

He slapped the bottom again. "Wake up anyway." He reached for the telephone on the bedstand.

The steward answered. "Good morning, milord."

"Good morning. What time is it?"

"One P.M., milord."

"I'll have some tea," he said.

Meg's voice came, still muffled by the covers. "I'd like some orange juice and coffee."

"And orange juice and coffee," Patrick added.

"Yes, milord. Right away."

Patrick put down the telephone and stared at the girl's bottom. "I say, you have a really cute little bum."

The girl stirred, turning, then sitting up in bed beside him. She shook her head, the long curling ringlets of red hair framing her face. Even her smile betrayed her Irish ancestry, crinkling her freckled white face and the corners of her blue eyes. "That's what you said last night, but then you were asleep before I came out of the loo."

He laughed. "That American friend of Lauren's seems to be handing out time bombs."

"It was your fault," she said. "You kept saying that you wanted a toke."

"I don't remember," he said. "What happened to Anne?"

"She got up early. She said she wanted to go to the beach."

There was a gentle knock at the door and the steward entered with a breakfast tray. "Good morning, milord.

267

Good morning, miss." He placed the tray on the bed between them.

Patrick looked up at the man. "Any messages?"

"Yes, milord. Miss Janette called. She said she would be arriving at the Nice airport on the six o'clock flight this evening with a friend and would you be kind enough to send the helicopter for her."

Patrick nodded. "Do that." He reached for the pot of tea. "Tell the captain to take the boat out to Maurea Beach. I promised some people I would meet them there at two o'clock."

The steward left the stateroom and Meg sat up in bed, the sheet that had been covering her falling to her waist. "May I pour your tea?"

"Please." He watched her pouring the tea, her firm full breasts swelling against her arms as she leaned over the teapot.

"Milk?"

"Yes, thank you," he answered, still looking at the richness of her breasts.

"That all right?" She glanced at him, still holding the small pitcher of warm milk. "You have a funny expression on your face."

"I'm slightly surprised." He smiled, throwing the coverlet from him, revealing his erection. "I have a hard on."

She put down the pitcher and then patted his penis lightly. "That's lovely," she said.

He smiled again. "How about giving me a little head?"

"Of course," she answered. "But can you hold it for just a minute? I can't eat a thing until after I've had my juice and coffee."

Everything seemed to change the moment Janette stepped out of the helicopter on the front lawn. The sun was falling into the mountains in the west behind Sainte-Maxime and it seemed to Harvey as if she had suddenly sprung from the earth beneath her feet as its golden rays

268

shot through the thin white dress whose skirt she held against her thighs as she ran from the downdraft of the slowing rotors.

A moment later, almost before she had finished greeting them, it seemed as if all Saint-Tropez had turned up. Cars began to appear in the driveway, people came as if from all over. Within an hour the quiet of the villa had turned into bedlam, everyone shouting and screaming and laughing, not seeming to listen to anyone else. Or maybe it seemed that way to Harvey because most of the time he did not understand what they were saying. He didn't speak a word of French.

He moved through the crowded living room toward the staircase. Champagne was not his scene. He was going to have himself a few tokes.

Lauren caught him at the foot of the staircase. "Where are you going?"

"I need a smoke," he said.

She glanced around the room, then smiled. "I think I do too."

It was quieter in his room as he closed the door. He rolled the joint quickly and lit it. He dragged on it, then passed it to her. "Is it always like this?"

She shrugged, taking the smoke deeply into her lungs. "I don't know. This is the first time for me."

"I liked it better when we had the place to ourselves," he said.

"It's her house," Lauren said.

"I know," Harvey said. "I'm not complaining. Your sister is something else. Is there anyone in town she doesn't know?"

Lauren giggled. She was feeling the grass. "I guess not."

"Do you like it?" he asked.

"It's not my scene. But, then, like you, I'm just a visitor here." She passed the joint back to him. "That's good. What number is that?"

"It's a new one. Number twelve. Straight up high," he said.

"What's happening with the seedless?"

"We're getting there," he said. "It's just taking time."

"Do you have any more of that Humboldt clay with you? It really works and I'd like Janette to have some."

"Sure," he said. "Is she staying down for long?"

"She's going to New York on Monday. Something just came up. Otherwise she would have stayed for the week."

"She's really into business, isn't she?"

Lauren nodded.

"Who's that girl with her? Stéphane?"

"A girl friend."

"A girl friend, girl friend. Or—?"

Lauren didn't answer.

"Hey, I don't mean to pry," he said.

"It's okay," she said. She walked over to the window. He followed her and they looked down at the helicopter on the lawn. "What do you think of Patrick?" she asked.

"I like him," Harvey said. "He's cuckoo. But he's okay."

"He wants Janette to marry him," she said.

"Oh." He dragged on the joint once more, then passed it again. "I thought he was having a thing with those two girls. You know they're both in his cabin with him."

"Yeah," she answered. "I don't really get it."

"That makes two of us," he laughed. "This is really another world. It sure as hell ain't Paradise Cove."

She laughed with him. "It sure as hell ain't."

It seemed as if no one ever slept. Dinner that night was late aboard Patrick's yacht, the *Fantasist*, in the port of Saint-Tropez. It was buffet style and people seemed to come and go at will. After a while Harvey lost count of the number of guests. At one point he had guessed that there were more than forty.

The noise of the music blaring from the stereo speakers throughout the boat was almost drowned by the sound of voices shouting above it. No one seemed to speak in a normal conversational tone. There was no point to it—if they did, they would not be heard.

The night wore on, the buffet table never seemed to empty, one platter being replaced by another as soon as the food was gone. By midnight everyone was high, and it couldn't have been the wine and champagne alone. There was a smell of smoking dope in the air, not the familiar odor of marijuana but more like opiated hashish to Harvey's trained nose.

It didn't take him long to discover that there was a great deal of rolled, fat English-style hash-and-tobacco mixture being passed around. He immediately tied onto one. It had a good kick to it but not as good as his own.

At one o'clock in the morning they moved to a discothèque called Papagayo at the far end of the port. The floor was jammed with jumping and sweating dancers. A live group blared from the small dance floor on the mezzanine. Here, too, the din prevented conversation and everybody shouted. Harvey, looking at the dance floor, couldn't tell one girl from another. They were all dressed almost alike. Sheer see-through blouses, their breasts showing clearly, tight hot pants or micro-mini short skirts, some with bikini panties underneath, some with nothing, and high-heeled stack shoes or boots, their hair either very long and falling to their shoulders and waists or cut very short in boyish style. In contrast, the men were almost plain, tight black or white slacks and brightly colored printed shirts. Here, too, the odor of hash hung in the air.

Harvey didn't dance. He sat at the uncomfortable little table, nursing a glass of champagne he had no taste for, watching the action on the floor. In France, boys danced with boys, girls with girls, or they danced solo and no one seemed to pay any attention. He watched Lauren moving on the floor; she seemed to stand out from the others. The French seemed to bob up and down to the music almost like puppets on a string, while she seemed to flow with the rhythm. She was smiling up at Patrick, who was dancing with her.

He searched the floor for Janette. Neither she nor her girl friend were on the floor. After a moment, he caught sight of them coming from the washrooms toward the table. Janette whispered something to her girl friend, who continued on to the dance floor and began to dance alone. Janette sat down beside him.

"Are you enjoying yourself?" she asked, her voice carrying through the din.

He nodded, looking at her. Her eyes were bright. He raised a finger, moistened it, then touched the side of her nose lightly. He tested his finger and smiled. "You waste a lot of powder."

She laughed. "How did you know?"

"It takes one to know one," he said. "Now, if you like, when we get home, I have some really special stuff."

"I heard," she said. "Lauren told me all about you. What we get here in France is not that good. But it's better than nothing."

"I guess so," he said. "But it's cut with speed or strych. I don't like it. You come down too hard."

Patrick and Lauren came back to the table. "It's getting dull here," Patrick said. "What say we go over to the Cave du Roi?"

Janette shook her head. "I don't think so. Jacques is coming down from London in the morning and we have some business to discuss."

"I thought you were down for a weekend of fun," Patrick said reproachfully.

Janette smiled. "I am having fun. You all go on. I'll go back to the villa."

"Wouldn't hear of it," Patrick said. "We'll all go with you."

By the time they reached the villa it was after three o'clock in the morning and there were more than fifteen people with them. Almost as soon as they entered, the record player went on and the hash bombers appeared. There was enough smoke in the room to get stoned just by breathing. They might just as well have not left the discothèque,

272

because the furniture was pushed back and they continued dancing. Soon everyone was hot and sweating and some of the girls began to remove their tops. First Meg and Anne, the two girls with Patrick, then the others, until only Lauren and Janette had their blouses on.

The party spilled outside onto the terrace, then suddenly everyone was naked in the swimming pool. Lauren came and stood beside him as he watched the others, splashing in the pool. "What do you think?" she asked.

He looked at her. "I see it but I don't believe it." She laughed. "You seem pretty straight," he said.

"I can't get off on their shit," she said.

"Like everything else, it's what you get used to," he answered. He glanced around. "Where's your sister?"

"She's gone to bed," Lauren answered. "Why?"

He gestured. "Her girl friend's going down on another girl over there at the far end of the pool."

Lauren followed his gaze. She was silent for a moment. "That's not my problem," she said.

Patrick came toward them. "I'm getting hungry. How about going down to Le Gorille for some ham and eggs?"

"Great idea," Lauren said. "I'm starved."

"Not me," Harvey said. "I think I'll turn in. I'm just a country boy. I'm not used to these hours."

Jacques had not lost any time. Janette was in the swimming pool at eleven o'clock in the morning when he arrived. Meticulously she followed her routine, the one she maintained throughout all the years she had spent time in the south of France. Every morning she faithfully swam fifty laps of the pool. Out of the corner of her eye she saw him approach, but she did not get out to greet him until she had finished the final lap. Then she climbed from the pool, the sun bathing her in its morning glow as she wrapped the large towel around her naked body.

"The body still looks fantastic," he said.

"It takes work," she answered. "I'm not getting younger."

He laughed. "You have a long way to go."

She walked to the table and picked up the bell lying on it. "Have you had breakfast?"

"On the plane," he said. "But I'll have coffee with you."

The houseman came out and Janette ordered coffee. She sat down in a chair opposite Jacques, towel-dried her hair, then shook it to finish drying in the sun. She reached for the pack of cigarettes on the table and lit one. "How did it go in London?"

"Better than we had hoped," he answered. "We have orders for approximately fifty thousand pounds."

She nodded. Ten, fifteen thousand pounds was their average in London. "We'll make money this year," she said. "But we still have the problem. Where do we go from here? Maurice wants me to talk to Johann."

"Maybe you won't have to," Jacques said. "I took a chance and called John Fairchild. He got very excited. As you know, he loved the collection. And he also loves the power of being a king maker. He himself made a call to the president of the Kensington Mills, and within one hour I was called back."

The houseman brought the coffee and left. She filled his cup, then her own. "Do you think they're really interested?" she asked. "Or are they just being polite to Fairchild?"

"They're hot," he said emphatically. "I could sense it in their voices. Why else would they set a full-scale meeting with the executive vice-president, the president and the chairman of the board? Kensington is a big company, the second-largest manufacturer of artificial fibers in the world after Du Pont, the second-largest manufacturer of cotton cloth after Burlington Mills. They have plants all over the world and turn out everything from the finest and most expensive quality to the cheapest. They're not just being polite to anyone. And, even more important, they're obviously not interested in going into anything they don't think has a major market potential for their product."

She was silent a moment. "I hope you're right. Yesterday it was almost as if the world was coming to an end."

"It wasn't," he said. "I'm returning to Paris tonight. I'll get our things together and meet you at Orly Monday morning."

After he had left, she stretched out on an air mattress to take in the sun. Less than a moment later, a shadow fell across her eyes. She opened them. Harvey was standing there. "Good morning," she said, making no move to cover herself.

"Good morning," he said. He held out a jar toward her. "Lauren thought you might like to have this."

She sat up and took it from him. "What is it?"

"It's a clay from northern California. The Indians used to use it to protect their skins and heal wounds. I found out that it's the best tanning stuff I've ever used."

She took the cork from the bottle. "It looks like dirt to me."

He laughed. "It is dirt. And don't pay attention to the smell. It goes away in a moment after you moisten it with water and put it on."

"Does it really work?" she asked doubtfully.

"It's worked on me and Lauren," he said. "It also seems to make you dark quicker without burning. Put some on now. You're all white. You'll see how quickly it works."

"Okay," she said. She dipped her hand into the pool, then mixed a little of the clay in her hands and began to rub it on her shoulders. "Like this?"

"Even thinner. You don't have to coat yourself. And you can use it on your face too." He straightened up. "Did Lauren come down yet?"

"I haven't seen her," Janette answered.

"She wasn't in her room," he said.

Janette smiled. "You sound worried."

"I'm not," he denied quickly. "But usually we meet early to go to the beach before the crowds."

"Did she go to the port with the others for breakfast?" Janette asked.

"Yes," he answered. "But that was at four this morning."

"Then she was probably too tired to come back and

stayed on Patrick's boat. Chances are they'll be at the beach by the time we get there."

He nodded.

She finished covering the front of her body with the clay and rolled over on her stomach. "Will you do my back?"

"Sure." He knelt and began to spread the thin film of clay over her. He stopped just short of her buttocks, skipped over them and continued on down her legs.

She turned her head to look up at him. "Don't do a half-ass job." She smiled. "That can get sunburned too."

Janette had been right. The *Fantasist* was anchored off the beach when they got there. Lauren, Patrick and his two girls were already stretched out on their mattresses. Lauren was the only one awake—the others were fast asleep.

Lauren got to her feet as they approached. There was a note of excitement in her voice. "Patrick wants to take us to Sardinia on the boat."

"Where's that?" Harvey asked.

"In Italy," Lauren answered. "Patrick says the beaches are not as crowded and the water is a lot cleaner."

"Wonderful," Janette said. "It will be fun and Sardinia is quite beautiful. We can all meet here next weekend. I'll be back by then."

Patrick opened his eyes, shielding them from the sun with the palm of his hand. He squinted at Janette. "Your sister is nuts," he grumbled. "She woke us up this morning at eight o'clock."

"You didn't have to get up," Lauren said.

"No one can ever accuse me of being impolite to my guests," he said. He turned back to Janette. "What's this about you going to New York?"

"I have to," Janette said. "But I'll be back by the weekend."

"Shit," Patrick said. He sat up. "I might as well give up ever expecting you to spend some time with us."

Janette smiled. "You never can tell."

He looked into Janette's eyes. "And after all the goodies I had in store for you."

She laughed. "Isn't it you English who have the saying 'Business before pleasure'?"

"I never heard it," he said.

"You never had to," she replied. "Now, be a good boy and don't sulk. You go to Sardinia and have a good time. Mama will come back on the weekend and we'll have our chance then."

Patrick shook his head. "Next week it will be something else."

Janette laughed. "Don't be a pessimist or you'll convince me you gave your boat the wrong name."

Patrick's two girls left the boat on the second day they were in Porto Cervo. Harvey came out on deck at eight o'clock in the morning and saw them standing on the rear deck while their luggage was being carried down the gangplank to a waiting car. "Hey, where are you two going?" he asked.

"Back to Saint-Tro," Meg answered.

"What's the rush? We'll be back there on the weekend."

Anne looked at him with a kind of contempt. "Patrick's decided to become a monk. He's kicked us out of his cabin."

"Besides we didn't come down here to lay around on the boat every night bored out of our minds. All he wants to do is smoke dope and talk philosophy with your girl friend," Meg added.

"I didn't notice them talking that much," Harvey said.

"How would you?" Meg asked scornfully. "You're always more stoned than they are."

The last of their bags went down the gangplank. Anne looked at Harvey. "Well, ta-ta, old dear. And if you want a little advice, keep an eye on your girl friend or Vicar Patrick will convert her out of your life."

He watched them go down the gangplank and get into the car. The car moved down the pier and then turned up

277

a road and out of sight. He went back inside the main-deck salon and then to the dining salon. He sat down at the table.

"Bacon and scrambled eggs, sir?" the steward asked.

He almost agreed before he remembered he was a vegetarian. "No bacon," he said quickly. "Just the scrambled eggs." Now that he thought about it, the girls weren't all wrong. It seemed that almost every time he was with them, Lauren and Patrick were in deep discussion. Absently he ate the eggs. What in hell did they have so much to talk about?

"All my life I've been hearing about my father," Patrick said. "From the time I first went to Eton they began making comparisons. And none of them were good.

"I kept telling them I wasn't my father. I was me. I was different. But that didn't matter to them. I had to be my father. So finally I told them all to fuck off."

Lauren lay naked on her stomach in the sand of the deserted beach. She turned her head on her arms so that she could look at him. "Didn't you ever want to do anything?"

"What was there left for me to do?" Patrick asked, his eyes studying the lovely curve of her derrière. "My father did everything."

Lauren put her face back in her arms. "There has to be something you want to do," she said.

"Of course there is," Patrick said.

"What's that?" she asked, her voice muffled by her arms.

"I'd love to run my tongue down your crack from your asshole to your quim and back," Patrick said.

She laughed. "I mean, seriously."

"I'm serious," he said.

"I told you I'm not into friendly fucking," she said. "I think it should mean something more than just a sport."

"Don't tell me you've never fucked Harvey," he said.

"I didn't say that," she answered. "But we're not into it on a steady basis. Once in a while, when we're in the mood. But not that much. We love each other but not that way."

278

"I'm not asking for that much either," Patrick said. "Just a little taste to sort of reassure me that you do like me."

She turned around, laughing. "I do like you," she said. "But I'm not ready to fuck you yet. So stop being a pain in the ass and give me that jar of Humboldt clay before I begin to fry."

"Why don't you just lie back and let me put it on you?" he asked.

She laughed again. "Oh, no. You'll only get turned on—then we'll have an argument."

"I promise to keep tight control of myself at all times," he said.

She looked at him. "You mean it?"

"Cross my heart," he said, making the gesture.

"Okay." She lay back in the sand and closed her eyes. After a moment, she felt the moist coolness of the clay on his hand as he spread it carefully over her. It was good especially over her sun-warmed breasts. She felt the warmth going into her. It was really a good feeling. In spite of herself she felt her nipples hardening and the warmth growing between her legs.

Abruptly she sat up and took the jar from his hand. "That's enough," she said in a firm voice.

"Why?" he asked in an injured voice. "I was keeping my word."

"That's right," she said, applying the clay to herself. "But I was turning on. And it's not time for me yet."

Suddenly he was angry. "You're getting to be more like your sister every day," he snapped. "You're nothing but a prick teaser."

She stared at him for a moment unable to speak. Then she felt the tears welling into her eyes and she turned her face away from him. "Is that what you really think?" she asked in a tight, hurt voice.

"What do you expect me to think?" He was still angry. "You parade naked in front of me like I'm not even human. How am I supposed to feel?"

"I didn't think it was anything," she said. "The other girls are naked all the time too. Nobody seemed to pay any attention to it."

"I don't give a damn about the other girls," he said. "That's why I sent them away."

"That's your business," she said in the same tight voice. "I didn't ask you to do it."

"No, you didn't," he said. "I never thought of that. Maybe you are more like Janette than I even thought. Maybe all you're into is girls or big pricks."

She jumped to her feet quickly, pulling on her bikini, then began to run down the beach away from him. He ran after her, caught her and spun her around to face him. "Where do you think you're going?" he asked.

"Anywhere!" she snapped. "Just to get away from you. You're really sick!"

He saw the genuine hurt and the tears in her eyes and was as suddenly contrite as he had been angry. "I'm sorry. I didn't mean it the way it sounded. I was angry."

She shook herself free of his grasp. "Leave me alone," she cried. "I want to go back to the boat."

"I'm really sorry," he said. "Look, I like you a lot. More than I even thought I did or could. Please don't be angry with me. It won't happen again."

She held the back of her hand to her nose and snuffled, looking up at him. "You didn't mean what you said about my sister, did you?"

"Of course not," he said firmly. "I was just getting as frustrated with you as I did with her. You know how I really feel about her."

"How do you feel about her?"

"I love her," he said slowly, meeting the searching look in her eyes. "But I'm not in love with her," he added softly. "I'm in love with you."

Book Four

Madame

W HEN HE CAME out of the bathroom she was seated, naked, on the edge of the bed, holding a small mirror in one hand while with the other she carefully restored her eye makeup.

He stopped, staring down at her, the towel tied around his waist still damp against his skin. "What are you doing?" he asked, his harsh Greek accent overriding his French.

"Putting on my makeup," she answered, without taking her eyes from the mirror.

"What for?" he asked. "I thought you were staying for the night."

"I changed my mind," she said, still not looking up.

"We had business to talk about," he said. "You don't expect me to decide on a ten-million-dollar deal with one quick fuck."

"That's right," she agreed. She stood up and looked down at him. She was a full head taller than he. "You've already got what you wanted. Now you don't have to waste your time on all the bullshit. And neither do I."

She walked past him into the bathroom and squatted across the bidet. Quickly she turned on the taps and the water began to swirl into the bowl.

He followed her and watched while she took the washcloth and began to soap herself. "Is that the only reason you went to bed with me? The money?"

She looked up at him, meeting his gaze without blinking. "Can you think of a better reason? I don't care if you're ten times richer than Onassis ever was. You're even uglier and not half as attractive."

"You're nothing but a whore," he said insultingly.

She didn't answer.

"Even if your cunt was lined with gold and diamonds, what makes you think it would be worth ten million dollars?"

"I don't think anything," she said evenly, letting the soapy water out and turning the taps on again. "You're the one that just ate it and fucked it. You tell me." She looked down and turned off the water, then up at him. "Besides, I came here to talk business with you. Not to fuck with you. That was your idea."

"Bitch!" he snapped and stalked angrily from the bathroom.

When she came out of the bathroom a few minutes later, he was in a dressing robe, seated in an armchair, sipping at a snifter of cognac. Silently he watched her pick up the camisole top and slip it on, covering her magnificent breasts, then snap the narrow garter belt around her waist and sit down on the edge of the bed facing him as she carefully put on her stockings. In spite of his anger he felt the heat rising again in him. The bitch knew all the tricks. No bikini panties ever covered her. Never wore them, she had said. She stood up and fastened her wraparound skirt and then buttoned the simple white silk shirt over it. She stepped into her high-heeled shoes.

"Janette," he said.

She looked down at him without speaking.

"I did want to talk business with you."

She spoke without rancor. "There's really nothing to discuss. You've had the papers for more than two weeks now. I'm sure your financial people have gone over it and that you've already made up your mind. And I think I've answered the only question that had been left open. Now all you have to do is to say yes or no."

"It's not quite as simple as that," he said.

"Maybe," she answered with a typically Gallic shrug. "Your problem may be complicated, but mine is simple. I need ten million to buy back distribution of my line before Kensington sells me out to the Japanese. *Au revoir,* Nico."

His voice stopped her at the door. "What will you do if I don't give you the money?"

She looked back at him and smiled slowly. "I'll manage," she said quietly. "This isn't the first time I've been in a situation like this. And it may not be the last. But I've always survived."

"I'll call you in the morning," he said. "Maybe something can be worked out."

"Don't bother," she said quietly. "I think I already know the answer. And so do you."

He watched the door close behind her, took another sip of his cognac, then went to the window and looked out into the street. She came out of the house and he watched as her chauffeur opened the door for her to get into the car. He stood there until the Rolls limousine turned the far corner and was gone from his sight then heavily walked back into the room. A strange sadness came over him. If only this could have happened when he was twenty years younger. There weren't many women like that a man could meet in one lifetime. It could have been quite beautiful.

She sank into the soft leather of the right corner of the passenger compartment of the Rolls and lit a cigarette. Thoughtfully she looked out the window at the empty streets of Neuilly as the car made its way toward the *auto-route* to Paris. Strangely enough she felt neither depressed nor disappointed at the outcome of her visit with the Greek. From the very beginning of their discussions she had known she would never get an answer until she had gone to bed with him. That was the way it had to be. A man like Nico Caramanlis would never be satisfied until everything had been checked out.

Still, it was worth the trying. One never really knew. And there weren't many men around who had the kind of money she was looking for. Greeks and Arabs. They seemed to be the only people who managed to prosper in this torn up economic world of chronic energy shortages.

And of the two, she preferred the Greeks. At least they weren't as foreign. They were European.

She glanced at the clock as the car moved onto the *autoroute*. The glowing dial read nine forty-five. She pressed a button and the window separating the driver's compartment from the passenger's rolled up and closed. She took the telephone from the console between the two jump seats and called home.

"*Résidence de la Beauville,*" the butler's voice answered.

"*C'est* Madame," she said. "Any messages?"

"Only one, Madame," he answered. "The marquis called and asked that you return his call as soon as possible whatever time you came in. He said it was very urgent and that he would be at home all night."

"Thank you, Jules," she said, putting down the telephone. She hesitated a moment before calling Maurice. She didn't really feel like talking to anyone just now. But then, she picked up the telephone and placed the call.

His husky voice came on the phone. "*Oui?*"

"It's Janette."

His voice grew excited. "Where are you? I've been trying to get you all afternoon."

"I'm on the *autoroute* from Neuilly," she said.

He chuckled. "You were fucking with the Greek. I could have told you that was a waste of time."

"How do you know that it was?" she asked.

"It's ten minutes to ten," he said. "If there was anything you would still be there."

She was annoyed. "I'm calling because you said it was urgent."

"It is," he said. "I must talk with you. Can you come here tonight?"

"Can't it wait until tomorrow?" she asked.

"No," he said. "Remember what we spoke about some years ago when I gave you the million francs?"

"We spoke about many things," she answered cautiously.

"I don't want to speak on the telephone," he said. "It has

286

to do with your mother and the Swiss banks. I have a man here who has some interesting information for us but he won't give it to anyone but you."

She thought for a moment, then she remembered. Maurice had some wild idea that her mother had a fortune in gold secreted away in a Swiss bank. He also had an idea that Johann had known about it and kept the money for himself. "I'll be there," she said. "It should take me about an hour."

She put down the telephone and rolled down the compartment window. "René."

"*Oui*, Madame," he answered without looking back.

"We'll go to the marquis' apartment on the Ile Saint-Louis."

"*Merci bien*, Madame."

She pressed the button again and the window went up. There wasn't any traffic on the *autoroute*. It shouldn't take more than an hour. Quickly she opened her bag and searched through it for the small vial. If she was going to deal with Maurice it wouldn't hurt for her to be more alert.

Cupping her hands so that she could not be seen in the rearview mirror, she took two quick snorts, then slipped the vial back in her purse and leaned back. A moment later she felt her head open up. A flood of memories rushed through her brain.

Six years ago. Then it was paying off Carroll and finding the money to stay in business. Now it was paying Kensington Mills so that she could retain control of her own business before they sold it down the river in a merger with another giant conglomerate. Nothing had changed except success.

And at this point in time, the net result of success was that it had driven up the cost of freedom. Ten million dollars. Six years ago it had cost only a little more than a million dollars. But then there were Lauren and Patrick.

Now there was no one but herself.

IT HAD BEEN six years since the night of the red collection, after which she and Jacques had gone to see Maurice. Oddly enough he was awake and seemed to be expecting her. He had come right to the point. "You blew the deal with Carroll?"

"Yes," she answered.

"Then you know that Philippe has signed with him?"

Surprise echoed in her voice. She glanced at Jacques, then back at him. "How did you know?" But even as she asked the question she knew the answer. The "pedes" had their own grapevine and there were no secrets in their world.

He smiled without answering. His man came in with a tray on which there were coffee and sandwiches, placed the tray on a coffee table and left the room. Maurice gestured. "I thought you might want something to eat."

She looked at him. "What else do you know, Maurice?"

"He got to Philippe through Marlon," he answered. "But that doesn't matter now. *C'est fait.* It is done." He went to the coffee table and filled the cups, then held one out to her. "Take some," he said almost gently. "A hot drink will do all of us some good."

"Thank you." She sipped at the hot coffee. He was right. She began to feel better.

"How much will it take to get Carroll off your back?" he asked.

"A million francs," she said.

He looked at her for a long moment, then, without speaking, he went to his desk and opened a drawer. Quickly he took out a checkbook and wrote in it, then held the check out to her.

She looked down at it. One million francs. Then at him. "I don't know what to say."

He smiled again. "You don't have to say anything. We're a family."

She shook her head in disbelief. This wasn't Maurice. She was silent.

"But that only takes care of Carroll," he said. "It doesn't solve the real problem. Where do you go from here?"

"I'll find another association," she said. "After tonight's collection there should not be too much of a problem."

"Patrick's company, the Reardon Group, just bought Kensington Mills in the States and I heard they're interested in going into *prêt à porter*," Jacques said. "I'm sure Patrick will be of help there. And there are others."

"It has to be fast," Maurice said. "You can't afford to lose the momentum this collection has given you."

"I know that," Janette said. "Jacques is going to London tomorrow morning to look into the situation there."

Jacques glanced at her but didn't speak. This was the first he had heard of it.

"In that case perhaps Jacques should go home and get some rest so that he can make an early start," Maurice said with a smile.

"I'll be all right," Jacques said quickly.

Maurice smiled again. "I'm sure you will be. But there are some things I would like to discuss with Janette. Personal family matters."

Jacques looked at her. She nodded almost imperceptibly. "I'll do that," he said. He held out his hand to Maurice. "I'd like to add my thanks to Janette's."

"You don't have to," Maurice said. He waited until the door had closed behind him, then gestured to a chair in front of his desk. "Sit down. You must be exhausted."

She sank into the chair and looked at him silently.

"Would you like a cognac?" he asked.

She nodded.

He filled two snifters, handed one to her, then sat down behind his desk. He raised his glass. "Cheers."

She sipped at the liquor. It felt warm and good going down. She still didn't speak.

"Is Lauren staying in Paris?" he asked.

She shook her head. "No. She's leaving tomorrow for Saint-Tropez with Patrick. I'm not going down until the weekend."

He nodded. "This collection should do well. With luck I think you might make some money this year."

"As soon as we do, you'll have your money back," she said.

He waved his hand. "It's not important. I'm really not concerned about it."

She took another sip of the cognac. "Okay, Maurice. We're alone now. You can stop playing games. Exactly what is it that you want?"

He laughed. Then the laughter faded from his voice. "Money. What other reason could I have?"

"How much?" she asked.

"Twenty million dollars," he said.

She stared at him. "You're crazy. There isn't that kind of money in my business."

"I'm not interested in your business," he said. "I want no part of it. I don't even care whether you pay me back or not."

"Then where do you expect me to find that kind of money?" she asked.

"In a Swiss bank," he said. "When your mother left France to go to Switzerland to meet the general, she left in an automobile whose sides and doors were filled with gold napoleons. None of that money ever turned up."

"How do you know that?"

"I know it," he answered. "I've never been able to prove it."

"Did you ask my mother?"

"Yes," he answered. "But of course she denied it. The way she felt about me, I couldn't expect her to say anything else." He was silent for a moment. "Johann knows where it is."

She stared at him. "What makes you think that?"

He smiled. "He bought you out, didn't he?"

"He got that money from his father-in-law."

"That's what he wanted everybody to think," Maurice said. "But I checked into it. He didn't get anything from his father-in-law. Not until after he took the company and merged it with the old man's."

"If it's true," Janette said, "how am I going to find out about it?"

"I don't know," Maurice said. "But sooner or later it will have to come out. In time, everything does. And when it does, I'm your partner."

She finished her cognac. "I can't believe it."

He smiled at her. "Believe it or not, is it a deal?"

She laughed. "If that's all you want, it's a deal."

"I'll have an agreement drawn in the morning," Maurice said. "We'll both sign it."

"You really believe it, don't you?" she asked.

"Yes," he said.

She rose from her chair. "It's been a long day. I think it's time for me to go."

He didn't get out of his chair. "Remember when you were a girl you used to wear black bikini panties for me? Do you still wear them?"

"No." She smiled down at him. "I'm a grownup now. I don't wear any."

He laughed, getting out of his chair and following her to the door. He held it open for her. She turned and kissed his cheek. "Good night, Maurice."

He looked up at her. "The next time you see Johann, why don't you just ask him about it?"

"I haven't seen him in almost ten years. What makes you think I might see him now?"

"One never knows," he said. "But if you do, just remember to ask him."

Then, a week later, after the weekend in Saint-Tropez, she did see Johann. But she never brought it up. It was all too ridiculous for anyone to believe.

She opened the door and he stood there, the shock of time running backward holding him immobile. Tanya. He almost spoke the name aloud. She was her mother.

"Johann!" she exclaimed, taking him by the hand and leading him into the suite. Closing the door behind him, she kissed him on both cheeks. "Johann," she said again.

Suddenly he felt awkward and stiff, just as he had felt with her mother. "Janette," he said. And when he spoke her name aloud, the strangeness he felt left him. He blinked his eyes rapidly. "I'm genuinely happy to see you," he said and meant it.

She smiled. And that, too, was her mother's smile. "I never thought you would be in New York."

"I came in for a board meeting," he said. "And when I heard you were in town, I had to call."

"I'm glad you did," she said. "Can I offer you a drink?"

"Just coffee," he answered. "I have other meetings this afternoon."

"You haven't changed," she smiled. "I have the coffee waiting." They went to the table and sat down. For a moment he glanced out the window. It was a hot summer day in New York. Central Park was crowded, and the buildings on the West Side shimmered in the heat, but in the enclosed suite on the twenty-second floor of the Pierre, the air conditioning was silent and comfortable.

She studied him as she poured the coffee. Johann had changed. There was a quiet sense of self about him that she had never felt before. Perhaps because his once-blond hair was grayer, perhaps because he was slightly heavier, perhaps because his dress was American, less formal than it had been in Europe. But even more perhaps because he was content.

"No sugar," he said smiling. "I have to watch my weight."

She laughed. "We all do."

292

He took the cup. "Tell me about Lauren. Is she enjoying herself?"

"I think so," Janette answered. "Right now, she's on the yacht of a friend of mine in Sardinia. I met them in Saint-Tropez on the weekend."

"Is her friend there?"

"Harvey?" she asked.

"Yes."

She nodded.

"Lauren's known him for years," he said. "Heidi always worries about him. She thinks he's a bad influence on her."

Janette smiled. "I don't think Heidi has anything to worry about. Harvey's a sweet boy and Lauren leads him around by the nose, not the other way around."

Johann laughed. "I keep telling her that."

"How is Heidi?" Janette asked.

"Very well," Johann answered. "We are both well. And very fortunate." He glanced around the suite. "I thought Jacques might be here."

"He had to go out to some meeting," Janette said. "He asked me to give you his regards and apologies for not being able to wait for you."

"I understand," Johann said. He looked at her. "What happened between you and Carroll?"

"Didn't he tell you?"

Johann nodded. "Of course. But that was his version. I would like to hear your side."

"There is no side," Janette said. "He just wanted me to do certain things I would not do."

"Such as?"

She met his gaze. "He wanted me to make a promotion through Lauren. I said that was not in our agreement—that what she did in the collection was a one-time thing for her and not a way of life. He became incensed at that and began to insist. I gave him back his money. That's the whole of it."

Johann nodded. He sipped at his coffee again. "He told me that Philippe Fayard is leaving you to join him."

"That's true," Janette said.

"Will that hurt you?" he asked. "Because I can stop him if you want me to."

Janette shook her head. "You don't have to do anything. Philippe's contract was up this year and I was not planning to renew it. In many ways I have outgrown him and I feel that couture is moving in a completely different direction. I want to be free to follow it without having to fight my own designer at every turn. That was one thing I learned from the last collection."

"But financially? I heard you were having problems."

"True enough," she said. "But I'll solve them. At least we'll make a great deal of money this year. That will help."

"You know, you can always call on me," he said.

She looked at him for a moment, then blinked her eyes and nodded. "I've always known that, Johann," she said. "Even when I was at my bitchiest."

Jacques sat morosely in his seat next to Janette as Air France 070 lifted from the runway at Kennedy International Airport into the skies over New York. Janette turned from the window to look at him. "We're passing over the Statue of Liberty."

"If I had my way, we'd take it back," he said, scowling.

In spite of herself, she had to smile. "We didn't lose anything," she said. "And we learned a great deal."

"Sure we did," he said bitterly. "We learned how stupid and naive we really are."

"You'll feel better when you have a drink," she said.

"I need more than that," he said. "As soon as they turn the seat-belt sign off, I'm going to the john and have a couple of strong toots."

She laughed. "I'll be right behind you."

"Damn!" he said. "How could we have been so stupid? It

was Givenchy they wanted all the time. They didn't even have the decency to tell us that the Reardon Group was already negotiating with him."

"I don't blame them for that," she said. "If I were in their position I would rather go with Givenchy than Janette. After all, he has already proven himself. And he is one of the best."

"They dragged us all the way over just to pick our brains," he said.

"We picked theirs too," she said. "At least now we know what they're looking for. Besides they haven't signed with Givenchy yet. Maybe they never will. He has a great deal more to be independent about than we have."

A faint bell announced the seat-belt light going off. Jacques got to his feet. "A double scotch on the rocks," he said to the stewardess as he started for the washroom.

"Champagne," Janette said, rising also. She waited outside the lavatory door and took the small vial from his hand as he came out. "Feel better now?"

"It helps," he said grumpily. "So far that's the only good thing about this trip."

She locked the door behind her and looked into the mirror. The washroom lights on airplanes were never the most flattering. She looked tired. There were faint dark shadows under her eyes. She opened the vial and, using his gold spoon, took a snort. She breathed deeply, letting the cocaine get into her. She felt the lift. She put a tiny bit on her finger and rubbed it into her gums. She liked the taste. She closed the vial carefully and put it in her bag.

She looked into the mirror once again. She did not appear so tired now. Quickly she checked her makeup—a little powder under her eyes on her cheekbones, lip gloss, and she was ready to go back to her seat.

Jacques rose to let her into her seat. He handed her the glass of champagne and raised his drink. "Cheers," he said. "You look better."

"Shows you what a little makeup will do," she laughed.

They both sipped at their drinks. "Now what?" Jacques asked.

She shrugged. "We'll see. At least we're making money this year so we're in no immediate trouble."

"Do you think Johann meant it when he told you that you can go to him for money?" he asked.

"I'm sure that he did," she said. "But I'm not going to. It would mean living in my mother's shadow forever and never being on my own."

He was silent for a moment. "Too bad your friend Patrick has nothing to do with his family's business. If he did, we probably could pull it off."

She looked at him thoughtfully. Patrick had his own quirks. But under the right circumstances they could be made to work for her. At this point there was nothing to lose. "Maybe we still can," she said.

The lights were on but the villa seemed empty when Lauren and Harvey came through the front door around midnight. Harvey put down their valises. "Maybe she's not back from New York yet," he said.

"She said she would be back on the weekend," Lauren answered.

Janette's voice came from the balcony at the top of the staircase. "Lauren?"

"Yes," Lauren called back. "I hope we didn't wake you."

"You didn't," Janette said. "I got a call from a friend at L'Escale about a half hour ago that you had just come into port, and I was getting dressed to go down and join you. Is Patrick with you?"

"No," Lauren answered. "Just Harvey. Patrick was going to turn in early. Everything go all right in New York?"

"Fine," Janette said. "I saw Johann. He sends you his love. Did you have fun in Sardinia?"

"It was great," Lauren said. "The beaches are big and quiet. Not like here."

Janette came down the staircase. She was wearing a Saint-Tro outfit, sheer black see-through blouse and a tight-fitting black leather micro-mini skirt. Her eyes were bright, and there were flecks of golden glitter on the makeup on her cheekbones. "What about the night life?" she asked. "I heard a great new discothèque opened there."

"We never went out at night. Once or twice to a restaurant but mainly we stayed on the boat," Lauren answered. "It never seemed as if very much was happening."

"That doesn't sound very much like Patrick," Janette said. "He usually never wants to stay in."

"I'm going to bed," Harvey announced. "It will feel good to sleep one night in a bed that isn't moving. I still feel as if I'm walking on a deck."

"You'll be over it in the morning," Janette laughed as he started up the steps.

Lauren waited until she heard the door of his room close, then turned to Janette. "I have a joint here. Would you like to share it?"

"Of course," Janette answered. She looked at Lauren as she lit the joint. "Is everything all right? You look very serious."

"Everything's all right," Lauren said quickly, passing the joint to her.

Janette dragged on it. "Are you having a problem with Harvey?"

"No." Lauren shook her head. She looked at her sister. "What do you think of Patrick? Seriously."

"Patrick's okay," Janette answered. "He's bright and up and likes to have fun."

"He said he was in love with you once and wanted to marry you," Lauren said.

Janette laughed. "He was either stoned or drunk or being silly, and I think the only reason he asked me was because he was sure that I would never do it." Then she saw the expression on Lauren's face. "Is he making a problem for you?"

297

Lauren shook her head. "Not really."

"Then what is it?"

Lauren looked into her eyes. "Are you in love with him?"

Janette laughed. "Patrick? Never. He's a nice boy but I can't see myself with him."

A kind of relief came into Lauren's eyes. "That makes me feel better."

"Why?" And then even before Lauren answered, Janette knew. "Are you in love with him?"

"Yes," Lauren answered, dropping her eyes for a moment, then raising them again. "And he says he's in love with me and wants to marry me. But I didn't want to give him an answer until I knew just where you stood. I didn't want to come between you."

"There's nothing between Patrick and me for you to upset," Janette said quickly. She reached for Lauren's hand. "But you're still a child, you're only seventeen. Are you sure you know about yourself, how you really feel?"

"I know how I feel about him," Lauren said. "I do love him. But I told him I wouldn't marry him right now. Not until I was eighteen."

"And what did he say?" Janette asked.

"He said that would be okay. But he wants to announce our engagement right away."

Janette was silent for a moment. "Have you made love with him?"

"Not yet," Lauren said. "I didn't want to until I knew exactly where I stood."

"What happened to his two friends?" Janette asked.

"They left the boat the day after we got to Sardinia," Lauren answered. "Patrick told me that he was through with all that. He was thinking seriously about going back into business as his father had wanted him to."

Janette dragged on the joint again, then gave it back to Lauren. She smiled slowly. "He must be serious about you then," she said. "Because for him to even think about going to work is one of the major miracles of all time."

"He really does know a lot about business," Lauren said quickly. "It was only that his father was so important that he ran away from it. But his father is dead now."

Janette nodded. She could understand that. She bent over and kissed Lauren's cheek. "It will have to be your decision, darling," she said. "Whatever that is, you can count on me to support you in it."

Impulsively Lauren hugged her. "I'm glad. Mother and Dad will go through the roof when I tell them."

"I'm sure we can make them see the light," Janette said. She nodded toward the staircase. "Does he know anything about it?"

Lauren shook her head. "No. I didn't want to say anything to anyone until I had spoken to you. Now I can tell him."

"It can wait until morning," Janette said. "He'll be upset. He's in love with you."

"Harvey?" Lauren's voice was happily unbelieving. "You don't really know about us. We've been pals for years. He won't be upset at all."

She said it. But then the moment the words left her lips she knew it wouldn't be like that at all.

The light was on in his room. It spilled under the closed door into the hall as she walked past it. She hesitated a moment, then knocked softly. She heard him moving around but there was no answer. She knocked again. Louder this time. "Harvey."

His voice was muffled. "Yes?"

"Are you going to bed?" Her voice echoed in the hall.

After a moment, he opened the door and stood there. "What do you want?" he asked. His voice was hoarse.

"I want to talk to you," she said.

He stood silently looking at her, then stepped back abruptly. "Okay."

His valise lay open on the bed, his clothing next to it. She turned to him as he closed the door. "What are you doing?" she asked.

He walked past her to the open valise and picked up a stack of T-shirts and dumped them into the valise. "What does it look like I'm doing?" he asked. He didn't wait for an answer. "I'm going home tomorrow."

She watched him silently as he placed some shirts in the bag. "There's no reason for you to go," she said.

He turned and looked at her. The hurt in his voice matched his eyes. "No? I'm not that stupid. You must think I'm a fool."

"I don't think you're a fool, Harvey," she said softly.

He turned his face away from her. He didn't want her to see the mist that was blurring his vision. His voice was strained and tight. "I didn't give a damn about coming to Europe. I came here to be with you."

"You can still be here with me," she said.

He looked into her eyes. "You know that I can't. And I know that I can't. So who are you trying to kid?" She didn't answer and he continued. "Do you think I didn't see what was happening? What was going on between you and Patrick?"

"Nothing happened," she said.

"No?" he asked with a sarcasm that he himself never knew he had. "I could have gotten off the boat with those two girls and you never would have known that I was gone."

"Harvey, Harvey," she said softly, going to him. She put her hands on his arms. "We're friends. I always want us to be friends."

He looked down into her face and then couldn't stop the rush of tears to his eyes. His arms went around her and he pulled her head tightly against his chest. "Look, Lauren," he said huskily. "I knew that we were both kids. But I always knew that I loved you. But kids don't talk about love. That's for grownups and I always thought there was time for that. Maybe I was wrong, but I never figured that you'd go for an old man."

300

Lauren was crying too. "He's not an old man," she snuffled against his chest. "He's not going to be thirty until next year."

"He's still twelve years older than you are. That's a lot."

"That's not much," she said. "My father is sixteen years older than my mother."

"And he talks funny," Harvey said. "I never can even understand a word he says. Half the time I have to guess at what he means. Why can't he talk English like the rest of us?"

"Because he is English," she said. "And they talk different than Americans."

"I bet there are a lot of things they do different than Americans," he said.

She placed a gentle finger on his lips to keep him from speaking and looked up into his face. "Harvey, I'm going to marry him."

She felt his jaw go slack against her finger and his mouth drop open as he pushed her away from him. He looked down at her in amazement. "Holy cats! Your folks'll kill you!"

"No they won't," she said.

He was still staring at her. "That's real serious," he said.

"I know. A little scary too."

"Yeah," he said. He thought for a moment. "Are you sure you're not overdoing it?"

"I'm sure," she said. "I'm in love with him."

"Oh, brother!" he exclaimed. "That's a real mind-blower. Getting married and all that. That's lifetime stuff."

"Yeah," she said.

He turned back to his valise and came up with a small vial. "This is the last I've got of number thirteen. I've been saving it for an emergency like this."

"What does it do?" she asked as he began to roll the joint.

"Gives you confidence," he said. "Makes you feel there's nothing in the world that you can't handle."

The Valium had put him away and he was aware of nothing until the leather strap slashed across his back, jolting him awake. "What the hell?" he mumbled, rolling across his bed to turn on the cabin lights.

"Jesus!" he yelled as the strap caught him again just as the lights went on. He stared up at Janette, standing at the side of his bed, her breasts heaving under her sheer black see-through blouse delineated by the cross-straps of her micro-mini leather skirt. She raised the belt in her hand and he caught a glimpse of her strong white thighs under the skirt as they fell into her almost hip-length black leather boots. He tried to roll away from the blow and caught it on his arms. "Are you crazy?" he yelled.

"You slimy son of a bitch!" she said in a calm, cold voice. "You said you like beatings? Well, you're going to get the beating of your life!"

The strap came down again and he jumped with pain. "Stop!" he yelled. He leaped naked from the bed and ran for the bathroom. Relentlessly she followed him, the strap slashing and cutting at him. He turned his face into a corner of the cabin, leaving only his naked back exposed to the stinging leather strap. After a moment he began to cry, then his legs trembled, and he sank to the floor, covering his face with his hands.

"Please," he said in a little boy's voice. "Don't punish me any more. I'll be good. I'll do anything you say."

Her voice was still cold. "Lick my boots, you little bastard!"

"Yes, yes," he said, still crying and crawling toward her on his hands and knees. He put his face against the nearest boot and began to lick it.

The strap slashed across his back. "Now the other."

"Yes," he said, moving to the other foot. "Let me be your slave."

The belt came down on his back again. "Is that all you want to be?"

"Yes," he whispered. "Your slave. That's all."

She slapped him across the face. "Eat my cunt," she ordered, raising the front of her leather skirt.

He rose on his knees and buried his face between her legs. She placed a hand on the back of his head, pressing him into her. "Lick it faster," she commanded.

Frantically he began to move his head against her, his hand going down to his erection and masturbating himself. Suddenly her knee came up, catching him under the chin and flinging him backward on the floor.

She brought the strap down across his arm. "I didn't give my slave permission to play with his little prick," she said coldly and walked across the cabin and sat in a small armchair, looking at him.

He pushed his back against a wall and, raising his knees to his chest, sat there staring at her, the tears running silently down his cheeks. She lit a cigarette and for a long time neither of them spoke.

Finally, it was he who broke the silence. "You're angry with me."

"I don't get angry with my slaves," she said. "Just disappointed."

He didn't speak.

"You're not even man enough to get yourself a real woman, you have to pick on a child." She ground the cigarette out under her boot in the carpet of the cabin. "Did you tell her what you really are like? That you like being a slave, that you love being a voyeur? And that is all that really turns you on?"

He was still silent.

"How do you think she is going to feel about you when she finds out? Then do you think that she'll believe your stories that you love her, that you're going to work and be a man like your father?"

"But I mean it," he cried. "I do love her. And I al-

303

ready sent a cable to the office that I'm coming in to work."

She laughed. "How long is that going to last? A month, maybe two. And then you're going to want to be a slave again."

The tears began to flood down his cheeks. He crawled toward her and knelt prayerfully, his hands clasped in front of her chair. "Don't tell her," he begged. "Please don't tell her."

She looked down at him without answering.

"I promise I'll be good," he said. "She's the only chance I have left."

"You said you were going to work?" she said.

"Yes," he said. "I am."

She took a deep breath. "Then I may give you a chance. But you'll have to prove yourself to me first."

"I'll do it," he said. "Just give me the chance."

"It involves your company," she said.

"I don't care," he said. "Just don't tell her."

She got to her feet and slowly began to undress. Finally she stood naked over him, except for her hip-length black boots. She raised the belt over her head and brought it whistling down on his back. The welts began to rise on his skin as she hit him again and again until finally he was cringing before her in full erection. Then she stopped, her breasts heaving with exertion. "Would you like to see me fuck with your African?" she asked coldly.

"Yes, yes," he said, beginning to masturbate himself violently.

She hit him again with the strap. "Then stop playing with your little prick until I give you permission, slave, and get him in here."

He looked up at her. "You won't tell Lauren?"

"Not if you do as I tell you, slave," she said contemptuously. "Now, get him in here."

She watched him pick up the phone. When he put it down she began to laugh. "What are you laughing at?" he asked.

"All of us," she said. "The whole world is crazy. We're all getting exactly what we want."

It was seven o'clock in the morning and the golden sun promised another day of unrelenting August heat as she drove into the courtyard of the villa and got out of the car. Wearily she went into the house, walking on heavy, leadlike legs. The African had been everything Patrick said he was. He wasn't human. He was nothing but a fuck machine. Her loins and anus felt swollen and aching and the sheer animal savagery of his pounding body had literally coerced her into a frenzied series of uncontrollable orgasms. Now all she wanted to do was sink into a hot tub, relax and then go to sleep. And she didn't care if she slept away the balance of the weekend. There was nothing more she could do than she had done last night.

She heard the footsteps on the staircase as she came into the living room and looked up. Harvey was coming down the steps, his single valise at his side. They stood there for a moment, each a little surprised at seeing the other.

"Good morning," she said.

He reached the bottom of the steps and put down his valise. There was embarrassment in his voice. "Good morning. I didn't expect to find anyone up."

"I'm just coming in," she said.

"Yes." He looked at her. "It must have been a hell of a party."

"It was," she said. She smiled. "I could use one of your high-quality toots."

"Of course," he said quickly. He fished in his jacket pocket and came out with a vial. He handed it to her with a small plastic straw. "The coke's already sifted," he said. "Just stick some in the end of the straw and snort."

She nodded and did as he said. The coke seemed to shoot back into her brain and explode. *"Mon Dieu!"* she exclaimed. "I feel as if the top of my head just came off."

He took the vial back from her with a half smile. "You had a good hit but you'll be okay in a minute."

He was right. Suddenly her weariness was gone. She looked down at his valise. "Does Lauren know you're leaving?"

He shook his head.

"Don't you think you ought to tell her?"

"I tried to last night but she only insisted that I stay."

"Why don't you then?" she asked.

She could see the hurt deep in his eyes. "What difference would it make? Really. She's into her own thing now."

"She'll feel bad if you just go like this."

"She'll get over it," he said. "Can I call for a taxi?"

"You could," she answered. "But you won't get an answer. It's too early in the morning and besides they have to come from Sainte-Maxime."

"What if I walked into Saint-Tro?"

"No taxis there. But you can get the ferry to the mainland. There will be taxis there."

"Okay," he said, picking up his bag. "Thanks for everything, Janette."

"You're welcome," she said. "What shall I tell Lauren?"

"Tell her I'll see her when she gets home," he said, starting for the door.

"Would you like me to run you into town?"

He shook his head. "No, thanks. You're tired. And the walk will do me good."

"Harvey," she said.

He looked at her. "Yes, ma'am?"

"How do I get in touch with you? I don't even know your last name or your address."

"Lauren can give it to you," he said. Then he thought for a moment. "Why would you want to get in touch with me?"

"One never knows." There was no point in telling him that the clay he had given her seemed to work and that at this very moment the chemists at the fragrance company laboratory were trying to analyze it. "I might be in California sometime and need a date."

306

A sudden grin cracked his face. "You can call me for that any time." He put down his bag and took a pencil and a piece of Zig Zag cigarette paper from his kit and scrawled on it, then handed it to her. "Just in case," he said. "Goodbye, Janette."

"Not that way," she said, taking the piece of paper. "The French way."

"How's that?" he asked.

She kissed him on both cheeks. "That's how." She smiled. "*Au revoir,* Harvey."

She went up to her room and turned on the water in the tub. While it was filling she went back into the bedroom and began to undress. In a moment she was nude. She turned and looked at herself in the mirror. Her eyes were glowing and her face showed no signs of the night. She half smiled to herself as she went to the window to draw the draperies against the light. There was nothing like a good fuck for making a woman look beautiful. Only one thing was missing. The warmth and tenderness you could get only from a woman. Stéphane should have been there. Then it would have been perfect.

From the window, she saw Harvey walking down the road, carrying his valise. For a brief moment she felt sorry for him and thought of calling him back. Then she decided against it and snapped the draperies closed. It was just as well he was gone. He could have only complicated matters by remaining. This way Lauren would have no one else to share her confidences. Everything would be easier.

She returned to the bathroom and poured some of her bath oil into the water and sank back into the tub. Strange, she no longer felt tired. Her mind wouldn't stop. There was much she had to do. Patrick didn't know it yet but the vacation in Saint-Tropez was over.

She didn't have the patience to soak in the tub. She got to her feet and turned on the shower. The cool water made her body tingle. A moment later she got out of the tub and wrapping her robe around her went into the bedroom and telephoned Jacques in Paris.

His voice was husky with sleep. "Yes?"

"Wake up," she said. "We're going to London."

"What?"

"We're going to London," she said. "I spoke to Patrick."

"He'll make the deal?" Jacques' voice was excited.

"That's what he said."

"But does he have the authority?"

"That's why we're going to London," she answered. "To find out. You go to London this morning and reserve a river suite for me at the Savoy. I'll meet you there this evening."

She put down the telephone and looked at the clock. It was eight in the morning. She set the alarm for eleven, then got into bed and pulled the sheets over her. Three hours' sleep should be more than enough.

She would call Patrick when she awakened and tell him to have his plane ready to take them to London. If he didn't already know, he might as well learn it now. She meant exactly what she said. If there was no deal for her, there would be no Lauren for him.

J ANETTE LIT ANOTHER cigarette as the car approached Paris. She leaned forward in her seat, looking out the window. At each exit of the *autoroute* there were four billboards. No matter what direction you came from, those four billboards were always there. And Janette had all of them. And each of them in its own way had its own story to tell.

The first billboard was coming up on the right bathed in bright light against the dark night. Black bold letters across the top of the billboard read simply: JANETTE JEANS. She was posed beneath the lettering, on her knees, derrière high in the air, with her head turned toward the camera, her hands cupping one cheek as she rested on her elbows. In smaller letters, reading vertically down the sign from the top of her derrière to her legs, was the phrase *Le vrai "Far West" français.*

The story behind it was simple. It had taken place one morning in New York shortly after the deal was made with Kensington. The president of the company came directly to the point.

"We have agreed to your every request, Madame. You will have your boutiques, all ten of them, as well as units in every major department store in America. But we have another problem and need your help."

"What is it?" she had asked.

"One million yards of surplus blue denim," he said. "Unfortunately we lost two of our largest customers to Burlington, and if we don't replace them, we'll be swimming in red ink this year. And up to now we haven't found any takers."

"And how could I be of help?" she asked.

"We've done a market study. We think there's room for jeans with a designer label at a popular price. St. Laurent is in the market but he's very expensive and his volume is negligible. We have figured the cost and we can make a good product to sell for twenty-five to thirty dollars. What we need is your name and six basic designs. We'll take care of everything else from manufacturing to sales. We already have thought of a name for them. 'Janette Jeans.' "

"And how does that fit into our agreement?"

"It's a separate item. We pay you a royalty of ten percent of our gross on every pair sold. There is no risk for you, no investment. All you can get is money. And we estimate there could be a lot of it."

"How much is that?" she asked.

"No one knows. But it could possibly reach a quarter of a million dollars a year."

"You have a long reach." She smiled. "It will be my pleasure to help you out." Even if she got only 25 percent of what he estimated she wouldn't complain.

But as it was, neither of them expected what was to happen. Her share of the gross sales for the year alone came to almost one million dollars. And that more than anything else established her in America.

The next billboard came into view. This time she was standing at an Air France counter handing her ticket to a reservation clerk. She was smartly dressed in a light suit for travel; subtly highlighted on the billboard were the gloves she wore, the shoulder bag hanging from a strap, the slim high-heeled shoes and the initialed valise at her feet. Again the bold lettering: POUR LE MONDE ENTIER. Beneath that in slightly smaller type: *Janette Cuir.* And then in smaller type opposite the items mentioned: *Le Gant, Le Sac, La Chaussure, Le Bagage.*

This opportunity had come soon after the success of Janette Jeans in America. Vito Montessori, an Italian who owned one of the largest leather-manufacturing companies in Italy, approached her with a licensing agreement. Be-

310

cause of the flight of many important names in Italian leather to manufacturing in the Far East to take advantage of lower labor costs, he wanted to develop a line of his own. Again, what he asked her to do was supply designs or give design approval, and he would undertake the fabrication and the marketing. But if she could obtain the cooperation of the sales outlets already established by Kensington in America, it would be even better. Needless to say, she could and did. This time her royalty was 15 percent, and a steady net income of almost a quarter of a million dollars a year was the result.

The third billboard featured not one but three photographs of her. Grouped together so that it seemed like one photograph, she was lying in a bikini, resting on hip and elbow in the sand, looking directly into the camera, then standing in a figure-hugging tank suit smiling up at the sun, and finally in a one-piece cutaway suit that came down over one shoulder, revealing more than it concealed. Again the bold type: JANETTE MAILLOTS DE BAIN. Below that in lesser type: *Pour le Soleil, Pour la Mer, Pour la Plage*. And then in a line that swept across the entire billboard: *Pour l'Eté Eternel.*

That had been her own idea. Buying a bankrupt manufacturing company in the south of France, she immediately entered into another distribution agreement with Kensington. Scaled at popular prices and aimed at the same market as the jeans, the bathing suits were another immediate success. The net income from that division was almost half a million dollars a year.

The last billboard coming up represented, in its own peculiar way, the biggest gamble of all. This, too, was all her own. For many years she had toyed with the idea, but it was the tremendous success achieved by Yves St. Laurent in launching his new perfume, Opium, during the last three years, that finally convinced her to move on her own.

Carefully analyzing the results of a market study she had ordered, she discovered some surprising facts. Of all the

311

perfumes sold, and there were hundreds of known brands, only two were widely enough known to be recognized by name as perfumes by the general public. The first was Chanel No. 5 with an 88 percent recognition factor, the second was Arpège with a slightly lesser recognition factor. None of the others came even close, but the closest to them proved to be Opium, with a 29 percent recognition factor, and that, as the market study pointed out, was due to the major and still current advertising and ongoing promotion. Two other interesting facts came to light. Both Chanel No. 5 and Arpège had been created in the twenties and belonged to the aldehydic floral group of scents, while Opium, a modern perfume launched in 1977, had its roots firmly in the oriental group, tracing its lineage almost directly from Tabu, launched by Dana in 1931, and Youth Dew by Lauder, marketed first in 1952. While Tabu had become something of a perfume classic, neither of the two had achieved the market recognition of Opium. But then, when they were introduced, they hadn't had the benefit of modern marketing techniques to create the kind of recognition that television could give them today.

Another interesting fact the study revealed was the importance of package design—both the bottle that contained the perfume and the package in which it was sold. That as well as the perfume itself had to tell its own story. And the story had to be embodied in the name of the perfume. It had to be simple, yet with a quick recognition factor.

She believed she had the name. *Soie.* The word for silk in French. The most intimate, most sensual fabric a woman could wear could also apply to her perfume. The other problem was not so easily resolved. Her original aromatic was too strongly based in the oriental and she felt that it could be regarded as an imitation of Opium. Working closely with the "noses," as they were called at the perfumery, she managed to combine the scents of both the floral, aldehydic group of Chanel No. 5 and Arpège and the sensuality of the oriental group. The result was a fragrance that was extraordinarily female yet feminine, sensual yet fresh and mossily floral. And the first decision she made was not to call it a perfume. *Soie* would be a fragrance, something that was a part of a woman, not a perfume she wore.

This last billboard was perhaps the most eye-catching of all. Upon seeing the bright sparkling bottle with the nude statue of a girl in Lalique crystal as the bottle stopper, one was not aware at first that in the shadows behind was another nude portrait of Janette. Painted many years ago by Dali, the artist had caught and exposed the many erotic facets of her body and personality. The shadowy pool of her dark eyes, the flush-red lower lip, the thrusting nipple tips of her swelling breasts, the curve of her belly falling into the shadow of her pubis almost lost in the swelling of her white hips and thighs. Almost by shock would come the realization that the portrait of the girl had been translated into the nude Lalique statue on the bottle. The name was etched into the cut crystal of the bottle in script, *Soie.* Beneath that in lettering almost too small to read, "de Janette." As on the other billboards, the advertising message ran down one side. *Le plus intime. Le plus sensuel. Le vrai aromate de la femme. Soie. L'aromate de Janette.*

And in its own way it was that perfume which led to her present situation. Determined to outperform St. Laurent in the market, she had committed more than five million dollars in cash to launch the perfume in the last six months, virtually stripping her own companies' cash reserves. Television advertising in America alone had run more than three million, the balance going to magazines and newspapers. And none of this money took into account the discounts and incentives given to the retail trade to gain their support. Their calculations had taken into account that it would be at least two years before the investment would be recovered and three years before they could realize a profit. To her satisfaction, the results were even more encouraging than had been predicted. An almost immediate market acceptance had led to a revision of the projected figures that cut their recoupment time in half.

But, as it turned out, it wasn't quick enough. The unexpected happened. The Reardon Group had been offered a tremendous profit for their controlling interest in Kensington Mills by a Japanese company anxious to get a foothold in the American market and had accepted.

At any other time this could have been the greatest opportunity she had ever had. For under the clause inserted at the last moment by her sagacious American attorney, Paul Gitlin, she had the option to buy back her contracts and agreements with the Reardon Group at the book value carried on its balance sheet should they sell or otherwise dispose of their interest in Kensington. And the ten million dollars at which it was carried was less than two times annual earnings. Ten times annual earnings would have been considered an equitable figure. But no matter how cheap, it did her no good. All the cash she had in her companies had been invested in the perfume. Now she was scrambling again. It was as if nothing had changed. Independence was as elusive as ever.

Maurice met her at the door to his apartment. He was visibly excited. "I was right," he said. "I knew all the time I was right."

"What the hell are you talking about?" she asked. "You're not making any sense."

"The money in the Swiss bank," he said. "Maybe now you won't have to fuck with the Greek for it."

"I don't know what you're talking about."

"You'll see," he said, taking her by the arm and leading her to the library. "You'll see."

He opened the door and a young man seated inside the room rose to his feet. Maurice introduced them. "Monsieur Thierry, my daughter, Madame Janette de la Beauville." He looked at Janette and explained. "Monsieur Thierry is with the Swiss Credit Bank in Geneva."

Janette extended her hand. "A pleasure, Monsieur Thierry."

314

The young banker kissed her hand politely. "An honor, Madame. I did not realize when I sought this meeting I would meet so famous a woman."

"Thank you, Monsieur," Janette said. "Now, if I may ask, why did you want to see me?"

The young banker looked at Maurice. He was obviously embarrassed. "I'm sorry, Monsieur le Marquis, but my instructions from the bank were very explicit. What I have to say is for her ears alone."

"I understand," Maurice said quickly. "Of course." Quickly he went to the door and closed it behind him.

"Now, Monsieur," Janette said, looking at the banker.

"If I may be permitted, Madame," Thierry said, taking a paper from his pocket and glancing at it. His voice took on a formal tone. "In accordance with the instructions given to the bank by your late mother, we have the obligation to inform you at the end of a period not less than twenty-five years after her demise that on October 10, 1944, she became the lessor of a certain group of safe-deposit boxes contained in the vaults of our bank." He stopped reading and handed the paper to her. "There are two copies of that information. If you will be kind enough to sign this copy, which acknowledges that you have received the information according to the instructions, we will have completed our business."

Janette took the paper and glanced at it. It was exactly as he had read it. She looked back at him. "Is that all?"

"Yes," he nodded.

"Does it mean I have access to those boxes?"

"If you have the key in your possession, certainly. If not —you do not."

"Then what is the purpose of telling me about it?"

"I do not know, Madame. We are only following instructions."

"Then who has the key?" she asked.

He shrugged his shoulders. "Under the Swiss banking laws protecting the confidentiality of our client relationship, I am not permitted to give that information."

"Then how do I go about establishing my rights to those boxes and their contents, as my mother obviously wanted me to have them?"

"You may file a claim in the Probate Court of Switzerland, which has the ultimate jurisdiction in matters of inheritance."

"How long would that take?"

"I'm sorry," he said apologetically. "I do not know. Sometimes years."

"Damn!" she said, looking down at the paper again. "Do you have any idea of the contents of those boxes?"

"No, Madame, what the clients place in their boxes is no concern of ours. I'm afraid I'm not being of much help. But there's nothing else I could do."

"What if I refuse to sign the paper?" she asked.

"Then you would have no right to lay claim to the boxes because you have not legally been informed of them and, again, under Swiss banking laws, we do not even have to acknowledge their existence."

She shook her head hopelessly. "Then I might as well sign it."

"Yes, Madame," he said, holding out a pen.

Quickly she signed the copy and gave it to him. "Thank you, Monsieur Thierry."

"You're welcome, Madame," he said, handing her the other copy.

She smiled suddenly. "It's late and I haven't had dinner as yet. Would it be a violation of Swiss banking laws if I asked you to join me for dinner?"

A slow smile came to his lips. "I think that is permissible, Madame. But I'm afraid I must refuse. I have a previous engagement."

"Then break it." She laughed.

"As much as I would like to, Madame, I'm afraid I cannot. My wife is waiting for me at the hotel."

She laughed again and held out her hand. "Monsieur Thierry, you're a gentleman. I hope we will meet again."

He kissed her hand politely. "So do I, Madame," he said, walking to the door.

A moment after he left, Maurice came back into the room. He stared at her face. "Well?"

"You were right," she said quietly, handing him the paper. "But merely knowing about it gives me no right to it."

He read the paper quickly. "Then who has the right?"

"Whoever has the key," she said. "And he wouldn't tell me who that was."

Maurice stared at her. "He doesn't have to tell me," he said. "I know who has the key. And so do you."

She was silent.

"You're going to have to do something about it now," he said. "Or remain a beggar and a whore the rest of your life."

She looked at him, still silent.

"You're going to have to bring Lauren into it," he said.

"Do I have to?" she asked.

"You know Johann," he answered. "Whatever is there is half hers. He won't do a thing unless he feels that she is protected. The only way you'll get anything is if the two of you approach him."

"I don't know," she said doubtfully. "Lauren doesn't give a damn about money. She never did."

"She's twenty-three now," he said. "She has to be getting tired of living on that stupid beach in California with no one except a five-year-old child to keep her company."

"That's the kind of life she likes."

"Then it's up to you to convince her that her daughter deserves a better chance in life than growing up to be a beach bum," he said. "Even if she doesn't want it for herself she has no right to deprive her child."

"I don't know," she said doubtfully. "Sometimes I think I've fucked too much with her head."

He laughed. "You don't believe that any more than I do, Janette. The one thing your mother and I had in common was our selfishness. We both wanted everything we could get." He went to the sideboard and took down a bottle of cognac. "You don't regret what you did. You got what you wanted, didn't you?"

She didn't answer as he poured the cognac into two glasses and came back to her. Still silent, she took a glass from him and sipped it.

He swallowed half his drink in one gulp, then put his glass down. "There's just one thing I never understood," he said. "Why you pushed Patrick off on Lauren. Wouldn't things have been simpler if you had married him yourself?"

She took another sip of the cognac before she answered him. "That's exactly what I intended to do when they came back from Sardinia."

"Then why didn't you?"

"She said she was in love with him."

He looked at her. "She was just a child. You could have blown that up."

"I suppose I could have," she answered, meeting his gaze. She took another sip of the cognac. "Maybe I should have."

Deep inside herself she always had known the marriage was doomed. And even while they exchanged wedding vows in the garden of Patrick's mother's home in Devon and Patrick's eyes searched her out as he looked over his bride's white veil, she knew it was doomed. And that she would be the cause of its destruction.

FROM HER WINDOW on the second floor of Reardon Manor, Janette could see the first of the wedding guests arrive. She glanced at her watch. Ten o'clock. The ceremony was scheduled for noon.

She glanced up at the sky. It was clear blue, not a cloud in it. Happy the bride the sun shines on today. She smiled at the thought. Especially on an English Sunday, she added. She went back into the room and picked up the guest list from the dressing table.

It wasn't going to be a large wedding, only sixty guests, but the list read like a Who's Who of British society and industry. Headed by the royal family represented by Princess Margaret and Lord Snowden, there were enough lords and ladies to fill the audience chamber at Buckingham Palace. The Lord Mayor of London would be there. France was represented by the Comte de Paris, her stepfather the marquis, and the French ambassador to the Court of St. James. Johann and Heidi had come from America and the American ambassador would also be there.

She put down the guest list and picked up another sheet of paper. This was her own schedule. Alexandre had flown over from Paris to do the bride's hair as a favor to her and she had brought Mme. St. Cloud to supervise and dress the bride. According to her schedule they should be in Lauren's room right now.

She slipped into a pair of pants and went down the hall. Lauren's room was a frenzy of activity. Heidi was already there and opened the door for her. Janette kissed her cheek. "How's the bride?" she asked, not seeing Lauren in the room.

"Nervous." Heidi smiled. "But not as nervous as I am. Right now she's in the bathroom having her hair washed."

"Good," Janette said. "Then Alexandre is already here."

"Yes," Heidi nodded. "He came with two assistants. He said that he would do my hair also."

"Lovely," Janette said. She looked across the room to where Mme. St. Cloud had just finished hanging the wedding dress on the form. "What do you think of the *robe de mariage?*"

"I love it!" Heidi exclaimed. "It's the most beautiful gown I've ever seen."

Janette glanced at her. The sincerity on Heidi's face convinced her. "Thank you," she said. "I wanted it to be something special."

"It is," Heidi said, following her across the room. "I've never seen anything like it."

Janette stopped in front of the dress form. She looked at Mme. St. Cloud. *"Tout va bien?"*

"Oui, Madame," she replied. *"Très bien."*

Janette turned back to the dress. In Paris this morning photographs of the dress were being released to the press. Tomorrow the pictures would be in half the newspapers in the world. What Heidi had said was true. There had never been another wedding dress like it.

In its simplest description it was three veils of delicate sheer silk embroidery, ivory thread on white. The first veil fell from the bride's head over her nude shoulders. The second veil was a strapless camisole top, almost lingerie-like, that gave a hint of nudity beneath it and fell just below the waist. The third veil was a skirt that began at the waist just under the camisole top, then fell in a clean body-clinging line until mid-thigh, where it began to flare out with ruffles of embroidery into a full skirt with a long train. The total effect was one of implied nudity—one thought he saw what he *thought* he saw, but in reality could see nothing.

She nodded in approval. "Call me when she is dressed," she said. "I want to make sure that everything is right."

"Oui, Madame," the dresser answered.

Alexandre came out of the bathroom and saw Janette. He came toward her and kissed her cheek. "Your sister is lovely," he said.

"And you are just as lovely to come here and do this for us, *chéri*," Janette said. "I am most grateful to you."

"It is nothing," he smiled. "My pleasure."

"Is she still in the bathroom?" Janette asked.

"Yes," he replied. "My girls are starting to give her a manicure and a pedicure."

"I'll pop in and see her for a moment," Janette said. "Then perhaps you can join me for a coffee."

"I'd love to," he answered.

Lauren was sitting in the bathroom, a towel on her head, her feet in a tub of water. She looked up at Janette and smiled. "Nobody told me it would be like this."

Janette laughed. "Well, you can't win them all. How are you feeling?"

"A little crazy with these people all over me. I could do with a toke of Harvey number six right now."

"Do you have any?" Janette asked.

Lauren nodded, indicating a cigarette case lying on the counter next to the sink. "Right there. But with Mother in the room outside and all these people around. You know."

Janette smiled. "We can take care of that." She spoke to the two girls. "Could you excuse us for a moment. My sister and I wish to talk privately."

"*Oui*, Madame," the girls replied.

They left the room and Janette locked the door. "See how easy it is," she said. She opened the cigarette case and took out a joint. Handing it to Lauren, she turned to the window. "Let me open this before you light up. It wouldn't do to have the smell of marijuana floating down the halls of Reardon Manor."

Lauren giggled. "That's right. Half those old fogies wouldn't know what hit them." She lit the cigarette and drew a deep toke into her lungs. She let it out slowly and handed it to Janette.

Janette took a toke and passed it back. "It's good."

Lauren nodded. "Harvey never misses. You've got him all excited about the clay cosmetics. Are you really going to do it?"

"I'm going to try," Janette said.

"I'm glad," Lauren smiled. "Harvey's a sweet boy." She took another toke. "I still can't believe it. I'm really getting married. It's like a dream."

Janette looked down at her, a strange sadness coming over her. "Yes," she said gently. "It is like a dream, isn't it?"

She was back in her room less than an hour later when there was a knock at the door. "Who is it?" she called out.

"Lord Patrick's valet, ma'am," came the answer.

She opened the door and peeked out through the crack. "What is it?" she asked.

"Lord Patrick would like to see you, ma'am," the man said.

"For God's sake, I'm not even dressed yet," she said. "Tell him I'll see him downstairs."

The valet's face was expressionless. "I think you'd better see him right now, ma'am."

Janette stared at him for a moment, then nodded. "I'll be right with you." She went back into the room and put on her slacks again and opened the door. She started down the hall.

"I think it would be better if we went the back way, ma'am," the valet said quickly.

Janette followed him through a door at her end of the hall, then through a long gray-painted corridor to the other wing of the building. He stopped in front of a door and opened it. "Lord Patrick's room, ma'am," he said.

She entered a small dressing room between the bedroom and the bathroom. "To your left," the valet said.

She went through an archway into the bedroom. He was seated, wearing nothing but his briefs, holding a glass of whiskey in his hand, staring into it. He looked up as she came into the room. "The wedding's off," he said. "You tell them."

322

"Have you gone mad?" she asked. "Why?"

He took another drink from his glass. "I changed my mind."

She stared at him for a moment, then turned to the valet. "Would you excuse us, please?"

"Yes, ma'am," the man replied and left the room.

When she heard the door close behind him, she walked over to the chair and looked down at Patrick. "Now tell me why," she said in a cold voice.

Patrick looked up at her. "Because she wants to have a baby right away. She said that she would throw her pills away on the day we were married."

"That's no reason at all," she said.

"It's enough reason for me," he said. "I don't want any squalling brats around."

"Okay," she said quietly. She turned and went back to the dressing room.

He got to his feet and followed her. "You can tell them that I got sick."

She spun back toward him. "I'm not going to tell them anything," she said coldly, taking a cane from the umbrella stand and moving toward him.

He dropped his drink, backing away, holding his hands in front of him to protect his face. "It won't work. You can't make me."

"No?" she asked, her voice cold as ice. The cane whistled down on his shoulders. He yelped in pain and tried to escape her but relentlessly she followed him, beating him across his back and shoulders, where red welts were springing up on his white skin.

He threw himself on the bed, sobbing. "Please, stop."

She dug the tip of the cane into his shoulder, forcing him to roll over and look up at her. He was already masturbating violently. Angrily she hit his hand away from himself with the cane. "I didn't give you permission to do that, slave."

"Yes," he sobbed.

"Now what are you going to do?" she asked.

He stared up at her. "Whatever Mother wants. Only I don't want her to go away from me just because I'm married."

"Mother won't leave you," she said. "She'll always be here. Now be a good boy, go in and shower and get dressed."

"But I haven't finished," he whined.

"If you're a good boy, I'll come back after the ceremony and give you permission to finish."

"Yes, yes," he said quickly. "Does Mother promise?"

"Mother promises," she said. "Now, get started."

He got out of bed and went to the bathroom. She stood there a moment and watched him turn the water on in the shower, then went out into the back corridor. The valet was waiting outside the door.

"Lord Patrick is taking a shower," she said. "You can go in now and help him dress."

"Yes, ma'am," the valet said. "Thank you, ma'am." He hesitated a moment. "Is the wedding still on, ma'am?"

"It is," she said.

An expression of relief came over his face. "Thank you, ma'am. It would have been turrible scandal what with Princess Margaret here and all."

"Yes," she said.

"Can you find your way back, ma'am?"

"I'm sure I can," she said. "You go inside and look after Lord Patrick."

It was an hour and a half later, as the ceremony ended, that Patrick looked at her. There was a strange smile on his lips as he lifted the veil from Lauren's face and bent to kiss her. The guests surged forward with cries of congratulations and Janette dropped back from her position as maid of honor to allow them to pass.

"You've surpassed yourself, Janette. It's a most beautiful dress." The woman's voice speaking French came from behind her.

Janette turned. It was Hebe Dorsey, the famous columnist of the *International Herald Tribune.* The attractive dark-eyed, perennially tanned woman with reddish-blond hair was one of the most important fashion reporters in the world, syndicated in many newspapers; she also contributed a monthly article to French *Vogue.* The Reardons hadn't wanted any press, but because she was a close friend of Janette's, an exception had been made in her case.

"Thank you, Hebe," Janette said.

"Wherever did you get the idea?" Hebe asked. "I've never seen anything like it. The ruffles on the skirt seemed to ripple and flow as she walked."

Janette smiled. "That's the effect I wanted to get. Actually I got the idea when I was in California several months ago and I watched Lauren surfing. I thought how wonderful it would be if I could capture the whitecaps of the waves as they sprayed around her."

"Do you have a photograph of the dress that I could use?" Hebe asked.

"There's probably one in your office right now," Janette answered.

"Good." Hebe looked at the crowd surrounding the bride and groom, then turned back to Janette. "I'm an incredible romantic," she said. "Is it really true that they first met at your collection last year and that it was love at first sight?"

Janette laughed. "Yes."

Hebe sighed, then smiled. "I think I have the heading for my story."

"Tell me," Janette said.

Hebe looked at her. "A fairy tale . . . come true."

Lauren was bewildered. The reality of the honeymoon was nothing like the promise. It began like a beautiful dream. After the wedding they had flown in Patrick's plane to Mykonos. The helicopter was waiting there to take them to the *Fantasist,* lying at anchor off the island. The whole idea had seemed like a romantic movie. A month-long honeymoon cruising the Greek islands. But something seemed to go wrong the moment they boarded the small jet at Devon.

The steward brought a bottle of champagne and two glasses as soon as they had taken off. He filled the glasses and went forward, disappearing behind the galley curtain.

She turned from the window, gave him a glass and picked up her own. "To us." She smiled. "Isn't it wonderful?"

He made no move to taste his champagne, just looked at her silently as she drank, then placed his glass back on the table between them and turned back to the window.

"Hey," she said. "You didn't touch your champagne."

He seemed almost angry as he turned to face her. "I've drunk enough of that piss to last me a lifetime." He pressed the call button. The steward appeared immediately. "Bring me a whiskey neat."

"Yes, m'lord." The steward returned in a moment, a glass of whiskey on the tray.

Patrick glanced at it. "How many times do I have to tell you that when I order a whiskey to bring a full bottle?" he snapped.

"Sorry, m'lord," the steward apologized. "Right away, m'lord." He went to the galley and returned with the bottle, which he placed on the table, then disappeared again.

He swallowed his drink in one gulp and refilled his glass without speaking.

He turned his face to the window without glancing at her as he lifted the glass again to his lips.

"What's the matter?" she asked in a puzzled voice. "Did I say or do anything wrong?"

He swallowed the drink and refilled his glass again before he answered her. "No," he answered shortly.

"You don't seem happy," she said.

He looked at her balefully. "What am I supposed to be doing? A tap dance on the ceiling?"

"You could at least act as if we're going on our honeymoon," she said.

"Middle-class shit," he snapped.

"You made the arrangements," she said. "I didn't ask for it."

He emptied his glass and began to refill it. She reached across the small table and placed a hand on his arm. "Don't drink any more, Patrick," she said gently.

He stared at her. "What else is there to do?" he asked truculently.

"We could move to the couch in the back and fuck. I always wondered what it would be like to make it on a plane."

"I've done it," he said. "It's not that great."

"But I've never done it," she said. "First, I can give you a little head, then you can give me a little head." She grinned suddenly, taking his hand. "Feel my pussy. It's soaking wet. I got all horny just thinking about it."

"Stop talking like a common whore," he said coldly, pulling his hand away. "Remember who you are now."

"I know who I am," she said, the hurt showing in her voice. "I'm Lauren. Who do you expect me to be?"

He poured the whiskey into his glass and drank it before he answered. "Lady Reardon," he said snidely. "Or is that too much to expect?"

She stared at him, unable to answer, the choking in her throat forcing the tears into her eyes. Quickly she rose from her seat and went to the couch in the back of the plane.

They completed the rest of the trip in silence and by the time they touched down in Mykonos, Patrick had drunk almost two bottles of whiskey and had to be helped from the plane to the helicopter. When they arrived on board the *Fantasist* all that could be done with him was to put him to bed and let him sleep it off.

She undressed and crawled, naked, into the bed beside him. Tentatively she placed a hand on his shoulder. But he was out. He never moved. An hour later she still hadn't been able to find sleep. She gave up the struggle, popped two Valium fives, smoked a stick of Harvey's number four, dream grass, as he called it, and was asleep before she felt her eyes close.

In the morning when she awoke, he was standing, his back to her, slipping into a pair of slacks. Her eyes widened. "My God, Patrick! What happened to your back?" she asked in a shocked voice.

He glanced at her in the mirror. "I slipped on the stone steps in the rear of the Manor yesterday morning," he answered without turning around.

She sat up in bed. "And you never said a word about it. Not even during the wedding. You must have been in terrible pain. You should have said something."

He didn't answer, still watching her reflection in the mirror.

"Now I know why you were drinking the way you did yesterday." She got out of bed and stood next to him. She looked up into his face. "You should have told me," she said sympathetically. "Then I would have understood."

He looked down into her face for a long moment. "I didn't want to upset you," he said finally.

She stood on tiptoe and kissed him. "I'm sorry, darling," she said. "We'd better find something to put on it."

He smiled his brave-Englishman smile. "It's really nothing, darling. It doesn't hurt that much now."

Two weeks later they were anchored off Corfu and she was lying nude on the sun deck, waiting for Patrick to finish his morning telephone calls. He spoke to his office twice a day, morning and evening. She picked up a spray can of Evian. The misty cool spray felt good against her warm skin. She squinted up at the sun. Patrick had better hurry. Another half hour and it would be impossible to stay in this sun.

She sprayed extra water into her hand and dipped her fingers into the jar of Sun Earth that Harvey had given her. It was Janette who had given it the name, and already she was working on a package design for it, planning to enter the market early next year.

She looked down at herself as she spread the thin layer. It really worked. Her body had never been so dark from the sun, and there never had been the slightest hint of a burn. By contrast, her hair had never been so white-blond, her eyebrows and lashes were practically invisible, even her pubic hair shone whiter than the skin beneath. She heard footsteps on the ladder and looked up. Patrick's head appeared first. He paused for a moment halfway up the ladder.

"I've ordered a drink," he asked. "Would you like one?"

"No, thanks," she smiled. "But you're just in time to do my back."

She rolled over on her stomach as he knelt beside her. She sprayed some water on his hand and then over her shoulders on her back. He dipped his fingers into the jar and began to apply the thin film of clay. She glanced sideways at his face. He was smiling. "You seem pleased with yourself this morning," she said.

"I am," he said. "I've finally gotten those bastards on my board of directors to admit that I knew what I was doing."

"That's great," she said. She knew of the skepticism and resentment he had faced upon going into the company. Everything he wanted to do was subjected to microscopic scrutiny and had been fought at every turn. "What made them finally see the light?"

"There were a couple of things but mainly it was the deal with Janette," he said.

"That makes me doubly happy," she said, rolling over, sitting up and kissing his cheek. "I'm proud of you."

He looked at her. "Do you know the biggest money-making item in our whole line is Janette Jeans? We've netted more than two million dollars in the States in its first year, and we've only been on the market eight months. According to projections we'll do six million next year. And even our experts had to admit that her idea of weaving ten per-

329

cent of stretch threads into the denim was brilliant and made the jeans fit even better. It even made fat asses look good. Then to top it all off, her collection at the beginning of this week showed Paris and the whole fashion world that last year's was no fluke. It put everybody away."

"I feel stupid,"she said. "All I thought about was the wedding. I forgot completely that it was collection time. She must think that I'm a real shit."

"I'm sure she understands," he said.

"Did she do it at the Lido again?"

"No. This time she had a circus theme. She took over a small circus and did it in a tent in Montmartre complete with ringmaster, clowns, acrobats, lions and elephants, the whole works. And this time it was all her own designs. It proved once and for all that she didn't need a Philippe Fayard or anyone to help her, that she could take her place along with St. Laurent, Givenchy, Bohan and all the rest of them as one of the top couturiers. In just the first three days after the showing, she had over a million dollars' worth of orders."

Lauren laughed happily. "I bet that son of a bitch Carroll is really kicking his ass."

Patrick laughed with her. "I'll bet."

"Bwana." The Negro's voice came from the ladder. Lauren grabbed at a towel to cover herself as he came up the ladder, the tall frosted glass of orange juice and vodka on a tray.

Patrick took the drink. He glanced down at Lauren. "Sure you won't change your mind, darling?"

She held the towel close to her. "No, thanks," she answered.

"That will be all, Noah," Patrick said.

"Yes, *Bwana.*" The African turned and went down the ladder.

Patrick sipped at the drink. "This is good," he said, holding it out to her. "Have a taste."

She shook her head.

He looked down at her. "Christ, you're almost as black as he is."

She sat up, throwing the towel around her shoulders. "I wish you'd get rid of him," she said. "He makes me uncomfortable."

"That's just your American prejudices," he laughed. "You don't like niggers."

"It's not that," she said quickly. "He's always staring at me. I can almost feel his eyes crawling all over me."

He laughed again. "What do you expect, walking around naked all the time? What do you think the rest of the crew does? The same thing. Only they're better at concealing it than he is."

"He's like an animal," she said. "You ought to tell him to wear underwear or something. You can always see the shape of his cock in those tight pants he wears."

The smile disappeared from Patrick's face. "You don't have to look."

"I don't look," she said. "You don't have to, it's so obvious."

Patrick put down his drink and unexpectedly slipped his hand between her legs, then raised his fingers to his lips and tasted them. "You're soaking wet," he said, excitement coming into his voice. "Admit it, his big cock turned you on."

"Don't be stupid," she snapped, annoyed. "I got turned on the minute you began rubbing my back."

"I want to eat you," he said.

"Then stop talking about it and do it," she laughed, pulling his face down to her.

She was lying in bed, watching him undress when she felt the vibration of the engines and the boat begin to move. She sat up and reached for the small traveling case in which she kept her stock of Harveys. Without looking up she asked, "Where are we going now?"

331

"Hydra," he answered.

"Another island?" she asked.

"Yes. It's about one hundred and fifty miles from here. We'll be there in the morning."

"Greek?" she asked, picking up each cellophane bag, squinting at it, then putting it down.

"Of course," he said coming to the edge of the bed and looking down at her. "That's all they have in the Greek islands."

"What's so special about this one?"

"I don't know," he said. "It's supposed to be very beautiful."

"All Greek islands look alike to me," she said, still picking and discarding cellophane bags. "I've got calluses on my feet from dancing the *sirtos,* and if I hear another chorus of 'Never on Sunday' I'll be willing to go deaf."

"Sounds like you're all ouzo'd out," he punned. It got no reaction from her. "What are you looking for?" he asked.

"Harvey said he put in a package of a new kind of grass," she said. "I found it," she said, holding it up triumphantly. "Number sixteen."

"What does he call that one?"

"Fantasy grass," she answered, already rolling a joint. "He said that gives you almost the same kind of high you get from mescaline or peyote."

"Fantasy," he repeated, intrigued by the thought. He sat on the edge of the bed, watching her lick the cigarette paper. "That's what every honeymoon should be. A time for fantasy."

"I'm not complaining," she said, lighting the cigarette. She drew two deep tokes, then passed it to him. "Try it," she said. "I can feel a buzz already."

He took several tokes. "Do you ever fantasize?" he asked, holding the cigarette.

"About what?" she asked, leaning back against the pillows.

He drew on the cigarette again, then passed it back to her. He let his fingers play with her pubic hair. "Like about

332

shaving your quim and having it all soft and pink like a little girl's."

She dragged on the joint. Harvey was right as usual. This grass did numbers on your head. She was really getting a buzz on. She giggled. "Would you like to do that?"

He nodded.

She gave him the cigarette, jumped out of bed and went to the bathroom. A moment later she was back, her pubis all covered with shaving foam, his razor in her hand. "Okay," she said. "Do it."

A few minutes later she was standing in front of the mirror, examining herself. She giggled. "My clit's like a little pink tongue sticking out between my lips." She turned to him. "Do you like it?"

"I think it's beautiful." He took another toke of the joint and passed it to her. "What do you fantasize about?"

She drew on the cigarette and giggled. "You wouldn't like it."

"Try me," he said.

"What you look like without your beard," she said. She giggled again. "Funny. Here I am married to you and I don't even know what you look like. Really."

He paused for a moment trying to gather his thoughts. He was having trouble remembering them long enough to speak them. "I look the same," he finally said.

"What is the same?" She giggled.

"The same as I always looked," he said. He began to laugh. "That's funny, isn't it? I mean. The same."

"It is funny."

"I'll show you what I mean," he said, going into the bathroom. She followed him and watched as he rubbed the foam into his beard. When he had shaved half his face, he turned that side to her. "See?" he asked, putting down the razor. "I look the same."

"Patrick, you're really beautiful," she said.

"I told you," he said reaching for the towel to wipe his face.

"You can't stop now," she said.

"Why not?" he asked.

"You can't go around with a beard just on one half of your face," she said, giggling. "That's silly."

He turned and looked at himself in the mirror. He laughed. "You're absolutely right. That would be silly." Quickly he added more shaving foam to his beard and shaved the rest of it off. He rubbed his fingers thoughtfully over his cheeks. "It feels strange," he said. "I've had that beard for eight years. I'd almost forgotten what it was like without it."

"You look younger," she said.

"Do you really like it?"

"I really do. I never knew it but you're very handsome. Now I'll have to worry. All the girls will be after you."

He turned back to the mirror, rubbing his face again. "It still feels strange."

"So does my pussy," she giggled. "What do you say we introduce the two strangers to each other?"

A few minutes later she held his face away from her. "I can't wait any more," she said breathlessly, trying to pull him over her. "I want you inside me."

He rolled over on the bed so that she was over him. "Get on it."

"Yeah," she said, rising to her knees. Then guiding him into her with her hand, she slowly lowered herself on him. The breath rushed out of her with a sigh. "Oh, that's good." Slowly she began to move on him. "Oh, man, I can feel it. It's like a hot rock in my pussy."

"Harder," he said. "I want you to beat it!"

She began to move faster, her body slamming down on him. She leaned over him, shaking her breasts in his face. "I'm beating you with my titties," she said.

"They're black like a nigger's," he said.

"You like that?" She pinned his arms to the bed. "Now you can't move. I'm going to nigger-rape you."

"Please don't!" he almost shouted, feeling his orgasm rising inside him.

334

"You can't stop me!" she said fiercely. Then her own frenzy caught up with her. "I can feel your cock shooting inside me!" Her body began to wrack with orgasms. "I'm coming and coming and coming!"

She slumped over him while they both caught their breath. After a moment, he made a gesture as if to move. She stopped him. "Leave it in there. Don't take it out yet."

"I want a cigarette," he said.

"In a moment." Her eyes looked into his. "Did you really fantasize that I was a nigger?"

He nodded without speaking.

"What else do you fantasize?"

"Lots of things," he said.

"Like what?"

"I want a cigarette," he said. She moved away from him and he got out of the bed and went to the dressing table for his cigarettes. He caught a glimpse of his face in the mirror and stood there for a moment staring at it. Then he touched his face with his fingers. "Oh, shit!" he said, turning to look at her. "What the hell did Harvey put in that grass? I really did shave off my beard."

"And I really let you shave my pussy." She laughed, getting out of bed and walking to him. She took a cigarette from his pack, lit it and gave it to him. "That was the best fuck we ever had. We should smoke that fantasy grass more often."

He dragged on the cigarette and then finally smiled. "It could get ridiculous," he said. "I'd look awfully funny with a shaven head."

"Can't you come up with any better fantasies than that?" She smiled.

He smiled slowly and went back to the bed. "I sure as hell can," he said. He looked at her. "I have the feeling that you've had it with the Greek islands."

She nodded.

He picked up the telephone and dialed the bridge. "Forget about Hydra," he told the captain. "Set course for Saint-

335

Tropez." He put down the telephone and looked at her. "How's that for a fantasy?"

She laughed. "Now you're really getting into it."

"I thought you would like it," he smiled. "We'll be there in three days. Janette's having her annual big bash Sunday night. We'll surprise the hell out of her and just walk in."

It was nearly three o'clock in the morning and the party was going into high gear. Lauren's head felt as if it were bursting with the noise. She could handle the grass and the coke but the champagne that Patrick had plied her with from the moment they arrived had put her away. She kept telling him that she couldn't handle it, but he had just laughed and kept refilling her glass. Now her head was spinning and she was beginning to feel nauseated. She began to search for him in the crowd. She wanted to go back to the yacht and sleep.

August was party month in Saint-Tropez and Janette had gone all out for this one. Catered by Félix of L'Escale, the giant buffet table set under the eaves on the terrace was bursting with all kinds of food. Magnificent roasts of beef and lamb, platters piled high with lobster and shrimp, baskets of *crudités* decorated all the tables. Before dinner had been served a half dozen waiters had circulated through the crowd, each with a bowl of caviar piled mountain high on a tray. There were candles on each table, and overhead under the eaves and around the garden, hanging from the branches of the trees, Chinese lanterns flickered. Los Paraguayanos played flamenco before and during dinner, and afterward two rock groups blasted the night for dancing.

The center of the large living room had been cleared for dancing and was impossible to cross because of the crowd. Slowly she made her way around the edge of the room to the corner where Janette had remained for most of the evening. It was a vantage point where she could see almost everything that was happening.

Janette was flushed and smiling as she spoke to the group

of people surrounding her. She didn't have to be told the party was a success. She knew that the moment the fogies from Monte Carlo began to arrive in their long gowns and smokings. That crowd wouldn't have undertaken the two-hour drive if they didn't feel the party was important. Not only that, Jack Nysberg, the official photographer for French *Vogue*, was there shooting pictures, and that was like the official stamp of approval.

Lauren touched her arm to attract her attention. Janette turned to her. *"Oui, chérie?"*

"Have you seen Patrick?" Lauren asked.

Janette glanced around the room. "No, I haven't. Maybe he's gone out on the terrace. Do you want me to send someone to find him?"

"No," Lauren said. "You have enough to do. I'll find him."

"Okay." Janette smiled and turned back to her coterie as Lauren made her way out to the terrace.

There were people still sitting at the tables, eating, when Lauren came out. A quick glance told her that Patrick wasn't there. Screams of laughter from the pool attracted her attention and she went out into the garden.

As she passed through the small cluster of trees that separated the pool from the house, she could see several couples on the grass obviously making it and either oblivious or not caring who saw them. She came out at the near end of the pool.

There seemed to be about twenty naked men and women splashing around in the water; another twenty-odd people stood at the sides watching them and screaming in laughter at their antics. Patrick wasn't with them. There was another crowd at the far end of the pool and she walked toward them.

Patrick was there, standing in a group of about nine people. He was holding a bottle of champagne in his hand and a glass in the other. She came up behind him and touched his arm.

He turned to her and smiled. "I was waiting for you to

come," he said thickly. He held the champagne glass toward her. "Have a drink and watch the show."

She shook her head. "I've had enough to drink. I think maybe you have too."

"Don't be a party pooper," he said, pushing her in front of him. "Then just watch."

At first she thought it was just three naked girls rolling over each other on the ground, but then she realized there was someone else. Maybe it was because he was so black that he blended into the semidarkness that she didn't see him immediately. Or because the naked girls were all over him almost hiding him.

"How did he get here?" She turned to Patrick angrily.

"I sent for him," Patrick said. "Even niggers are entitled to have a little fun."

She started to move away from him but he held her fast. "Look at that," he said laughing. One of the girls was lowering herself on Noah. "A hundred pounds she can't take him. He's too big for her," he shouted.

"You're on," one of the men said.

Patrick looked down at her. "How's that for a fantasy? Wouldn't you like to join them?"

"I want to go back to the boat," she said, pulling herself free angrily. "I don't feel well."

He stared at her. "The car and chauffeur are out there. You can go if you want to but I'm staying. I'm having the first good time I've had in a month."

She half ran back to the house, blinking back her tears. She would have to go through it to get to the parking area out in front. But when she got into the house, the body heat and the noise hit her and she felt the nausea rising in her. She knew that she could never make it to the car if she had to go through the crowd. She ran up the staircase into the room she had occupied last year and through it into the bathroom.

Kneeling on the floor, her hands supporting her by holding the rim of the toilet, her body was wracked by spasm after spasm as she vomited into the bowl. It seemed as if she were throwing up everything that she had eaten in the last week. Finally, it was over and she sank back, exhausted, to her haunches.

For a moment she rested until she felt strong enough to get up. She made her way to the sink and stared at herself in the mirror. She looked terrible, her makeup running, her face pale with sweat. She turned on the cold water and taking a washcloth began to clean her face. Afterward she held the washcloth to the back of her neck and rinsed her mouth to get rid of the awful taste.

Wearily she opened her bag and began to repair her makeup. But it was slow going. She still felt weak and exhausted. It had to be all the champagne she had drunk. She had never been this sick before. It even seemed to be an effort to put on her lipstick.

Even when she had finished with the makeup and started from the bathroom, she felt as if she had no strength, her body still trembling. She went into the bedroom and stood there a moment looking down at the bed. A few minutes' rest and she was bound to feel better.

She sat on the edge of the bed and kicked off her shoes, then stretched out. She was right—she was beginning to feel better already. Gratefully she closed her eyes. Gradually the trembling ceased. Much better, she thought. Then she was asleep.

She awoke to the sound of voices in the next room. It took a moment for her to remember where she was. It was still dark in the room but there was a faint hint of the coming daylight at the windows. Slowly she got out of bed and went into the bathroom. She washed her face again with cold water and looked in the mirror. The color had returned to her face. It was just as well she had fallen asleep. She had needed the rest.

She opened her purse. What she needed now was an upper to get her moving. Then she remembered that she had left her pillbox on the boat and had given the coke to

Patrick to carry. She heard the voices in the room next door again. Janette was still awake. She could get some from her.

She went into the bedroom and stepped into her shoes. She opened the door and stepped out into the hall. The house seemed strangely silent. She went to the railing and looked down. Through the archway she could see into the living room. It was still a shambles but no one was there.

Again the sound of voices came from Janette's room. She went to it and knocked softly. The voices continued as if they hadn't heard her. Tentatively she opened the door slightly and looked through. One whole wall of Janette's bedroom was completely mirrored and from where she stood she could see the whole room reflected in it. A numbingly cold wave ran through her, freezing her into momentary paralysis.

Three naked figures were framed in the mirror as if on a giant screen. Patrick, on his knees before the African, was masturbating himself violently while with the other hand he held Noah's phallus in his mouth. He writhed in pain as Stéphane, lashing his back with a riding crop, her face contorted with a strange hatred, snarled, "*Plus dur!* Scum! Pig! *Suce plus fort!*"

For a moment she felt as if she would faint, then her anger brought an unsuspected strength from somewhere inside her. Slowly she closed the door and leaned against it, fighting to regain her self-control. Suddenly she understood many things. The welts on his back the day after they were married. Why he always wanted her in the dominant position whenever they were making love. Why he refused to part with the African. It all came together now. She had been a fool not to see it before.

Then the hurt came up in her and her eyes began to fill with tears. She moved toward the staircase and went slowly down the steps and toward the front door.

It opened just as she reached it and Janette came in through the door. She stopped and stared at Lauren in surprise. "I just came back from breakfast at Le Gorille," she said. "I was told that you went back to the boat early."

Suddenly Lauren felt ashamed. Her eyes dropped. "No," she said.

"Then where were you?" Janette asked.

"I fell asleep in my old room," she said, still looking at the floor.

"Oh," Janette exclaimed.

Lauren raised her eyes. "Did you know that Patrick is up in your room with the nigger and your girl friend?"

Janette's eyes never wavered as she lied. "No." But she did know, because she had arranged it. She started for the staircase. "I'll throw them out."

Lauren stopped her. "Don't bother," she said dully. "It won't change anything."

"Then what do you want me to do?" Janette asked.

"Take me to the boat," Lauren said. "I'm going to pack and go home."

Silently they went to the car and got into it. It was almost daylight as they turned out of the driveway onto the narrow road leading to the village.

Lauren looked at her sister. Janette's eyes were squinting against the sun as she watched the road. "Why didn't you tell me he was like that?" she asked.

"He promised he was going to change," Janette answered without taking her eyes from the road. "After all, he did go back to work."

Lauren began to cry, the hurt rising even more in her. "You still should have told me. I feel like an idiot. Everybody had to know but me. I bet they all think I'm the jerk of all time."

"They're all jealous of you," Janette said. "There isn't one of them that wouldn't exchange places with you, even right now."

"I don't understand it," Lauren cried softly.

"When you get older you will," Janette said. She glanced at Lauren. "Things like this happen all the time. Men are

341

strange animals, they act in strange ways, but eventually they straighten out."

"He won't," Lauren said with conviction. "He's not only kinky, he's a closet queer. They never get over that."

"Half the women in Europe wouldn't be married if they objected to that," Janette said. She glanced at Lauren again. "Patrick's father and grandfather were noted pedes in their day. Their wives knew it and accepted it. It didn't keep them from making a successful marriage and raising a family."

Lauren had stopped crying and stared at the road in silence.

"Perhaps Patrick didn't hate his father as much as he hated his father in himself. At least, he tried to break the pattern." Janette slowed the car to allow a farm truck loaded with just-picked corn to turn onto the road in front of them, then crawled slowly along the road behind it. "You waited a year to get married. Do you think you're being fair to yourself deciding to destroy it so quickly?"

"Then you think I should stay married to him?" Lauren asked directly.

Janette hesitated a moment, then glanced at her sister. "Yes."

"Why?"

"Because it could be a good marriage. Patrick's family is one of the best in Britain, the title has spanned four generations. And when his mother dies, Patrick will be one of the richest young men in the world."

"If it's really that good, why didn't you marry him? He asked you first."

Janette glanced at her quickly then back at the road. She answered in a low voice. "Because I couldn't give him what the marriage would eventually require to be successful. Heirs. I had an accident when I was a young girl and I can't have any children."

Impulsively, Lauren touched her sister's hand. "I didn't know, Janette. I'm sorry."

"*C'est la vie.*" Janette shrugged, then glanced across the car. "But you're all right. You have choices. You can make it work if you want to."

Lauren met her gaze. "Maybe you'll think I'm naive. Or stupid. Or both. But the money and the title never meant anything at all to me. They still don't." She was silent for a moment as the car entered the narrow streets of the village leading to the port. "I guess I'm more American than I thought. I can't play the games that you Europeans play. To me, a marriage without love is no marriage at all."

She made the seven thirty morning flight from Nice to Paris and the ten o'clock polar flight from Paris to California. And it wasn't until six weeks later, two days after she had received her interlocutory decree of divorce in the courtroom at Santa Monica, that she found out she had been pregnant for two months.

THE DOORMAN AT Maxim's opened the door of the Rolls. He touched his cap. *"Bon jour,* Madame," he said, then hurried to hold the restaurant door for her. She went inside, pausing for a moment as the maitre d' hurried up to her.

"Madame de la Beauville." He bowed. "Monsieur Caramanlis is waiting for you. Please follow me."

She walked through the corridor into the restaurant, her eyes adjusting to the dimness from the bright sunlight outside. Maxim's at luncheon was very different from Maxim's at dinner. At luncheon, all the important regular clients occupied the front room, many of them at the same table each day, while the tourist and occasional client were seated in the back room, the dance floor of which was also covered with tables. At night, the opposite was true—the important clients were seated in the back room near the orchestra, while the others were seated in the front room.

Caramanlis was one of the regulars. He was seated alone at a large round table near the window in the far corner, not far from Robert Caille, the editor of *Vogue,* who always had the center table, who was deeply involved in conversation with several men and did not see her as she walked by. Caramanlis rose as she approached the table.

He kissed her hand and gestured to her seat, then turned to the maitre d'. "You may open the champagne now."

Janette smiled and sat down as the maitre d' held the chair for her. She looked at Caramanlis without speaking. After what had happened between them last night, she had not expected to hear from him again.

It had begun that morning, as she was sitting down to

breakfast at home. Promptly at eight o'clock she heard the chime at the front door. A few minutes later, the butler came in with a box of roses and held them while she removed the card and read it. There was no message, just the handwritten name. Caramanlis.

Then, exactly at ten o'clock, as she sat down at her desk in the office, Robert, her secretary, came into the room. He, too, was bearing a box of red roses. This time there was a velvet-covered jewel box inside as well as a card. She opened the jewel box first.

Inside the box, lying on black silk, was a choker of square-cut emeralds, set in gold and linked to each other with small round white diamonds. She stared at it silently. After a moment, she snapped the box shut and reached for the card.

"Wouldn't Madame like to wear it?" Robert's voice was almost shocked.

"No," she answered shortly. "It's too Greek."

This time there was a message on the card. "Luncheon. Maxim's. One o'clock." But no name. Only the initial "C."

She shook her head. For a moment, she was tempted to send it back to him without even a note, but the subtlety would be lost on him. An ego such as his had no limits. She would meet him for lunch and see for herself the expression on his face as she gave it back to him. She looked up at her secretary, still there, the box of flowers in his hands.

"Stop standing there with that silly expression on your face," she said in an annoyed voice. "Go and put the roses in water."

"Yes, Madame." He began to hurry from her office.

"And, Bobby," she called after him, stopping him at the door, "have them placed on the reception desk outside. I don't want them in here."

The maitre d' placed the chilled champagne glasses in front of them and poured a little in Caramanlis' glass for

345

him to taste. Caramanlis nodded without tasting the wine. Bowing, the maitre d' filled both glasses and left.

Caramanlis raised his glass to her. "I owe you an apology and an explanation."

She didn't touch her glass. "You owe me nothing," she said quietly, taking the jewel box from her purse and pushing it across the table to him. "Especially trinkets like this."

"But—but you don't understand," he said, almost stammering in his surprise. "I wanted you to know—that after last night—there were no hard feelings."

"You don't have to tell me that," she said sarcastically. "It never got hard enough last night for me to feel anything."

A veil seemed to drop over his eyes. "You bitch!" he said, unsmiling.

She knew she had scored. She was smiling sweetly as she rose from the table. "Goodbye, Monsieur Caramanlis," she said and walked away.

He didn't turn to look after her. He felt the flush creep up over his collar into his face, and he kept his eyes down, looking at the jewel box lying on the tablecloth. He was sure the sudden silence in the restaurant meant that their conversation had been heard throughout the room. He picked up his champagne glass, his hand almost trembling with the anger surging through him.

As quickly as it had stopped, the conversation level in the room went back to its normal heights. Slowly he sipped the champagne. Through the window he could see the doorman holding open the door of the Rolls as she entered. Then he closed the door and the car moved away.

A waiter appeared and quickly removed Janette's glass of champagne and place setting. A moment later, the maitre d' was standing next to him. "Is Monsieur Caramanlis ready to order his lunch now?" he asked as if nothing out of the ordinary had occurred.

"I'll have the grilled Dover sole, lemon, no butter, no potatoes, and plain green salad with just lemon." The maitre d' left and he picked up the jewel box and slipped it

346

into his jacket. He felt his lips tighten again. This trinket, as the bitch had called it, cost him a quarter of a million dollars. For the first time since she had left the table, he lifted his eyes and gazed around the room.

No one seemed to be watching him; they were talking to each other with their usual animation. But he knew better. By cocktail time, all Paris would be talking and laughing about him.

The champagne suddenly tasted bitter in his mouth. He put his glass down. She was like every other French whore that he had known, playing out their games in front of an audience, thinking that their cunts made them inviolable.

But this one would discover that she was wrong. In the small Greek village in which he had been born they knew how to take care of whores who had overstepped their privileges. It was a lesson they usually never forgot for the rest of their lives.

"You're getting old, Jacques," she said, looking across her desk at him. "At one time you were always urging me to push—now all I hear from you is 'Slow down.' What could be wrong with owning all the results of our work ourselves?"

He returned her gaze, not allowing his face to express the hurt her words had given him. "I'm sorry you feel that way, Janette," he said. "But I'm not saying there is anything wrong in wanting to own it all. What I'm asking you to consider is whether it is worth ten million dollars.

"Right now, without any investment at all on our part, we're earning between four and five million dollars a year and most of it just on licensing agreements and royalties. Kensington had to make the investment in stores, inventories, manufacturing facilities, sales organization and advertising. All we contributed was our name and designs."

"My name and designs," Janette said sharply.

"That's right." He nodded. "That's our real investment

347

and I think we should stick with it and protect it. Just look at what it cost us just to get *Soie* on the market. Twenty-five million of our own hard-earned francs. And it will be three years before we can even hope to see a significant profit. And that is a successful promotion.

"Also take couture, where we also own it all. We are doing more business than we ever dreamed. We are as successful as any of them—Dior, St. Laurent, Givenchy. Still, operating expenses manage to eat up everything we make. If we break even each year, we're happy.

"It's not just the ten million dollars which at the moment we haven't got that I'm objecting to, Janette. It's what lies beyond that. More money will be needed to create and operate all the various services that Kensington now performs for us. That could be another ten million dollars. And what I am saying is that even if we had the twenty million dollars to do it, are we equipped for it? What do we know about manufacturing in South America and Asia? About operating a chain of retail boutiques in America? Nothing. We'd be worse than amateurs. Even the professionals run into trouble there they never expected. Look at Agache-Willot, one of the most successful retail operators in France. Just a short time ago they bought Korvettes in the States, also a most successful operation. But something went wrong. Almost in no time at all they managed to lose forty million dollars, and because of it, they face the possibility of losing control of their own company here at home to the banks." He paused for a moment to catch his breath.

"Finished?" Janette asked coldly.

"No," he said. "Not yet. I want you to hear me out. Then you can decide whether you think I'm getting old or not." He paused again, then continued without waiting for a word from her. "And even if we are successful, what do we gain?

"We have heard that they make more than twice the profit that we do. But we don't know how that profit is broken down or from where it comes. Don't forget they made this deal with us because they already have the plants

348

and facilities to manufacture their own textiles as well as finished goods. They make them from every step of the operation, and I'm willing to venture that the greatest portion of their profit comes from that end rather than the retail. They can, if they want to, even operate the retail division at a loss because it can be absorbed into their manufacturing profits.

"If I am right, the most we can gain, if we buy our way out, and if we are successful in doing all the things I have said we must do, will amount to about two million dollars a year. That means it would take us ten years just to recoup the twenty million dollars we would have to invest. And that is without even knowing what we have to pay for the twenty million dollars if we could get it. It is entirely possible that the four or five million dollars a year we do make will disappear entirely, eaten up by the operations of a business we know nothing about. It happened to Agache-Willot. It can happen to us."

He took another deep breath. She was still watching him silently. "I am your friend, Janette. We have fought many battles together, side by side, so I don't think I have to prove either my friendship or devotion to you. I have watched with admiration the fierce drive within you that brought you from a girl to the strong and important woman that you are today, second to none in our business. So, as a friend, I feel free to caution you. No one in this world can own it all. Always leave something for others to do and profit by, and you will profit.

"Do not let your own ego and blind ambition lead you to your own destruction."

They were silent for a long while, just looking at each other. Finally she spoke. "That was quite a speech."

He nodded slowly. "It was. I don't know where it came from. I didn't expect it."

"Neither did I," she said. They were silent again for a moment, then she met his eyes. "Do you really mean that? What you said about my ego and blind ambition?"

He was embarrassed. "I don't know. I guess so. I don't

know what else it could be that is pushing you. We're making all the money we really need. Up to now, everything we've done has been a challenge and fun to do. But suddenly it's not fun any more."

"And if I were to give you another ten percent of the company?" she asked. He already had five percent. "Would it become fun then?"

"I thought you knew me better than that, Janette," he said, shaking his head slowly. "I don't want any more. I have all that I need. What I said, I said for your sake, not to gain something for myself."

"What would you say if I told you I was going to do it despite your advice?"

He looked at her. "I would say, 'Good luck, Janette.'"

She met his eyes. "And that is all?"

He rose from his chair heavily. "No, Janette. I would also say for that you would need someone far more capable and knowledgeable about those matters than I."

Suddenly she was angry. "I was right!" she snapped. "You're not only getting old, Jacques. You've become a coward, afraid to fight."

This time the hurt showed on his face and echoed in his voice. "I'm sorry that you feel like that, Janette." His voice broke and he went quickly to the door so that she could not see the sudden blurring in his eyes.

At the door, he turned and looked back at her. She looked at him in stony silence. He shook his head sadly. If only she would say one word. He didn't want it to end like this. But she remained silent. It was over.

He opened the door, still looking at her. She returned his gaze as if he were a stranger. "Goodbye, Janette," he said. And silently closed the door behind him.

She stared at the closed door. God damn him! What right did he have to sit in judgment on her? Her anger began to dissipate, replaced by an impulse to run after him and bring him back. But that was what men always wanted. A woman to run after them, begging them to come home.

She wouldn't do it. She would wait. He would come back. He would think it over and in the morning he would be in his office as if nothing had happened.

But then the tone of finality in his farewell echoed in her mind and she knew it was not to be. A strange sense of loss came into her. He was never coming back. In a way, he was the only real friend she had ever had. He had always been there. Now she was truly alone.

Lauren could hear the car horn blast in front of the white beach house on the Pacific Coast Highway clear into the kitchen at the other end of the house. She put down her coffee cup and got to her feet. Before going to the front door, she glanced out the terrace window at the beach. Anitra was naked, sitting on the sand, playing with the two puppies. Sitting in the shade of a beach umbrella, her nanny, Josefina, a Mexican woman in her forties, was knitting and watching the child.

Lauren ran through the house, out the front door into the courtyard, and opened the front gate. The car was right in front and Harvey was already opening the straps that held the surfboard to the roof. She laughed and went to help him. Nothing had changed about Harvey except the car. It was a Porsche 918 now instead of a Volkswagen. He had not achieved his ambition to become a millionaire at twenty-one, but now at twenty-five he was getting close. And he had never become a dealer as he had planned. Instead, everything was very straight. Sun Earth had really taken off.

He turned to look at her as she came next to him and began to tug at the next rack strap. She was tan and lithe in her cut-off jean shorts and bikini top, her hair long and white from the sun, her blue eyes sparkling in her tanned face. "You're looking good," he said, kissing her upturned cheek.

"How, paleface," she said mockingly, holding up a hand face out, Indian style.

He laughed, tugging his strap loose. "Some people have to work for a living," he said. "They can't afford to lay around on the beach all day."

"That ain't the way you used to tell it," she said, pulling her own strap loose. "Things sure have changed."

He lifted the surfboard from the roof carefully. "How's the surf?"

"Not bad," she said. "Running at six feet according to the radio. You might have some fun."

"Great," he said, holding the surfboard under one arm and pulling a small bag from the jump seat with the other. "I can't wait to try it. It's been too long."

"A month and a half," she said.

He followed her into the courtyard. "How's Anitra?"

"You won't recognize her," Lauren laughed. "She's getting so big. She's having a ball with those two Dalmatian puppies you gave her. She hasn't realized yet that they're getting bigger than she is."

She led the way along the path next to the side of the house to the beach. They came out at the terrace. Harvey leaned the surfboard against it in the shade and followed her up the terrace steps. He squinted at the water, then up at the sun. He began to strip off his shirt and turned to Lauren, smiling. "This must be the place for the good life. What I dreamed about as a boy. Nothin' but surfin' an' smokin'."

She laughed. "That hasn't changed. It's still here. The kids are still doing it."

He looked over the terrace railing and saw Anitra playing in the sand. He held up his hand, waving. "Hey, Anitra!" he yelled.

The child never looked up, continuing to play with the puppies.

"Hey, Anitra!" he shouted again. "It's Uncle Harvey."

Nothing. The child gave no sign that she had heard him, still playing with the dogs.

He turned to Lauren, a hurt look on his face. "She's ignoring me. She never even looked up."

"She's a woman," Lauren smiled. "She's playing hard to get. After all, you haven't come to see her in a long time."

"Oh," Harvey said. Then he grinned. He opened his bag

and took out a box. Holding the box in the air over his head, he called to the child again. "Hey, Anitra! It's Uncle Harvey and look what I got for you!"

The child looked up. A moment later she was running on her little brown legs across the sand to him.

Harvey turned to Lauren with a triumphant smile. "She's a woman all right. A present will get them all the time."

After dinner that night, they moved over to the living room and stretched out in front of the fire on the woven Mexican floor rug. The child was already asleep and Josefina was finishing off in the kitchen.

Harvey rolled over onto his stomach and looked out of the floor-length windows at the ocean. He could hear the pounding of the surf but he couldn't see it. Fog had rolled in, up the beach almost to the windows. "Fog's really comin' in," he said. "Spooky."

"You get used to it," she laughed, throwing a log on the fire. She watched it for a moment, then added another log as a shower of sparks went up the chimney. "It was hot today. But in November the nights can get real cold."

"Yeah," he said. He took a pouch from his pocket and began to roll a joint.

"Something new?" she asked.

He shook his head. "Nothing new any more. Johnny's so busy scoopin' up the dirt, he don't have time for planting no more. He's got more'n twenty people working for him now an' his mother won't even let him grow lettuce. She says they're doing so good they don't want to do anything that will bring the law down on them. I feel lucky if he gets good grass from his neighbors for me."

He finished rolling the joint, licked it, then smoothed it with his fingers and lit it. He took two deep tokes, then passed it to her. "This is good," he said appreciatively. "Try it."

She did the same thing, holding the smoke in for a long

354

time before letting it out slowly. "It's not bad," she commented, returning it to him. "But it's not a Harvey special."

He grinned, dragging on the joint again. "Them days are gone forever."

"Too bad," she said. "They were fun."

"Yeah." He looked at her. "I guess we can forget about ever getting our investment back. We never made it to the grass we wanted."

She laughed. "Do you think we can write it off our income tax?"

He laughed with her. "We can always try. But the IRS might have some other ideas." He passed the cigarette back to her and grimaced as he sat up. "I think I got sunburned today."

She stared at him. "You sure did. That's terrible. How do you think it will look when the president of Sun Earth walks into the office Monday morning looking like a lobster? Nobody will believe that it really works."

"You're right," he said. "But I was havin' such a good time out there, I forgot."

"Remember next time," she said with mock sternness. "Rule number one. Physician, heal thyself."

"I'll put some on now," he said. "It will take out the sting and by morning I'll be okay." He got to his feet and went to his room. A few minutes later he was back, his shirt off and the familiar Sun Earth jar in his hand. "You'll have to do my back," he said. "I got it pretty good there too."

She took the jar from his hand and looked at it as he sat on the floor, his back to her. The blue earthenware ceramic jar in the shape of a mercator of the world was highlighted by the continents in green on its surface, and the gold-painted ceramic cork holder fitted to the top representing the sun told you exactly what it was even if you couldn't read the clear black lettering on the gold. SUN EARTH. *Pour le Soleil. de* JANETTE. She began to spread it on his back. "Janette knew what she was doing," she said. "She said the most important thing was the package."

"Nobody's arguing with her," Harvey said. He glanced back over his shoulder at her. "By the way, do you know that Jacques is no longer with her?"

"No, I didn't." She was surprised. "I haven't spoken to her in months. What happened?"

"I don't know," he said. "We got the news just last month when I called to make an appointment to go over and talk to her about our new cosmetic line. Jacques wasn't there and I was pushed off to the new guy."

"Who is he?" she asked.

"I don't know," he said. "But they tell me he's a hotshot that used to work for Revlon in France. A real cold-ass too. He didn't even wait for me to finish explaining to him that we got the three basic shades and colors all worked out the way Janette wanted so that they could be blended to achieve any makeup color wanted. He just cut me off and said that their market study had shown that it had too limited a market for them to achieve a worthwhile gross and that women wouldn't go for the idea of having to blend their own shades of makeup. Besides they were already planning to introduce their own line of makeup next year."

"You never talked to Janette?" she asked.

"No. He said she was away on some promotion trip or something but that she would be in the States sometime in November and would probably see me to talk about a new distribution contract."

"What's the matter with the one you have?" she asked.

"Nothing," he said. "But it was only for three years. That's over next month at the end of December. He also said that they would probably require a doubling of their fees, that costs have gone up so much, their study reveals, that they're losing money on every jar they sell."

"What happens if you don't agree to give them more?"

"He already as much as told me that they would come out with their own. I told you he was cold-assed."

"Can they do that?" she asked.

"Sure they can," he said. "All they have to do is monkey with the formula a little bit."

"But the name?" she asked. "Are they entitled to that too? Janette was the one that thought it up."

He faced her, smiling. "They're fucked on that one. It's a registered trademark of our company and they can't touch it."

"Good," she said. "You don't seem worried about it."

"I'm not," he said. "As a matter of fact I'm hoping they don't renew our contract. As soon as I hung up on the Frenchman I called Squibb and made a deal for the cosmetics. And if I can move Sun Earth over to them, they'll give me an even better deal."

She closed the jar and put it down. "Roll another joint," she said.

"Okay."

She watched his hands expertly fashion the cigarette. He lit it and passed it to her. She took a deep drag. "I feel sad about Jacques," she said. "It seems to me that he's always been around. I remember him from when I was a kid. I wonder what happened?"

He took the joint from her. "You can ask her when you see her. If cold-ass is right, she'll be here sometime this month and we'll hear from her." He took a drag on the joint. "What are you planning for Thanksgiving? It's in two weeks, you know."

"I promised the folks I would spend it with them," she said. "They're dying to get their hands on Anitra and spoil her. They feel terribly deprived that I don't live right next door to them. What are you doing?"

"Nothing," he said. "My folks are still on that world cruise my Dad promised to take when he retired. They won't be back until the end of January."

"That's what Mother thought," she said. "She told me to ask if you would join us."

"Hey, that's great. Does that mean she's finally decided I was respectable?"

Lauren laughed. "If she has it's only because she doesn't know you as I do."

They were on their dessert, pumpkin pie and coffee, when Johann looked across the table at Lauren. "I forgot to tell you. Janette's in town at the Beverly Hills Hotel. Did you know?"

Lauren shook her head. "She never called me."

"That's funny," Johann said. "She seemed to know that you were going to be here. I asked her to come for dinner but she said she had another engagement and that she would come for a drink about six o'clock. She wanted to talk to the two of us. I wonder how she knew you would be here."

"I probably told her," Harvey said. "I had a meeting at the hotel with her yesterday."

"What happened?" Lauren asked him.

"Nothing much," he said. "Beginning January first, Sun Earth will be distributed by Squibb."

"Then you didn't renew with her?"

"That's right." Harvey smiled. "She has a new system now. She doesn't talk business, she leaves that all to her new managing director. After we said hello, we went down to his room. He told me what they wanted. I said I wouldn't pay it. He said that in that case they had no choice but to place their own product on the market. I said it was okay with me. Then we went back to Janette's suite and told her. I think she was surprised. She never expected me to turn them down flat like that. They must have thought they had me by the short hairs."

Johann laughed. "I wouldn't be surprised. I know her new managing director. He's telling everybody how they're going to take over the world."

"Maybe the world," Harvey grinned. "But not Sun Earth."

"How did she look?" Lauren asked curiously. It had been several years since she last saw her.

"Fantastic," Harvey said. "But you know Janette. Did she ever look any other way?"

"She doesn't know how," Lauren said. "Was she alone?"

"She had a girl friend with her. A dark-haired French model type. I never saw her before and we weren't introduced, so I don't know her name. She wasn't there when we first met but she was when I came back with the managing director."

"I wonder why she wants to see both of us?" Lauren looked at Johann.

Johann shot a glance at Heidi, then turned back to Lauren. "I think I have an idea," he said. "But let's wait and see what she has to say."

Promptly at six o'clock the doorbell rang. It was Janette. She was alone. It only took one look and Lauren knew that she was wired. Another glance at Harvey confirmed it. He saw it too, but Johann and Heidi would never notice.

They sat in the living room and made small talk. Janette couldn't get over how Anitra had grown. Very tall for a five-year-old. Five and a half, Lauren pointed out. Besides, American kids were bigger than French. It had to do with diet or something. Janette agreed with her and reminded them that Patrick was also very tall.

Then Lauren remarked that she had heard Jacques was no longer with her and asked what had happened. Janette seemed a little embarrassed as she answered that Jacques had grown tired of business and wanted to go back to his first love, which was writing. She thought he was going to do a monthly article for French *Vogue* and a book on the history of French couture.

Heidi politely asked if she had eaten. If not, she could have a plate prepared for Janette. There was plenty of turkey and the trimmings left over. No, Janette had eaten. Then she glanced at her watch. It was getting late and she had another appointment soon. She would like to discuss a very personal matter with them.

"Of course," Johann said, getting to his feet. "We can do

that in the library." He looked at Harvey. "Would you excuse us?"

"Go ahead," Harvey said. "I'll catch up on what happened in today's football games on TV."

Johann sat down behind his desk. Heidi sat down at the side of the desk, Lauren and Janette in chairs in front opposite him. Johann nodded at Janette. "Please, begin."

Janette opened her purse and took out a letter. "Some months ago I received this notice from the Swiss Credit Bank of Geneva." She gave it to Johann. "I would like you to read it."

Johann took out his glasses and put them on. He read it quickly, then gave it to Heidi. "When you've finished, give it to Lauren to read."

They were silent until Lauren finished reading. Then Lauren looked up. "What does it mean?" she asked.

Janette looked at her. "Obviously Mother placed something very valuable in that bank and it's been there all these years."

"Do you know what it is?" Lauren asked.

"Not exactly," she answered. "But I have a good idea."

"Then why didn't you go right up there and take it out?" Lauren asked.

"The only one that can do that is the person who has the key," Janette said. "And I don't have it."

"Then who does?" Lauren asked.

Johann's voice was unexpected. "I do."

"But you never said anything," Lauren said.

"I didn't have to," Johann said, "until I thought it was necessary." He took a file folder from his desk drawer and opened it in front of him. From the folder he took a photocopy of the letter that Tanya had left in the vault for him. He handed the letter to Janette. "I think that will be self-explanatory."

Janette read it quickly and passed it to Lauren, who read it and looked up. "But I still don't know what it is."

"Gold," Janette said. "A fortune in gold coins."

"How do you know that?" Lauren asked.

"Maurice told me," Janette replied. "Half of them belonged to him but before the war was over General von Brenner had Mother smuggle them out of France and put the coins in a Swiss bank."

Johann looked at Janette. "Since when do you believe what he tells you?"

"What reason would he have to lie?" she asked. "He told me the whole story. About how the general stole the companies from him and put everything in Mother's name."

Johann shook his head sadly. "It's a lie. Nothing but a lie. Everything Maurice has today, even his title, was bought for him, either by the general or given to him by your mother."

"Then why didn't you tell us about this before?" Janette demanded.

"You read the letter," Johann said. "I didn't think it was necessary."

"Were you ever going to think it was necessary?" Janette said coldly. "Or were you planning to keep it all for yourself?"

"You bitch!" Heidi's voice was angry. "If it weren't for Johann, you would have nothing, be nothing but a whore on the streets of Paris today. It was Johann who kept Maurice from stealing everything from your mother, it was Johann who protected you all the years you were growing up."

Johann held up his hand. "Don't get upset, dear," he said soothingly. He turned to Janette. "And what would you like me to do now?"

"Give me the key," she snapped.

"I can't do that," he said. "Half of it belongs to your sister."

"Maurice was right," she snapped. "There's nothing left. You used it all for yourself."

Johann looked at her. "I took nothing except what I was entitled to."

"That's the money you used to buy the company from me!" she said.

"No," Heidi said. She ignored Johann's restraining gesture. "It's time you learned some truths. The money was in the bank in your mother's name but it wasn't your mother's money. It belonged to the general. And when the general's widow and sons came to Paris intending to bring a suit against you and your mother's estate to recover the property that the general had owned, which included the vineyards, the perfume factory and the mineral water company —all of which was now in your name and Lauren's—Johann took that share of the money which belonged to him and paid them off." She looked at Johann. "Show them the release you had the von Brenners sign."

Johann took another paper from the file and gave it to Janette. Janette read it and looked up at him. "How do I know this is true?"

Lauren's voice was shocked. "You can't believe that Daddy would lie, could you?"

"Anyone could write a piece of paper," Janette said contemptuously. "That doesn't mean anything. Don't be naive. We're talking about millions of dollars."

"I don't care about the money," Lauren said. "I can't seem to make you understand I never did."

"You can't be like that any more," Janette snapped. "You have a child to protect."

"I'll protect my own child in my own way," Lauren answered angrily. "I don't like what you're saying and I don't like what you're doing."

"I need that money," Janette said. "And I need it now. And I mean to have it if I have to go into the court and tell the whole world that Johann Schwebel was in the Nazi army of occupation in France and together with his superior officer looted the helpless French of their possessions."

Lauren shook her head. "I don't believe it. You're really not saying those terrible things." She looked at Janette. "You can't be willing to ruin so many lives just because of money."

Janette stared back at her silently.

Lauren turned to Johann. "Give her the key, Daddy. If that's what she wants, let her have it."

"It's half yours, child," he said.

"I don't care." She was crying. "It's dirty money covered with blood and hate and I don't want any of it now."

Johann looked at Heidi. She nodded. "Lauren is right. It's blood money. Give her the key."

Johann hesitated for a moment. Then looked at them. "No, I won't do it. I don't give a damn what Janette wants. Half of it belongs to Lauren and will remain there until Lauren decides what she wants done with it." He looked at Janette. "I will meet you at the bank in Geneva next week and turn over your share to you. Is that satisfactory?"

Janette nodded. "It has to be. I don't have any choice, do I?"

"No choice at all," Johann said.

Heidi got to her feet. Her voice was angry. "Now get out of my house. I never want to see you again."

Janette got to her feet. She looked down at Lauren. "I did it as much for you as I did it for myself."

Lauren raised her head. She brushed the tears away from her eyes with the back of her hand. "I'll bet," she said sarcastically. "You've never done anything for anyone in your whole life unless there was something in it for you. I agree with Mother. I don't ever want to see you again."

"But—" Janette hesitated. This wasn't what she had wanted. Lauren was supposed to be with her.

Lauren's voice was suddenly strong. Janette had heard it like that once before. When she left Patrick. "No buts. Goodbye, Janette."

Janette looked at her for a moment, then turned toward the door. Lauren had meant it when she said she was leaving Patrick. And she meant what she said now.

J OHANN WAS WAITING for her when she arrived at the
bank. She shivered as she got out of the taxi and hurried inside, the mink-lined hood of her parka shielding her face against the sleeting December rain that always
seemed to be falling on Geneva streets.

The young man who had brought the notice to her in
Paris greeted her at the door. "Madame de la Beauville, so
nice to see you again."

Frantically she searched her memory for his name and
found it. "Monsieur Thierry." She smiled.

"Herr Schwebel is waiting in my office," he said. "Please
follow me."

He led her to an office at the rear of the bank, through a
door marked "Private." Johann was standing at the window,
looking out at the sleet. He turned when he heard them
enter.

"Good morning, Johann," she said.

He didn't return her greeting. "I suggest that you rent a
vault before we go downstairs," he said abruptly.

She looked at him for a moment, then turned to Thierry.
"I suppose that's a good idea. Monsieur Thierry, please."

"Of course, Madame," the young man said. He took some
papers from his desk. "If you will be kind enough to fill
these out, it will only take a moment."

She sat down in the chair he indicated and quickly filled
out the forms and pushed them across the desk to him. He
glanced at them.

"Very good," he said, turning the papers over. "There is
a form on this side on which you can designate a beneficiary
to whom the vault will be given in the event of your demise.

If you should wish to use it, however, we shall need two witnesses who will attest both to your signature and the name of your beneficiary. Of course, everything will be held strictly confidential under the terms of the Swiss banking laws."

She thought for a moment. "I'd like to use it."

"Very well," Thierry said. "I will call in two bank employees to attest the document."

"I'll wait outside," Johann said.

"Is it necessary?" she asked the banker. "Can't you and Monsieur Schwebel act as witnesses?"

"Of course," Thierry replied. "But in that case you must understand that the bank cannot guarantee confidentiality." He turned to Johann. "With all due respect to Herr Schwebel."

"I'm not concerned about that," she said.

"Very good," the banker said. "Fill in the names of the beneficiaries and their relationship to you in the space indicated. Then sign your name where indicated." He gave Janette the pen again and looked up. "Herr Schwebel, will you be kind enough to observe Madame de la Beauville's writing?"

Johann came next to her and stood there looking at the form as she filled it out. She wrote quickly on the lines designated for the beneficiaries. Lauren Reardon, sister, and/or Anitra Reardon, niece. Then on the line below, her own name. The banker pushed a stamp pad toward her. "We'll need your thumbprint," he said apologetically. She held out her hand and he guided her thumb and pressed it on the pad, then guided it to the paper. "Roll your thumb from side to side," he said. "Now, Herr Schwebel, your signature."

Quickly Johann signed it. Then the banker himself signed the document. He got to his feet. "If you will excuse me for a moment, I'll get a vault assigned to you and come right back with the key."

The door closed behind him and they sat there in silence

for a moment. She took out a cigarette and lit it. He went to the window again and looked out. He spoke without turning to look at her. "Every time I think I finally have you all figured out you do something to surprise me."

"I have no intention of dying," she said.

Thierry came back into the office. He gave the key to Janette. "Now if you'll be kind enough to follow me."

They went down into the vault. Quickly he checked the number on Johann's key, and placing his key in the lock, turned it, then waited while Johann placed his key in the other lock and turned it. The door swung open. He did the same thing for Janette. The two boxes were almost next to each other. He turned to them. "I'll leave you alone," he said. "When you're ready to leave, press this button near the vault door and I'll be back to let you out."

"Thank you," Johann said. He waited until the vault door had closed behind the banker, then turned to Janette. He nodded and quickly began taking canvas coin bags from the deep box and piling them up on a wooden table just behind him. Finally there were thirty-three of them. Then he searched around in the box until he found what he was looking for—a canvas bag slightly smaller than the others. He peered at the markings on it, then placed it on the table with the others. He looked at her. "That's it."

Wonderingly, she picked up the last bag and opened the cord that held it shut. She turned it over on the table and the gold coins began tumbling out. Holding her breath, she picked one up and looked at it. It was a coin she had never seen before, but despite its small size it was heavy in her hand. "What is it?" she asked breathlessly, her heart beginning to pound.

"Gold napoleons, louis they're called, after Louis Napoleon, who ordered them struck," Johann answered.

"My God," she almost whispered. "What are they worth?"

"Your share is thirty-three thousand three hundred and thirty-three of them," he said. "At today's gold price they have a value of about five million dollars."

366

"Five million dollars," she said. Maurice had tricked her. He had pushed her into doing what she did because she thought there would be enough money to buy back her freedom from Kensington. It wasn't worth it.

"It's a lot of money," he said. He gestured to his open vault. "Would you like to check this box? There is exactly the same amount of money in it as you have there on the table."

She shook her head. "I don't have to do that. I trust you."

"Finally," he said drily. He snapped the door of his box shut and straightened up. "I suggest you place your bags in your vault."

She was still staring at the money. "Yes," she said.

"Do you want me to help you?" he asked.

She looked at him. "Please."

Quickly they began to put the bags into the box. At the end there were just the coins she had emptied on the table. She began to put them back into the bag.

He stood there watching her. "You don't have to answer if you don't want to, Janette, but what happened that made you feel you needed this money so desperately?"

"I wanted to buy my freedom from Kensington," she answered in a low voice. There was no point in telling him now that it wouldn't be enough.

"What on earth for?" His voice was incredulous. "They've done a fantastic job for you. You have to be netting at least four million dollars a year."

She didn't answer.

"I don't have to give you this advice," he said. "But I'm going to anyway. I've been responsible for you so many years that it's a habit I can't get out of that easily.

"Gold is increasing in value every day. Two years ago what you have there was worth only one million. It's gone up five times since then. And I've heard the U.S. government is planning to inflate the market and then place some of its own gold reserve on sale. And then gold will go

367

through the roof. By this time next year the value of what you have may well be five times what it is today."

She stared at him, still silent, the last of the coins in the bag. She pulled the string shut.

"What I'm saying to you is—keep the gold. Forget buying out Kensington. That gold will be worth twenty-five, thirty million dollars in about a year. You won't live long enough to make that much more money from buying out Kensington."

Without speaking, she placed the bag in the box and snapped the door shut, taking out her key. She looked at him. "How will I know when to sell?"

"The minute it goes over eight hundred dollars an ounce," he said. "It might go to a thousand but it doesn't matter. If it gets to the eight hundreds, that's when I'm planning to sell Lauren's share."

She nodded slowly. In effect he was saying the same thing that Jacques had said. It would take too many years to get any real gain from buying out Kensington. And she didn't have that much time to spend struggling. Jacques was right again. What was the point of working if it wasn't fun?

He reached for the button and pressed it. "My hotel is just around the corner," he said. "Would you like a coffee?"

"No, thanks," she said. "I flew up from Paris this morning and I'm booked to return on a two o'clock flight. I'll just have time to make it."

Thierry appeared in the door and opened the vault gate with his key. They followed him upstairs to the main floor. They thanked him and he bowed. He was happy to be of service to them, he said, opening the door for them.

They stepped out into the street. The sleet slammed into them. Janette threw her hood over her head. A taxi came crawling by and Johann stopped it. He opened the cab door and let Janette climb in.

She looked out of the cab up at him. "I'm sorry, Johann," she said. "But—thanks."

He gestured with his hand. "I'm sorry too. Goodbye, Janette." Then he closed the door and straightened up. For a moment he watched the taxi go down the road. Then he turned and resolutely began to walk to his hotel. He didn't know whether the blurring in his eyes came from the tears or the sleeting rain. But all he kept seeing in front of him was that sleeping infant nestled in her mother's arms the first time they entered the general's house in Warsaw.

It was raining when she arrived in Paris. But at least it wasn't sleet, as it had been in Geneva, and not as cold. René was waiting as she came out the airport door and held the door of the Rolls for her. He closed the door and got into the driver's seat. The big car moved quietly away from the curb. "Where to, Madame?"

She glanced at the clock. It was just past four. "The office, René," she said.

"*Oui*, Madame," he said. His eyes met hers in the rearview mirror. "Was it a good flight, Madame?" he asked politely.

"It was, thank you." She nodded. Then she pressed the button and the partition window rolled up. She didn't feel like speaking and leaned back against the seat, closing her eyes. God, she was tired. It was beginning to seem as if she was always tired, always suffering from jet lag, always getting off one plane and on another.

It used to be that she would have some time for herself. But not any more. For the first time she began to understand how much of the day-to-day routine Jacques had spared her. The new man was brilliant, the office and the plants seemed to operate more efficiently under him, but there was only one thing wrong. The people she dealt with, the important buyers and executives who used to be willing to talk with Jacques, all now wanted to talk to her. And the days were never long enough for her to fit them all in.

"We're here, Madame." The chauffeur's voice coming from the open door startled her. She had fallen asleep. She smiled, getting out of the car.

"Thank you, René. You can pick me up at seven." She stepped under the umbrella the doorman held for her and walked up the few steps that led to the office door. He opened the door to let her pass, then followed her inside and pressed the elevator button for her.

Robert followed her into her office and took her coat. "Was it a good flight, Madame?"

"Very good, thank you," she said, walking behind her desk. "Have the final sketches come up from design yet?"

"They should be on their way up now, Madame," he said. "I'll check on them right away."

"Thank you," she said. She sank into her chair.

"The telephone messages are on your desk, Madame," Robert said.

She glanced at the desk. The messages were there all right—laid out neatly, one overlapping the other in rows of five. This way she didn't have to pick them up to see who had called. A quick glance would give her the name. She grimaced. There had to be at least twenty of them. She made no move to look at them. Instead she looked up at her secretary. "Anything important, Bobby?" she asked.

"Not really, Madame," he said. "They can probably hold until morning."

"Good," she said. "I really need the time to go over the sketches."

As soon as he closed the door behind him, she opened a drawer and took out a vial of cocaine. She did two snorts in each nostril and leaned back waiting for it to kick in. She felt her head begin to clear. It helped but it wasn't enough. She took a Dexamyl from the pillbox in the drawer and swallowed it with some water from the carafe on her desk. The combination did the trick. By the time the artists came in with their final sketches, her eyes were bright and she really was going. She worked with them until six o'clock without a stop.

When the last of the artists had filed from her office, she leaned her head back against the chair. Jacques was right.

370

It wasn't fun any more. Now she was beginning to feel better about not getting enough money to buy out Kensington. As bad as this was, she could imagine how much tougher it would be if she did go through with it.

Robert came into the office. "Monsieur le Marquis is outside."

She looked down at the messages, then at her appointment calendar. His name wasn't on them. "Did he call?"

"No, Madame," Robert said. "But he said that he had to see you. It was very important."

She thought for a moment, then nodded. "Show him in."

Maurice was smiling as he entered. She didn't rise and he came around the desk and kissed her upturned cheek. *"Bon jour,* Janette."

She gestured to the seat in front of the desk. *"Bon jour,"* she said wearily.

He sat down and looked at her, still smiling. He nodded his head for a moment before he spoke. "Well?" he asked.

She stared at him. "Well, what?"

His smile grew even broader. "Don't play games with your dear Papa," he said. "The suspense is killing me. I know you met Johann at the bank in Geneva at eleven o'clock this morning and that you both came out at one o'clock and he put you in a taxi to take you to the airport."

Her voice was incredulous. "You've been having me followed!"

"Of course," he smiled. "Wouldn't you do the same thing if you were in my circumstances? After all, you did come back from California early this week and you never called me. And I know that you saw Johann and Lauren on the Thursday before. Come now, the suspense is killing me. Tell your partner how many millions we have to share."

She stared at him for a long moment. The vision of the gold coins gleaming in the lights of the bank vault ran through her mind. That was where the freedom lay, not with Kensington. And there was no reason for her to share it with him for a lousy million francs, not after all he had done to her from childhood on. Perhaps if it hadn't been for him, she could have been like Lauren, happy and with a child of her own. A sudden wave of hatred for him steeled her resolve. "Nothing."

He stared at her in disbelief. "Nothing?"

"That's what I said. There was nothing," she said coldly. "I don't know from where you got your information. But it was wrong. There's no Kensington there for me. It was a beautiful dream while it lasted but now it's over."

"I don't believe you!" His voice began to rise. "There had to be something there. You're lying!"

"There was something there," she said. "Papers that the general gave my mother to keep for him. Papers showing the things he had bought and given to her. Including your title, which he bought in order for you to marry my mother."

"It's not true!" His voice grew even more shrill. "Everything was cash."

She laughed, knowing that the information she got from Johann was verified. "But the general was German. And you know how they are. They keep detailed records. Even of information that might be detrimental to them. We found that out at the war criminal trials."

"You're lying!" he screamed. "You're trying to throw dirt in my eyes. There was money and now you want to keep it all for yourself!"

Suddenly all the hatred of him inside her came out. Whatever agony she could cause him would be as nothing compared to what he had caused her. Her voice went cold. "Maybe I am," she said, enjoying seeing him squirm. "But you'll never know, will you? And there's nothing you can do about it." She rose from her chair. "Now, get out!"

"Nothing?" he screamed, suddenly leaping from his chair at her, his hands grabbing at her.

She was too quick for him. She stepped back, her hand picking up the razor-sharp, stiletto-shaped letter opener from her desk. He stopped suddenly in front of her, its needle point at his throat just over his collar between his Adam's apple and his chin. Their eyes burned into each other's in mutual hatred. Her lips were drawn back over her teeth in an animal-like snarl. Her voice was an animal's growl. "Don't stop now, Maurice! Give me a chance to finish what my mother began!"

He took a deep breath and stepped back just as the office door behind him opened and people began to crowd into the doorway, staring into the room. "You won't get away with it!" he said shrilly, trying to control his voice. "The general tried to screw me and he's dead, your mother too. And she's dead. You won't get away with it."

She looked up and saw the people in the doorway staring at them. Suddenly she was exhausted. "Get out, Maurice," she said in a weary voice. "Before I have you thrown out."

Then he became aware of the people behind him. He glanced back at them, then at her. "This is not the end of it," he said, his voice quiet once again. "Someday when you least expect it, you will pay. Just remember that!" Then he turned and walked out with as much dignity as he could muster. The people stepped aside silently to let him pass, then filled the doorway again.

Robert came to her as she sank into her chair. "Are you all right, Madame?"

"I'm fine," she said. She looked at the people in the doorway, their white, frightened faces staring at her. "Go back to your desks!" she snapped. "It's not seven o'clock yet."

The faces disappeared from the doorway quickly. She looked up at Robert. "Close the door," she said. "Then I'll have a cognac."

"Yes, Madame," Robert said. He was back in a moment, the brandy snifter in his hand. He watched her swallow half the drink in one gulp. "Is there anything more I can do for you, Madame?"

She felt the liquor burning its way down her throat. "No, thank you, Bobby," she said. "Just leave me alone for a while. I'll be all right."

She watched him close the door behind him, then put her head on her hands on the desk. She still felt the trembling inside her and knew if she hadn't sat down when she did, her legs would have gone out from under her.

Nothing had changed since she was a child. The moment he started violently for her, she was at the point of orgasm and her legs grew weak. The terror she felt was the pleasure she felt. Her hatred of him could only be measured by the desire she had for him to punish her. Her thighs were soaking wet from the juices that had poured from her.

She opened a drawer and took a handful of Kleenex from the box inside, then raised her skirt and began to wipe the moisture from her. Her dress was stained and she would have to change it. Slowly she got up and went to the bathroom. She would take a quick shower. She smelled of her own sex.

For the second time that year she was the topic of conversation at the cocktail parties of Paris. First it had been the Greek. This time it was her stepfather.

As UNBEARABLE AS the cold had been that winter, the heat of the summer during the collection in Paris at the end of July and the beginning of August was equally unbearable. And in the large reception room of the Hotel de Ville it was even more so. Air conditioning hadn't been invented as yet for French government buildings.

More than two hundred people had been packed into the room whose capacity was less than half that number. The champagne wasn't even cold and the hors d'oeuvres were limp with the heat. The photographers and reporters crowded their way to the small platform at the end of the room. A collective sigh rose from the crowd as a man perspiring in a heavy black suit climbed up on the platform. The ceremony was about to begin. Soon they would all be able to leave.

He spoke into the microphone. *"Messieurs et Mesdames."* No sound came from the public-address system. He tapped the microphone. No sound. He tapped again. Still nothing. He shrugged his shoulders and gave up. This time he almost shouted. *"Messieurs et Mesdames,* the Mayor of Paris."

Applause rose through the room as the mayor entered through a door from his office. He looked cool and comfortable, as he should—his office was air conditioned. He held up his hand to still the crowd and smiled.

"Ladies and gentlemen," he said, his voice carrying through the room even without the microphone. He knew how to project. He was a professional. "I know you are all anxious to leave and go on about your business. Many of you have dinners and other important affairs to go to, so we will be as brief as possible. First, I would like to thank all of you for taking the time to be here and do honor to this woman who has done so much to keep the name Paris as the most important city in the world of fashion. A young woman, born and raised in this city, who has risen to the top of her profession as one of the great couturiers of the world. A woman in the grand tradition of Coco Chanel and Elsa Schiaparelli who will leave her mark in the fashion world for many years to come.

"So I would like you to join me in welcome and applause to this year's recipient of the Médaille d'Honneur of the City of Paris, to a woman who has contributed so much to the culture and dress of the world and has been one of the greatest exponents of Parisian industry and charm ever known. Ladies and gentlemen, may I present to you Madame Janette Marie de la Beauville!"

The door to the private office opened again and Janette came out on the platform. She too was cool and smiling. She, too, had been in the mayor's air-conditioned office. She crossed the platform and stood next to the mayor.

An usher appeared with the medal attached to the traditional red, white and blue ribbon, lying on a velvet cushion. The mayor picked it up and held it over her head, pausing to let the photographers get their fill; then, finally, he placed it carefully over her shoulders without disturbing a single hair of her coiffure. He was a professional.

"Madame Janette," he said, turning his face to the audience so that the photographers could get the pictures. "I call you Madame Janette because I know that is how all your friends and colleagues address you. It is with great honor that I present to you this medal in appreciation of all you have done for Paris, and for France. Your name will grace our history with the beauty you have created for all of us." He bent over her, kissing her on both cheeks. "Keep it brief," he whispered in her ear. "They're sweating like pigs and the room stinks."

Janette smiled at him. *"Monsieur le Maire."* She turned to the room and smiled again. *"Mesdames et Messieurs."* She paused for a long moment, then laughed aloud. "I, too, will be brief." Another pause. She raised both hands to her lips and threw them a kiss, her arms opening wide. "Thank you. I love all of you. Thank you."

The photographers kept shooting pictures of Janette, of Janette and the mayor, but the people were already leaving. It was over. And when the photographers stopped taking pictures, the mayor kissed Janette's hand and left. It was over for him too.

Janette sank into the back seat of the Rolls. René looked at her in the rearview mirror. "Congratulations, Madame," he said. "It is a beautiful medal."

Suddenly she remembered she was still wearing it on the sash the mayor had placed around her shoulders. Quickly she took it off and looked at it. It was gold plate over copper. "Yes, it is," she said thoughtfully. "Thank you."

"Where to now, Madame?" he asked.

She looked up in surprise. How stupid. Her publicity department should have arranged for a dinner to follow the presentation. They really blew it. Another free one hundred thousand dollars' worth of press had been lost. If she didn't think of it herself, nothing happened. That never would have happened if Jacques had been here. "Home," she said in an annoyed voice. "Home, of course."

She undressed and had dinner in her robe in front of the television set. She caught the late news on all three channels. There was nothing about the presentation on any of them. That was the end of it. Tomorrow she would have a new publicity director. This one didn't know which end was up.

She switched off the set a few minutes after eleven o'clock when the last channel went off the air. She was so angry she couldn't sleep. Restlessly she paced up and down the bedroom. No way she could go to sleep.

Finally she picked up the phone and called René. "Bring the mini around, René," she said. "I'm going out."

"Would you like me to drive you, Madame?"

"No," she said. "I'll drive myself."

She slipped into a cotton shirt and a pair of jeans, then tied a cashmere sweater over her shoulders. She pulled on a pair of boots and tucked the jeans into their tops, then took several thousand francs from the dresser and stuck it in her jeans pocket. At the last moment, she took a small vial of coke with the spoon attached to its top and put that in her blouse pocket. She glanced at herself in the mirror before she went out. She smiled. No one could possibly guess that she had done so much for *haute couture* if they saw her now. Then she went downstairs. René had the car in front of the door. She got into it and tore out into the street.

Two hours later, she was sitting alone at a table in a lesbian bar on the Left Bank, sipping a brandy. Two bull-dikes were sitting at the bar nursing their drinks, another was dancing with the waitress, who was so tired she could hardly lift her feet.

Janette gestured to the bartender, who came over to her on heavy, slippered feet. "Yes, Janette?" she asked.

"What's happening in this town?" Janette asked. "This is the third place I've been to in two hours and they're all like this. Zero."

"It's August and it's too hot," the bartender said wearily. "All the talent's gone south."

"Shit," Janette said. "I might as well go home."

"Might as well," the bartender agreed. She smiled, showing two gold teeth. "I'm going to close up anyway. It doesn't pay to keep the place open just for the beer drinkers."

Janette took a hundred francs and dropped it on the table. "Good night," she said.

"Yeah," the bartender said, picking up the bill and putting it under her apron. She watched Janette leave, then waddled back to the bar. "Drink up, ladies," she said. "We're closing for the night."

Janette pulled the mini up on the sidewalk in front of her house, then got out and locked it. As she walked around the car to go to the steps, two men came out of the shadows of the house next door.

"Madame Janette de la Beauville?" one of them asked.

"Yes," she answered, pausing for a moment. Then a sudden cold dread ran through her and she turned to run up the steps to the door.

But the moment's hesitation had been enough. One of the men caught her by the arm and pulled her brutally back. She stared up at him, trying to see his face in the dark. "If it's money you want," she said, fear almost choking the voice in her throat, "I'll give it to you. It's all in my back pocket."

"We don't want your money," the man said in a strangely accented, almost amused voice. "We have a message for you from an old friend."

They were the last words she heard for a long while. Almost at the same moment, she felt a fist crash into her face. She felt her nose and her cheekbone crack. "Oh, no," she remembered thinking, then the blood poured into her mouth and she began to fall.

It was all a haze of pain after that. She heard occasional moans without realizing they were her own; the sharp continuing blows on her face and body never seemed to come to an end. She tried to scream for help but her voice drowned in her throat. Never quite unconscious but never conscious either, all she could do was grunt in pain with each blow. Then she was lying on the concrete sidewalk feeling their heavy boots kicking into her sides. Then as suddenly as it had begun, it stopped.

She felt rather than saw the men bending over her. "That should do it," one of them said, laughing. She remembered thinking what a strange accent he had and felt his hand searching the breast pocket of her shirt. She wanted to tell him the money wasn't there, it was in her back pocket. But then he drew away. He laughed again. "Goodbye, Janette."

After a few moments she tried to move. The pain knifed through her body and she screamed but there was no sound. Slowly she began to crawl up the steps. It seemed to take years of agony to reach the door. Finally she made it. It took another thousand years for her to reach up and press the doorbell. And then a million years for it to open.

She could only hear the shocked horror in the voice of the butler. *"Madame!"* Then she went headlong into the night.

It was six weeks later and she was sitting in the darkness of her room watching a stupid afternoon movie on the television set. There was a knock at the door and the butler came into the room.

"Yes?" she asked.

"Monsieur Jacques is here to see you, Madame."

"Send him away," she said sharply. "I don't want to see anyone."

"You can't send him away," Jacques said. "He's already here."

Quickly she pressed the remote control she had in her hand and the television set went dark. The butler left the room, closing the door behind him. Jacques came toward her. Quickly she turned the wheelchair away from him.

"Don't turn away from me, Janette," he said.

"I don't want you to see me," she said in a husky, unused voice. "I'm not very pleasant to look at."

"I'm not concerned about that," he said. He walked around in front of her. "Do you know what day this is?"

She turned away so that he could not look into her face. "It's a day just like any other. What difference does it make?"

"A big difference," he said. "It's your birthday. I brought you flowers."

"So now I'm forty as well as ugly," she said in a bitter voice.

"You'll never be ugly to me," he said. "Besides, it's only a matter of time. The doctors perform miracles today."

380

"They'll need all they can find to help me," she said.

"You have the faith, Janette," he said. "And they will find them. You have to want to be healed before they can heal you."

She was silent.

"You're not a coward, Janette," he said. "You never were afraid of a fight before."

She began to cry almost silently. "That was because I never really knew what fear was. When those two men were hitting me I was never so afraid in my life. And it wasn't only the pain I was afraid of, I was afraid that it would stop. Because when it stopped and I would feel nothing, I would be dead."

Gently he took her hand. "Who did this to you, Janette?" he asked softly. "I know the police haven't been able to find out anything, but was it Maurice? If it was, you tell me and I'll kill him."

She shook her head. "It wasn't Maurice."

"How do you know?"

"Because I know who did it," she said. She remembered finding the card that had been stuffed in her shirt that night when she had thought they were looking for her money. It was on her dresser when she came home and the maid said it had fallen from her shirt when she had taken it to be washed. It was a simple white card with only a name printed on it. Nico Caramanlis.

"It doesn't matter now," she said. "It's over and I just want to forget it."

He was silent for a moment, then got to his feet and walked to the windows. Quickly he pulled back the draperies, letting the sunlight fall into the room. As quickly she raised her hands to her face, hiding it.

He came back to her and, kneeling before her, took her wrists in his hands and slowly moved them away from her face. "Let the daylight in, Janette," he said gently, looking into her eyes. "You can't spend the rest of your life hiding in the dark."

Her eyes searched his questioningly.

"You still have too much to give," he said. He paused for a moment. "See, it's not so bad, is it?"

She began to cry again, the tears falling silently down her cheeks. Slowly he drew her down to him and held her head against his chest.

"I would have come sooner had I known," he said. "But I was in China and I didn't see a French newspaper until three days ago. Then I knew I had to come home. You see, Janette, I was hiding too."

"Jacques," she whispered. "Jacques."

He kissed the top of her head softly. "Yes," he said. "I'm back. And it will be the two of us again. You and me. And we'll have fun again and laugh again and love again."

"Yes, Jacques, yes," she whispered. "Tell me."

He looked down at her, the tears filling his own eyes. "I'll never stop telling you, Janette."